*older books or movies. The individuality of Martin's work will be, for many readers, the quality that stands out above all else. An Unexpected Treasure is a book for people who enjoy historical romances a cut above the average fare.*

*The ending is satisfying on every level. Readers, especially devotees of this style, will never feel cheated with how Martin ties together its assorted strands. We need books like this in 2021, imaginative and involving fictional works brimming with the life characterizing the best entertainment. There's little question Martin will continue producing such works in the future. Her eager and growing readership will greet this book with ample interest and few, if any, will express disappointment with this latest offering. It is a thrilling and breathless ride that will expand her readership. An Unexpected Treasure further solidifies her reputation as one of the best historical novelists writing today.*

**—Jason Hillenburg, Reprospace Editorial Reviews™**

# Endorsements

*"This delightful seventeenth-century tale took me on a journey to the heart of rural Leicestershire in England. An intriguing romance which unfolded at a gentle pace like an elegant old fashioned tapestry being stitched and coming to life before my eyes.*

*Celia Martin's vast knowledge of history and her meticulous research into the period is evident throughout and her proficient use of colloquial language transports the reader back to the time and place, presenting a charming sensitivity for the era.*

***

*Born before her time, Selena D'Arcy is a down to earth, strong-willed young maiden with a heart of gold and with a reluctance to conform to what is expected of a young woman of her social status. Sent to stay with her aunt and uncle where her aunt is to train her in the many skills and etiquettes of how to behave in a more acceptable ladylike fashion and how to manage the running of a grand estate...it is with the hope that this will prepare and steer her towards a suitable marriage. Shortly after her arrival, however, Selena falls in love with a neighbouring farmer, the handsome Calder Grantham, a widower with a young son. Although in her family's eyes, they would not be considered a suitable match, knowing her own mind, Selena is resolute that he will, one day, become her husband.*

*Engaging the hearts and affections of everyone she meets, Selena embarks on a project of organising and rallying support and funds for the building of a local grammar school in the village, not only for the benefit of the locals but in mind of any future sons she might bear once Calder has taken her as his wife. Selena not only becomes popular with her numerous new neighbours, but she has also been blessed with a natural gift of winning the trust and friendship of the copious animals which cross her path.*

*Her compassionate manner and aptitude to perceive people's hidden talents and uncover their potential always finding ways to improve their lives become prevalent throughout the story. Selena sees the good in everyone she meets, including those who do injustice towards her. One cannot help admire this kind-hearted young woman and as I reached the end of the book, I felt a great fondness towards this loveable and charismatic young woman.*

*Martin is a skilled author who captures the period well. Her brilliant flair for character building brings to life a multitude of engaging personalities which are entwined throughout the story and makes for a highly satisfying read. An absolute gem of a historical period romance with an endearing ending."*

**—Lilly Adam,**
**Renowned Author of The Victorian Saga Romantic Series**

*Celia Martin continues her streak of impressive historical fiction with another entry in her series revolving around the D'arcy family and other assorted characters. Her use of Restoration-era speech is an abiding hallmark of her work and, once again, present throughout An Unexpected Treasure. She invokes the upper-crust English milieu of the era without striking a false note. Her writing deserves praise for bringing the period to life without saddling readers with too much detail.*

*Her command of storytelling fundamentals never fails. It is beyond question Martin read much before exposing her fiction for public perusal and it shows in many ways. One of the more prominent examples of this strength is the tight grip she maintains over the plot development. Her characters face numerous obstacles and trials along the way and Martin places several dramatic scenes within the narrative inciting you to read further.*

*Martin's characters recall several stereotypes, but she concocts compelling personalities for major and minor figures alike. She does not attempt to satisfy us with cardboard characters and scenes culled from*

# An Unexpected Treasure

## Celia Martin

KITSAP PUBLISHING

***An Unexpected Trasure***
First edition, published 2021

By Celia Martin

Book Layout: Reprospace

Copyright ©2021, Celia Martin

ISBN-13 Softcover:  978-1-952685-28-6

This is a work of fiction. Names, characters, businesses, places, events and incidents are either the products of the author's imagination or used in a fictitious manner. Any resemblance to actual persons, living or dead, or actual events is purely coincidental.

All rights reserved. No part of this book may be reproduced or transmitted in any form or by any means, electronic or mechanical, including photocopying, recording or by any information storage and retrieval system, without written permission from the author, except for the inclusion of brief quotations in a review.

Published by Kitsap Publishing
P.O. Box 572
Poulsbo, WA 98370
www.KitsapPublishing.com

# Also by Celia Martin

## To Challenge Destiny

"Exquisite passion and breath-taking action! A historical romance feast!"

**—Curt Locklear, Laramie Award Winner**

"Martin proves she has the vision and talent to make bygone times come alive for modern readers."

**—Anne Hollister, Professional Book Reviews**

## A Bewitching Dilemma

"A willful heroine cornered by a relentless foe and a dashing sea captain tormented by his past cast their lots against the tides of a history dark with treachery. A compelling read cover to cover."

**—Michael Donnelly, Author of False Harbor**

## With Every Breath I take

A love story laced with fun and surprises.

# Taking A Chance

*"I've no hesitation to recommend this five-star read to new or old readers of historical fiction."*

**—Trisha J. Kelly, multi-genre award-winning author of children and middle school books, and of cozy mysteries and crime thrillers.**

*"Celia Martin captures the complex landscape of people dealing with Puritanism which squelches the fun out of life for ordinary people. A great backdrop for the heroine to shine as she strives to marry the man she loves"*

**—C.A. Asbrey - author of the 19th century murder mysteries, 'The Innocents' and of articles on history for magazines and periodicals.**

# Precarious Game of Hide and Seek

*"Celia Martin's historical romance ranks as above average fare in the this genre.*

**—Jason Hillenburg, Reprospace Editorial Reviews™**

# Fate Takes a Hand

*"Each character, lovingly written, pulls the reader into the story, contributing to the elegance of this beautiful work of fiction. Love stories like this are timeless. If you are looking for a wonderful historical romance with a truly satisfying conclusion, I highly recommend Fate Takes A Hand."*

**—Kristen Morgen, Author of Behind The Glass**

*"Celia Martin's Fate Takes a Hand provides a reading experience any devotee of historical romantic fiction will enjoy and holds up under multiple readings."*

**—Jason Hillenburg, Reprospace Editorial Reviews™**

# And The Ground Trembled

*"Celia Martin is an engaging storyteller. I absolutely loved And the Ground Trembled. It is beautifully written, entertaining, and a lot of fun"*

**—Vonda Sinclair, USA Today Bestselling Author**

*"I see fans of the historical romance genre flocking to Celia Martin's And the Ground Trembled. Lush descriptive passages, a vivid rendering of the historical period, and strong characterizations highlight this novel. Martin feels a strong personal connection with this era in history. The book shows her familiarity with even the smallest of details about its fashion, a keen ear for human speech of the time, and more than a nodding acquaintance with its history."*

**—Mindy McCall, Reprospace Editorial Reviews™**

# Perfidious Brambles

*Perfidious Brambles is a delight. Readers will love the plot with its high romance and touch of intrigue. If you are looking for a lovely novel in which to get lost, you have certainly found it in Perfidious Brambles.*

**—Riana Everly, Recipient of two Jane Austen Readers Awards**

---

## https://tinyurl.com/cmartinbooks

---

To the many authors I have met on Facebook who have helped me in a multi-tude of ways, and who have also introduced me to their wonderful books and hours of fun reading.

# A Collection of Romantic Adventures

Follow the romantic adventures of the D'Arcy, Hayward, and Lotterby families, and their captivating friends in seventeenth century England and the American colonies. In An Unexpected Treasure, Lady Selena D'Arcy is to be trained to be a lady of quality as befits her station, but she has other plans, and they involve Calder Grantham, neighboring yeoman. Will she manage to surmount numerous obstacles and win Calder's love? Or will her parents' disapproval forbid her that love? Be sure to watch for Deceptive Deceptions when Calantha Matherly, better known as Marvelous Marvella Blessing, famed London actress, runs away to Italy with her lover, as her two sisters arrive for a season in London along with their hopes of finding suitable husbands. But all is not rosey for the sisters, for shortly before arriving in London, Agrippina witnessed a murder. Now, it seems the murderer intends Agrippina to be his next victim. And will Calantha's return to London hinder or aid her sisters' hopes of finding love and marriage?

## Excerpt from

## *Deceptive Deceptions*

## At the end of the book.

---

**Visit my web site at:**
**tinyurl.com/celiamartinbooks**

---

# *Prologue*

## Derbyshire, England 1681

Lady Flavia D'Arcy groaned as the coach hit yet another rut in the poorly maintained road. Her traveling companion, the dove-like Carola Mead, echoed her groan. Across from Flavia, her personal maid, Gertrude, widened her large blue eyes, crinkled her perky nose, and clamped her prominent front teeth down over her lower lip. The ride was not only rough, it was boring. They had little they could do but sleep, yet sleep was made near impossible by all the bumps. If her parents had sent the better coach to retrieve her from Tuftwick Hall, she would not be suffering as much. Brushing a curl of her light brown hair off her cheek, she could well imagine she would be black and blue by the time she arrived at her home, Whimbrel Hall.

The muslin shades were drawn to keep the dust out, but Flavia still felt her face, eyes, and tongue were coated in grit. She envied her brother, Ewen, and his friends. Riding their horses, they were out in the fresh air, not cooped up in a moving box. Ewen's brown eyes, so like her own, had glistened with mirth when he joked she could be like her cousin Selena and ride astride. That had set his friends to laughing. The memory of that quip brought her thoughts back around to Selena. Pooh! She had worked so hard to rid herself, at least temporarily, of thoughts of her annoying cousin. Thinking of Selena made her even more miserable.

Why her mother believed she would be able to have any influence on Selena was beyond Flavia's comprehension. No one had any influence on Selena. Selena had influence on everyone else. Flavia had not a doubt in the world that Selena would lead her into some kind of trouble. Oh, why could her mother not have let her go to London with her Aunt Phillida and her cousin Elizabeth to find a husband? But no, her mother said she was too young. Well, she was eighteen, after all. Plenty old enough to marry. Her mother had married her first husband when she was but fifteen and had her first child by the time she was sixteen.

Gads, but she would be glad when they reached their evening's destination. Her father had arranged for them to stay each night with a friend or acquaintance of his. But for their noon meals, they were forced to stop at village inns. The food was seldom appealing, but at least sitting down to the table was a respite from the pounding she was receiving in the coach.

She felt sorry for Carola Mead. Carola had traveled in this hideous coach all the way from Whimbrel Hall to collect Flavia, and now the poor, unassuming dear was having to travel back over the same bumpy road. Carola was a distant cousin of her mother. As Carola had no immediate family or means of support, Flavia's mother had taken her in, given her a home, and treated her as a member of the family. Flavia believed Carola, in order to show her gratitude, often volunteered for egregious tasks no one else wanted to do. This had to be one of those tasks. And Carola was no younger than Flavia's mother who was now in her mid-fifties.

Flavia was grateful she was at least to be allowed a week's visit with her two half-brothers who had estates outside the town of Derby. Their wives would coddle her and make over her and understand all she had endured on this wretched journey. When Aunt Phillida and Elizabeth left for London, Flavia had been sent to stay with Aunt Phillida's sister-in-law, Lady Tuftwick. That dear lady had also coddled her, and Flavia had loved her time at Tuftwick Hall. She had enjoyed flirting with Lady Tuftwick's older son, Algernon, and the young son, Doran, when he was home from school on holiday, and she had treated Lady Tuftwick's thirteen-year-old daughter, Lexina, like a sister.

Then came the letter from her mother telling her she was being sent for so she could help turn Selena from a hoyden into a lady. Impossible! Ewen knew it was impossible, but he admitted, he liked Selena the way she was.

"Not that anyone with any sense would want to marry her," he proclaimed to his friends.

"I found her a regular pixie," Ansel Yardley said. He had met Selena four weeks earlier at Crossly Oaks, Flavia's half-brother's manor in Derbyshire. "Right pretty, too," he added.

"True enough. A bright spirit, she is," Ewen agreed, "but would you want your wife riding astride? Would you want her ignoring her duties because she is off riding or walking or bringing home stray animals or people from who knows where? She does that, and a lot more. Animals and children love her. They follow her about like she was some kind of Pied Piper."

Algernon LaBree chuckled. "I look forward to meeting her. She sounds amusing."

"Amusing, yes. One of the fellows, but not wife material, I swear to you," Ewen said.

"She has a good portion coming to her," Yardley said. "A manor in Lincolnshire, am I not mistaken."

"Aye, that she has. But I will say no more on the subject. Are any of you foolish enough to fall in love with Selena, 'tis your misfortune. You have all been warned."

Ewen's companions had laughed at his sally, but Flavia could find nothing humorous about the subject. Her mother had asked Ewen to bring a couple of his friends to Rotherby that Selena could practice being more genteel around gentlemen. Flavia guessed her mother might also have hopes Selena might find a mate. But here was Ewen, warning them off. Not that she could blame him. They were his friends, and he could not wish them tied to Selena.

Flavia liked all three of Ewen's friends. Ansel Yardley was the funniest. When he laughed, which was often, his dark eyes fairly twinkled. He had a strong chin and firm mouth, but his grin was so infectious, she doubted he could ever seem stern. Algernon LaBree was the most handsome of her brother's new friends, with his bright blue eyes, dark hair, and Greek god facial features. Though ever courteous, he was a flirt, and Flavia was drawn to him. She could see herself falling in love with him did she not ever so often conjure up the fleeting image of Ewen's childhood friend and their neighbor, Orland Darnell. She wondered if Orland might also be invited to Rotherby to help with Selena's civilizing lessons. She hoped he would be.

Silvester Preston, Yardley's cousin, was intriguing in that he seemed always to be studying everyone from under his lowered eyelids. His eyes were a light-colored hazel, almost a pale green, and his dark hair was incredibly thick. His thin, aquiline nose gave him an aristocratic appearance, though he was but the son of a baronet. While Carola rested for a week after her arrival at Tuftwick Hall, Yardley and Ewen rode to Nantwich in Cheshire to collect Preston, because Yardley was certain his cousin would be delighted to join them.

"He is ever bored," Yardley proclaimed, "and eager to escape his mother, my Aunt Arcadia. She wants him to marry and produce a son, an heir to the baronetcy. If she thinks he is going to meet a potential mate, she will pack him off herself." So Silvester Preston, the future Baronet of Britteridge, had joined them, but Flavia was not certain Preston was at all interested in finding a mate. Fact was, from snippets of conversation she had overheard, but should not have, she believed he fancied himself a dallier, in no hurry to limit himself to one woman.

Another bump, another pair of groans. Wretched road. None of the counties maintained their highways as they should, though her father swore they were far superior to what they used to be, especially the new toll roads that had been built. Settling back against the cushioned seat, Flavia wished it was plusher. Was she ever to ride in this coach again, she would be certain to provide herself with more cushions.

Closing her eyes, she tried to sleep, but again, Selena swam through her mind. She wondered what Selena would do that would get her into trouble and prove to her mother that she was not as grown up as she considered herself. She wished she was stronger willed. Wished she could say no to Selena, but Selena had a way of making everything sound or appear reasonable. Oh, well, she might as well just face up to it—Selena meant trouble.

# *Chapter 1*

**Leicestershire, England – Whimbrel Hall**

Rowena D'Arcy, Lady Rotherby, lightly drummed her fingers on the small table beside her cushioned chair. Her drumming caught her husband's attention.

Next to her in a matching armchair, Nathaniel D'Arcy, Lord Rotherby, asked, "All right, Row, what is troubling you?"

"Look at her, Nate," she said, nodding to the young woman sitting in the window seat across the parlor. A book rested in the girl's lap, yet she did naught but stare out the window at the fading night sky. "She has done nothing but mope since she arrived here. Again this evening, she barely touched her supper, nor her dinner earlier today. That is not like Selena. In all the years I have known the child, she has always had a more than hearty appetite. But now, in the three weeks she has been here, she is losing weight. The maid, who is seeing to her, says does she lose more weight, she will have to take in some of her gowns."

"I would say our Selena is a very unhappy young woman," Nate answered.

Frowning, Rowena turned to him. "I can see that, Nate. 'Tis what I am to do about it that puzzles me. Her dear mother sends Selena to me, trusting me to turn her into a lady, and all I have done is make her sick. How will it look to Angelica if I must send her daughter back to her, ill and looking like a rail?"

"Selena cares not for her lessons?"

"She says, could she but understand the need to learn the things I am attempting to teach her, she might be better able to apply herself, but she can see no reason to learn what she needs to learn about how to run a home. She cannot understand why she cannot have a competent housekeeper or steward manage the running of her house."

"And is there a reason she cannot?"

Rowena rolled her eyes sideways at her husband. "We have a wonderful housekeeper as well as a butler and a steward, but which one should I allow to do the seating arrangement for a formal dinner? Which one would you like to choose the fabrics for your next breeches or coats? Which one should have chosen the furnishings for our bedchambers? Or for any of the rooms in the house? Yes, the butler keeps order and gives the footmen their duties. He sees we are appropriately served at our meals. But he informs me," she stressed the me, "when your wine supply is running low and must be replenished by ordering from France. Sugar, spices, salt, pepper, any number of items must be ordered in a timely fashion, and the correct amount must be ordered or we will run out of the items."

Her husband tried to interrupt her by agreeing she had a point, but Rowena would not be stopped. "Yes, our steward sees our meat is cured and stored, he works with the gamekeeper who supplies our game and fish. He works with the head of our dairy and our brew-house and insures we have the wood or coal we need for fires in our rooms and for the kitchen. He keeps the books, but I go over them with him on a weekly basis. You see them but once a month. I know when we can afford special treats, a new gown for Flavia or coat for Ewen.

"And though our housekeeper is in charge of directing the maids …"

"Enough!" Nate said, his voice raised to a measure Selena turned to look at him. He lowered his voice. "Enough, my dear. You have convinced me."

"I have not told you the half of it."

His blue-green eyes danced, and the smile Rowena loved spread across his face. "Of that, I have no doubt. But I think, do you believe you can teach these things to Selena, you will be sadly disappointed. The question to ask is, do these things that matter to us, matter to Selena."

Rowena returned her gaze to her niece. With her dark hair and blue-green eyes, Selena looked more like Rowena's husband than his own children did. Both their children looked like her with their brown hair and brown eyes. Selena, on the other hand, had the typical D'Arcy coloring, and a straight nose, high cheekbones, and a firm chin. The golden tan of her skin was fading slightly as Rowena had the girl spending most of her time indoors with various training activities. Slowly shaking her head, Rowena wondered if her husband could be right. Was any attempt to convince Selena of the importance of learning to care for a house and home useless.

Just this morning she had been trying to teach Selena how to properly make a bed. "But why must I know how to make a bed?" Selena asked. "The maid will do it, as she does now."

"You need to know how, so that you may show a new maid how to do it."

"Why would not the housekeeper or another of the maids show her?"

"Mayhap the housekeeper is ill, and you have guests coming. All your maids are busy cleaning, and the new maid is to make the beds."

"I would simply tell the new maid to do the cleaning. Surely I would not have hired a maid who had no knowledge of cleaning, and the old maid could then make the beds. Mother never has to show maids how to make beds. Of course, she cannot. So if a new maid needs training, the housekeeper or Mother's maid, Esmeralda, trains her."

Selena was right about that. Due to a terrible accident, when her coach overturned, Angelica D'Arcy, Lady Rygate, was left paralyzed from the waist down. Confined to a chair or her bed, the lovely woman had been unable to give Selena the guidance she needed in her early years. Consequently, Selena's father, doting on his daughter, spoiled her and allowed her to run wild with her four brothers. Selena had even shared her brothers' tutors. Lord Rygate had kept all his children at home in their youth. He had not sent any away to foster homes or to schools until the boys were old enough to be sent to Oxford.

What training Selena did receive in proper decorum came primarily from her father or her mother's devoted personal maid. Selena could dress appropriately when forced to do so, she could dance, could sit at a table and not embarrass herself with unladylike behavior, but that was about it. She could not sew a stitch, she could not plan a meal or a social gathering. She could curry a horse or train a dog to hunt, but she had no idea how to insure a table was properly set or in what order the dishes or wines should be served.

"Mayhap you could work out a compromise with our unhappy lass," Nate said, interrupting his wife's thoughts.

Rowena turned to him. "What might you suggest?"

"Well, at present, Selena is allowed to go riding in the morning before she breaks her fast. That means, if she wants that treat, she must rise early, which our girl hates doing. She does it, though, because she loves her horse and loves to ride. Then the remainder of the day, she is locked into activities with you that to her seem senseless."

Nodding, Rowena admitted all her husband said was correct.

"Suppose you limit her lessons to just the mornings. Then, after dinner, the afternoons can be hers to use as she pleases. To take walks, to read, maybe take her rides, does she choose not to get up so early in the morning." He held up a hand as Rowena started to interrupt him. "These new privileges would be contingent upon her willingness to learn the lessons you are attempting to teach her. Does she work hard and cooperate in learning her lessons, she has her freedom in the afternoons."

Rowena eyed her husband from under lowered lids. "Nate, my love, that might just work. I know you think does a man love Selena, he should love her as she is, but that would not be fair to either of them. A man needs his wife to properly run his home."

"That may be true, but Selena need not marry. She will someday inherit a very nice estate, so she will never be destitute. Her brothers love her. She will always be welcome in their homes. Does she not find a mate, would it be so terrible?"

Picking up her husband's hand from the armrest of his chair, she placed it on her cheek. "Would you have her miss the joy that we experience every day? Would you have Selena never know love?" Rowena shook her head. "That would be sad. That is why her mother asked me to train her to be a lady. Angelica and Ranulf know the kind of love we know and share. Can you wonder Angelica wants that for her daughter?"

"Not to know a true love would be sad. But I am not certain it is worth changing Selena. She has a way about her that delights children. And the way animals take to her is uncanny. Should she lose that luster, that joy of living that has always encompassed her ..." He shrugged.

"Well, I shall think about your suggestion. Could be it would produce results. It could be worth trying, anyway."

"Good," he said, looking at her in a way that told her his desire for her was mounting. He had been home from London for but two days and was due to return to London in three days. His older brother's daughter, Elizabeth, was to be married, and as neither her mother nor her father could be with her, due to her mother's illness, Nate had volunteered not only to give the bride away, but to help Elizabeth and her future husband secure a home and other items they would need to set up housekeeping together. He would then accompany the newlyweds to Wealdburh in Cheshire to visit Elizabeth's parents. It would be a homecoming for him, and he was looking forward to seeing the home of his youth. But it meant he would be gone from Whimbrel for near three months. By far the longest they had ever been separated. Rowena dreaded his absence.

"All that talk of love has stirred my need for you my dear," her husband, leaning closer, said in a low voice. "I find my love for you has not dimmed one bit over our years together. If anything, it has grown stronger. What say, we hasten our niece to bed and head to our bed."

Smiling, Rowena said, "You are right, Nate. If anything my love for you, my need to be one with you is as intense as it was when first we wed." She tilted her head to one side and glanced at him out of the corners of her eyes. "As intense as before we were wed."

"That does it," he said, rising. "Selena, your aunt and I are planning to make it an early evening. Think you, you are ready for bed?"

Closing her book, Selena said, "Aye, Uncle Nate, but do you not object, I will just go see how Brigantia fares. She seemed a little off when I rode her this morning."

"That is fine, but be back in the house ere it grows dark."

"Yes, sir."

Rowena watched Selena leave the room. The girl walked with a firm step, more like a man would walk than a young lady. One more thing she needed to work on with Selena. But with her husband taking her arm, thoughts of Selena slipped away, replaced by thoughts of her amorous husband. His body still enticed her. Strong and muscled. Though she was tall, he towered over her. She decided this evening, she would send her maid on to bed and would let Nate help her undress. And she would help him. Hmmm. Sweet love.

# Chapter 2

Selena believed she could well be floating on air, except for the fact she was so enjoying the leaf and moss padded woodland path beneath her feet. After she returned from her morning ride and grabbed a quick bite to eat, she found her aunt awaiting her in the parlor. Her aunt had a proposition for her, and as soon as Selena heard it, she agreed to it wholeheartedly. Did she work diligently in the mornings and not complain about the subject of her lessons, she was to have her afternoons free.

She breathed in deeply, rejoicing in the earthy woodland scents. Finally, she had some freedom. She learned the new plan had been her uncle's suggestion, and she remembered to thank him when they sat down to dinner. Her aunt, pleased with her morning's performance, praised her, and said she was happy to see Selena had regained her appetite. Selena appreciated her aunt's compliments, though she had seen no sense to the morning's exercise. Her aunt decided she needed to learn how to walk like a lady. Selena thought she walked just fine, but she forbore mentioning her own opinion. She but did her best to do exactly as her aunt directed her, foolish though it might seem.

"Selena, dear, you are light on your feet, that is good. But you stride across a room like a man. Now watch me." Her aunt had proceeded to walk across the parlor and back, her gown swishing ever so softly with each step. "You need to take smaller steps. Now you try."

Selena obeyed, but her aunt had not been satisfied. "Let us try it with a book on your head," Aunt Rowena said. Selena giggled when her aunt placed the book atop her head. Keeping it balanced on the head was a bit of a challenge, and it did cause her to slow her pace. "Now try turning your toes in just a smidge while you walk. Should make your hips sway."

Selena could not think why she needed to learn to walk more mincingly, but to have her afternoons free, she was not about to question her aunt. After the lessons in walking, they had returned to the task of fine stitching. "There are times," Aunt Rowena said, "when a lady needs to keep her hands occupied, her eyes lowered, and her tongue in her mouth. You may find this most often necessary when men start arguing religion or politics."

Selena wondered why she would have to keep quiet rather than enter in on the discussion, as she did with her father and brothers, but again, she refrained from asking. She but did as she was bid, and attempted to take tiny delicate stitches on the lace hanky her aunt had given her to practice on. Sewing, she decided, was about the only thing so far that she could see a use for. Oh, not the delicate stitching Aunt Rowena was expecting her to learn, but being able to tighten the waist on a pair of her brother's breeches to make them fit better could come in handy.

So the morning had passed, and now she was free. Free to explore her uncle's estate. Aunt Rowena thought a footman should accompany her, but Uncle Nate said, "Why? When have we ever had any cause to think we have anything to fear on our estate. Do let the girl have her afternoon to herself." Her aunt acquiesced, and no sooner was dinner ended, and Selena excused herself and hurried to her room to don a plain gown and sturdy shoes.

The day was perfect for a walk. The sun was shining, a gentle breeze cooled the air, and the birds were chirping. She had wandered about the meadows for a while but then headed for the woods. The path she followed was well worn. It looked to have seen a lot of use over the years. Uncle Nate told her the woods housed its share of hares, squirrels, coneys, and foxes, but he thought few deer ever wandered through, and no boars. He believed the only deer on his estate were to be found in his fenced deer park. He promised her, come fall, she could go on a hunt with him and Ewen.

She was looking forward to Flavia's and Ewen's arrival. Four weeks earlier, she had seen Ewen briefly at his half-brother's home in Derbyshire, but she had not seen her cousin, Flavia, in three years. Not since the last family reunion at her Uncle Kenrick's Walling House outside Wallingford in Oxfordshire. Those family gatherings were always such grand fun. She was glad the large D'Arcy family enjoyed a close relationship.

Stopping at various clearings and taking the occasional side trail, she had no idea how long she had been hiking when she came to a small brook. It was narrow enough she could hop across it. As the path continued on the opposite side, she chose to continue her hike, though she guessed it was nearing mid-afternoon. She had not gone far when she saw a man dressed in clothing denoting him to be a farmer. His wide-legged breeches, woolen stockings, sturdy square-toed shoes, and a plain brown coat with rolled back cuffs showed wear but were clean. A flat-brimmed hat sat atop his loose, short, brown hair. He was pulling a coney from a trap. A poacher, she thought, and without giving her action a second thought, she confronted the man.

"You are lucky I am not my uncle's gamekeeper," she said, assuming a firm voice. "You must know poaching can run you a hefty fine, do I report it."

At the sound of her voice, the man straightened and turned to face her. At that instant, she fell in love. He had to be the most handsome man she had ever seen. His eyes were the bluest, blue under straight, brown eyebrows. His face had the tanned hue of a farmer, and his features, though rugged, were perfectly proportioned. But it was his smile that near made her swoon. It was a smile that reached his eyes, causing them to twinkle.

"Well, now, Lady Selena," he said, his voice rich and vibrant.

He knew her name! How was it he knew her name?

"You accuse me unjustly," he continued. "You see, you are on my property. That brook you would have hopped over a short ways back is the boundary line between my farm and your uncle's manor. But do please consult Lord Rotherby, do you not believe me."

"How do you know who I am?" she blurted out, it being the first thing she could think to say to this incredibly handsome man.

He chuckled. Oh, she liked the sound of his laugh. It rumbled up from his throat. "Everyone knows Lord and Lady Rotherby have their niece visiting this summer. As you referred to your uncle, I assumed you must be Lady Selena."

"How is it everyone should know of my visit?" She advanced closer to this wondrous farmer. "I have been nowhere but to church, and I have met but few people. I cannot remember seeing you there." Had he been in church, she would have noticed him, of that she was certain.

He smiled. "I fear I am often absent from Sunday services. My housekeeper and son normally attend. Both told me of you, but even had they not, Rotherby parish and surrounding community is not large. Does someone of prestige come to our area, word soon gets around."

She laughed, and he cocked his head and looked at her with a curious expression on his face. A happy expression, it seemed to her. "'Tis strange to think I would be considered a person of prestige," she said. "I cannot think why."

"You are an earl's daughter. That gives you prestige."

"Does it? How interesting. But, sir, you have me at a disadvantage. You know my name, but I have not learned yours."

He bowed slightly. "Forgive me, my lady. My name is Calder Grantham." He pointed off to his left. "That farm in the valley, as well as a portion of this hillside, belong to me."

Looking past him, she could see a valley, but to see more of it, she walked past him, then took a deep breath. "Oh, 'tis lovely. I cannot think when I have seen a more lovely valley." The hillside sloped gently down into a lush green valley. Rock fences and low hedgerows kept sheep and cows pastured and out of a couple of grain fields. A number of out buildings, some of stone, some of wood, were a short distance from the loveliest, two-story, stone house with green shutters on a multitude of windows.

She turned back to the man who had just stolen her heart. His farm was as beautiful as he was. "You must forgive me for mistaking you for a poacher."

"Easily forgiven, but I would say in the future, should you ever encounter a real poacher, you should refrain from making any threats. Fact is, 'twould be wise did you carry a good strong walking stick with you. Just to be on the safe side."

"Uncle Nate seemed to think there was no threat on his property."

"Ordinarily, I would say he is correct, but of late, one of our neighbors has been allowing a number of his dogs to roam free. He says, 'tis because his steward discovered several illegal traps on his property. If 'tis true, poachers might be in our area. But to my way of thinking, 'tis the dogs to be wary of more than the poachers. They have already killed one of my lambs."

"Oh, no! I hope the man letting his dogs run loose has paid you for the lamb."

"Not yet. I may have to take him to the next quarter session court in Melton-Mowbray, do I choose to travel that far, since I might not get a fair judgement from our local justice."

"Why is that? Is he not respected?"

"Oh, the squire, our Justice of the Peace, is respected. But 'tis his dogs that run lose."

Selena put her hand to her mouth to cover her smile. "Oh, dear," she finally managed. "I suppose that is a tad unfair. I wonder if Reynard Bardwith could help. He is my Aunt Rowena's son-in-law, and he is the current constable in Rotherby. Might be he could speak with your squire. A constable to a justice."

"Nay, 'twould not be fair to Mister Bardwith. I know him. Have known his family for years. Bardwith is a good man, a fair man, but I would not put this on his shoulders. But here now." He changed the subject. "If you have walked all the way from Whimbrel Hall, 'tis over two miles. You must be thirsty. Would you care to stop in my home for a mug of ale, or perhaps some buttermilk?"

Indeed she would like to see his home. See more of him. Sudden fear! Dear God, please, he cannot be married. Thoughts ran riot in her brain, but she managed to answer, "Thank you, yes, I would like something to drink, but I cannot say I remember drinking buttermilk since I was a young child."

"Ah, then you could be in for a treat. On a warm day like today, nothing is better than fresh buttermilk kept cold in the spring." He nodded to her. "Shall we go? I need to get this rabbit to my housekeeper, is she to prepare it for our supper."

# Chapter 3

Her heart thumping about in her chest, Selena followed Calder Grantham down the hillside. He had a housekeeper, but he had thus far mentioned no wife. Surely, was he married, he would have mentioned his wife. He said his son and the housekeeper went to Sunday services in Rotherby. Again, no mention of a wife. Oh, he must be a widower. Had he loved his wife deeply like her parents loved each other? Was he so greatly saddened by her death he would never be able to love again? Such questions darted about in her head. At the same time, she felt a pain in her heart that this man had lost his wife, yet she could not but hope he was over his grief.

The walk across the lush meadow covered in grass and clover was like a tour as Calder – she was already thinking of him by his given name – pointed out the various aspects of his farm. She enjoyed listening to his vibrant voice, pitched neither too high nor too low. 'Twas obvious he loved his farm and took pride in it. He waved to a couple of laborers. One was weeding an herb and vegetable garden, another was trimming one of the hedgerows. She could hear the sound of a Jew's harp being played, and in the distance she saw a shepherd seated on a low rise keeping watch on the sheep and their lambs.

Noticing the direction of her gaze, Calder said, "Abner needs keep watch on the flock in case the dogs return. I cannot well afford to lose another lamb. I would prefer Abner could be helping Joseph with the hedgerow trimming. I like to keep the hedgerows at a low enough height I can hop over them am I needed in a hurry." He smiled his vibrant smile at her. "I also want them low enough that your uncle's and his friends' horses and dogs have no trouble jumping over them when they chase after a fox or a hare."

Surprised, she stopped, and touched his arm that he would stop. "My uncle goes fox or hare hunting here on your farm?"

He nodded. "Aye, he and other neighbors go dashing across whatever property they wish when they follow their prey."

"But does that not ruin some of your crops or scare your animals?"

"The hunting never starts until harvest season ends, but yes, the hunters have been known to scatter the sheep and cattle, do they chance through the pastures. Your uncle always warns me in advance when he is planning such a hunt, but not everyone gives us warning."

"Hmmm," she said, and started walking again when he did. "Seems inconsiderate to me. At home, we have never ventured off our own estate when we hunt."

"Well, at least deer hunting is reserved to deer parks," Calder said. "Any deer not in parks have long since left the area or have been killed by the locals to provide for their families."

"We have a substantial commons on our estate," Selena said, "but we have few tenants. They grow fruits and vegetables for the London market. Like your farm, our land is good for sheep raising. 'Tis our tenants who see to their care. We also have thick forests, and make a good profit from the sale of wood. So between the woods and the sheep pastures, we provide the perfect landscape for the fallow deer. But we and our tenants hunt only on our land."

"You are saying your tenants are allowed to hunt your deer?"

She laughed. "The deer are not ours. Once there were numerous deer parks in Surrey, but they were allowed to fall into disrepair. The deer escaped, and now roam at their will."

"The venison must be a nice treat for your tenants," Calder said, stopping in front of his house as a boy came running toward them. "My son, Pascal," he said. "He has been minding the bee hives, watching do they swarm. Mid-day being the most likely time for them to swarm."

"I have seen the scouts out," the boy said. He looked to be about five or six. He was a small image of his father. His features had not yet that rugged look, but he had the same vibrant blue eyes, same straight eyebrows, and his brown hair was but a shade lighter. His head cocked to one side, he looked at her curiously. "Are you not Lady Selena?" he asked.

"Aye, she is," Calder said. "Make your bow, son."

The boy bobbed at his waist and Selena smiled and said, "Pleased to meet you, Pascal."

With a pat to his son's head, Calder said, "I have invited Lady Selena to have some buttermilk. Might you run to the spring and fetch us a crock?"

"Oh, yes, Father," Pascal said, his voice bright and chirpy. "I will be right back." And he took off toward a small stone building next to the brook that bubbled down from the hill.

Opening the door to his house, Calder said, "Do come inside, Lady Selena."

Upon entering the house, her arm brushed against his arm and a tingle shot up her spine. Calder Grantham had her head in a most pleasant spin. The spin continued as she looked around the large open hall. She could not be more pleased with the interior. Everything about it bespoke friendly warmth. The diamond-paned windows had cream-colored curtains spread open to let in the sunlight, the table in the center of the room was covered in a clean white cloth, brightly woven rugs hung on the stone walls, and a low crackling fire in the larger of two stone hearths had a black iron pot sitting on a tripod over it. A heavenly scent of something baking wafted through the air.

A strongly built woman with graying hair tucked into a bun turned from a long work table snug against the wall next to the hearth when Calder said, "Hannah, we have a guest. And I have that coney you wanted." Stepping over to Hannah, he plopped the rabbit on the work table.

Her hands and forearms covered in dough, Hannah eyed Selena. Her pale blue eyes beneath sparse blond brows and lashes looked surprised. Wiping her arms on her large apron, she dropped a curtsy. Her thin lips spread in a small smile. "Why, am I not mistaken, 'tis Lady Selena. I recognize you from church."

"Indeed it is," Calder said. "Lady Selena, may I present my housekeeper and cook, Hannah Burbage. I cannot rightly think how Pascal and I should manage without her."

At the compliment, Hannah shook her head. "I but do my best. But Lady Selena, you have caught me at an awkward time. Today is my day for baking bread. At present I am up to my elbows kneading the last batch. Do I not persist, could be it will not rise as it should."

"Oh, by all means, continue with your bread. I am but here for a drink of buttermilk. But I must say, something is smelling heavenly already." Raising her chin and sniffing the air, Selena wondered what the housekeeper might be cooking.

"Ah, 'tis the currant buns you be smelling," Hannah said. "Master Pascal likes to break his fast of a morning with a currant bun and fresh churned butter."

"Hmmm, I cannot say I blame him. It sounds wonderful, and they smell yummy."

"Would you like a bun, hot from the oven," Hannah said, "they will soon be done."

"I would love a taste. But only does it not interfere with your work, Mistress Burbage."

Hannah chuckled. "No one has called me Mistress Burbage in many a year. Hannah works for me just fine, Lady Selena."

"Then you must call me Selena."

Hannah vigorously shook her head. "Oh, no, milady. That would not be fitting. You be quality. Now you sit yourself down there at the table, and Calder can get you a noggin and serve you soon as Pascal comes with the buttermilk."

As she spoke, the boy came through the door, a heavy clay crock cradled in his arms. "I have the buttermilk, Father," he said.

"Splendid, Pascal," Calder said, taking the crock from his son. After bidding Selena take a seat at the table, he joined Hannah at the work table. Shelves above the table held various sizes of wooden plates, cups, and bowls. Taking three wooden noggins down, he filled them with the buttermilk. He handed one cup to Pascal, the other two he brought to the table.

Setting the noggins on the table, he said, "To my way of thinking, buttermilk tastes best from a wooden noggin." She had noted a rough wooden hutch against the back wall. It displayed pewter mugs, plates, platters, and bowls as well as a large carving knife and fork. "Seems the pewter adds its own flavor to the buttermilk," he continued, pulling out a chair and seating himself opposite Selena. "You want to saver the buttermilk at its best."

She took a sip. Oh, it was delicious, cold, thick, and slightly sour. She licked her upper lip. "Thank you, Mister Grantham. 'Tis perfect."

"Good. But, please, I am not called Mister. I am but Calder or at times, Goodman Grantham. I am but a yeoman. I work my own land," Calder said with a smile that set Selena's heart to spinning. "The buttermilk," he continued, "not only makes a refreshing drink, Hannah often uses it when cooking baked goods. Makes them lighter and fluffier."

The creamy liquid sitting on his upper lip, Pascal said, "On occasion, Hannah makes our puddings with buttermilk."

"Oh, that sounds good," Selena said.

"Near as good as her currant buns," the boy said, and Selena laughed.

Pascal laughed, too. "I like your laugh," he said. "'Tis all tinkling, musical. Makes me think of bells tinkling."

"He is right," Calder said. "You have a most merry laugh."

"Laughter is good for the soul," Selena said. "I am glad does my laugh sound merry, for certainly, I feel merry."

Enjoying herself immensely, Selena asked, "You then know my uncle?"

"To speak to him," Calder said. "I understand he treats his tenants well. Like us, he is heavy into sheep and cattle. 'Tis good pasture for them. And wool can line a pocket with coin, does the wool merchant pay a fair price for the wool."

"Aye, that is what my father says," Selena said. "We had a merchant came down from London that Father worked with for many a year, but he passed on two years back, and the man Father works with now is not as satisfactory."

"Where are you from?" Pascal asked.

"I am from eastern Surrey near the town of Reigate."

"Why are you here?"

"Pascal! You should not ask such a question," Calder said. "'Tis rude."

"Oh, I am sorry." The boy hug his head, but looked up with a smile when Selena laughed.

"Never you mind, Pascal," she said. "I find nothing wrong with the question. I am here staying with Lord and Lady Rotherby so Lady Rotherby can turn me into a lady."

"Huh!" The boy's blue eyes widened, and so did his father's.

"Seems I have much to learn am I ever to manage a home," Selena said, donning half a smile. "I fear I much prefer riding and walking about in the woods and playing with animals when I should be learning which earl should sit next to which baron or whether fish should be served before pheasant or any number of things, that frankly, I really cannot care about."

Pascal laughed. "What happens if the earl sits beside the wrong baron?"

Joining in his laughter, Selena shrugged. "I have no idea, but it must cause some big problem because my aunt has a book she uses, if she wonders who should sit where."

Calder was smiling. "Etiquette can be important, I am certain." He looked at his son. "'Tis not something we are ever likely to have to worry about."

"I wish 'twas nothing I had to worry about," Selena said before finishing her buttermilk. Setting the noggin on the table, she rose and Calder rose with her. "I suppose I must be getting home so not to worry my aunt. 'Twas so wonderful to meet all of you. Might I visit you again?"

"We would be honored," Calder said, and Selena prayed he meant it.

"Here now," Hannah said. "These currant buns are done. I have wrapped one in a napkin. You take it with you. Save it to break your fast in the morning, do you wish. It will keep."

"Thank you," Selena said, taking the proffered bun. "'Tis most kind. When next I visit, I will return the napkin."

"You will come back, will you not?" Pascal asked. "I like you."

Bending closer to Pascal, Selena said, "I like you, too. So yes, I will come back soon."

"Here," Calder said, handing her a sturdy walking stick. "I can easily get another stick. You never know when it might come in handy. Those dogs could be on the prowl."

"Thank you," Selena said, taking the stick, but doubting she would need it against the dogs. However, it would give her something that belonged to Calder, and that she was pleased to have. Pascal and Calder both came out and waved to her as she marched back across the field toward the hill. When half way up the hill she turned around. Pascal was still watching her. He waved, but his father was nowhere in sight. Well, he most likely had work to do.

Hugging the stick, she set off down the path. She liked knowing what Calder would be eating for his supper. Stewed rabbit and fresh baked bread. She wondered if his laborers sat down to table with him and Pascal. She guessed they did, and most likely Hannah did also. She wished she was sitting down with them instead of with her aunt and uncle.

Not that Aunt Rowena and Uncle Nate were not good company and often amusing, but since she was in training, everything she did was scrutinized by her aunt. Plus she had to dress for dinner and for supper. After supper, they retired to the parlor. A couple of nights she had played chess or backgammon with her uncle, but for the past several nights, she had been too low-spirited to do anything but read, or try to read. This evening, though, her spirits were buoyed, but rather than play any games, she wanted just to think about Calder and his wonderful home and family.

She decided she would not tell her aunt and uncle about Calder. Not yet, anyway. She could not say why, but she feared they might not approve and might forbid her from visiting him. She picked a safe place near the path to leave her walking stick, then struck out across the meadow to the house.

The house was pretty, and like her parents' home, it was new. The building had been started in sixteen sixty-two, a year after King Charles II awarded the estate and the title to her uncle for his aid to the King while the King was in exile on the continent. The house had all the newest modern attributes. Built of a pretty red brick, it had new sash windows, wainscoted walls and decorative stucco ceilings, painted canvas coverings for the floors, and a gallery stretching the length of the ground floor to house family portraits and other pieces of art.

A parlor, two dining chambers – one for entertaining guests, one for just the family – a library and an office were on the ground floor, and besides the grand hall, the house had a grand entry with a beautiful staircase leading up to the bedchambers on the first floor. The nursery and rooms for the house servants were on the second floor, and the basement contained the kitchen and the cook's quarters, the wine cellar and the buttery. Like Selena's father, her uncle had gone into debt to build his house, but he managed his land well, and he was now free of debt.

When guests were not in attendance, the family ate in the small dining chamber at the rear of the house. As soon as she changed, that was where Selena headed. Arriving but a few minutes after her aunt and uncle, she took her seat and smiled brightly. "'Twas a wonderful afternoon," she said before they could question her. "I had a lovely walk in the woods. Our woods are not near as extensive, that is, they are more scattered, not one big woodland."

"You may have noticed," her uncle said, "a number of the trees are young. 'Twas sad to cut down so many of the older growth, but 'twas needed to pay for the building of this house."

"I noticed, sir, but the young trees have such vivid green foliage, they quite catch the eye. Plus they allow more sun to filter through, casting beautiful displays of shade and sunlight."

"You enjoyed yourself then?" Aunt Rowena said, as the footmen set bowls of mushroom soup before the members of the table."

Selena beamed at her aunt. "Yes, as I said, 'twas wonderful. Thank you for devising this plan. Indeed, tomorrow morning I will work doubly hard at whatever you wish to teach."

Her aunt laughed. "That sounds most promising. But while you were out this afternoon, you had your first caller."

"I did? I had no idea I knew anyone to be paying me a call."

"'Twas Mister Orland Darnell. The son of our neighbor, Lord Edgerton. You met Mister Darnell at church last Sunday."

"Oh, yes, I remember him. He made me a pretty bow."

Uncle Nate chuckled. "That would be Orland. He and Ewen have been the best of friends since their early youth, but I fancy since returning from Middle Temple, Orland has become a bit of a dandy."

"Indeed, he was dressed very prettily," Selena said.

Aunt Rowena smiled. "I invited him to join us for dinner tomorrow. So you shall at last have some company. In fact, you may ride out with him, do you wish. Mayhap ride over to the village. I have allowed you little chance to see how lovely northern Leicestershire is, and I believe that should be remedied. We will cut your lessons a tad short that you may dress a little more formally tomorrow. I will tell Louisa to do your hair in a more intricate mode rather than your usual bun."

Selena was at first disconcerted. She wanted to return to Calder's farm, but she hid her dismay and thanked her aunt. She saw her uncle watching her. Had he caught her moment of disappointment? He was shrewd and missed little. Maybe she could still visit Calder. She could get Orland Darnell to ride over with her. No, that might not be wise. Darnell might well mention the visit to Aunt Rowena, and though she was not certain why, she had no wish to tell her aunt about her visit to Calder Grantham's. She would simply have to delay her next visit.

# Chapter 4

Calder dumped his last pail of milk into the barrel secured in the cart. Abner had finished hitching the horse to the cart and was ready to take the milk over to White Acres Tower. Calder's four dairy cows produced more milk than his small household could use, so every day, Calder sent the excess milk to their neighbors, the Huddlestons, caretakers for White Acres Tower. White Acres had a large dairy herd and several dairy maids. The butter and cheese they made from the milk was transported to Leicester to furnish the town's residents' needs. In lieu of coin payment for the milk Calder sent to White Acres, he received butter and cheese for his household, sparing Hannah a time consuming and sometimes onerous job of producing the needed provisions.

The Huddlestons were related to the Granthams, and like the Granthams, their ancestry, if through the occasional female ancestor, could be traced back to before the Conqueror, before any families had permanent surnames. Calder's surname dated from the early fourteenth century when Geoffrey of Grantham married the heiress to the farm. Since Geoffrey, there had always been a male heir to the ancient holding. Someday, Pascal would inherit the farm and hopefully have a male heir to continue the Grantham name.

Calder knew he should have married again to produce more heirs should, God forbid, anything happen to Pascal. Hannah had told him he should marry again, give Pascal a mother. "All you need do is crook your finger, and any number of girls would hasten to be your bride," she said. But he had never wanted to crook his finger. When he married Pascal's mother, Mary Hadrian, he had been young and in love. He and Mary had wanted a large family. They had been blessed with Pascal. Then two years after Pascal's birth, Mary and the infant she carried inside her died of a fever that attacked many households that year.

The loss had left him devastated for more than a year. How he would have managed without Hannah, he could not say. The Huddlestons had cared for Pascal that year, and the boy was still close with the family. Stalking from the cow and horse barn to the sheep stalls where Abner had herded the sheep for the night to keep them safe from the squire's dogs, Calder chided himself. Four years since Mary's death and in all that time, no woman had caught his eye. No woman until Lady Selena. A lady! What a fool he was. She was above his touch, yet he could not get her out of his mind.

He liked everything about her; her lively blue-green eyes, her direct way of speaking, her humorous, self-depreciating manner, and her light, bubbly laughter. Laughter full of joy and delight. Pascal liked Lady Selena, too. He was hopeful she would return. Though he knew he should not wish it, Calder, too, hoped she would return. Not that he had any hopes of marrying an earl's daughter, but he would not mind if he could enjoy her company from time to time.

What a shame Lady Rotherby wanted to change Lady Selena. He thought Selena perfect as she was. He would not change a thing about her. But then, he would never be entertaining earls and needing to make certain they were properly seated next to the appropriate baron. From the limited time he had spent with Lady Selena, he could not think she would have much fun at such entertainments. He could almost pity her. An earl's daughter who would rather be a yeoman's daughter. A most interesting young woman.

❧ ❧ ❧

Settling into her usual chair in the family parlor, Rowena admitted to being greatly pleased with the new plan concerning Selena. One day, and Selena was back to her disarming self. Happy and laughing her tinkling laugh and eating a hearty supper. How smart Nate had been to suggest giving Selena more time to enjoy herself. She had been co-operative during her lessons. Had made no complaints no matter how many times she had walked back and forth across the parlor floor with a book on her head.

Rowena could tell Selena would have liked to complain, but the fact that she forbore doing so indicated how much the girl wanted time to be free to do as she pleased. Mayhap now, with this new arrangement, Selena might finally begin making some progress. She had thought Selena might have shown more excitement at the prospect of having a guest to dinner and then to get to ride out with him. Orland Darnell was a personable young man. No doubt he would charm Selena. That was what Selena needed, an interest in suitable young men instead of thinking about dogs and horses and who knows what menagerie of animals.

Selena already had a rooster, a cat, and two dogs attempting to follow her about whenever she stepped outside. Somehow, though, when she bid them bide, they did as ordered. The girl had such a way with animals. Nate declared it uncanny, and she had to agree with him. But what husband would want animals forever following his wife around. Well, that was an issue to be addressed at a much later date. For now, the object was to get Selena to accept the limitations placed on a woman. She could no longer be one of the boys.

❉ ❉ ❉

After going out to see about her horse – Brigantia seemed to need regular reassurance in her new home – Selena joined her aunt and uncle in the parlor. Her aunt sat in her usual chair, her hands busy with the mending in her lap. Her uncle was in his chair beside his wife, reading a recently arrived newspaper from London. The evening was warm, not even a low fire was needed in the hearth. Summer was upon them.

Taking her spot on the window seat, Selena opened her book, and though she stared down at the pages, she was not seeing the print. She was seeing Calder Grantham. She liked his strong, sun-bronzed hands, the twinkle in his eyes, and the gentleness of his voice. He was proud of his farm, proud of his family. She looked forward to learning more about his family. They had obviously prospered over the years. He might not be a country gentleman, but from what she had seen, he was not lacking for any comforts.

She liked his son, Pascal, and she liked Hannah. Both were congenial, and neither acted constrained in her presence, though Hannah did insist on calling her Lady Selena. She supposed she could not expect otherwise. It did keep a distance she would prefer not to have. Hopefully, with Pascal and Calder, she would get past the need to be Lady Selena and could just be Selena.

Selena knew she had been spoiled all her life. Servants had always been there to do her bidding, and she had never questioned it. They had made her bed, seen that her clothes were cleaned, cooked her meals, and cared for her horses, though over the years, she had often helped with currying her mares. But she had never had to do any real work. Never had to get up in the cold mornings and light fires or haul heated water up the stairs or used water back down. Never had to empty or clean chamber pots or scrub dishes or bake bread. Now that Aunt Rowena was teaching her about the management of a household, she was having to see much more clearly all the things that other people were doing for her.

She had always tried to be courteous to servants. But she had never considered the onerous tasks they were expected to perform day in and day out, often even when they might not be feeling well. One's station in life was all but a matter of how a person was born. Some were definitely more lucky than others. She was one of the lucky ones. Yet, she could not help but wonder what it would be like to get up in the morning and go out to feed the animals and milk the cows or goats, then come back inside and eat breakfast before going out to hoe the garden or help harvest the crops.

Had Calder's wife done all those things? Had she made the beds and emptied the chamber pots, or helped Hannah bake the bread or clean the rabbit? The duties of a yeoman's wife would be very different from that of a gentleman's wife. Selena was not certain she would make a good yeoman's wife, but she knew she wanted to learn more about the possibility.

Smiling, she gazed down at her book. In two days she would visit Calder's farm again. Until then, she would keep the memory of two brilliant blue eyes clutched close to her heart.

$$\text{❦ ❦ ❦}$$

Nathaniel saw the winsome smile spread across his niece's face. That his plan to give her more time to herself had raised her spirits was evident, but something more than just a raising of spirits was behind that smile. That she had no interest in Orland Darnell was obvious. So what was the cause of that smile? Intriguing.

# Chapter 5

"Shall we ride into the village?" Darnell asked.

Holding Brigantia to a trot beside Darnell's large roan, Selena said, "Yes, that would be delightful. I have had little time to see much of the area. Aunt Rowena keeps me busy with my lessons."

"What are these lessons Lady Rotherby is teaching you?"

Selena laughed, and Darnell joined in her laughter.

"When you laugh," he said, "I cannot help but laugh also. Your laughter is so light and merry, 'tis contagious."

Selena liked Darnell. At twenty-one, he was a year older than her cousin, Ewen. Ewen and Darnell, having been the best of friends from their early youth, had shared many an adventure. At dinner, Darnell had entertained her and her aunt and uncle with some of his and Ewen's more tame episodes. Darnell was a handsome lad with round gray eyes, a slim nose, curvaceous lips, and light-brown hair that he wore, in Selena's opinion, overly long. His riding costume was impeccable, from his high black boots to his cocked-brim hat to his white cravat at his neck and his gold-handled sword at his hip.

After dinner, she had changed into her riding attire, a peach-colored, close-fitting jacket with side vents and large cuffs, and a matching skirt with a long train. Her black cocked hat had a pink plume, and she wore white gloves. She hated having to ride sidesaddle, but anytime she was atop Brigantia, she could not help but feel her spirits rise. And Darnell was a personable fellow, good company. He reminded her of her cousin and her brothers, so she was pleased her aunt had invited him to dinner, even though it meant her visit to Calder's farm had to be delayed. Mayhap when Darnell next visited, and she had little doubt her aunt would invite him again, she would take Darnell with her to visit Calder.

"So what are you studying?" Darnell again asked.

"How to be a lady," she answered and watched the expression on his face change from curious to surprise.

After a shake of his head, he said, "What can you mean by that?"

"I fear I am very unladylike, Mister Darnell. I would far prefer to be riding astride like you than riding side-saddle, as I now must do. I detest needing to be concerned with the running of the house. I would far prefer to be outdoors taking walks, riding, playing at tennis or pall mall, or swimming. Oh, yes, I know how to swim. I could care less who is seated where at a dinner party, or if my stride across the room looks more like a man's than a lady's. My poor, dear aunt's job is to teach me how to do these things despite how much I may dislike doing them."

By the time she finished her lists of her lessons, Darnell was chuckling merrily. "Have you really ridden astride?" he asked.

"Oh, yes, most of the way here. Most of my life. Does that repel you?"

"On the contrary, I find it amusing. I cannot say I have seen anything about you that I would consider unladylike, from your attire to your table manners. However, I can see how you might have the need to learn to manage the concerns of your home. Just as Father says I must learn more about the management of the Edgerton Court as well as our smaller estates in Rutland and Lincolnshire. 'Tis one of the reasons he insisted I spend a couple of terms at the Middle Temple to learn more about laws."

"There, you see, that is what I mean. You get to manage the estate, while I am meant but to manage a house. There are so many boring details, too."

"One might not expect a woman to manage an estate. 'Tis a major task."

"Queen Elizabeth capably managed to run the country. I should think it should not be too great a task for a woman to manage an estate."

He chuckled again. "You are right. But Elizabeth was a Queen with many able men to advise her. I can see your aunt will have her hands full in trying to teach you the importance of managing and directing your staff. However, having known Lady Rotherby for many a year, I cannot but think she will prevail, and you and she will come to a happy understanding."

Selena shrugged. "I hope you may be right, Mister Darnell. 'Tis important to my mother, so I will do my best."

"I have no doubt you will," he said.

Selena thought he spoke in rather a condescending manner, but she would not have her afternoon ruined by his remarks. After all, he but believed, as most men did, that a woman had limited capabilities. Limited to running the home, but not an estate. At least, not unless she was widowed, and then, somehow, she seemed to gain more capabilities. Selena found the whole thing amusing and was in good spirits when she saw they were nearing their destination.

Having seen the village of Whimbrel from the coach window when passing through on the way to and from the town of Rotherby for Sunday services, Selena was pleased to have the chance to actually visit the village, small though it was. She spotted a blacksmith shop and heard clanging and banging. A couple of ale houses had signs signaling they had freshly made ale. The village also sported a shoemaker, a farrier, a pottery maker, and a baker. A short way from the village, on a bend of the local stream, was her uncle's mill. Adjacent to the mill was the miller's substantial stone house. Between the mill and the village was the village green and the community well. A few cows were grazing on the green, and a couple of women appeared to be washing clothes at the stream.

The village was busy on this sunny, mid-afternoon day. A cart loaded with hay and with a barking dog perched atop the load rumbled along the dusty street. It was chased by several young children—children too young to be at work. A youthful girl with thick-blond hair herded a gaggle of geese across a plank bridge over the drainage ditch that ran along beside the street. Selena had to admit, her uncle made certain his tenants maintained the road running through his estate grounds. No deep ruts, no clogged ditches.

She had learned the village once had a church and a tiny nun's convent, but with the dissolution of the Catholic Church under Henry VIII, the property had gone to ruin, and most of the stones had been carted off and used for other buildings. Where the convent once sat, a new owner had built a granary storage building. The church ruins, next to the granary, looked bare and lonely, but the graveyard near the ruins appeared to be maintained, though it had no new residents. Burials were now in the consecrated churchyard grounds in Rotherby.

Selena hoped to meet some of Whimbrel's citizens. Most of the village inhabitants were her uncle's tenants, but a few were independents and had their own small parcels of land where they raised sheep and rye or oats. Crofts varied in size, but besides the houses, each croft had its own little garden plots, and most sheltered chickens and a pig or goat or some animal in a barnyard behind the house. Most of the houses were built of stone or wood or a combination of the two, but some were wattle and daub with thatched roofs.

"Might we stop in one of the ale houses?" Selena said. "I find my throat dry."

"Why not?" Darnell said. "Let us visit Widow Forester. I see she has her sign out. Ewen and I always prefer her ale."

Reining up in front of the widow's cottage, Darnell hopped off his horse and hurried to help Selena down. She hated having to wait to be handed down from her horse, but that was part of being a lady, and she was trying hard to be a lady. At least while with Darnell. That would please her aunt, did he give her a good report.

The cottage door opened before Selena's feet touched the ground, and a woman with graying hair sticking out from under her cap merrily greeted them. "Why, Mister Darnell, I have not seen you in some time. Have you been away to school again."

"Aye, Widow Forester. I was away at Middle Temple, one of the Inns of Court, but I am now finished." He turned to Selena. "Lady Selena, this is Widow Forester."

Selena smiled and reached out her hand to the woman. "How nice to meet you. I will tell you I am very thirsty, and Mister Darnell assures me you make the best ale in the village."

The woman wiped a work-worn hand on her apron before cautiously taking Selena's hand and at the same time bobbing a curtsy. "'Tis an honor to serve you, Lady Selena. My home is humble, but I bid you welcome."

Opening the door wider, Widow Forester stood back to allow Selena and Darnell to enter. The interior was dim, no candles burned, the only light came from the three small windows of the main room. The half-stone, half-timber-framed and plastered house had a stone chimney and a steep narrow staircase wedged in on one side of the hearth, with a door to another room on the opposite side. A trestle table was set up in the center of the room with a bench on one side and three stools on the other. Under one of the side windows, a sturdy oak work table held two small casks. Shelving to the side of the window held a number of wooden noggins.

"Do please have a seat on the settle. 'Tis more comfortable than the bench or stools," Widow Forester said, indicating a high back settle near the hearth. She hastily moved a spinning wheel away, and fluffed a cushion on the seat.

Selena took the proffered seat and smiled. "Thank you," she said. She guessed on cold nights, the high back on the settle kept cold air off the neck, and being next to the hearth, fingers busy with spinning could be kept warm. No doubt every home in the village had a spinning wheel. Spinning wool into thread provided additional income to families.

"Where are your sons?" Darnell asked while Widow Forester filled two noggins with a creamy ale.

"Benjamin is in the shop. Ralph has had to travel to Rotherby to purchase more wood." Handing Selena a noggin, she said, "My sons are barrel makers, Lady Selena. The village blacksmith makes the hoops they need for the barrels and pails, but they must get the wood they need from Rotherby. They then have to cut the slats to size and shave them to fit together tightly that nothing leaks out. They are quite accomplished."

"Was your husband also a cooper?" Selena liked the woman. She liked knowing the widow's sons were skilled workmen.

"Nay, 'twas my brother who trained my sons. My husband, God rest his soul, came from a long line of woodsmen. He logged trees, large and small, and carted them to market. Like his father before him, and his grandfather before him, he was a forester. My husband was the forester for Mister Darnell's father, Lord Edgerton. My husband cared for his woods. Planted new stock. Made certain no more trees were harvested than the woods could support.

"This house was my brother's house. When my husband died, my brother invited us to move in with him, his wife having recently passed on and them having had no children. I took to making ale to please my brother. He likes a creamy ale, he does, and 'twas one way to thank him for him taking me and me boys in. My brother passed on last year." The widow blushed. "Sorry if I do babble on."

Selena smiled up at the widow. "No need to apologize. I am sorry you lost your husband and your brother, but I am pleased you have two fine sons."

The widow nodded her thanks, then looked at Darnell. "Mister Darnell and your cousin, Lord Sutherlin, have been good customers for several odd years now."

Selena's cousin, Ewen, being the son of an Earl, was given the honorary title of Viscount Sutherlin, but his family members and close friends never addressed him by his title. He was just Ewen. After tasting the ale, Selena could understand how her cousin and Darnell chose Widow Forester's ale over others. It was rich and malty, and indeed, creamy enough to make Selena lick her upper lip. She loved it, and so she told Widow Forester.

Before the widow could answer, the door opened, and a plainly dressed woman wearing a fresh apron entered. "I saw your sign out, Widow Forester, and thought to buy a noggin of ale."

Widow Forester chuckled. "Nay, Sibyl, you saw Lady Selena is my guest, and you came to meet her, but I will take your coin and serve you the ale once I introduce you."

Selena was delighted to meet Sibyl, Goody Abel. She learned the plump, dimpled woman was the baker's wife, and she promised she would stop by sometime to try one of the baker's biscuits. Meeting the villagers was exactly what she wanted to do, so she was delighted when next the shoemaker's wife arrived, then a couple of the farmers' wives. One wife, with a babe in arms, came shyly forward to meet her. Rather than hold court on the settle, she suggested she join the women at the table, but Darnell intervened.

"Nay, Lady Selena, do you stay here any longer, Widow Forester will have no ale left for the men when they return from the fields. Soon every woman in the village will be crowding into the house. We must go. Your aunt will be wondering, do I not get you home in a timely fashion. I would not want her to forbid me to ride out with you again."

Selena laughed at his speech, and set the women in the room to laughing. "Very well," she said, "if we must go, we must go." She looked each woman in the eyes before departing and promised she would return soon and hoped to get to know each one of them better. She chucked the baby under the chin, and it grinned up at her. That delighted her young mother, who cooed, "Oh, look how she tikes t' Lady Selena."

Selena would have asked to hold the baby, but Darnell, having dropped a couple of coins in Widow Forester's palm, took Selena by the arm and urged her out the door. He gave her a boost up onto her mount, flung himself onto his, and said, "Let us go afore anyone else can claim your attention."

Selena laughed but gently set her heels to Brigantia and headed off at a trot. She waved to a couple of children who waved to her as she and Darnell exited the village and started back down the road toward Whimbrel Hall. She had liked meeting the women. On her father's manor, she knew every tenant and their families and had always found them engaging people. She believed her uncle's tenants would be no different. How much more pleasant it was to meet and speak with the villagers than to work at learning to be a lady.

# Chapter 6

Selena scurried down the gentle slope leading from the wooded hill to the Grantham farm. She was eager to see Calder. Eager to determine whether she still found him the most handsome man she had ever encountered. Eager to talk with him, to watch the way his vibrant blue eyes lit up when he laughed. She saw Joseph working on another section of hedgerow, Abner was with the sheep, but in a different pasture, and the third man was not to be seen. Nor was Calder or Pascal.

Hurrying to the house door, Selena rapped as loudly as she could. It was promptly answered by Hannah. "My goodness, Lady Selena, I was not expecting you. Will you not come in. You look thirsty. I have some ale I can serve you."

Selena entered, thanking Hannah, and agreeing she was thirsty. First she told Hannah how much she had enjoyed the currant bun, then while accepting the noggin of ale, she asked, "Is Calder not to home?" She hoped she was not being presumptuous in using Calder's given name, but he had said he was not to be addressed as Mister Grantham.

Apparently no offense was taken, for Hannah said, "Calder is in the cow barn. One of his cows, a young one, not full grown, cut her lower hip on a rough branch of the hedgerow. He is aiming to stitch up the cut."

"Poor thing," Selena said. She gulped down the ale in what she knew her aunt would consider a most unladylike fashion, and stated, "I will go see can I help."

"But Lady Selena …" Hannah said, reaching out a hand as Selena set her noggin on the table. "It might not be …"

Hurrying out the door, Selena failed to hear the remainder of Hannah's sentence. With two barns on the farm, she hesitated, but hearing a bawling sound from the stone barn, she headed for the open door.

Upon entering, the smell of fresh hay and manure assaulted her, and in the dim light flooding in from the large open doorway, she saw the shadows of two men and a boy struggling with the wounded cow.

"Easy there you poopnoddy. I am trying to help you."

Selena recognized Calder's voice. He sounded frustrated.

"Jared, can you not keep her still?"

"I be trying, Calder, but she be powerful scared since you poured that vinegar on the cut," the second man answered.

"Might I try to calm her?" Selena said. Both men and the boy turned to stare at her.

Pascal spoke first. "Lady Selena, you did come back. I knew you would."

"Indeed, I did tell you I would. But Calder," again she felt strange addressing him so informally, but he took no notice, and she continued, "do let me try to calm the poor dear. I have found I have a way with animals."

"She might step on your foot, milady," the other man said.

"'Twould not be the first time my foot has been stepped on. Do let me try," she said again, advancing cautiously forward and crooning, "Easy, poor dear, easy girl."

❦ ❦ ❦

Calder had been surprised to see Lady Selena. Though he had wished it, he had not let himself believe she would return. Now, to see her dressed in a plain gown and sturdy walking shoes and looking perfectly at home in his barn, he at first could do nothing more than stare. He then realized the cow was no longer straining against the rope. As Lady Selena spoke quietly to the animal and advanced to take the rope from Jared, the cow seemed to be mesmerized.

Lady Selena dropped the rope and placed both her hands on either side of the cow's head, then she placed her forehead against the cow's muzzle and nuzzled her. She next caressed the cow's nose and mouth before reaching up to stroke and cuddle her ears. All the time she was speaking softly to the cow, calling her poor dear, and telling her she must be brave. In a matter of moments, the cow seemed completely calm. Her hands still lightly caressing the animal, Selena said, "I do think you may stitch her wound now, Calder."

Standing behind Lady Selena, Jared said, "Well, I will be damned. Ne'er saw anything like that."

Calder agreed with Jared. He had never seen any animal react in such a fashion. And not only was the cow now as gentle as a lamb, the barn cat, that never had anything to do with anyone, its only job being to keep the rat and mice population under control, was rubbing around Lady Selena's legs and purring loudly.

"What do you stitch her with?" Lady Selena asked.

Her question returned him to his senses, and he held up a large threaded needle. "'Tis a needle we use to repair leather, like harnesses or such, and hair from her tail is the thread. I poured vinegar over the cut first to clean it. That frightened her so badly, we could not get her calmed. But I must say, you have done an unbelievable job at steadying her."

"She but needed someone to understand her fear," Lady Selena said. Looking down at the cat winding around her feet, she added, "Not now tabby. Let us finish here first."

"Ne'er saw that cat take to nobody afore," Jared said.

"Me neither," Pascal said. "It will not let me near it. 'Specially if it has new kittens."

Selena laughed that delightful tinkling laugh of hers. It set Pascal off, and Jared's face spread wide with a grin. Calder had to grin, too, even though he needed to keep his mind on stitching up the cut. The cow's flank flickered, but the animal remained still.

"Little boys, and sometimes little girls, often move too quickly for cats," Selena was telling Pascal. "Mayhap, when we are done here with the cow, we can sit for a bit and see if the cat might let you pet her. Has she a name?"

"We just call her the barn cat," Pascal said.

"Well, she should have a name. You think on a name, and we will christen her today." She addressed Calder. "Has the cow a name?"

He glanced up for a brief second. "Nay, she is not one of our milk cows. When she is full grown, she will be taken to market along with most of the other cows in the pasture. We keep a bull and several of the cows for breeding, butcher one for our own needs, but market cows are not given names any more than are the sheep."

"I suppose that is how it is with my uncle's cows and my father's," Lady Selena said. "Did we name them, we would not then want to sell them or eat them."

"That would be right," Jared said, his thin lips pursed thoughtfully. "Had me a piglet when I was a boy. Named him Henry. Raised him good, fattened him up. I was that proud o' him. Then come the chill fall season, and me father said 'twas time to butcher him. Near broke my heart. Ne'er named me another animal again."

"Oh, how sad," Selena said. "I understand how you felt. I have ever tried to stay distant to any of the animals that might end up on the table. But once, when I was not that much older than Pascal, I raised ten baby ducks. Their mother had been killed by a fox. Fortunately, my father indulged me. Their wings were not clipped, and when grown, they eventually flew away, though some did hang about for a time."

"I like the baby ducks and the chicks," Pascal said, "but I never raised any. I have played with them some, though. They are so soft and fluffy."

"That they are," Selena said, "but poorly suited to live in the house."

"You had your ducks in the house!" Jared asked, his deep sunken eyes widening. The look on his laborer's face almost caused Calder to miss a stitch.

"Until the maids complained," Selena answered. "Father had the village carpenter make a special cage for them to be kept outside the door at night or when I went indoors. But whenever I was outside, those ducks would follow me anywhere."

Pascal laughed. "That would be fun."

"Oh, it was," Selena assured him.

Calder completed stitching the cut and patted the cow on the rump. "There now you poopnoddy, all done. Jared, you can take her back to the field. Then see does the oat field need weeding. I fear the thistle has returned."

"Aye, sir," Jared said, picking up the rope and attempting to lead the cow away.

The cow seemed unwilling to budge until Selena scratched her nose and said, "Go on with you. Back to your friends you go, and no more cutting yourself." She gave the cow a gentle push on her neck to turn her, and with a lowing moo, the cow turned to follow Jared. At the barn door, she looked back, blinked her large brown eyes, and mooed again before allowing Jared to lead her off.

At this point, the cat was demanding attention, and Selena sat down cross-legged on some hay in the middle of the stall, and the cat jumped into her lap. Pascal immediately sat down beside her, and reached out a tentative hand toward the cat, but Selena caught his hand. "Let us give her a moment to feel secure before you try to pet her. We shall think of a name for her. Have you named a cat or a dog before?"

"Nay," Pascal said. "Father named Rollo when I was but small. Rollo is our dog."

Wishing he could sit down beside Lady Selena, but feeling her family would frown on that, Calder remained standing. He imagined Selena's aunt would frown on everything she was doing, but he doubted Selena much cared as long as she was not caught.

"Rollo is a fine name for a dog," Selena said while softly petting the cat from head to tail. "'Tis perfect for a dog, but we must have just the right name for this cat. She is, after all, the protector of this barn. She is noble. We should name her for a queen, should we not?"

"Oh, yes, a queen," Pascal agreed.

Watching his son, seeing his glistening eyes, his glowing cheeks, Calder smiled. He could not remember when he had seen Pascal so animated.

"She is a brave warrior," Selena said. "What would you think, do we name her for the Celtic queen, Queen Guinevere?"

Pascal cocked his head. "What is a Celtic queen?"

"Are you not familiar with the King Arthur legends?"

Pursing his lips and shaking his head, Pascal said, "Nay."

"Ah, then sometime I will tell you a couple of the tales. Arthur was king before the Saxons came, and long before the Normans came to rule England. Guinevere was his queen. A brave queen she was."

Calder chuckled quietly when his son said, "Oh, then I like the name."

"Good." Selena raised her hand in a pledge and Pascal followed suit. "We do christen thee, Queen Guinevere," she proclaimed, then glanced at Pascal. "However, I do think because our queen is so small, we should call her by a shorter name. We shall call her Ginny."

Pascal nodded. "Yes, Ginny is good."

"Wonderful," she said, and taking his hand in hers, she placed it on the cat's back. "Rub her very gently. Hear how she purrs. She must like you."

"Oh, do you think so. I hope she likes me."

"I think she does, but she may still be frightened of you until she gets to know you."

"I think we have spent enough time with the cat," Calder said. "Lady Selena, allow me to help you up." He held out his hands to her. "Would you care for some buttermilk, again?"

"I would. And another of Hannah's currant buns, does she still have any," she said, and setting the cat off her lap, she held up her hands for him to grasp and pull her to her feet.

She had strong hands. Not rough, work-hardened hands, but hands that could hold a horse in check or wield a walking stick as a weapon should the need arise. She was a self-assured young woman, but that could lead her into trouble was she too bold, as she had been when he first met her. He knew he held her hands longer than he should have after he pulled her to her feet, yet he had been reluctant to release her. It could well be the only time he would ever get to touch her. Feelings were rising in him he knew he needed to suppress. And he would, but he could still treasure the moment of innocence.

# Chapter 7

When Selena entered Calder's house just ahead of him, Hannah greeted her with an exclamation. "Lady Selena, gadzooks, would you be looking at you! Straw all over your gown. Would you be coming with me, I will take you upstairs that you may refresh yourself." Grabbing a pot of water off a stand in the hearth, she poured some into a large leather pitcher and directed Selena to the stairs.

Selena obediently followed Hannah. She was happy to get to see more of Calder's house. The stairs of sturdy oak were well built. The steps turned at a landing halfway up, then exited onto a narrow corridor. Two doors opened off the side of the short corridor. A third door was situated at the end of the corridor. Hannah directed Selena to the first door. "This be a guest chamber, does Calder's sister ever come visiting. 'Twas her room when she lived here, afore she married Mister Tusket, the vintner in Rotherby."

Selena loved the room. The stone walls were covered in samplers and bright rag rugs. The counterpane on the four-poster bed was a patchwork of colors. Cream-colored curtains, like the ones downstairs, hung at the single, diamond-paned window. A lovely maple chest sat at the foot of the bed, and a heavy oak cabinet, below a framed looking glass, held a white crockery washbowl. Hannah poured the warm water from the leather pitcher into the bowl, then opened the cabinet and pulled out a cream-colored towel.

"Should you need it, there be a chamber pot under the bed. No need for you to hurry yourself." She shook her head. "What Calder was thinking, letting you muss yourself in such a fashion. When you are done tidying up, come back down, and we will have some buttermilk and a currant bun."

"Hannah, you are too kind."

"Nonsense. 'Tis not every day we have a real lady come to visit."
Pulling some straw off the back of Selena's skirt, Hannah said, "Is
there anything else I can be helping you with?"

"No, but thank you, Hannah."

Hannah harrumphed and exited and Selena set about repairing the
damages to herself. She was glad to have the chamber pot. She maybe
drank a tad too much wine at dinner. In the future, she needed to be
wary of what she drank before setting off on her outings. When she
felt orderly, she tiptoed to the door and quietly opened it. Good door. It
made not a creak or a squeak. She wanted to see the other two rooms
before she went back downstairs. Cautiously making her way down the
corridor, she peeked into the next room.

It was obviously Pascal's room. A bed large enough to hold two
people was pushed into the corner and curtained off, and a narrow,
one-person bed, but little bigger than a cot, occupied the center of the
room. A small, skinny-legged stand holding a candle sat next to the
bed, a cedar chest sat at the foot of the bed, and a sturdy cabinet holding
a red crockery washbowl stood against the wall. The room had its single window and cream-colored curtains, but where the first room had a
small hearth, Pascal's room had but an iron brazier to offer warmth to
the room when the weather turned chill.

Moving on to the room at the end of the corridor, Selena peered into
the brightly-lit interior. The large room, being the width of the house,
sported four windows hung with bright blue curtains. A window on
each side of the hearth, and one on each side of the room let in a vast
amount of sunlight. The coverlet on the four-poster bed was also blue.
Matching spindle-leg stands were on either side of the bed. A lovely
maple chest rested at the foot of the bed, and a tall black maple cabinet
graced the far corner of the room. A blue crockery washbowl sat atop
a cabinet that matched the tall corner cabinet, and a lovely framed mirror hung above it. The hearth was spotlessly clean, obviously not used
during these warmer days.

Fearing someone would find her poking about, she scurried downstairs to find Calder and Pascal awaiting her at the table. Noggins of
buttermilk and red-crockery plates holding currant buns rested on the
white cloth spread over the table.

"Ah," Calder said. "All repaired I see. I hope you found all you needed."

"I did, indeed, but I fear I made more work for Hannah in cleaning up after me."

"Nonsense on that," Hannah said. "Be a pleasure to clean up after a lady after all these years o' cleaning up after naught but a couple of men."

Selena laughed and Pascal joined in her laughter. She smiled at him. He was an endearing little boy, and she was already more than a little fond of him. Both Pascal and Calder had risen from their seats when she drew closer to the table. A cane-back chair had been pulled out for her, and neither father nor son resumed their seats until she sat.

"Be you comfortable there, milady?" Hannah asked.

"Aye, I am just fine, thank you, Hannah. And I am eager to have another currant bun. You are a masterful cook."

Blushing, Hannah said, "Now, I would not be saying that."

"I would," Calder said. "We lack for very little here, and 'tis your doing, Hannah."

"Enough of such flattery. I have me work to do. Eat up." Turning from them, Hannah returned to her work table, and with a wooden spoon, started beating something in a heavy bowl.

In between bites of the currant bun and sips of buttermilk, Selena learned more about Calder's farm. Two of his laborers lived on the farm in housing above the sturdy oak barn. The third man, Abner, lived with his wife and three children in a small hamlet between the Whitaker manor, it being White Acres, and a section of the squire's manor, bordering to the north of Calder's farm. At harvest time, Calder hired men, women, and children from the hamlet and from Whimbrel. "During harvest time, we, meaning all the crofts, farms, and estates in our parish, also get help from Rotherby. A good harvest means lower prices for everyone."

"We a'ready got the hay reaped," Pascal said, the pride in his voice obvious. "I helped this year. And I have helped weed the fallow field, have I not, Father?"

Calder tousled his son's hair. "You have indeed. You even helped with the hemp."

His mouth full, Pascal nodded, but he glowed under his father's praise.

"I understand you have a way with the animals, Lady Selena," Hannah said. "'Tis a special gift few have."

"I do love the animals," Selena answered. "They are such innocents."

Calder chuckled. "I would not be calling the squire's dogs innocents."

"Have they been about again?" Hannah asked, concern in her voice.

"Aye," Calder answered. "Abner had to chase them off with his crook. Having to keep Abner minding the sheep instead of helping with other chores is getting costly."

"I would think so," Selena said. "Can you not speak with the squire about it?"

"I have. It has done no good. He seems more worried about poachers than my sheep."

Selena shook her head. "Most unreasonable I should think. He should have his dogs trained to stay on his own estate, or at the very least, they should be trained not to attack sheep."

"In another week we will wean the lambs and prepare the sheep for shearing. We will then keep some penned for milking. Sheep milk brings a better price than cow milk. There are those who swear cheese made with sheep milk is the tastiest."

"What happens to the lambs?" Selena asked.

"A few will be saved for our meal needs or for breeding. The rest will be sold in mid-summer when people are ready for mutton."

"Sad," she said, frowning, "but then Father did the same. People must eat, and the poor animals must play their role in our meals. I do admit, I like a good beef roast or ham or roasted chicken or duck, and yes, lamb as well." She sighed. "Such is the animal's lot in life. But are they treated kindly while alive, that is important."

"Our animals are always treated kindly," Pascal said. "Father would never let an animal be cruelly treated, would you, Father?"

Calder smiled at his son, and Selena's heart did a little flip. Oh, how his smile set her head to spinning.

"We try to insure our animals are kindly treated." He looked at Selena. "And I thank you again, Lady Selena, for your aid with that poor cow."

"'Twas naught. She was but frightened." Selena had been about to take a final sip of her buttermilk, but she set the noggin back down. "I wonder, might I visit when you are shearing your sheep. Father always let me watch, and was any sheep badly frightened, I helped calm them. The men doing the shearing seemed to appreciate my help."

"I think I, too, would appreciate your help, but would not your aunt object. 'Tis not exactly something a lady should be doing."

Selena shrugged. "She need not know."

"Humph!" Hannah said. "Do you go home smelling of sheep, she will know. Sheep smell, there is no way around it. Even after they have been well washed before shearing."

"Hannah is right," Calder said with a chuckle.

"I have no doubt I can return to my room and wash and change ere she ever sees me," Selena said. "Besides, I could end up smelling of sheep just by petting them. Certainly my uncle has two pastures filled with sheep." She scratched her head. "Hmmm. I wonder if he has had any trouble with the squire's dogs. I have not heard him mention it, but then he has had much to do since he returned from London, and he leaves again for London on the morrow."

She smiled brightly. "My dear cousin Elizabeth is to be married, does her father give his approval, and Uncle Nate is certain he will. Uncle Nate is returning to London to help Elizabeth find a home and various other items she will need in her new life with a husband. Then they are to go to Wealdburh, that is in Cheshire, to visit her parents, and Uncle Nate is to go with them.

"Sadly, Elizabeth's mother has the consumption so is too ill to go to London, and Uncle Kenrick will not leave his wife, so Uncle Nate will give Elizabeth away. 'Tis sad Aunt Blanch is dying." Her gaze met Calder's. "Life is so fragile. You lost your parents and your wife. My mother is an invalid, and her life is sadly restricted. I feel we must grab what happiness we can and not let it slip through our fingers ere it disappears." She picked up her noggin again. "So, do you allow it, I will be here for the sheep shearing."

"Yea!" Pascal said, clapping his hands.

Calder bent his head toward her. "Very well, Lady Selena. I would not want your enjoyment of life to slip through your fingers, but I give you no guarantee you will be coddling the sheep. You may be willing to risk your aunt's ire, but I am not."

Selena just smiled. If she could in any manner help this man she had already determined she loved, she would do so. The fact that she had a way with animals was a blessing. And did God give her such a blessing, she should use it to be helpful.

# Chapter 8

Standing in the cow barn, and peering out from behind the door, Calder secretly watched Lady Selena disappear into the woods at the top of the hill. Watching her until he could no longer see her meant he was behind in his milking, but he had not been able to help himself. Gads what a fine woman she was. If only she was not the daughter of an earl.

Knowing Abner would soon have the sheep penned and would be hitching up the team and cart to take the milk to the Huddlestons, Calder hurried to get his milking done. At supper, he would look forward to hearing what Pascal had to say about Lady Selena. The boy had walked with her to the hillside. He could tell the two had been talking animatedly. Selena was as good with children as she was with animals. But she was not meant for a yeoman. He needed to stop thinking about her, yet he feared he could not. Nor did he want to stop thinking about her. She could never be his, but he could still enjoy her company for as long as it lasted.

He was just finishing with his final cow when Abner called to him. "All hitched," Abner said. "But I got me a problem, Calder."

Calder came out with the final pail and dumped it into the barrel. "What is your problem, Abner? Tooth still bothering you?"

Abner nodded and put his hand to the graying stubble on his chin. "Bain't no better. Giving me worse pain each day. I am afeared, do I not go into Whimbrel and have the smith pull it, I will not be able to help with the washing and shearing of the sheep come next week."

Heaving a long sigh, Calder scratched his own chin. Middle-aged, Abner had started working on the Grantham farm before Calder was born. Long years of hard labor had left him with bent shoulders and rough, work-hardened hands being twisted anxiously while he waited. "You got the coin to pay the smith?" Calder asked his laborer.

"I got it. I was planning to get me daughter a ribbon she has been begging after, but she will have to wait."

"Shame, that," Calder said. "Gals can set such store by little pretties. You buy her a ribbon when you are in Whimbrel, and I will see you have an extra ha'penny in your pay this time around."

"That be right kind of you, Calder. My little Nancy will be mighty pleased, she will. You want I should leave off the cart on my way to Whimbrel come morning?"

Each evening, Abner took the milk to the Huddlestons, then Calder let him take the cart and horse home with him. He knew Abner sometimes used the cart to transport goods for others, and picked up extra pennies that way, but Abner took good care of the horse. Fed him well, rubbed him down, and had a nice clean stall for him next to his own family milk cow, so Calder could not begrudge Abner the use of the cart or the horse.

"Does your family want an outing, you may use the cart to take them into Whimbrel with you. But do you go by yourself, bring the cart by here afore you go to the village."

"Good of you, Calder. By the by, Jared was telling me 'bout that Lady Selena and how she calmed that cow down. That the truth?"

"Aye, she has a way with the animals, it would seem."

"Was she not a lady, one might be thinking her a witch. Never heard of no ladies being witches, though. Have you?"

Calder hid his smile and shook his head. He had never believed in witches, but he knew many of the locals did. "Nay, never heard of such," he said.

Abner rubbed his jaw again. "I best be getting this milk to Huddlestons. Do I decide to take the family with me, I will have the cart back here by this time tomorrow afternoon."

"I hope when the smith pulls the tooth, it will not hurt too much."

"Guess I will have me a couple of ales afore I have it done."

"Good idea."

Abner nodded, went to the horse's head, gave a pull on the lead rope, and off they went. Calder turned to his next task, feeding all the sheep. Keeping them in the barn and feeding them hay was creating another problem. He was using up the hay he would need to feed the animals he meant to overwinter. Did he not have enough hay stored up, he would not be able to maintain as many animals through the winter. Fewer sheep meant less wool, fewer lambs, bad for the purse. Could he but find the time, he needed to try talking to the squire again.

With Abner absent on the morrow, what was he to do with the sheep? He needed to do a second ploughing and harrowing of his fallow field, and he needed Joseph and Jared to continue with their tasks. The hemp had been pulled, but still needed to be washed and dried before the fibers could be sold to weavers to turn into thread or rope. Peas and beans were ready to be harvested and dried, and his last bee hive might swarm at any time. He could use Pascal to mind the sheep, but then he had no one to watch the bees. For the past month, Pascal had been watching the hives during the mid-day when the bees were most like to swarm. He even ate his dinner out by the hives. The honey the bees produced brought a good profit and also sweetened the pastries Hannah made, sugar being an expense he could seldom justify. He wondered if Pascal could mind the sheep. The boy was but six. Young to be put in charge of such a large flock. Counting ewes and lambs, he had just over a hundred sheep. Still, what choice did he have? Surely with help from the dog, Rollo, he would be able to manage. The boy would like having the responsibility. He liked to help. Liked to prove himself no longer a baby.

By the time he finished his last chore, Calder saw Jared and Joseph coming in from the fields, their work tools slung over their shoulders. They would clean and wash themselves before coming into supper. Pascal had already finished herding the chickens and ducks into their coops and secured them for the night. The geese were allowed to find their own night-time nesting, as few foxes wanted to take on an angry goose, and the geese, with their raucous cries, were as good as any watchdog in signaling prowlers, whether man or beast. Hungry men, some just passing through the parish, others out of work and needing to feed their families, were often worse predators than a fox. Though roguery happened less often in the summer and autumn harvest seasons, when more hands were needed on the farms and estates.

When he returned to the house, he found Hannah had supper ready. He but needed to wash up and change to a clean shirt. Once he had refreshed himself, he felt more positive about the morrow, and he hurried back downstairs. Pascal, Jared, and Joseph were at the table, and Hannah had set out a trencher of bread and a bowl of butter. Mugs, brimming with ale, were at each place but Pascal's, and Hannah was bringing over a large blackened kettle of pottage to set in the center of the table. She ladled heaping spoonsful onto each red, crockery plate. Pheasant, potatoes Calder had started growing the previous year and was not yet certain he liked, though they were filling, peas, leeks, parsley, and rosemary for seasoning, fresh out of the kitchen garden, made up the pottage. Bread leavings from the previous meal thickened the gravy.

At first, no one spoke. They were all hungry, and filling their rumbling stomachs was the priority of the moment, but after he had shoveled in a number of spoonsful, Calder turned to his son. "Pascal, Abner's tooth pains him to the point he must go to Whimbrel on the morrow and have the tooth pulled. I cannot afford to have Jared or Joseph stop their work to mind the sheep. Do you think you could shepherd them? You and Rollo?"

His son's eyes were like large, shining saucers. "Oh, aye, Father. I know I could."

Calder nodded slowly. "All right then. I will have Jared help you herd the sheep into the lower pasture tomorrow morning. Hannah will pack you some bread and cheese and a jug of buttermilk for your dinner. No napping. You must stay alert to keep the squire's dogs away."

"I will, Father. I will!" Pascal promised.

Turning to Jared, he saw both he and Joseph were smiling. Joseph's big toothy grin and wide blue eyes showed his approval of his young master. Jared's darker eyes, gleaming in the candlelight, showed a merriment the laborer was seldom without. Both men, now in their early thirties, had been in his father's, and now his, employ since they were little older than Pascal. Both being younger sons of a couple of the squire's tenants, they had no hope of inheritance, so they had been pleased to find permanent employment on the Grantham farm. Calder had grown up with both men. Jared had a sweetheart, but he had not saved enough to marry. Possibly never would. Being a laborer with no land of his own made marriage a near improbability.

Knowing Jared's sweetheart was a dairymaid at White Acres Tower, Calder made a request he felt certain Jared would not find unfair. "Jared, with Pascal minding the sheep tomorrow, I yet need someone to watch the bees. Would you mind popping over to White Acres and asking Mister Huddleston if either his daughter, Molly, or his son, Derwin, could watch the last bee hive for me. Pascal believes he has seen the scout bees going out this week. I feel certain they will swarm any day now. Cannot afford to lose a swarm. I baited several potential hives with honey and mint, but there is no guarantee they will not decide to nest somewhere else."

As Calder suspected, Jared beamed. "Aye, Calder, I would be right happy to ask Mister Huddleston to send one or the other over. I think Derwin, though he be but five, is a bright boy, from what I have seen of him. I think he could do the job, though Molly might be better."

"I agree," Calder said. "Molly, being a year older than Pascal, has her wits about her. However, I would trust either child to follow the swarm and mark where they settle." Once the bees settled in their new hive, come evening, he and Jared and Joseph would drop all else, and while the bees were still docile, they would close up the hive and move it to a safe place where no animals could molest them, and the hive would be protected from the north wind. They would then open two holes. He could but hope a queen would have swarmed with the workers.

Calder sighed. "I worry something could go wrong. I want not to lose a swarm. Besides the honey, the wax brings a good profit from those who can afford wax candles."

Jared and Joseph nodded in agreement. Wax candles were seldom used in modest households. Calder only used them for celebrations like Christmas or his son's birthday. He was hoping to be able to send Pascal to school in Leicester when he was a couple of years older. That would be expensive, so every penny he could put aside was needed. He had attended the grammar school in Rotherby until he was twelve, but he wanted a better education for Pascal. Times were changing, and a man had to be careful of his property. He needed to know the law. After grammar school, he wanted Pascal to attend one of the Inns of Court. Mayhap even have a year or two at a University first.

He took a long swig of his ale. So much needed doing. Mayhap, he would continue to have Pascal shepherd the sheep, then he could put Abner back to work on more important tasks. That hemp had to be washed and beaten and the fibers separated and dried soon or it would be worthless, and he could not afford to have a crop go to waste. He should probably see if he could hire a couple of girls from Whimbrel to see to the hemp. He wanted that job done right after he finished washing and shearing the sheep.

On the morrow, when Ware Huddleston took his milk and cheese to market in Rotherby, he would pass through Whimbrel on the way. Most likely he could leave word at the baker's that the Grantham farm needed a couple of girls to wash and beat hemp. Sooner or later, most villagers visited the baker, it being easier to have him bake their bread than to fire up their own ovens, did they even have an oven. Word would spread about his need, and surely one or two gals needing some extra pennies would show up for work. After supper, he would write a note to Huddleston asking for Molly or Derwin to watch his hives and asking Huddleston to leave word at the baker's for him.

When all was done, he would settle for a time on the step outside and watch the moon come up over the horizon. Foolishly, he would let himself think about Lady Selena. Surely, just thinking about her would cause no harm. She was a delight, and at the present, he needed a delight in his life.

✹ ✹ ✹

Selena had managed to slip up to her room without being seen. She had used the servants' back staircase. Her skirt showed grass stains on the hem, but when she removed the gown, she found no straw clinging to it. She changed into a clean shift and stretched out across her bed to await her maid. She could have dressed herself, but she needed to wash again after her hurried hike home. Besides, she was happy to have the time on her own to think about Calder.

Having seen his room, she could picture him in it. Come night, when she crawled into her bed, she could envision Calder in his. Most likely he would leave the curtains open and let the moonlight seep into the room. She decided she would do the same. Then it would almost be like they were going to bed together. How wonderful that would be.

Her thoughts were interrupted by the maid opening the door. "Oh, milady, had the cook not told me you had returned, I would not have known it. I am sorry I missed your return. But I have warm water here, do you wish to wash."

Selena hopped off the bed. "Yes, Alice, I do wish to wash, but you have naught to be sorry about. I slipped in through the back entrance because I was a mess, and I feared Lady Rotherby would scowl. You must not tell her what a disgrace my gown is."

Selena helped Alice pour the pail of water into her pitcher and some into her washbowl. The pretty blond girl, but a year older than Selena, dimpled and promised she would breathe not a word to Lady Rotherby. "I will see can I get some of the worst grass stains off the hem afore the laundress sees it," she said. "Goody Hilton grumbles a lot lately. Her back and knees hurt her, and is she in bad spirits, she might well complain to Lady Rotherby."

"You are too kind to me, Alice," Selena said, dunking a wash cloth into the water and squeezing it out.

"Oh, no, Lady Selena, 'tis you who are kind to me. Choosing me to be your personal maid was very kind."

Selena had not brought her own maid from her home in Surrey. The maid had a beau and had not wanted to leave him. Her Aunt Rowena had given her the choice of either of the upstairs maids to be her personal maid, and Selena had immediately selected the bubbly Alice. It had not taken long for the two to become co-conspirators.

While washing her forearms, legs, hands, and face, Selena asked, "Alice, are you familiar with the Grantham farm?"

"Ohhh," Alice purred, "I know the farm, and everyone knows Calder Grantham. He is a lovely man. Not an unmarried woman I know would not like to become Goody Grantham, but he has never shown an interest in any woman since his wife died. Broke his heart, they say."

Selena readily understood how every unmarried woman, and perhaps some married women, could secretly wish to be married to Calder Grantham. "Did you know Calder Grantham's wife?" she asked.

Alice shrugged. "Not really, she was several years older than I am. My older sister knew her. Mary Hadrian was the daughter of Squire Nibley's most prosperous tenant." She dimpled. "But Goodman Hadrian is old now, and 'tis his son who manages the property. The son, Jonah, is married to my sister's good friend, Elsa."

"Did you not tell me your sister lives in Rotherby. That she married a merchant?'

"Yes, Anna lives in Rotherby, but her husband is not exactly a merchant, though he makes a good living. He herds cattle and sheep to market in Leicester. There, a merchant buys them from him. Some of the cattle and most of the sheep, the merchant sells to butchers in Leicester, but others he adds to a growing herd that is driven to London. That is how Anna's husband made enough money to become a cattle and sheep buyer. He helped drive the cattle to London a couple of times. He saved his pay until he had enough coin to start buying a few head of cattle. He drove them to Leicester, made a profit, and bought more. Now, he is the main cattle and sheep buyer for the parish and has a couple of men working for him. I know your uncle sells to him. The squire and his tenants do. And Calder Grantham sells to him.

"But why do you ask about Goodman Grantham? Have you met him?"

Selena was glad Alice, turning to shake out Selena's petticoat, would not see her face. Her face would give away her feelings. "On my walks, I chanced upon him in the woods. He invited me to see his farm. 'Tis a lovely farm."

"That it is," Alice said, fluffing up Selena's skirt. "When I go home to visit my family, I cut through the woods. Most likely the path you took. Then I go down the slope to Grantham's farm, and take the path below his fields to my parents' home."

"Oh, yes, I believe you said they were the squire's tenants."

"That is right. Though my older brother, Laban, is the primary tenant now, my parents being too old to do all that is needed on the croft." Looking around, Alice asked, "Which shoes would you like to be wearing, milady?"

"The red, calf-hide ones. They are soft and my feet are tired."

"You walked far today, milady?"

"Yes, I walked to and from the Grantham farm as well as round the lake beforehand." She watched Alice to see if the girl's face would show surprise, but Alice turned to find the requested shoes.

When she turned back with the shoes in hand, Alice said, "Aye, that is a goodly walk. As I well know. As I told you, that being the way I must go when I visit my home."

"How did you come to be working here, Alice?"

Tilting her head to one side, Alice said, "My dowry is small. Do I ever hope to marry a man of some means, as did my sister, I must have a decent dowry. Squire Nibley's wife needed no additional maids, but I learned Lady Rotherby did. So I sought work here, and I was hired. I was twelve when I started. Lady Rotherby liked it that I could read and write more than just my name. My parents sent me and my siblings to petty school in Whimbrel. Lord Rotherby is so good to pay the school usher, so the local children, even girls, can go to petty school."

"I was not aware Whimbrel had a school."

"'Tis only open after the fall harvests are completed, then closes come summer, when even small children are needed on the farms."

"I never saw the school. Is it in the village?"

"Aye, 'tis in Goodman Osgood's parlor. Though 'tis terrible crowded. Goodman Osgood is a freeholder. Has near a hundred acres, I have heard. He is also the farrier."

"'Tis good of him to let the school be held in his parlor."

"'Tis his younger brother is the school usher, and when he is not teaching, he helps work Goodman Osgood's farm."

"'Tis still generous of Goodman Osgood. The distance from your home would have been quite a walk for you as a little girl. Whimbrel is a goodly distance from the squire's."

"Aye, but my parents were determined we should all know how to read, so even was it so cold the chill went right into the bones, off we marched. Each of my three brothers also attended the grammar school in Rotherby. And!" Alice puffed out her chest and raised her chin. "My third oldest brother, John, is now the schoolmaster at the Rotherby grammar school."

"Is he now! He must be very smart if he is anything like the tutors who taught my brothers and me."

"Oh, he is smart. The previous schoolmaster helped him get a scholarship to the university, and when the schoolmaster moved to a larger school in Leicester, he recommended John for the Rotherby schoolmaster. John has been the schoolmaster there for five years now."

Sitting down to let Alice fix her hair, Selena said, "Seems your family has all done well. Your parents must be proud."

"Well, my second oldest brother Wally is but a laborer. He works at whatever job he can find. Sometimes he herds cattle for my sister's husband. Sometimes he works here at Whimbrel or for the squire. He does what he can, but he has yet to find a permanent position."

"That is a shame. Where does he live?"

"He lives with my parents, but my oldest brother Laban is not that happy to have him there, he and Honor having three children and another on the way that they must house."

"Is Wally a good worker?"

Alice shrugged. "Like I said, Wally will do whatever job he can get, but I think he is more a dreamer. He likes to make up stories. Most are quite entertaining. Everyone likes them, but Laban says Wally needs to stop dreaming and find a permanent position."

"Hmmm," Selena said. "I would like to meet Wally."

Alice stopped with a pin ready to be placed in Selena's hair. "Why would you want to meet Wally?"

"I would like to hear a couple of his stories. Are they truly good, could be they could be published, and he could make enough to pay for his own home."

Her eyes wide, Alice asked, "You think people might want to read his stories?"

"I will not know until I hear a couple. Now, do please finish my hair. I wish not to be late for supper as 'tis Uncle Nate's last night here. He leaves again for London on the morrow."

Alice returned to her creation. She took pride in the hair arrangements she did for Selena each evening, but during the day, Selena preferred to tuck her hair in a bun. Aunt Rowena was pleased to see Selena looking more stylish when she came down to supper each night, and Selena enjoyed making both Alice and her aunt happy.

She hoped Wally's stories were truly good, truly entertaining. In her opinion, too many books were dry and humorless. Her oldest brother, Giles, had a close friend from his days at the university who had recently opened a publishing house in London. Giles had helped finance him and helped him find an honest bookseller for his partner. Were Wally's stories good, she would have him write one out, and she would send it to Malcolm Postgate. Could be Wally could also become an apprentice with Postgate or the bookseller. Certainly, more lighthearted books were needed to help encourage the English to become more literate.

Her hair and attire complete, Selena rose, thanked Alice, and hurried down to supper. Her aunt and uncle were awaiting her in the parlor. She would miss her uncle. His presence made life more pleasant because Aunt Rowena was always happiest when her husband was near to hand. The love that existed between them was the kind of love Selena's mother and father had. It was the kind of love she wanted. She believed she could find that love with Calder. Only problem was, how to make Calder fall in love with her. Was she as beautiful as her cousin, Elizabeth, who would soon be getting married, or even as sweet and lovely as Flavia, she thought she might have an easier task of winning Calder's love. However, she knew she was far from plain, and though she might not be as beautiful as Calder's deceased wife, Mary, she sensed Calder was not immune to her.

What appealed greatly to her was that he seemed not to find her unladylike actions scandalous. He was accepting of her as she was. That meant so much. She wanted to be loved for who she was, not for the person her mother and Aunt Rowena wanted her to be.

# Chapter 9

Nearly jogging along the woodland path, Selena was in a hurry to get to the Grantham farm. She would not be able to visit Calder the next day because Lord and Lady Edgerton and their son Orland Darnell were coming to dinner. Aunt Rowena had informed Selena that Lady Edgerton was anxious to meet her, having heard from Darnell a glowing description of her. Aunt Rowena was very pleased Darnell had been so flattering in his description. It made her think Selena had behaved herself nicely on her outing with Darnell.

After dinner, Selena would be expected to join everyone in the parlor for music or games, so she would not be able to take her usual walk. Or even go off on a ride with Darnell. Never having had the patience to practice, Selena could play no instrument, but she was considered to have a good voice. Aunt Rowena played the harp, and a couple of nights, they had favored Uncle Nate with a few numbers. Could be they would have no music but would simply play cards. She found cards a bit boring, so had never been very good at any game. However, could be she and Darnell would play chess or backgammon, and Lord and Lady Edgerton and Aunt Rowena could enjoy a cozy chat. No doubt about her and possibly her dowry, which was one of her mother's manors, left to her mother by her parents who died when Selena was barely ten.

Selena had only pleasant memories of her grandparents. Her mother had been their only child and had been born late to them. They had adored Selena's mother, and her mother's father, Lord Hartguard, left her mother three substantial manors, several small manors, and a house in Bath. Lady Hartguard left Selena's mother a manor in Scotland that Selena's brother Artemas would inherit. Selena would one day receive, as her dowry, a manor in Lincolnshire. She had only seen it once. It was quite old, dating back to the fourteenth century. It was not a pretty place like Calder's house.

Hopping over the narrow brook, Selena knew she had almost reached her destination. She stopped to straighten and smooth her skirt, then hastened on. At the edge of the hill above the Calder croft, she was met with a surprise. In the lower field, closest to the hill, she spotted Pascal atop a stump. He was holding a good-size lamb in his arms, and his dog Rollo was barking and darting around three larger dogs that were jumping up trying to get at Pascal and the lamb.

Without a second thought, Selena dropped the walking stick, grabbed up the hem of her skirt, and went racing down the slope. Pascal saw her coming, and the look on his face showed both alarm and relief. Clambering over the stone fence, she yelled, "Hey, hey!" as she neared the disturbance. "What is the meaning of this. For shame! For shame!"

At the sound of her voice, the dogs looked around at her, but as she neared, they stopped barking, and one hung his head and tucked his tail between his legs. "What kind of a thing is this to be doing? You naughty dogs," she said when she reached the stump. The dogs were eyeing her cautiously, so she gave them time to assess her, to recognize she was not an enemy, would not harm them. After a moment, the largest dog, a long-legged, yellow dog with floppy ears, took a few steps toward her.

"That is right," she said. "Come meet me."

"Oh, do be careful, Lady Selena," Pascal cried. "He might bite you."

Not taking her eyes off the dogs, she answered, "I will be careful, but you call your dog to heel. He is making these dogs skittish with his darting and bouncing."

"Rollo! Come here," Pascal commanded, and the lively black and white, sheep-herding dog bounded over to the stump but continued his antics.

Selena smiled. Fortunately the three dogs that Rollo had been attempting to intimidate were ignoring him and were thinking they wanted to get acquainted with her. The two smaller dogs were spotted, one with brown spots, the other with red spots. The one with red spots seemed truly sorry for its misbehavior. As it inched its way toward her, it kept its eyes down and its tail tucked between its hind legs. "At least you know to be ashamed," she told the red-spotted dog. "You other two should be just as ashamed. I have no doubt your job is to catch poachers, not to frighten small boys and smaller lambs. Am I not right?"

The other two dogs were beginning to look contrite. The three had all come up to her, all were stretching their necks out trying to get their heads patted or ears scratched. She obliged each one of them, and soon their tails were wagging, ears were perked, and tongues were lolling out of happy grinning mouths.

Rollo started whining, announcing he too would like some attention, and Selena laughed. "Oh, you good dog, Rollo. How brave you are." She looked up at Pascal. "How brave you are. Let me take that lamb from you. Your arms must be very tired."

"Do you think 'tis safe?"

"Aye, I would say 'tis safe." She walked past the three dogs, and all three turned to stay close to her. With another laugh, she gave Rollo a pat on the head, then reached up to take the lamb from Pascal. Holding the lamb in her arms, she looked down at the dogs. "Be good dogs. I must put this poor scared lamb down that it may return to its mother." She noted the rest of the flock were all bunched together at the distant corner of the field. One sheep, most likely the lamb's mother, was bleating plaintively.

The dogs payed no attention to the lamb as it bolted away. Reaching up to Pascal, she said, "Let me help you down. I can see you are so tired your legs are shaking."

"Thank you, Lady Selena. I will use your help. I am powerful tired. And my throat is tired from yelling, first at the dogs, and then for help. But no one heard me."

Lifting him down and setting him amongst the dogs, Selena saw he at first looked scared, but as the dogs were still wagging their tails, in fact, more like wagging their entire rear ends, he relaxed and smiled. "I cannot think how you got them to be so nice," he said.

"Ah, they are not mean dogs. They are but bored, so they are doing things their owner should train them not to do. Tell me. If I follow that path the other side of the fence, will it lead me to Squire Nibley's?"

"Aye, but what do you mean to do?"

"I mean to take these dogs home, and to take Squire Nibley to task for not having them better trained."

"Gads!" Pascal said, his eyes wide. "You mean to tell the squire about his dogs?"

"I do indeed. You do please tell your father, if I cannot make it back here today, that I will not be here tomorrow either, as my aunt is having Lord and Lady Edgerton to dinner. Then the next day is Sunday, and I doubt not we will spend time in Rotherby with Aunt Rowena's older daughter. But I will be here next week to help with the shearing. You will tell him?"

"I will, Lady Selena, but you be careful." He glanced down at the dogs. They no longer seemed ferocious, but he still looked wary.

Selena laughed and tousled his hair. "Go find your cap, young man. And be certain you tell your father how very brave you were. Praise Rollo, too." She reached down and gave Rollo a scratch behind his ears. That set the other three dogs to nudging her, each wanting an approving pat, and she readily gave each one a nose scratch.

"Come, dogs, let us take you home." As she set off for the path that would lead her to Squire Nibley's manor, the dogs bounced and pranced around beside her. When she got to the fence, the dogs bounded over it, and she crawled over it, then turned and waved to Pascal. What a brave little fellow he had been. When next she saw Calder, she would tell him how proud he should be of his son.

From her maid's description of the time it would take to walk to the squire's manor, she knew she would not have time to see Calder. Once she took the dogs home, she would have to make haste to be back home in time to ready herself for supper. Supper without Uncle Nate would not be as much fun. She understood why he needed to return to London. Her cousin Elizabeth would need his help. She wished she could go to the wedding, but Aunt Rowena was unwilling to travel to London for but a couple of days, then turn around and come back to continue Selena's training.

"No," her aunt had said. "I love Elizabeth. She is a delight, but I simply will not make that journey. I will meet her husband at your brother Giles's wedding this fall. That wedding I must attend as Giles is your father's heir."

Traipsing along the well-worn path, Selena talked to the dogs and occasionally gave each one a pat or a scratch. The walk was pleasant, the fields green with growing crops or meadows of grass and grazing livestock. "Why did you not attack your master's sheep, you naughty dogs?" she asked before spotting a shepherd in the distance. "Ah, ha, you probably did, and the shepherd chased you off. You have got to learn better manners."

When she spoke to the dogs, their ears perked up. Well, the yellow dog with the floppy ears tried to perk his ears. He did bob his head from side to side which at least made his ears flop about his face. She laughed at him, and that, too, set the dogs to dancing. She enjoyed their company, but she knew when she returned to Whimbrel Hall, the cat and the two dogs who were always running up to greet her would be jealous. They would be sniffing and nuzzling her skirt and hands. Animals were so endearing. 'Twas a shame people were not always as endearing. Certainly Squire Nibley had not been fair to Calder, refusing to pay him for his lamb after the dogs killed the poor thing. She intended to address the issue.

She was arriving at the Nibley estate by the back entrance. In the distance, she saw several tenants' houses bunched together, and one larger house slightly away from the others. She guessed that might be Calder's deceased wife's family's house. Alice had said the Hadrians were the most prosperous of the squire's tenants. She wondered which house might be Alice's family's. She was surprised that the squire's manor was yet unenclosed, at least the grain fields were not enclosed. The parallel strips in the fields with ditches between them meant each tenant's crops were spread over several different strips in several different fields. She had learned from her uncle that it was an uneconomical method of farming, and time consuming to the tenants who had to go from one strip to another in a different part of each field.

Her uncle told her many estates in Leicestershire, including his, had gone to enclosure. He also told her, that, sadly, some landlords, when enclosing, had unfairly taken more than their share of the woods and commons, leaving their tenants with less land to pasture their animals or to gather needed wood for their fires or to repair their homes or outbuildings. Some tenants prospered from the enclosures, others did poorly, and some lost their homes entirely and became landless laborers, not unlike Alice's brother Wally and the men who worked for Calder.

Selena saw several women working outside their homes, some weeding their gardens, some washing clothes, their skirts tucked up at their waists to keep them out of the fires that heated the cauldrons of water. Others were scouring the drainage ditches around their crofts. Hard but necessary work were they to stay dry when the rains came. A couple of women glanced her way or stared at her, but she continued on toward the manor house.

She spotted the dog kennel, but ignored it. She meant to speak directly to the squire. With the dogs dancing happily at her side, she aimed for the front of the house, but her progress was halted when a man dressed in the garb of a laborer, flared breeches, coarse hose and scuffed shoes, plain brown patched coat and waistcoat, hallooed her. She stopped and waited for him to approach. Sitting beside her, the dogs waited with her.

"Good day t' ye, pretty maid, but those would be Squire Nibley's dogs there with you."

"That I know. I mean to speak to the squire about them. They have been ill-behaved."

The man scratched beneath his scraggly hair, making his cap bounce on his head. "Well, now, Squire Nibley wants them dogs out protecting his woods. He has had poachers."

"Indeed. Unfortunately, these dogs have not been patrolling his woods. They have been harassing farmers and killing lambs. I intend to talk with Squire Nibley about the problem."

The man narrowed his eyes and leered at her. "And what farm might you be from?"

She raised her chin and looked down her nose at him. "I am Lady Selena D'Arcy, and I am currently residing with my uncle, Lord Rotherby." She had trouble keeping a smile from her face as the man's features changed, and he grabbed off his cap. At times, there were definite benefits to being a Lady of the Realm.

"Beggin' ye pardon, milady. Comin' here by foot and with the dogs, I mistook ye for a yeoman's wife. I will go fetch the squire for ye. He is not to the house. He is in the stable seein' t' a mare what was late comin' to foal."

"Thank you," Selena said, giving him a bright smile.

The man blinked, bobbed his head, and went running off. She and the dogs followed more slowly after him. No reason to stand around waiting. She was interested in seeing more of the grounds. It was a neat manor. The brick house displayed many modern features, including numerous chimneys, which meant all rooms other than maybe the servant quarters would be heated. It had new sash windows and clean lines reflecting just a hint of metropolitan tastes. The landscaping behind the house was open except for a wall blocking out any view of the majority of the outbuildings. Garden paths meandered through low shrubbery and blooming flowers, and a pond in the center of the garden had a small cupid statue spouting water.

Strolling along and admiring the garden, Selena looked up when one of the dogs yipped. A pudgy man in riding boots and a green frock coat was hurrying toward her, the laborer, who had gone to fetch him, trailing at his heels. His hat askew from his hurried walk, his cheeks a bright red, the squire puffed out a greeting.

"Lady Selena, what an unexpected and delightful surprise!" He turned to the man behind him. "Deaver, the dogs, the dogs, take them to the kennel." He looked back at Selena. "I am so sorry, Lady Selena, that my dogs have been a nuisance to you."

Selena laughed and patted the yellow dog's head. "No, Squire Nibley, the dogs have not been a nuisance to me. They have been a terror to a small boy and a lamb. I chanced by Grantham's farm on my walk and saw these dogs had young Pascal stuck on a tree stump and clinging to a lamb. That is not proper behavior for these dogs, sir. They should be better trained. If you are going to allow them to run loose, they should know not to attack sheep. They should also stay on your property, if you are meaning them to keep poachers at bay."

The squire was looking from Selena to the dogs to Deaver. "I had no idea the dogs had ventured off my land."

Selena cocked her head to one side. "Did you not? I believe Calder Grantham told you the dogs had killed one of his lambs."

"Oh, yes, yes, that is right. Though I was not certain was my dogs what killed the lamb."

"Considering where I found your dogs, I believe you can believe 'twas your dogs that killed the lamb. I feel certain you will now compensate Goodman Grantham for his loss. I must wonder have your dogs killed any other farmers' animals."

Nibley looked at Deaver questioningly.

The man scratched his head and frowned. "Old Goody Jenkins said they chased her cow and scared it so bad she got no milk that night." He shrugged. "Cannot always know is she tellin' the truth. Her head is a bit off of late."

"Anyone else?" Selena asked.

Looking rather sheepish, he glanced at the squire. "One of the tenants, Hacker, said the dogs attacked his calf, but Goody Hacker came out with her broom and drove them off."

"I see," the squire said, and he looked back at Selena. "It would seem you are correct. My dogs have not been doing their duty. Normally I would have a gamekeeper, but I had to let him go. I found he was poaching. Caught him with two of my finest pheasants." He shook his head. "I would not begrudge him a coney, but a pheasant, no.

"But where are my manners. Dear Lady Selena, will you please come inside and take some refreshment after your long walk. I tell you, my wife has been hoping to meet you."

Selena, being nudged by the dogs, periodically patted one or another. "I am hardly dressed to be greeting your wife, Squire Nibley, but do you attend Sunday services, I will make it a point to greet you and meet your wife. Right now, I think I should help get these dogs back in their kennel. I trust they will not be out on their own again."

"No, no. I will not have them loosed again. But Deaver can put them back in the kennel. You need not bother yourself."

Laughing, Selena said, "He can try, but I am doubtful he will succeed."

Deaver had been trying to get the dogs to go with him, but they were having none of it. They would not leave their new friend. "They seem unwilling to be parted from Lady Selena."

"Well, take a stick to them, man!" Nibley said, and Selena cried, "Oh, no. You should never hit these dogs. That is too cruel. They will follow me."

With a pat to each dog, she started walking toward the kennel. The dogs, as well as Deaver and Nibley, followed after her. Three other dogs in the kennel started baying as they neared. "Goodness, what a racket," she said, stopping by the gate and allowing Deaver to open it.

Deaver managed to keep the other three dogs inside while Selena urged her three companions to return to their home. "Be good dogs. You have had a very adventuresome day. 'Tis time you have yourselves a nice rest." Selena snapped her fingers, and the dogs reluctantly entered the kennel, but they looked back at her with sorrowful faces as Deaver darted out and closed the gate. Selena laughed at them, and they yelped and jumped against the fence, but she shook her head. "That is it. I bid you three a goodbye. I must return home or be late for supper."

"Might I not give you a ride home, Lady Selena," Nibley said. "It would not take me long to have my coach hitched."

"A kind offer, but I dropped an item in the woods when I saw your dogs attacking Pascal, and I must retrieve it. Besides, do I start out now, I will have no trouble getting home in time to refresh myself before supper. I do trust you will be seeing Calder Grantham about his lamb, and I hope that I may see you Sunday in church."

Nibley nodded, "Aye, I will see Grantham is compensated. And my wife and I will look forward to seeing you and Lady Rotherby in church come Sunday."

"Splendid," Selena said. "Now I must hurry." She set off at a good clip with the dogs' yowling ringing in her ears. Looking back, she saw the squire standing where she had left him. She gave him a wave, which he returned. Bringing her focus back to the well-worn path, she let her thoughts shift to Calder. She hated that she would not be able to see him for three days, but at least, she believed, he would not again have to worry about dogs attacking his lambs.

She was not sure what she thought of Squire Nibley. He seemed not to be aware of his dogs' transgressions. She remembered seeing him and a short wife, near as pudgy as he, in church, but her aunt had not introduced her to them, though on one occasion, they had hovered near to hand. Could be an oversight on her aunt's part, or could be her aunt had no real liking for the couple. She had heard her aunt refer to the squire but once, and that in passing. She would have to tell her aunt of this encounter. And she would have to greet the Nibleys on Sunday.

Upon reaching the top of the hill above the Grantham farm, Selena picked up the walking stick she prized because Calder had given it to her, and looked out over the farm. Smoke rose from the main chimney. Hannah would be fixing their supper. The sheep in the lower pasture were grazing peacefully, but no one was shepherding them. Calder must know they were now safe from the dogs. She saw someone come from the stone barn, but she could not tell who – except she knew it was not Calder. Him she would recognize at any distance.

Turning from the view, she resumed her homeward journey. Tonight, she was definitely ready for her supper.

# Chapter 10

Calder knew he should get his cows milked, but he sat contemplating his feelings for Lady Selena, and wondering what he was to do about them. Though he had not seen her this afternoon, events concerning her actions were foremost in his thoughts. He revisited them once more, starting with Pascal's tale. Having heard his son's voice, Calder had hastened from the barn where he had been repairing the harness for the plough horses. Something had to be wrong for Pascal to have left the sheep. "Father, where are you?" the boy cried.

"Pascal, what is wrong? Why have you left the sheep? Did the dogs attack again?" Squatting on his haunches to be at his son's level, he caught Pascal by the shoulders.

Panting, Pascal worked to catch his breath, then said, "Yes, Father, they did, and I called and called for help, but no one heard me. But Lady Selena came and saved me and the lamb."

"What!" He half rose and looked over Pascal's head, expecting to see Lady Selena. He could not help the little jump in his heart at the expectation. Not seeing her, he asked, "Where is she? Did you leave her with the dogs?" Might Lady Selena be in trouble?

Straightening, he took several running steps toward the pasture, but Pascal called after him, "Lady Selena is taking the dogs back to the squire."

Abruptly stopping, he turned. "What?"

"Lady Selena said she was taking the dogs home, and that she meant to take the squire to task." His eyes round, he looked up at his father. "Will she really take him to task?"

Giving his mouth a wry twist, Calder slowly nodded. "I could see she might. But tell me all that has happened. Did the dogs hurt you?"

"Nay. They just scared me. They came bounding over the wall, and Rollo started barking at them, but they ran past him and chased the sheep all around. Rollo and I chased them. I threw rocks at them and hollered at them. Then all the sheep bunched up in the far corner. All but one lamb that ran a different direction. The dogs saw the lamb and made to get it, but I caught the lamb up and climbed atop that big stump in the pasture. Then I tried calling for help. The dogs kept jumping up, and the lamb was squiggling, and I was certain I might fall or drop the lamb, but then I saw Lady Selena running down the slope from the woods."

Admiration in his voice, Pascal shook his head. "She can really run. She had her skirts hiked up, and she was over the fence in a thrice and was telling the dogs they were naughty dogs. I could not believe it, but they began acting just like Rollo does around her. Wanting her to pet them. They forgot the lamb, and Lady Selena took it from me, set it down, and they paid it no mind. It just ran off, and Lady Selena helped me down because I was so tired." Running out of breath, he abruptly finished his speech.

Calder smiled at his son. "I am glad you are all right. And I am very glad Lady Selena arrived to help you. So she left with the dogs?" He wanted to know more. Hear more about the amazing young woman who had entered their lives and was turning his thoughts upside down and inside out.

"She said she would not have time to come here after taking the dogs back to the squire's. And she said tomorrow Lord and Lady Edgerton are coming to dinner, and the next day is Sunday, and they will be visiting Lady Rotherby's daughter after church. But she said she would be here for the sheep shearing. She said I was to tell you so." He ducked his head then glanced up at his father. "She also said I was to tell you I was very brave."

"Indeed you were. Fact is, I believe you deserve a treat for being so brave. Go tell Hannah I said you were to have one of her cross buns with butter on it. Do you wish, you may take one to Molly. As she has been minding the bees since mid-morning with naught but bread and cheese for her dinner, she is most likely hungry and would enjoy a treat."

"Thank you, Father, but do I not need to return to the sheep?"

Shaking his head, Calder said, "Nay, if Lady Selena has the dogs with her, the sheep are no longer in any danger. Rollo is there to mind them. Go have your treat."

Hitting his fist into his hand, Calder had watched the boy scamper off. He had put his son at risk. Abner, a grown man with a stick, had no trouble driving the dogs away, but Calder kicked himself for not realizing his small son would be no match for the dogs. Not that the dogs would have deliberately tried to hurt Pascal. They were but doing what hunting dogs do, going after prey. But Pascal, in trying to save the lamb, could have been accidentally hurt. Thank God Lady Selena had come along when she did.

He had headed back to the barn to finish mending the harness, but a tiny smile had crept across his face. He wished he had seen Lady Selena racing down the hill to rescue Pascal and the lamb. Wished he had seen her calming the dogs. Even more, he wished he could see her taking the squire to task. And she would do it, he had no doubt. God, but she was a treasure. He hoped when someday some man won her heart, that man would appreciate her for herself.

His thoughts returning to the present, he shifted his weight on the three-legged stool. Staring out the open door at the ducks wandering about the croft, he sighed. Dreaming about Lady Selena would not get his work done. He had best get to it. Abner would be returning from having his tooth pulled and would be looking to deliver the milk to White Acres Tower.

Rising, he picked up the stool, determined to get the milking done. Enough day dreaming.

❦ ❦ ❦

"Yes," Aunt Rowena said, dabbing her mouth with her napkin, "you are correct. I have not made you acquainted with the Nibleys for good reason."

They were finishing their supper, and Selena had finished telling her aunt about her day's adventure. She told her aunt only what she told Squire Nibley. She had come across Pascal and the lamb being attacked by the dogs while on her walk. She was not yet comfortable with telling her aunt, she was going as often as she could to the Grantham farm.

"You were astute to notice I failed to introduce you." Aunt Rowena said. "Now it seems I will have to do just that." She shrugged. "Sooner or later I would have had to do so anyway. They are members of the local gentry, and he is the Justice of the Peace."

Curious as to why her aunt chose not to introduce her to the Nibleys, Selena asked, "So what is wrong with them?"

"Little is wrong with Squire Nibley. 'Tis Mistress Nibley I have trouble countenancing." She fluttered her hand. "Oh, not that she is a bad person. She is just such an incredibly boring person. She can talk of nothing but clothes or the new furnishings for her house or her problems with various servants. Has the woman ever read a book, I am unaware of it.

"She is Squire Nibley's second wife. His first wife died some five years ago – the recurring fever, if I am recalling correctly. She was a good neighbor. She knew her tenants, could discuss various problems in the parish that needed addressing, and she had read a book or two besides the Bible. I believe Nibley's son is in school at Eton or maybe he is at the University by now. Nibley's daughter is living with her grandparents in London. From what I have heard, she is not comfortable with her new stepmother. A plain girl, but sweet tempered and bright. A good head on her shoulders, as the saying goes."

"I thought the house was very lovely," Selena said, "and the grounds and gardens were most pleasant. Mister Nibley must run a profitable manor."

Aunt Rowena chuckled. "The remodeled house, the improvements to the manor are all thanks to the new Mistress Nibley. Her grandfather was but a tavern owner, but his son made a fortune, so they say, in smuggling French wines and brandy during the Puritan reign. Mistress Nibley, being an only child, her father lavishes his wealth on her. I heard he had hopes of marrying her to a peer or at least a baronet, but as she remained on the marriage market year after year, he settled for Squire Nibley. At least Nibley's great, great grandfather was a knight."

"Is Squire Nibley a good Justice of the Peace? Is he fair?"

"I have not heard anything that would make me think he was not fair. Not that we have had anything that needed to come before him. Why do you ask?"

Twisting her mouth, Selena said, "His dogs caused damage to various people, and I wondered if he would compensate them. 'Tis all."

"I would hope he will, but 'tis not our concern, Selena. Sometimes you do get too involved in matters that you need not poke your nose into."

Giggling, Selena said, "Father has often told me the same thing. I do try not to get involved, but oftentimes, I simply cannot help myself." She raised her hand. "However, I do so pledge I will try not to get too involved in things that are none of my business."

"Ah, that would be a blessing. Besides, you have enough to do with your lessons. By the by, when Lord and Lady Edgerton are here tomorrow, do be on your best behavior."

"I will be, I promise. Will I like Lord and Lady Edgerton? Do you like them?"

"Lord Edgerton is a large man. Not just in height, but in girth. But his weight is not offensive. His shoulders are so broad, he has not the look of a fat man. Lady Edgerton is tall and slim. A good match for her husband. Orland is their only child and is slightly spoiled, as you may have noticed, but he is still a good boy. He and Ewen have been close friends since they were small. As to whether I like Lord and Lady Edgerton, yes. I do.

"Lord Edgerton is generally a jolly man, and Lady Edgerton, though fussy about etiquette and their family's reputation, is for the most part a sensible woman, and one I can converse pleasantly with. As to whether you will like them, I would see no reason you should not."

"Splendid. I already like Mister Darnell. I very much enjoyed our visit to Whimbrel. The tenants seem prosperous."

Aunt Rowena grinned. "They should. I would think they have the lowest rents of any tenants in the parish. Mayhap in the shire, but Nate says our wants are simple, so we need not raise the rents. Fortunately, we have some income from my dowry, and we get a sufficient amount from Nate's other two manors that he inherited from his mother. So, we are comfortable, and so are our tenants."

"Seems fair to me. They are, after all, the ones doing the work."

Aunt Rowena threw back her head and laughed merrily. "Oh, dear Selena, please make no such remark to Lord and Lady Edgerton. I believe they treat their tenants fairly, but they are not apt to think the tenants deserve more because they are the ones doing the work. Lord and Lady Edgerton, like most people of peer or gentry status, believe they are deserving of their wealth, and that the tenants are lucky they lease them land to farm and to live on. After all, they could enclose everything, and just grow sheep and cattle, as some landowners are doing."

"I suppose that is true, but did no one grow the wheat and rye or the various herbs and vegetables, would we be eating nothing but sheep?"

"I know, and you know, that farming the land is vital work, but because we know it, is not a reason to be telling other people what they should be doing with their land. Much of our land is devoted to raising sheep. We make more off the sale of wool than off our tenants' rent, but we also have acres of wheat, rye, oats, and barley. We have a mill to grind the grains, not only for ourselves and our tenants, but for other local manors and farms."

After taking a sip of her wine, Selena changed the subject and asked, "Why is there no church in Whimbrel? I saw the church ruins?"

Acknowledging the sudden change in the conversation, her aunt said, "Nate considered trying to rebuild the church, but the population is not large enough to support a church here and in Rotherby. Going into Rotherby to attend services is not difficult for us in our coach, but it can be hard on the tenants and on our servants in the winter. Is it too bleak, some choose not to attend. I cannot blame them."

Selena nodded thoughtfully. "Yes, and services are but one day a week. However, I have learned the boys, if they are to go beyond petty school, must go to Rotherby to attend grammar school. Would not a school closer to their homes, say in Whimbrel, be more beneficial? Especially in the winter."

"I suppose it would be, but what are you thinking?"

"Do you but remember how Cousin Timandra helped get a school built for her husband's grandfather's and uncle's tenants? I was thinking, might not the old Whimbrel church be rebuilt and made into a school. The foundation is there and a portion of the walls."

"Selena." Aunt Rowena shook her head and sighed. "Not only would there be the expense of rebuilding the church as a school, it would need furnishing with seats and tables and books. A schoolmaster would need to be paid. He would need a home."

Drawing in a deep breath, Selena cocked her head and narrowed her eyes. "Yes, I can see that creates a dilemma. There is obviously no easy solution. I must think on it."

Aunt Rowena frowned. "No, Selena, you need not think on it. In fact, 'tis better do you not think on it. You but need to be thinking on your lessons. That holds doubly for tomorrow when Lord and Lady Edgerton are here."

"Yes, Aunt Rowena," Selena agreed, but her mind was already on a plan. Whimbrel needed a school. The second Mistress Nibley needed to be accepted by her community. Selena decided she needed get Darnell to ride with her to Whimbrel again. She needed to learn more about the village housing. Could be one of the tenants would be pleased to rent out a room to a schoolmaster. Many schoolmasters had hard lives. They could so easily lose their positions. Many had no permanent living. Such a person should happily accept a position in Whimbrel.

Raising the money would be the only problem, but that problem could be solved by Mistress Nibley. What better way to become a pillar of the community than to see to the building of a school. Looking at her aunt, Selena smiled and said, "Might we adjourn to the parlor. I have a book I hope to finish this evening."

Rising, Aunt Rowena said, "Splendid. I have a book I am just starting. Some quiet time will do us both good."

Selena agreed. Quiet time would give her time to formulate her plan. If her Cousin Timandra could have a school built. She could do it, too.

<h1 style="text-align:center">Chapter 11</h1>

Selena found Lord Edgerton a delight, but Lady Edgerton, seated next to her at the dinner table, seemed disconcerted by almost everything Selena said. Aghast upon learning Selena had ridden most of the way to Whimbrel on horseback and not in a coach, the lady, her eyes wide, clutched her hands to her chest. Then, when she learned Selena had ridden astride, the lady launched into a tirade of enumerations of what was or was not proper behavior for a young woman. "Indeed, for any woman!" she declared and looked to Aunt Rowena for confirmation.

Frowning at Selena, Aunt Rowena said, "Certainly in this day and age, there can be no good reason for such actions."

Selena accepted the frown as chastisement, and turned to converse with Lord Edgerton. He seemed to enjoy talking to her about horses, but soon Lady Edgerton, scowling at her husband, announced she believed such conversation was hardly fit for the dinner table, or at least not fit for discussion by a lady at the dinner table – if at all fit for a lady to discuss, at any time. Again she looked to Aunt Rowena for confirmation, and sighing, Aunt Rowena said she believed other subjects might prove more suitable.

Trying yet another subject, Selena quickly discovered Lady Edgerton was not pleased to hear she took walks on her own without a footman or someone accompanying her. Then to learn Selena had accosted Squire Nibley about his dogs' behavior, well that was inappropriate deportment. Lord Edgerton was not so disapproving. He laughed uproariously and claimed he would have dearly loved to see Nibley's face.

But surprisingly, Lady Edgerton seemed most upset with Selena's depiction of the rooster that awaited her every morning at the back entrance to the house. The rooster insisted on trotting along beside her to the stables. It would then fly up to the wall separating Brigantia's stall from the adjoining stall and would not stop crowing until Selena took him in her arms and gave him a cuddle. "Then the cat, Smokey, and the dogs, Biscuit and Piff, must receive their pats before I get to take my ride," Selena said with a bright smile.

Lord Edgerton laughed, but Lady Edgerton sat there shaking her head. "Such familiarity with barnyard animals hardly seems wise, Lady Selena. They have been known to carry various diseases." She looked to Aunt Rowena. "Dear Lady Rotherby, I cannot recommend too strongly that this sort of behavior should be halted." Waving a hand at her son, who had been very quiet through most of the dinner, Lady Edgerton added, "Orland has told me, that according to Lady Selena herself, you have been entrusted with training her in more maidenly ways. I can see you have not an easy mission ahead of you."

Selena was having some difficulty controlling her laughter, especially when the pompous, but, Selena believed, well-meaning, Lady Edgerton turned to her and said, "Lady Selena, you are a lovely young woman. Heed your aunt's wise counsel, and hopefully you will blossom into as lovely a lady as your aunt."

Biting her lower lip, Selena nodded. She dared not glance at her aunt for fear she truly would burst into laughter. Regrettably, she realized she had not exhibited the kind of behavior Aunt Rowena had wanted. She should have stuck to mundane subjects like the weather or the lovely Whimbrel Hall gardens or mayhap the floral design Aunt Rowena had her stitching. But then, would she not have been as boring as the poor second Mistress Nibley?

❦ ❦ ❦

Selena was relieved, when they adjourned to the parlor, to find she and Darnell were given the choice of joining in a card game or of playing a game of backgammon. Both quickly chose backgammon, and Lord and Lady Edgerton and Aunt Rowena settled down to a three-handed game of Ombre.

"You have been very quiet today," Selena said, once she and Darnell started the game.

He glanced at his parents. "'Tis not always easy to converse with my parents. Father is boisterous, and Mother seldom likes anything I say."

Selena smiled. "Your mother seemed not to like much of anything I said today." Making a move, then sitting back to watch Darnell study the board, she added, "I do hope she will forgive my bluntness. I meant to be on my most lady-like behavior at dinner, but I fear I have not yet learned to curb my tongue."

Looking up and wryly twisting his mouth, Darnell nodded. "You said little that would meet with her approval. She thinks she must keep up certain appearances. We are not an old barony. Father is but the second Baron Edgerton. My grandfather bought the title from Charles I when the King needed funds. Which I hear was often." He shrugged and chuckled. "Anyway, Grandfather already owned the manor. His father bought and sold various monastic properties and greatly increased his wealth. Before he became a trader in land, great-grandfather was simply in trade, anything from lumber to horses to wool. 'Twas his wise land investments that made him rich. Rich enough to buy three thousand acres of prime land here in Leicestershire with a good woodland and with a good woodland and' should be with a good woodland and access to the Wreak River.

"Mother's family dates back to Henry VIII. One of her ancestors was an Earl, but she is from a younger son's branch of the family. The branch that went into trade. Made good money, but had no prestige, and prestige is important to Mother. That is one reason she so enjoys her friendship with your aunt, the wife of an Earl, whose family dates back to the Conqueror."

Selena laughed. "Both my father and Uncle Nate are younger sons. You must know they are newly made Earls. Being favorites of the King, both having helped Charles when he was in exile, he rewarded them with titles and estates. Whimbrel and Rygate were once manors belonging to the crown."

"Yes, I know it, and Mother knows it, but even as younger sons, Lord Rotherby and your father are descendants of the D'Arcys, a family known to have come over to England with the Conqueror. That ancestry makes a big difference. Especially as your father and uncle are but one step away from the direct line of descent."

"Yes, but on my mother's side, her father's ancestors were once woolen merchants. Fact is, the manor in Lincolnshire that I will someday inherit, though 'tis ancient, was acquired by a merchant ancestor during Queen Elizabeth's reign. Unfortunately, it was old when purchased, and little has been done to update it. It still has a medieval gate and inner courtyards, but I think during the reign of King Henry VIII, Gothic windows were added, so at least there is some light. I find it a dark, hulking place. But then, I have only been there once, and I was quite young. Could be I would not now find it so intimidating."

Darnell rolled the dice, made his move, and then said, "Your father must have a steward or bailiff caring for it, I suppose."

"Yes, he has stewards or bailiffs for all Mother's manors. From Grandfather, Mother inherited three large manors and several small ones. From her mother she inherited a manor in Scotland. The manor I am to inherit, is from Mother's father's mother. I can tell you nothing more about my future manor. I know not whether it is enclosed or open field, if it has a vast number of tenants or next to none. I just never thought to ask Father anything about it. It has never been of great interest to me."

Picking up the dice, she gave them a toss, scowled at her three and two, then laughed and moved two checkers. "I am beginning to think this will not be my game. Should we go best two out of three."

"This game is not half over. You could well improve, but whether you do or not, yes, we should do best two out of three." Glancing over at his parents, he added, "Or even best four out of five. My parents both love playing cards, so they may be there for the rest of the afternoon."

"Very well. So now, Mister Darnell, what can you tell about the Nibleys? As you heard, I had a brief encounter with Squire Nibley, and I expect to meet his wife at church tomorrow."

"Ah, the squire is a good man, the present Justice of the Peace. He is well respected. The Nibleys have been at Nibley Hall for any number of generations. A Nibley ancestor was knighted by Edward IV. Nibleys have long been seated on their manor."

"And what of Mistress Nibley?"

Narrowing his eyes and pursing his lips, he looked thoughtful. "I know her little. She is neither fair nor plain. Where the squire is a tad portly, she is more plump, rounded I guess I would have to say. In fact, everything about her is round, her eyes, nose, mouth, shoulders, and err… bosom. Her laughter is annoying, rather screechy." He shrugged. "That is all I know of her. As I said, I have had little contact with her. Father and Mother did dine with them once. Mother said never again. Said the food was acceptable, the table well set, but she said Mistress Nibley's chatter was too inane."

"How long have the Nibleys been married?"

Cocking his head to one side, he again looked thoughtful. "Close to three years now, I would guess. But for near two years, they were involved in remodeling their house and grounds."

"Oh, poor Mistress Nibley, three years and not yet accepted."

"Why your concern about Mistress Nibley?"

Selena offered Darnell a small smile. "'Tis ever sad when someone is not accepted, and the someone has no idea why. To please my mother, I must learn to be more ladylike. But I have Aunt Rowena to teach me. Mistress Nibley needs to learn to chatter less, and read more. Could she discuss Shakespeare or Moliere with Aunt Rowena or your mother, they might find her of more interest."

"Hmmm. 'Tis possible. But here, let us return to our game." Picking up the dice, he rolled and got two sixes. Chuckling, he moved his checkers on the board.

"Not fair! Not fair!" Selena cried with a giggle. But her mind was not truly on the game. Her thoughts were on Mistress Nibley and the building of the school in Whimbrel village.

# Chapter 12

Goblet in hand, Rowena eyed her niece. As both she and Selena were still full from dinner, she had ordered a simple supper of bread and butter, boiled eggs, and sliced beef be served in the parlor. Deciding that, over the course of dinner and the afternoon of games, they had been drinking enough wine, she ordered a sweetened cider to go with their plain supper. Sharing the intimate drop-leaf parlor table with Selena would make conversation easier, and they had various things to discuss, starting with Selena's behavior.

Selena took a sip of cider then smiled. "I know what you are thinking, Aunt Rowena. You are thinking I promised to be on my good behavior, yet everything I said seemed ill advised. I cannot think I offended Lady Edgerton." She cocked her head to one side. "Nay. For I was never rude. I was but honest. When she asked about the journey from Rygate, expressing her own opinion of a despised coach ride to London, I but told her I preferred to ride my horse. Sadly it went on from there. I realize, I should not have mentioned I rode astride, wearing men's clothing, but 'twas too late when I did realize my error.

"I never thought my little anecdote about the animals would be seen as something unladylike. You have never forbidden me from befriending them, so I had no way of knowing I should not have mentioned them. Uncle Nate said 'tis safe for me to take my walks on my own, so I never thought that information to be off limits for discussion. Or the mention that Squire Nibley should not be allowing his dogs to run free and terrorize his neighbors.

"Surely you cannot fault me for discussing the different merits of horses with Lord Edgerton at the dinner table. Why, at the supper table on Uncle Nate's last night here, he and I, and you also, had a rousing conversation about Brigantia and Uncle Nate's large black stud and your favorite mare, Diera, and whether either mare should be bred. So you see, Aunt Rowena, I had no way of knowing I was committing etiquette blunders."

Rowena listened quietly to Selena's excuses, and sadly, she had to agree with the girl. Other than her admission that she had ridden astride in men's clothing, or that she had chastised the squire for the wrongful actions of his dogs, nothing Selena had said or done could be construed as improper conversation or activities. Animals were drawn to Selena, and she to them, it was that simple. Nothing would change that.

And Selena was correct, a discussion of the merits of various horses was often a topic of conversation in her home. No, the problem lay in Selena's directness. She seemed unable to judge when a particular subject might be inappropriate in certain situations. Rowena realized this was where the real challenge lay. Selena could behave like a lady, dress like a lady, but she had not learned to think like a lady. She was kindhearted, almost to a fault, even tempered, generous, and would ever look for the good in people and animals. But could she become the kind of lady her mother hoped she would become, so she could win the love of a peer or at least a gentleman?

Rowena had no doubt she could teach Selena to manage a home, hire and train servants, even keep the larder and wine cellar stocked. But she was beginning to think Nate might be correct. Mayhap, to try to change Selena's personality would destroy the girl they so loved. She would have to give that a good deal of thought. In the meantime, she would continue with the household management and decorum lessons.

"You are correct, Selena, certain things you could not know would be deemed inappropriate for dinner conversation. We will try to work on that. I cannot think Lady Edgerton was offended. But I cannot think she believes you to be a potential mate for her son."

"Oh, that is good, for I would have no interest in Mister Darnell. He is much like Ewen, and I can see how they would be the best of friends. Both are youthful, yet."

Rowena chuckled. "And you are not?"

Selena giggled, then sobered. "Oh, yes, I am youthful, also, but in a different way. I see the whole world, the real world, and all its people and animals, their needs, their heartaches. Ewen and Mister Darnell see the world as a joyous playground for those of wealth. True, I have been pampered all my life. Servants are always at my beck and call, but I recognize that they are people with needs, and feelings, and hopes and dreams. The tenants that grow the crops and mind the sheep and cattle and drive the animals to market and see to their feed, their worth is as grand as mine, in God's eyes, anyway.

"Yes, I am often frivolous. I am callous about the manor I will someday inherit. I have never needed to be concerned about having clothes to wear or food to eat or having to walk two or three or more miles to go to church on Sunday. On cold days, the fire in my chamber is always lit and warm water awaits my morning ablutions. My clothing is laundered and pressed, my hair is combed and dressed. I have all these things and more, simply because my father is an Earl, and my mother is very wealthy. I avail myself of these many advantages. Yet, I know they are not mine because I am superior to my maid, Alice, or anyone else. I was but more fortunate to have been born into the D'Arcy family."

Rowena nodded. "Yes, child, in many ways you are more wise than my son or Darnell. Certainly you are more aware of the privileges you possess. I can see that you want a man who shares your outlook. You are correct, Darnell is not that man. Would it not be a shame, if you find that man, but you cannot fulfill his needs of someone to manage his home and raise his children? In other words, you need to be an asset to your husband. That may sometimes mean minding your tongue. At least giving more thought to your statements, before you make them."

Watching the thoughtful expressions flitting across Selena's face, Rowena hoped her words might have an impact on the girl. Selena was such an endearing child. Always had been. But could she ever attract a man that suited her needs and his?

"I will try to do better, Aunt Rowena. I know I have promised you such before. Truly, I never intend to embarrass you. It but happens. I promised Mother I would do your bidding, and I shall. You shall see. I will learn to manage a home."

❊ ❊ ❊

Selena had every intention of learning to manage a home, and the home she intended to manage was the Grantham farmhouse. She would, of course, never interfere with Hannah, but she would add another servant or two to help Hannah. Once she and Calder had children, they would have to have a nurse, and she would have Alice, her maid, but she had no intention of needing to entertain earls and barons or anyone else of that ilk. She would simply be a farmer's wife. Now, she but needed to make Calder fall in love with her. How to go about achieving her goal, she was not certain, but the first step would be to visit the farm as often as she could.

She had never had a vision of what kind of man she would someday marry. Fact was, she had wondered if she would ever meet any man who might stir longings in her, like she knew her mother experienced with her father. But, from the moment she set eyes on Calder, she had felt he was the man for her. In talking with him, seeing his home and his son and servants, seeing his farm and animals, but most of all, in looking into his eyes, her first impression had been confirmed. She would marry Calder Grantham or no one.

She knew her cousins would be arriving in little more than a week. They were presently staying with Aunt Rowena's oldest son by her first marriage. Her Cousin Flavia had sent a note, begging she and Carola Mead, her chaperone, be given a respite before traveling on to Whimbrel, and Aunt Rowena had acquiesced. Once Flavia and Ewen and Ewen's friends arrived, Selena worried her freedom to visit Calder might be jeopardized. Well, if need be, she would drag Flavia along with her. Ewen she could count on to take his friends off on various outings, so they should not create too much conflict. And most likely, Ewen and his friends would make dinner and supper entertaining. She had already met Ansel Yardley and found him diverting. No doubt Ewen's other friends would be equally amusing, or at least interesting.

With the simple supper finished, Selena and Aunt Rowena settled with their books, but Selena continued to let her mind wander. She meant to finish her book, *Love's Victory*, by Lady Mary Wroth, so she might pass it on to Mistress Nibley. Was the poor woman ever to be accepted by Aunt Rowena and Lady Edgerton, she was going to have to become better read. Selena found the situation amusing. Here she was learning to be a lady, and at the same time, she was hoping to teach Mistress Nibley to be a more entertaining lady. Suppressing a giggle, she looked over at her aunt. At some point her aunt would have to learn about Calder. What would happen then, she could not guess, but did her aunt attempt to restrict her visits to the farm, she would have to disobey her. That she would not like to do.

Soon it would be time for bed. On the morrow, they would attend services, formally meet the Nibleys, and then go to dinner at Aunt Rowena's older daughter's house. Selena liked Cecily and her husband and three children. Reynard Bardwith was the constable of Rotherby, though he insisted he would serve but one year. It was a demanding, thankless job, but was passed around to the stable members of the parish, and no one was stuck with the position for more than a year. Being a lawyer, and used to traveling to Leicester and Melton-Mowbray, and occasionally even to London with his cases, the office of constable was imposing numerous difficulties on Reynard. He was paying a bailiff, out of his own pocket, to fill in for him when he had to be away from Rotherby and was allowing the bailiff to collect the petty fees for various infractions.

In her determination to marry Calder, Selena knew she had one big thing in her favor. Reynard. He was the son of a yeoman. He became a gentleman when he became a lawyer, but he was still of yeoman stock. He inherited a two-hundred acre farm from his father, and he leased another two and a half hundred acres. The farm was operated by a cousin who lived in the farmhouse that had once been Reynard's home. Reynard had a substantial house in Rotherby and seemed not to want a house in the country. If Aunt Rowena could let her daughter marry a man one step away from the farm, surely she could not object to Selena wanting to marry a farmer.

Could she get Aunt Rowena to approve of her marriage to Calder, that would help her gain her parents' approval. She would soon be twenty-one, and would not need her parents' approval, but she would prefer it. She loved her family, and would not like anything to come between her and her beloved parents and brothers. But she was getting ahead of herself. She had yet to win Calder's love. He had to want to marry her, as she wanted to marry him. Somehow she had to convince him that she would make a good farmer's wife. That she had to do. She would. She just knew she would.

# Chapter 13

With the Sunday services ended, Selena and her aunt made their way to the door. The weather was glorious, bright and sunny, so attendance had been good. All the same, Selena knew many of the parishioners would be footsore by the time they returned home. She and Aunt Rowena complimented the vicar on his sermon, exchanged polite greetings with Lord and Lady Edgerton and Darnell, and Aunt Rowena accepted the Edgertons thanks for the previous day's dinner and entertainment. Finally, she took Selena's elbow and turned to greet the Nibleys who were waiting anxiously a few steps away.

"Selena, dear, allow me to make you known to Squire Nibley and Mistress Nibley," Aunt Rowena said. "Squire and Mistress Nibley, may I present to you my niece, Lady Selena." Selena smiled brightly at the pair as Aunt Rowena continued, "I understand from my niece, she has already informally met you, Squire Nibley."

"Indeed she has," the squire said, his red cheeks puffing in and out, his pudgy hands fumbling with his gloves. "Seems my dogs were on the rampage." He looked at Selena. "I have taken care of all complaints, and have paid Grantham for his lamb. And for the scare the dogs gave his son. I gave the lad a sixpence to spend as he may please."

"How kind of you," Selena said before addressing the Squire's wife. "So pleased to meet you, Mistress Nibley."

"Oh, Lady Selena, when my husband told me you had been to the hall, and he had not insisted you come in to rest and have a drink, I was mortified."

"Oh, he did insist I come in, but I refused, considering my appearance after my walk. 'Twas no way to meet you. Short of throwing me over his shoulder and carting me inside, he could not have changed my mind."

The squire chuckled nervously, and Mistress Nibley emitted a grating titter at Selena's comment. Selena found Mistress Nibley much as Darnell had described her. Everything about her was round, from her face and her features to her bosom and her waist and the dainty hands fluttering expressively when she spoke. But she would not call Mistress Nibley plain. Her round mouth was spread in a pretty smile, displaying neat little teeth, and her round eyes, a deep dark brown, were very expressive. She was dressed in the first of fashion with perky curls of light brown hair peeping out from under her headdress, a cap with a standing frill and long lappets, that perfectly matched her gown. She had to be near twenty years younger than her husband, but being a second wife, that was not surprising.

Not being very tall, Mistress Nibley was forced to crane her neck to look up at Selena and her aunt. "I was thinking, Lady Rotherby, to welcome Lady Selena to the parish, I would like to invite you and her to dinner. Mayhap you would be free this Tuesday?" Her hands stilled their fluttering, and she pressed them to her bosom.

"I do believe we are free Tuesday," Aunt Rowena said, "but I will need to be certain. I will send you a note tomorrow morning, if that will not be inconvenient for you."

"Oh, tomorrow morning will be fine," the woman gushed. "Just fine, will it not, Florian?"

Bobbing his head up and down, Squire Nibley said, "Oh, yes, fine, just fine."

"Good," Aunt Rowena said. "I see my daughter is waiting for us. We dine with her today. You will excuse us?"

"Of course, of course," Mistress Nibley said. Looking at Selena, she added, "So lovely to meet you, Lady Selena."

Selena reached out and took Mistress Nibley's busy hand. "Lovely to meet you, Mistress Nibley. I do hope we will be able to dine with you on Tuesday."

The lady sighed deeply. "Oh, yes, I do hope you can make it. Good day to you."

Selena gave Mistress Nibley's hand a pat, gave Squire Nibley a smile and a nod, but instead of trailing after her aunt, she hurried over to Pascal and Hannah. They had been standing patiently waiting for her to join them. She knew they hoped to speak to her, for Pascal had not taken his earnest young eyes off her. Even from a distance, she could see the excitement radiating out of him. "Greetings, Hannah. Greetings, Pascal," she said.

"Oh, Lady Selena, I had to talk to you," Pascal exclaimed. "Hannah said you might not have time to stop to talk, but I knew you would."

"Of course, I would stop to greet you and Hannah," Selena said, giving the boy a bright smile. "I can tell you are excited. Tell me why."

"I saw you talking to the Nibleys. Did the squire tell you he paid Father for the lamb?"

"He did."

"Besides paying Father, he gave me a sixpence. Said was as an apology for the dogs giving me a fright. But I was not terribly afraid. At least not of the dogs."

"I know, you were very brave. But you are still deserving of the sixpence. I hope you will spend it wisely."

"Father says I may spend it as I like, but I mean to save all but one penny."

"Saving is good, but what are you saving for?"

"For new shoes. I will be turning seven this fall, and Father says I need attend school in Rotherby once the harvest is over. 'Tis a fair piece to walk, and I will need good shoes."

"Indeed, it is a fair piece. All on your own?"

"Oh, no, I will walk with Molly Huddleston's two older brothers. On days when the weather is really bad, Mister Huddleston lets Tom take the cart."

"Boy, you have been blathering on long enough," Hannah said, clamping a hand on Pascal's shoulder. "I can see Lady Rotherby looking this way. I think she is wanting Lady Selena to join her."

Selena looked over her shoulder. "Yes, Hannah, you are correct. She wants me to hurry. I will say good-bye for now, but do tell Calder I will be there tomorrow to help with the sheep." Both cried God speed to her, as she hurried back to her aunt.

Aunt Rowena was frowning, but her petite daughter, Cecily, who, with her pale-blond hair and vivid blue eyes, looked not at all like her mother, gave Selena a hug. "You are not to let Mother chastise you,"

Cecily said. "I have told her I am in no hurry. I sent the children home with their nurse, and Reynard knows I am riding home with you and Mother. Reynard, poor dear, as constable, has a call he must make before he can have his dinner."

"How much longer is his term as constable?" Selena asked, following her aunt and Cecily into the Rotherby coach.

"Six more months. What an expense it has been on our budget. I was hoping to have some of that new wallpaper put up on the walls in our parlor, but that cannot be this year. Mayhap next. We shall see."

The short trip from the church to the Bardwith's home on the outskirts of town was entertaining, as Cecily had a bright sense of humor and a treasure trove of tales centered around her three children. Brilliana, her older daughter, at fifteen, was blossoming into an absolute beauty. She had her mother's coloring, and her grandmother's height. At ten, Teagan, a slim boy with his father's dark hair and his mother's blue eyes, was a typical boy, active, curious about near everything, and forgetful. Seven-year-old Ampora, being a bright and studious child, had excelled in petty school. She was to have a tutor, as girls were not allowed to attend the grammar school. The image of her dark-haired, dark-eyed father, she seemed to be the one to take after him in other ways as well. She loved to read, and finding reading material suitable to a young girl was not easy.

"*Aesop's Fables and Arabian Nights* are favorites," Cecily said. "And like her siblings, she is reading *Orbis Pictus* in Latin and English and enjoying the pictures. I could wish the book had been around when I was her age. She also loves to listen to her father tell about his cases, and she can spend hours contemplating a puzzle her father puts to her.

"Were she a boy, we would have no doubt she would be headed for a profession in the law," Cecily said. "As is, mayhap she will marry a lawyer."

"'Tis a shame so many restrictions apply to girls and women," Selena said. "Ampora cannot become a lawyer, and I am here, learning to be more ladylike, when instead, I would like to be equal to a man in word and deed, but I am told no man wants that in a wife."

Aunt Rowena frowned and shook her head, and Cecily chuckled. "The trick, dear cousin, is to learn to hide the fact that you are equal to your husband in stamina and intellect, if perhaps not in bodily strength. Men have fragile egos, and 'tis the wife's job, does she love him, to protect that ego. When you meet the right man, you will want to do all in your power, not just to be his helpmate, but to be his confidant, his conscience, and his soul."

"I know you are all these things to Reynard," Selena stated before looking at her aunt. "And you are those things to Uncle Nate, as Mother is all those things to Father."

Aunt Rowena and Cecily both smiled and nodded.

"But are you not concerned, Cecily, that Ampora, simply because she is a girl, cannot be a lawyer, even if she is smart enough?"

Cecily gave a half smile. "I have many wishes for all my children. Mainly I wish them to be happy. To live their lives, wishing for things that cannot be, is not what I want for them."

"You must learn, Selena," Aunt Rowena said, "that life is far from perfect. Not just for you or for Ampora." She raised her eyes. "Our coachman started with us, a youth in the stables, before he became a postilion and eventually our coachman. He is good at what he does. He is loyal, and when he is old and needs to retire, he will receive a good pension. Our cook, too, is most satisfactory, though he is aging and may not be able to do some of the heavy work in the kitchen for that many more years. Neither the coachman, nor the cook, nor my personal maid, who has been with me since King Charles made Nate an Earl and gave us Whimbrel, will ever advance beyond their current positions. Is that fair?" She shrugged. "I but know it is life. They accept the role in life they have been dealt. You must learn to accept yours."

Before Selena could answer her aunt, Cecily said, "Some people advance beyond the station they were born into, as did my Reynard. His father, as you know, was a yeoman, a freeholder, who wanted his only surviving child to be a gentleman. Reynard's father scrimped and saved and did without many items, that he might send Reynard to school. Now, Reynard is a respected lawyer and gentleman, not only of Rotherby, but of the entire shire. We have a comfortable home. Nicely furnished, thanks to my generous dowry from Mother and my deceased father. However, we will never be excessively wealthy, our income being dependent upon Reynard's various cases, and a small sum we get from his farmland. Much of the farm's income goes to Reynard's cousin, who cares for and operates the farm. But 'tis doubtful any of Reynard's cousin's four children will have the opportunities Reynard had, or that our children will have. Reynard's cousin, being the son of a younger son, had no land, and he might have no home, was he not working Reynard's land and living in Reynard's home of his youth. What will become of the cousin's children, I cannot know. The older boy may stay on the land and work it for Teagan someday. As Mother said, we cannot say it is fair. It is but life."

Again, Selena had no chance to answer as the coach drove up in front of the Bardwith home, and the footman opened the door and lowered the steps. He reached out a hand to help Cecily, then Selena, then Aunt Rowena from the coach.

"After you have stabled the horses," Cecily said to the footman, "see the cook about your dinner. He knows he is feeding extra mouths today."

"Thank you, Mistress Bardwith," the footman said, giving her a slight bow.

Selena sighed and followed Cecily and Aunt Rowena up the steps of the modest, yellow-brick house with its symmetrical proportions and multiple windows. It was a comfortable, if unimposing home, and Selena believed it was filled with love. She knew her aunt and Cecily were giving her wise advice. She needed to accept that she could not do all the things a man was allowed to do, but she could not help but resent the fact. Maybe, had she led a more restrictive life as a child, she might be more accepting of her plight in life. But she had known so much freedom, 'twas hard to contemplate giving it up. Did her plans to marry Calder come to fruition, she believed she would be able to retain many of those freedoms. And yes, she would be more than happy to protect Calder's ego, did it need protecting.

# Chapter 14

Having overslept in the morning, Selena missed her morning ride. She knew Brigantia needed her exercise, but she hated to have anyone else ride her. She decided she would ask the groom assigned to ride with her if he knew how to get to the Grantham farm by way of the road. That way, Brigantia would get her exercise, and she could get to the Grantham's sooner. Her maid, Alice, had tried to awaken her at her usual time, but she had grumped at her, and had turned over and gone back to sleep. When she did finally arise, after Alice returned to try for the second time to get her up, she barely had time to scarf down a biscuit and some warm ale, and join Aunt Rowena for her lesson.

The first portion of the morning lesson, as it turned out, was on polite conversation. What was acceptable in a family situation, and what was acceptable as a guest, or when entertaining guests. The second portion was centered on the various duties of servants, how they should be addressed, and how they should be treated. "Naturally, some servants are more special than others," Aunt Rowena said. "I recollect you have formed a fondness for Alice, as I have for my personal maid. That is to be expected. Lord knows I love my former nurse, Liverna, who was also my maid and my children's nurse, and even now she is nurse to Fonda's children." Aunt Rowena chuckled. "You and I both know Fonda's nursery, and perhaps her whole house, would be in utter chaos if not for Liverna."

Selena laughed, too. She loved Fonda, Aunt Rowena's daughter-in-law. She found Fonda entertaining and had enjoyed the days she had spent in Fonda's home before continuing on to Whimbrel. She knew all too well that Fonda was not a disciplinarian, nor did she make any attempt to be. If not for Liverna, Fonda's three children would grow up experiencing the same kind of freedom Selena held so dear, but now

Selena was beginning to think having such freedom was not necessarily a good thing. It led to discontent with one's lot in life. Even if one had a very good life, as she did.

At last the lessons ended, and she and her aunt had dinner. That, too, finally ended, and she was at last free to visit Calder. Fortunately, the groom, Jimmy, knew exactly how to get to the Grantham's, and soon they were cantering off down the road. Normally Jimmy trailed a little behind Selena, but as he was guiding her, he was riding beside her. Selena knew this would not normally be acceptable behavior, but 'twas necessary in this case. As long as they were riding side by side, she saw no reason she should not converse with him.

He was a personable youth, with a bright, freckled face and bulging biceps. Selena had no doubt her uncle had chosen Jimmy to be her groom because of his acknowledged strength. Did she get into any trouble, Jimmy should be able to extricate her. He also carried a small club at his waist. When riding with her, Jimmy wore her uncle's livery, but when working in the stable, he donned the plain garb of a stableman, loose flared knee breeches, a woolen waistcoat, linen coat, and heavy leather shoes.

"Jimmy," she said, "how long have you been at Whimbrel?"

He grinned, showing a mouthful of strong, straight teeth. "This be my sixth year here, milady. Came here when I was twelve and had finished at the grammar school. Me father is one o' Lord Rotherby's tenants. He is a leaseholder. I have two older brothers, so no chance to inherit any land, but Lord Rotherby is good about hiring those on his estate who might be in need of a job. I figure I can work meself up, and mayhap, become the coachman when old Bertie retires." He rubbed his upper arm. "I got me the strength to keep coach horses in check."

Selena agreed. He looked quite powerful. "Both your parents are still living?" she asked.

"Aye, milady. They are both yet full of vim and vigor. Father recently had to add onto the house when me oldest brother, Henry, and his wife had their second child. It cost more than Father liked to spend, him wanting me youngest brother, Arn, to continue in school, but he cannot afford to send him back to the grammar school in Leicester this year. 'Tis the board that cost, but 'tis a better school than the grammar school in Rotherby. Father hopes next year Arn can return to Leicester, but this year he will have to attend the Rotherby school. Not that Alice's brother bain't a good teacher, but there are things he cannot teach, like bookkeeping. Arn is the youngest of me brothers, and to my way of thinking, he is spoiled. But he is also smart. Fascinated by the stars he is. Wonders are people living on the moon and looking down and wondering if anyone is living on earth. Always full of questions."

"I am sorry he will be unable to attend the Leicester school this fall. I hope he will be able to go back there when your father has completed building the addition."

"Does Mother have anything to say about it, he will. He is her pet."

"Have you any sisters, Jimmy?"

"Aye, two, milady. Both married. "Sara has been married three years now, and Mary just got married, which is another thing what took the schooling from Arn. Mary had to be given a dowry. Bain't much, a cow and a calf, and her linen chest, but Willy has a small leasehold over to Lord Edgerton's manor, so Mary did all right by herself. Sara's husband is the Whimbrel village shoemaker, so she did all right by herself, too. Mother is pleased for the both of them."

"Do they look like you?" Selena wondered if they had his fair hair and freckles.

"Mary looks like me. We both take after Father. But his face is so lined and bronzed, you cannot see does he have freckles or not." Reaching up and scratching under his cap, Jimmy asked, "Would I be impertinent, milady, did I ask why you would be asking all these questions about me family?"

Nodding her head, Selena said, "You are not impertinent. At home, I knew all our tenants and a number of the neighboring tenants. All good people. All hard working, as I am certain your parents are. Wanting to give the best they can to their children. The sacrifices many parents are so willing to make for their children seems a wondrous thing. I admire the tenants who work the fields, and shepherd the sheep and cattle, and milk the animals, feed them if they are not out to pasture, shear the sheep, and pluck the geese feathers. Oh, and so many things that I have not the knowledge of. Just in talking with you, Jimmy, I have learned of the many things your parents must contemplate on a daily, as well as a yearly, basis.

"Yet, here I am, never needing to lift a finger for myself. I have the freedom to spend the afternoon riding or visiting a friend. Tell me honestly, Jimmy, do you resent the genteel class?"

Vigorously shaking his head, he proclaimed, "Good heavens, no, milady. I was born to me station, and I know 'tis what God wanted, or else I would have been born to a different class. But Arn, now, does he complete his schooling and go on to university, he may become a gentleman, like Mistress Bardwith's husband. But that, too, would be God's will."

"I see," Selena said. She wished she could learn to be as accepting of God's will, but she feared she never would be. Certain things God willed, she simply could not understand. Like why God had willed her mother should be crippled in an accident and forced to spend the rest of her days in her bed or on a chair. Never to walk or run again. So many other things that seemed so completely unfair and unnecessary – children dying, animals suffering from mistreatment, ships lost at sea and sailors drowning, older sons being given land and younger sons having to find a means of living on their own, some never to know their own home. God's will was indeed most incomprehensible.

"That be the track to the White Acres Tower," Jimmy said, interrupting Selena's pondering. He pointed to a well-maintained wagon path that swept through a field of white daisies. "'Tis why it has its name of White Acres," he continued. "The flowers first bloom in the spring, but some continue to bloom all through the summer and sometimes into the fall. Each year, on orders from Lord Penhaligon, this section of the estate must be left fallow so to preserve the flowers and the name of the estate.

"You seem to know much about the manor," Selena said.

"Right I should. Me oldest brother's wife's family be tenants there. Have been for more generations than they can count. Likely been there longer than the Huddlestons. Mayhap before the Normans came."

Selena had not yet met the Huddlestons. They probably attended services in Rotherby, but were they not in Aunt Rowena's social circle, they would not be introduced. Aunt Rowena nodded to many people, and the men doffed their hats, and the women curtsied, but none seemed to think they should be introduced. None but the squire and his wife. But they were in Aunt Rowena's social class, and could not be ignored, even if she cared little for them.

"There ahead," Jimmy said. "There is the Grantham farm."

The track leading into the farm was as well maintained as the one on White Acres, but it passed through fields of growing grain rather than white daisies. The horses splashed through the stream that wound down from the hill and eventually curved off toward White Acres. Selena saw Calder and his laborers engaged in shearing the sheep. Much baaing was going on as the wary sheep struggled against their captors. Calder's laborers were doing the shearing, and Calder, Pascal, and Hannah were gathering up the wool and stuffing it into linen sacks.

When Pascal saw her riding up, he stopped what he was doing and went running up to her. "Oh, Lady Selena, what a lovely horse," he cried as he neared her.

Jimmy had dropped back behind her, no longer her companion, but her servant. She pulled up on her reins as Pascal approached. Jimmy hopped off his horse to help her dismount, but she was on the ground before he could reach her. She gave him her horse's reins and knelt to pet Rollo. The dog had been torn between doing his duty, keeping the sheep bunched, and greeting her. His feathered tail wagging, he stayed for a quick pat then raced back to herd an errant sheep back with the others. An amazing dog. She had learned from Calder that Rollo's mother had been bred on the Scottish border where sheep and cattle were a mainstay for the families living there. The dogs were near part of the family, so valued were they, because they were naturally skilled at herding. Calder had purchased Rollo as a puppy from the Huddlestons, who had received his mother as a gift from the Earl of Penhaligon, Lord of White Acres, to help with the dairy herd.

Laughing as Rollo returned to work, and with her hand on Pascal's shoulder, Selena headed over to the barn area where the sheep were being shorn. Jimmy tied the horses to the hitching post, then slowly followed her. Selena greeted Calder, Hannah, and his laborers, and was heartily greeted in return. She then said, "Do you wish, I can see if I might calm the sheep."

Jared looked up for a moment and said, "Could you keep this one from wriggling like ye done the cow, I would be grateful. She be a young one and has ne'er been shorn afore."

Squatting, Selena placed her hands on either side of the upside down sheep. Its eyes were rolling in its head, its feet kicking wildly, but she rubbed its jaws, and using her fingertips, worked her way up to its tiny ears. The sheep relaxed. Jared whistled low. "A marvel," he said, resuming his clipping. When he finished with the sheep, he flipped it back onto its feet, and with a backward glance at Selena, the sheep joined several other shorn sheep at a mound of hay that had been spread out to reward the sheep after they endured their shearing.

"How did you do that?" Jimmy questioned, shaking his head. "'Tis like the animals what follow you around at Whimbrel."

Rising, and glancing over her shoulder, Selena said, "I seem to have a way with animals. I believe they sense I mean them no harm. They accept my touch, and it calms them."

"'Tis like nothin' I ever saw," Abner said, finishing his sheep. Setting it free, he looked to Calder to bring him another.

Noting the bunched sheep, especially the young ones, were fretting, Selena walked into their midst and began speaking softly to them. She gave various sheep a pat or a rub. "'Tis what I always did with Father's sheep," she said when Calder selected another sheep for Jared, and then one for Abner. "They but need to know they are not to be harmed."

Calder laughed, his eyes glowing brightly with warmth and cheer. Selena was hard pressed to remember what she was doing until he carted off one of the sheep. His three laborers sat on low stools, and with sharpened shearing scissors, they turned the sheep this way and that and deftly clipped off the wool. Between the sheep already shorn, and those waiting to be shorn, she counted fifty-two sheep. A goodly number for a farm the size of Calder's. A small number compared to the sheep her father kept on his estate.

She had always enjoyed helping calm the sheep. Most sheep were gentle animals, and they kindly provided mankind with wool for their clothing and milk and meat for their tables. She wondered how Adam and Eve, when they left Eden and needed clothing, figured out the sheep's wool could be shorn and spun into thread to be woven into clothes. And where did they get the scissors? As a child, she had once questioned the Reigate vicar. He said God would have told them how, but she wondered about that. Since God was mad at them, and kicked them out of Eden, why would he then help them. If he meant to help them, why not let them stay in Eden?

Her Father said he believed Adam and Eve at first wore animal skins like the Indians in the American colonies, but how they learned about the wool, he could not answer. She had numerous questions about how Adam and Eve learned to do things, like making a fire or milking a cow or making tools or building a house. As she got older, she gave up asking how these various skills were learned, if they had no one to teach them, because no one she asked seemed to know the answers to her queries, not even her brothers' tutor. The tutor knew Latin and Greek and French and some arithmetic. He knew geography, and knew about the many countries and continents depicted on the globe her father purchased for their studies. He taught them about the Kings that ruled over England from the time of the Conqueror and before. He could quote scriptures from the Bible. But he could not explain how Adam and Eve or any of their children learned to shear sheep and spin the wool.

"You have done a fine job of calming the sheep, Lady Selena," Calder said, leading the last sheep over to Jared. Abner and Joseph were finishing their final sheep, and Hannah and Pascal were bagging up the last piles of wool. Having no other job required of him, Jimmy had helped with the bagging.

"'Twas my pleasure. The sheep are dear animals." Selena wrinkled her nose. "Yours have little smell. Did you use your spring to wash them?"

"We divert the stream into a pond," Calder said. "When all are washed, we release the water and let it flow out over the field. It would not be taken kindly by the Huddlestons or other neighbors downstream did we wash the sheep in the stream."

She laughed. "Oh, I suppose not. Father has quite a large pond that his tenants use to wash his sheep and theirs, but the pond is there year round. Ducks and geese flying south often stop to feed and rest at the pond. Some of them end up as a meal for us or our tenants." She glanced around. "Where are the lambs?"

"In the barn," Calder said. "We will start weaning them soon. Then we will cull the flock and decide which sheep and which lambs need be sold. I cannot feed more than fifty through the winter. And that depends upon the harvest doing well."

He turned to his laborers. "The sheep are content to be eating, and Rollo can keep any from wandering off. Hannah has a hearty repast prepared for us. Wash up at the well and come inside. Hannah will soon have it all set out."

He looked back at Selena. "Lady Selena, do you and Jimmy join us?"

Smiling a little sadly, Selena said, "I wish we could, but I fear my aunt has an early supper planned for this evening. She invited the vicar and his wife to sup with us, and they will want to return home before dark. So now, I must hurry home to clean up before they arrive."

"Will you be coming back tomorrow?" Pascal asked.

She shook her head. "Nay. We dine tomorrow with the squire and his wife." She looked to Calder. "But I hope I might visit again soon, am I not interfering in your work."

"You are welcome any time, Lady Selena. 'Tis always a pleasure to have you stop by."

Smiling more brightly, she thanked him and asked Jimmy to fetch the horses. Hannah bid her good-bye before hurrying to the house to set out the meal for the laborers. The laborers, too, bid her a good day, and thanking her for her aid with the sheep, they went to pull up a bucket of water from the well to clean themselves. Selena spotted soap and towels set out on a stand beside the low rock-rimmed well. The sheep were enjoying their feed, chickens and geese mingling in amongst them. Everything was orderly and peaceful. How she wished she could stay.

Jimmy brought the horses over, but before he could give her a foot up, Calder grasped her hips and lifted her gently up onto her horse. His hands rested momentarily on her hips once she was seated on her saddle, before he jerked them away. "Have a safe ride back, Lady Selena."

Her heart thumping in her throat, she had difficulty answering him. "Thank you," she managed. "I hope to see you again soon."

"Yes, come back soon," Pascal cried.

"I will," she promised, with a wave to the boy.

She started to turn Brigantia, but Calder caught the reins. "I near forgot to thank you for getting the squire to pay me for my lamb." He grinned. "He even apologized. Wish I could have heard what you told him."

"I but told him the truth. He seemed concerned that his dogs had bothered some of his tenants as well. His kennel man had not told him of the other complaints."

"Well, I thank you." He looked from her to Jimmy. "I thank you, Jimmy."

"Happy to help. Used to do the bagging for me father," Jimmy answered.

As she rode away, Selena glanced back. Pascal and the laborers were heading into the house, but Calder stood looking after her. She waved and he waved. That was good she thought. Yes, that was good.

# Chapter 15

"Ne'er saw anythin' like what Lady Selena can do with calmin' them animals," Abner said, shaking his head as he spoke. Seated on the bench at the table, he poked another piece of mince pie into his mouth.

"'Tis uncanny it is," Jared agreed. "Almost like she bewitches the animals."

"Think she could be a witch?" Joseph asked, his round eyes growing rounder.

"If she be a witch, she be a good witch," Jared stated.

"Enough o' that," Hannah said, coming back to the table with another pitcher of ale. "Lady Selena is no witch, good or bad. She is like me aunt's first husband, Cathal, the Irishman. He had a way with the animals, especially horses. 'Tis something comes from bein' of Celtic ancestry, he claimed. Whatever Celtic means." She shrugged. "But 'tis my guess, Lady Selena has some distant relative what was Celtic like me aunt's first husband."

Calder was glad Hannah had stated in clear terms that Selena was no witch. He had been about to lecture his laborers on their foolishness. Witches were no longer hunted or prosecuted in England. Fact was, people of science, he had heard, believed the whole idea of witchcraft was fantasy. No more real than elves and fairies. But 'twas better Hannah should take Selena's part, even if her notion that Celtic ancestry gave Selena her power over the animals was just as ridiculous. Best it not be bandied about that Lady Selena might be a witch.

"I will ask her about her ancestry," piped up Pascal.

"She might not know all her ancestry, son," Calder said.

"Yes, but she might," his son answered with a bright grin.

"She also might consider ye rude, young man," Hannah said.

Pascal looked up at Hannah in surprise. "Oh, I would not want her to think me rude. But why should she think it rude. Is it bad to be Celtic?"

Familiar with the Celtic term, Calder said, "Nay, 'tis not bad. Am I not mistaken, it but means people with ancestry from Ireland, Scotland, and Wales. King Henry VII, having ancestry from Wales, had Celtic blood in his veins. As did King James, being from Scotland. That means King Charles II has Celtic ancestry. All the same, 'tis not really our business."

"Still, I would like to know," Abner said. "Better to know she has that Celtic ancestry Hannah speaks of, than to be wonderin' if she be a witch."

Shaking his head, Calder changed the subject. "I am hoping several girls from Whimbrel will come tomorrow to wash and beat the hemp. Do we wait any longer, the hemp will be too old to fetch a decent price."

"I am set to help sort the wool," Hannah said. "And I am wonderin' should you hire a girl to stay on for a couple of months to milk the sheep, what with it being time to wean the lambs? Or mayhap you want to hire Wally Shandy again, like you did last year?"

"Yes," Jared said. "Hire Wally. I like the stories he tells."

"Oh, I do, too," Pascal said.

Calder nodded. "All right, Pascal. Tomorrow, you run over to Nibley Hall and see if Wally Shandy is to home and wanting work. If he does, tell him to come as soon as he can. I want to start weaning on the morrow. We can then put the sheep out to pasture on the wheat stubble to fatten them up. Abner," he looked to the older laborer, "you start passing the word we will have sheep and lambs ready to sell to the locals come the middle of next month, do they want to buy any before I sell them to Wally's brother-in-law, Guy Hamon. Hamon will herd any he buys to Milton-Mowbray or Leicester and no doubt make a goodly profit."

"Aye, but you will make a goodly profit off the sheep's milk," Hannah said. "'Tis no cheese more prized than the cheese made with sheep's milk. The Huddlestons are always eager for you to wean the lambs so you can start milking the sheep."

"Makes for some extra income through early September," Calder said, then thinned his lips. "Still, Wally must be paid out of the profit. Another year or two and Pascal will be able to do the milking."

"The good thing is," Abner said, "the boy no longer has to watch the bees. Frees him to do other chores. Lucky you was to hand when that last hive swarmed on Sunday." He chuckled. "They took no notice 'twas the Lord's day."

"Aye," Calder answered with a short nod, "their hive is secured, and Jared is that certain a queen is with them. One less thing to be worrying about, and the extra honey can be sold in Rotherby when we drive the sheep, lambs, and geese to market end of next month. With this year's new hives, we will still have plenty of honey for our own use."

"I know you got your heart set on sendin' Pascal off to school in a year or two," Abner said, settling back a bit from the table and rubbing his full stomach. "I know 'twill cost ye to board him in Leicester. That is why I thought you might be interested in knowin' old man Buxton is thinkin' o' leasin' out his acreage. Got just over a hundred acres. Told me t'other day when he come by the hamlet hopin' to sell a brace o' rabbits he killed. He says he cannot face another winter o' mendin' fences and ploughin' and sowin' his winter wheat. Says he groans with achin' bones each time he rises from his pallet. Says he cannot think how he can face the cold to bring in enough wood to keep his fire goin' for warmth or even to cook his pottage.

"He has no family left. Wife died two winters back. Both sons died afore they ever had a chance to marry and have children. Daughter run off near ten year ago now, and he has not heard from her since. Knows not is she alive or dead."

"'Tis a sad state for the old fellow," Hannah said. "Not that he has ever been anything but an irascible old goat. Used to pity his wife. To my thinking, 'tis no wonder the daughter run off. Girl never had a decent gown nor decent shoes to wear. Used to see her in the winter with naught but a skimpy cloak to keep the cold from chillin' her bones. Hands were blue once when she stopped by here to warm up after her father sent her to Whimbrel to fetch him some tobacco. Shame it was, the way he treated her."

"Well, that may be," Abner said, looking again at Calder. "All the same, Calder, ye might want to have a chat with Buxton. His property bein' just t'other side o' White Acres. Close enough to this farm that you could tend it with but one more hand, cause Buxton has a cottager, Olly Keat, what has several more good years in him. The extra hand could live in Buxton's house. It bain't a large house, but 'tis solid built."

Contemplating Abner's news, Calder rubbed his chin with his thumb and forefinger. Homer Buxton had good land. Over the past couple of years, since his wife died, Buxton had let more of the land lay fallow, raising but a few sheep and goats on those sections.

"Might you know is any of his land freehold?" Calder asked.

"Nay. I know not. Guess ye would have to ask him. I know some is leasehold, because last year, I remember him complainin' that his lease had come due, and Lord Penhaligon had raised his rent. But knowin' Buxton, it could not have been raised too much, or he would not have renewed the lease, him feelin' poorly lack he does."

"Mayhap I will go talk to him tomorrow. Learn what he is asking. And how much land is freehold." Calder was interested in the possibility of adding to his acreage. He knew he should not be looking forward to Selena's visits, but the fact that she would not be paying a visit on the morrow, as she would be dining with the Nibleys, made it easier to leave the farm. Of his five hundred acres, three hundred were freehold, and two hundred, he leased from Lord Penhaligon.

"Do you and Buxton come to an agreement," Jared said, "I could be your man to run the farm. I know Buxton can be cantankerous, but I would take no guff off him."

Calder could understand Jared's wish to take on the added responsibility. If he moved into Buxton's house, he could marry his sweetheart. Calder guessed the pretty Huddleston milkmaid to be in her mid-twenties. She would be looking to get married, and was Jared unable to marry her, by rights, she might find someone else. A woman who failed to marry could face a sad and cold future, come old age. Were she and Jared able to combine their incomes, they could put away enough to start having children.

"Jared would be a good one to run the Buxton farm," Abner said. "My older boy, Billy, has been workin' on and off for Buxton for near four years now. Billy is fourteen, and I know no reason he could not take over for Jared here. He is big for his age, and strong. He even did some o' the plowin' this year for Buxton."

102

"Abner," Calder said, "you have given me much to think on. I will ride old Cob over to Buxton's. Get me there a bit faster so I can return sooner. So much needs doing." He looked around at all the people at the table. "Let me see, now." He looked first at his son. "Pascal, you will go first thing and ask Wally does he want the milking job. Hannah, I know you plan to start sorting the wool. Jared, you and I will divert some of the spring water into the pond before I leave. Do no girls from Whimbrel turn up, you start soaking and beating the hemp. Pascal can help you when he returns. If the girls do arrive, get them started, then you can begin spreading the marl and manure on the ploughed fields. Pascal, when you return, you help him."

"Yes, Father," Pascal answered, his eyes bright in his enthusiasm for his increased duties.

"Abner, you need to separate the lambs from the ewes. When I return, we will cull out those we will not over winter, but you know well enough which ewes are past their prime. Once you have them separated, you could start with the culling."

"Aye, that I will do. I can bring my younger son, Lyell, with me tomorrow. He be ten now and through his schoolin'. He will be doin' what jobs he can from here on. Do you add Buxton's farm to yours, he could do some of the chores me son, Billy, was doin' for Buxton. That is, do you take Billy on here."

Calder nodded his head. "Good idea. Bring both boys. They can help Jared. Fertilizing the fields is never a fun job."

"You can say that again," Jared stated, wrinkling his nose.

"I will have them here," Abner said.

"What am I to do?" Joseph asked.

"I need you to start chopping down the trees I marked." He chuckled as Joseph groaned. "Go on with you now, you have a good strong back."

"Aye, but it will be less strong by the time I finish."

"Well, it must be done, are we to have the wood we need for the winter. Wood is better, does it have more time to dry. Does Jared, with the help of Abner's boys, finish fertilizing the nearer fields, the next day, he can help you, and Abner and his boys can continue the fertilizing."

He looked again at Hannah. "How are we set for tomorrow's noon meal? You will have Abner's sons and hopefully several Whimbrel girls to feed."

"I have six loaves of bread, four mince pies, the big kettle of porridge will be kept simmering, one of our last two ham hocks I have been soaking for three days, and 'tis ready for roasting. I could use more cheese, does Abner bring some from the Huddlestons' when he comes in the morning."

Calder glanced at Abner, and Abner nodded. "Aye, when I take the milk tonight, I will ask for the cheeses, so I have them."

"Good," Calder said. "Speaking of the milk, we had best get back to work. Abner, I need you and Pascal, with Rollo's help, to herd the sheep and lambs back into the hay field. We will give the lambs one more night with the ewes. Jared, you and Joseph need continue weeding the barley and the oat fields. Get what you can done ere night falls. I know you have had a busy day already, but we lost a good week what with Abner having to mind the sheep."

"Guess since we had this repast," Hannah said, "we will be having a late and small supper? Mayhap just some of the porridge and some rye bread?"

Nodding, Calder agreed. "That will be fine. Give you some time to make sure all is ready for tomorrow's meals."

"I mean to kill me a couple of hens," Hannah said. "I will pluck 'em, then put them on to slow boil tonight. They will be fallen off the bone come morning. Be good added to the porridge. Besides, I was wanting some more feathers for my pillow. It has been rather flat of late."

Calder grinned. "I guess you would know which hens have been laying poorly and will not be missed. I must get to my milking. Abner, I will see to harnessing the horse and hooking up the cart. Let us go to our chores."

Stools scraped, and all but Hannah marched out the door. Calder was pleased with his day's accomplishments. The morrow would be another busy day, but on the following day, Selena could well return for another visit. She was a remarkable young woman. Except for her clothing, that fetching riding outfit she had worn, no one would guess when she squatted down to calm a sheep that she was the daughter of an earl.

Gads, but he knew he should not be dreaming of her, longing to see her, but he could not help himself. She stirred feelings in him he had not felt for many a year. Better he should keep his mind on the farm and his son's future. The possibility of taking on more land was both intriguing and a bit frightening, but it could give him the income he would need to send Pascal on to the University.

Shrugging, he hurried on to the barn to milk his cows.

# *Chapter 16*

With Jimmy heading back to the stables, Selena decided to give Brigantia a quick run. Giving her horse her head, they raced across Uncle Nate's field before returning to the stables. Selena had no worry she might scatter the sheep. They had been herded up for their washing and shearing. She had made no attempt to help calm the sheep for her uncle's laborers. Her aunt would have been shocked had she suggested such an action. Aunt Rowena would have said, "You are here to learn to be a lady. Working with sheep is not something a lady would do."

At least her aunt had not known how she had spent the afternoon at the Grantham farm. Jimmy would not tell on her. When she arrived back at the house, she snuck in the back entrance and asked the scullery maid to find Alice and send her to her at once. Having made it safely to her room, Selena hastily slipped out of her riding habit. Looking it over, she could find no rips or tears. The hem was muddy, but Alice could take care of that for her.

Holding the coat up to her nose, she sniffed. The odor was faint, but the smell of sheep existed. After cleaning the hem of her skirt, Alice would have to find a place outdoors where the costume could be aired. Selena was grateful she had two riding habits. She preferred the peach-colored one, but she wished she had worn the dark brown one instead. It would not have shown stains as much. Oh, well, what was done, was done.

"Lady Selena," Alice said, breathlessly entering the room, "you must have come in the back entrance again. I begin to wonder if I should not await you there."

Selena laughed. "Nay, you must continue with whatever are your other duties. Aunt Rowena must not suspect I am sneaking up to my room to avoid being seen. She will think I want not be told I have not the appearance of a lady. Which is true, I do so admit."

Alice nodded and said, "My duties are simple, milady. I take care of your clothing and keep your room orderly. But when all is done here, I go help the maid, Antha, with the cleaning. Today we cleaned the library. Lady Rotherby said she wanted every book carefully dusted, and she wanted the lamps cleaned, and the rug that is displayed over the trunk taken out and beaten. That is where Nelly found me. I was helping Antha beat the rug."

"Well, I hate to tell you, Alice, but you must see to this riding costume." Selena held up the skirt and coat. "It smells of sheep, and it has a muddy, dusty hem."

"No offense, milady, but so do you. That is, you smell of sheep. I asked Nelly to heat me some water. She will bring it up directly. We mayhap should wash your hair. I will see to your shift and petticoat and stockings. I fear they will all need washing. Thankfully the laundress is still here. Do you strip down, I will run these out to her immediately. She will not be happy, but she will do them, do you have a coin I can slip her."

Beginning to strip down as Alice spoke, Selena went to her chest and pulled out a coin purse. It was no longer brimming with coins. She had used a number on her journey from Rygate to Whimbrel, but she found a sixpence and handed it to Alice. "If you have a way to make certain she has no reason to tell my aunt about this, that would be appreciated."

Alice looked at the coin. "I think this will convince her she should have no reason to speak to Lady Rotherby about your garments. Now, here is your robe, milady." Alice handed Selena a silken robe as Selena slipped out of her shift.

"I will run these garments out," Alice said, "but I will first tell Nelly to bring the warm water up to you."

"Thank you, Alice, I cannot think what I should do without you."

Alice, bundling the clothing up under her arm, smiled, bobbed a curtsy, and hurried out the door, leaving Selena to pace the floor until Nelly arrived with the water.

An hour later, her hair still damp but neatly arranged on her head by Alice's nimble fingers, Selena arrived in the parlor just before the guests arrived. Eager to speak to the vicar about her plan to rebuild the church in Whimbrel village and turn it into a school, she had been looking forward to the informal supper. Having the vicar's support could go a long way toward getting donations. Striving to be on her best behavior, she tried to curb her tongue and think long before she spoke. When the kindly-eyed vicar and his slim, waifish wife departed, after expressing their pleasure in the meal and the company, Aunt Rowena complimented Selena.

"Were you always this circumspect, my dear child, I would say we are at last making progress. However, seeing that you chose not to listen to me concerning your ideas about the old church, I will say, the vicar seemed much impressed with your wish to have the old Whimbrel church rebuilt as a school. As it seems you are intent on this idea, his promise to bring your plans up to the parishioners seems a good sign."

Relieved her aunt did not seem as annoyed as Selena feared she might be, she nodded. "I was much impressed with the vicar. I feared he might think it would hurt the Rotherby school, but he seemed to think the Whimbrel school a grand idea."

"The Rotherby school draws from a large area. The vicar believes children need to be educated, that they may better understand the Bible. If Whimbrel has a grammar school, it could mean more boys will be able to attend school."

Frowning Aunt Rowena continued, "But Selena, I do think you should have paid my concerns more heed, or had, at least, again consulted with me before rushing head long into this time absorbing plan. You yet have your lessons."

"I am sorry, dear Aunt. I thought 'twould not hurt to at least question the vicar on what he thought of my idea. Then when he seemed to like the idea, I just got carried away. I promise, though, I will continue with my lessons in the mornings. Indeed, I shall work very hard. I will only work on plans for the school in the afternoons."

Aunt Rowena sighed. "Well, I suppose what is done is done."

"Thank you, Aunt Rowena," Selena said, then expressing her wish to rise early in order to give Brigantia her run, she excused herself shortly after the guests left. Settling into bed, she began formulating her plan of attack on Mistress Nibley. She meant to convince the squire's wife to head up the launching of a drive to raise funds to build the Whimbrel school. Once she was married to Calder, and Selena fully expected to marry him, she had no wish for their sons to go all the way to Rotherby to attend grammar school.

Her thoughts of the future subsiding, she drifted into a deep sleep and woke with a start when Alice drew back the curtains on her bed. Morning already. Having given Alice strict orders to force her to rise in the morning, she struggled out of bed, donned her brown riding habit, and reached the stables a little after sunrise. Jimmy, awaiting her, had his horse and Brigantia saddled. Both horses were prancing about, ready to set off on their morning exercise.

Jimmy's horse was no match for Brigantia. It trailed a goodly distance back. Brigantia took several low fences with a graceful ease before she finally slowed of her own volition. At that point, Selena turned Brigantia, and, at a gentle trot, they headed back toward Jimmy. It was a fine day, a bright sunny day with only a few clouds, and Selena decided they should circle through Whimbrel before returning to the house. She wanted to see again what was left of the church, and she still had plenty of time before she had to ready herself for dinner at the Nibley's.

※ ※ ※

Giving a nudge with his heels to his horse's ribs, Calder hoped to speed up his progress to Buxton's. A few clouds hung low in the bright sunny sky, but they had not the look of rain. Riding past White Acres, he decided, after he talked to Buxton, before he made a final decision of taking on more responsibilities, he would discuss the merits with Ware Huddleston. Ware was ten years Calder's senior, and having attended two years at Clifford's Inn of Chancery, he had a good grasp of potential benefits or pitfalls to increasing acreage and sheep flocks or cattle herds. Ware's management of White Acres provided Ware and his family, and Lord Penhaligon, owner of the manor, a goodly income.

When Calder rode up to Homer Buxton's house, he saw Olly Keat, Buxton's cottager, chopping wood. "Where is Buxton?" Calder asked.

Stopping his work and wiping his brow, the gristle-haired man pointed toward the barn. "He be bagging the wool. We just finished shearing the sheep yesterday, but by the time we finished, we were too tired t' bag the wool."

"Thank you. I will look for him in the barn."

"Be ye here t' talk t' Homer about leasin' his acreage?"

Calder frowned. "I will discuss my reason for being here with Buxton."

The older man shrugged. "Not meanin' t' be jumpin' in. Just wanted ye t' know, I got a number of good years left in me."

Calder nodded and rode off to the barn. He could not blame Keat for being anxious. As a cottager, he had no real right to the little plot of land he lived on, and that offered him a hearth and home. Finding Buxton busily sorting his wool, Calder stood in the barn entrance until the man noticed him. Buxton, once a burly man, was looking shriveled and shrunken. His long dark hair under his grubby cap was matted and streaked a dull gray. His hands, dirty and gnarled, looked to pain him as he maneuvered the wool into bags.

Lash-less, watery eyes looked up at Calder. "Well, Grantham, what do you here?"

"I heard you might be interested in leasing out your acreage. I came to learn more about what you have and are you truly thinking of leasing it?"

"That would be Abner Oldfield what told you I was thinkin' I be needin' to retire?

"It would."

"'Tis the truth." He held up his hands. "Look at these miserable claws. I can scarce get them to pull up a pail of water from the well, let alone do all the other jobs that need doin' 'round here. I got me just over a hundred acres. Little over thirty be freehold. The rest I lease from Lord Penhaligon. Just renewed the lease for another five years, but my guess is, Huddleston would extend it to twenty, was it put to him, you wanted it. The White Acres land borders on my freehold. For two years now, I have left three thirty acre fields fallow. Let the sheep and goats graze on them, but last year, I sold most of my sheep to buy the winter supplies I needed. Me, bein' unable to plow the acreage to grow enough grains to feed myself, let alone a large flock of sheep, I kept but ten sheep last year. Kept all my goats. They can eat anything through the winter. Matters not to them, and their milk makes a good cheese."

"How much are you wanting for the lease of your acreage?" Calder asked.

"Enough to keep me body and soul together through my old age," Buxton said, rising to his feet. "I would want to live out my days in my house. Mayhap have a body could help see to me was I sick and could see to me meals. I was thinkin' a tenth of the profits would be fair."

Calder cocked his head. "Would the lease include the animals you now have on the land? Including your plow horses?"

"It maybe could."

"What happens if you up and die? If I invest in sheep and cattle to put on the acreage, I would want to know I have the lease after your death."

"I got no family. My daughter run off. I know not is she alive or dead. I got no reason to leave nary a mark to her. I could make out my will leaving my freehold and my lease to you."

Pursing his lips, Calder nodded, then asked, "What if the man I choose to work this acreage wants to live in the house with you? May-hap bring a wife?"

"My house bain't large, but I got me two bedchambers besides the hall. Fact is, come those lonely winter nights, I would not mind havin' company."

"How much acreage does your cottager, Keat, have?"

"When his wife was alive, he had four acres. Wife was barren. When she passed on, I could see no reason he should need more than three acres. 'Tis enough for him to keep his cow and a couple of goats, some chickens and a pig. He plants one acre in peas and another in barley, and it serves him well enough. To my thinkin', he has a few more good years in him."

"No doubt he does," Calder said. "I would like to take a look around the croft. Want to see your draft horses. Take a look at your fields."

"Help yourself. I got to finish sortin' this wool, then I got some briars came up in the field, I need to tackle."

Calder was pleased to get to roam on his own. The croft and toft were not in the best of shape, but they would need little major repair. Ditches needed cleaning, barn and hen house needed some repairs, but they were minor. The fallow fields really needed harrowing before they could be plowed, but the ground looked healthy. The six head of cows appeared well fed. Buxton had only four draft horses, but they looked strong and sturdy, and his plow, shaft, and harnesses were in good enough shape to last a couple of years before needing replacing.

Did Buxton do as he said, and make his will out to him, Calder could well be looking at a truly great investment. Jared and his sweetheart could see to Buxton's meals and to his laundry and other needs. Calder thought he might even have Abner's youngest son, Lyell, move in with Buxton and Jared. That way the boy would be there to give Jared a hand and to run errands. A pallet in the hall in front of the fire would no doubt be as good as his accommodations at Abner's. It would mean two fewer mouths Abner would have to feed if his son, Billy, took Jared's place and roomed with Joseph in the loft above the barn, and Lyell lived at Buxton's.

Having spent the morning examining Buxton's farm, he told Buxton, he would get back to him on the morrow as to his decision. Was all satisfactory to both of them, they would go into Rotherby and have Reynard Bardwith write up the contract and the will. Buxton nodded his approval, and Calder headed back to White Acres. He would be arriving at the Huddlestons' dinner hour, but he knew he would be welcomed and invited to join them. He had told Hannah not to wait dinner for him, not knowing how long he would be gone. His three laborers, plus Pascal, Wally, and Abner's two sons and the three Whimbrel girls who had arrived just as he and Jared finished diverting water from the stream to a pond, would all be hungry for their meal.

He liked the three Whimbrel girls. They had all worked for him for several years. He found if he paid a fair wage, and Hannah prepared a good meal, the same laborers were apt to return year after year, and that was good. It meant no time need be wasted training new help.

Feeling the nip of hunger himself, he smiled. The future looked promising. Indeed it did.

# Chapter 17

After being warmly welcomed into Nibley Hall's richly appointed parlor by Squire Nibley and his wife, Selena drew Mistress Nibley aside and handed her a book. "This is a book I feel certain you will enjoy, Mistress Nibley. *Love's Victory* by Lady Mary Wroth."

Mistress Nibley accepted the book, but looked at it with apparent misgiving. Before she could say anything, Selena added, "You must know how much my aunt and Lady Edgerton enjoy discussing the books they have read. No surer way to win their approval than to be well read. My aunt has a fine library."

Glancing at Selena's Aunt Rowena, engaged in a discussion with Squire Nibley of the tepid weather they had been experiencing, Mistress Nibley said, "Your aunt enjoys reading?"

"Indeed she does. In fact, every evening before retiring, we remove to the parlor, and we each relax with a book. The book I am loaning you, I just finished last night. When you finish it, you would be welcome to peruse Aunt Rowena's library to find something else of interest. I know Aunt Rowena would be happy to help you with your selection."

Mistress Nibley held the book out and frowned at it. "I have never been a big reader. Father had a couple of books, but they pertained to his business."

"Well, I believe you will become engrossed in this book." Selena tapped the book in Mistress Nibley's hand. "Then we must discuss it. I shall ask Aunt Rowena to invite you over one afternoon for just such an occasion. Mayhap we will have some sherry and biscuits and make a party of it."

Mistress Nibley brightened. "Oh! I should enjoy that."

"Splendid. Let me know when you have finished reading the book, and I will arrange for the discussion party. Mayhap Lady Edgerton would like to join us."

Flushing, Mistress Nibley fairly bounced on her toes. "Indeed, indeed, I shall start reading it this very evening."

Selena smiled inwardly. The first step in drawing Mistress Nibley into the parish social unit seemed successful. She had little doubt but what Mistress Nibley, eager to be accepted by her peers, would take to the reading whether she enjoyed it or not.

The Nibley footman, in full livery, appeared at the door to the parlor to announce that dinner was ready to be served. With the squire conducting Aunt Rowena, Selena fell in beside Mistress Nibley, and they advanced into the dining chamber. Its stucco walls were ornate and painted a pale off white. The long table covered with a white cloth and three lighted candelabras was set at but one end. Squire Nibley seated Aunt Rowena at his right, and Mistress Nibley indicated she and Selena should sit side by side to his left.

"Much cozier this way," Squire Nibley said. "We could scarce be able to converse were you seated at the far end of this table."

"Indeed, you are correct," Aunt Rowena agreed.

"Yes," Mistress Nibley said with a nod. "We could not decide whether to serve dinner here or in our common dining chamber, but I feared it was too informal."

"You should not worry about formality with us," Selena said, but a glance at her aunt told her she should have minded her tongue.

"What Selena means," Aunt Rowena said with a smile to Mistress Nibley, and then to the squire, "is that we appreciate the trouble you have gone to on our behalf."

"'Tis our pleasure, our pleasure," the squire asserted. "You know, Lady Rotherby, I believe you have not dined here since we had our home remodeled. We have all the most modern conveniences now."

Selena guessed he was acknowledging in a tactful way that her aunt had not dined there since he remarried.

"Well, you have certainly furnished your home beautifully," Aunt Rowena said.

"Yes," Selena agreed. "These gold cushioned chairs are not just lovely, they are very comfortable. And your floral arrangement is magnificent."

"Ah," the squire said, "Claudia did the arrangement herself. The one in the parlor as well. She says she has found no one to do them to her satisfaction."

"You have quite a talent, Mistress Nibley," Aunt Rowena said. "You have never mentioned this skill before."

Mistress Nibley blushed and smiled. "I have always loved flowers. Even as a child, I liked making arrangements. Mother enjoyed the arrangements. She was bedridden the last years of her life, and she said the flowers brightened her days." Mistress Nibley's smile turned wistful. "Father thought perhaps the arrangements should be left to the servants. He said ladies had no need to be involved in such activities." Turning her dark expressive eyes on her husband, she added, "But Florian says an appreciation of beauty is the mark of a lady, and we now have a lovely garden with roses, daffodils, pinks, peonies, lilies, violets, marigolds, primroses, and many other flowers, and I do enjoy making the arrangements."

"Was I as skilled as you are," Aunt Rowena said with a soft smile, "I would enjoy making the arrangements also. Not having the skill, I leave the arranging to my housekeeper. However, I do enjoy puttering about in the garden and selecting the flowers I would like to have in the arrangement."

Two footmen had begun serving the meal, so conversation was halted as a platter of bread and bowls of soup were placed on the table. "'Tis a pheasant soup," Squire Nibley said. "Had a good hunt Monday."

"Very tasty," Selena pronounced, and Mistress Nibley beamed.

The next course was fish from the squire's own pond, then came fresh lamb, then pigeon pie in a pastry crust, and the last course was a roast of beef. Each course was accompanied by a vegetable dish. Selena thoroughly enjoyed the fried cucumbers and the carrot pudding, and expressed such to her hostess, who again beamed at each compliment as though she and not the cook had prepared the dishes. More than likely, Mistress Nibley had consulted with her cook as to what was to be served.

When Selena thought she could not eat another bite, dessert was served. Not one dessert, but three; a raspberry flummery, a lemon pudding with whipped cream, and a baked custard. She chose a dish of the custard, though she could eat but a few mouthfuls. Aunt Rowena chose the lemon pudding and managed to finish enough of it to be polite, but the portly squire and his plumpish wife had a tasting of all three. Finally the dishes were cleared, the cloth removed to expose a gleaming Mahogany table top, and a bowl of nuts was set on the table. Wine had been served with each course, and an elderberry wine was poured to accompany the nut serving.

Sipping her wine and feeling a touch light-headed, Selena declined the nuts, but she resumed the compliments to Mistress Nibley that she had begun during the second course. She had complimented the orderly servings, which meant Mistress Nibley's staff was well trained. She praised the arrangement of the furnishings in the dining chamber, from the placement of the sideboard to the decorative screen before the hearth, and she applauded Mistress Nibley's admission of her charitable donation of clothing to the parish. At the same time as she was complimenting Mistress Nibley, Selena, knowing how her aunt had complained of Mistress Nibley's inane chatter centered only on herself, strove to redirect the conversation. Any time Mistress Nibley started to discuss her newest clothing acquisitions or the most recent fashions she had seen when on a visit to Leicester, or any problems she might be having with her servants, Selena broke in on her prattle with one of her compliments. Mistress Nibley would blush and giggle a little and thank Selena for her kind words.

"I do believe you are a most accomplished woman, Mistress Nibley," Selena said with a bright smile while watching the woman pop a walnut into her round mouth. "I think Aunt Rowena is quite correct in her belief that you would be the perfect person to organize a drive to raise funds to build a grammar school in Whimbrel. We would build the school on the foundation of the old church, so that would reduce the cost to some extent."

Her eyes locked on Mistress Nibley, Selena refused to look at her aunt, though she knew Aunt Rowena was staring at her. Or might she be glaring? Aunt Rowena had made no such comment pertaining to Mistress Nibley's abilities, but Selena knew if Mistress Nibley believed

Lady Rotherby thought her to be the perfect choice, Mistress Nibley would be more likely to take on the task. And Selena did believe Mistress Nibley was the perfect choice.

Was Mistress Nibley to lead the drive, she would have an opportunity to become better acquainted with her neighbors. Two purposes would be served. Funding for the school would be advanced, and Mistress Nibley would become an accepted member of the community. Best, Selena thought, when she married Calder, their future sons would not have to travel all the way to Rotherby to attend school.

Naturally Mistress Nibley and her husband were surprised by the proposition, but Squire Nibley said he thought it a capital idea. "My grandfather once said he remembered, when as a boy, he used to attend church in Whimbrel. That was when James was on the throne, am I not mistaken. Whimbrel became a crown estate with Henry VIII's dissolution of the monasteries and nunneries. The nuns of Saint Agnes's, being but a small group, held but a small benefice. Anyway, the church in Whimbrel survived up through James's reign. But the manor was neglected. Run by a bailiff. More of the land was enclosed for the rearing of sheep. Whimbrel tenants moved away, and the church fell into ruin with not enough parishioners to support it."

Looking at Aunt Rowena, he smiled broadly. "Lady Rotherby, until you and Lord Rotherby were granted the Whimbrel manor by King Charles II, I thought the village of Whimbrel could well disappear. Especially after the Puritans logged off so much of the park and raised the rents on the few tenants left. What a difference you have made. So I say, yes. A school is just what Whimbrel needs." He looked at his wife. "And Claudia, I believe Lady Rotherby is right. You would be perfect to head up the drive. Let me say right now, I will be happy to be your first contributor."

Flushing almost a purple, Mistress Nibley looked both pleased and confused. She began stuttering, but finally managed to say. "Well, Florian, if … if both you and Lady Rotherby think I am capable of taking on such a grand responsibility … then, yes, I accept."

For a moment, Selena met Aunt Rowena's eyes. She thought her aunt's eyes were filled with humor. At least, she hoped that was what she saw in her aunt's dark eyes. But the glance was brief before her aunt turned to Mistress Nibley and, smiling sweetly, said, "I compliment you on your acceptance of the responsibility, Mistress Nibley. As Squire Nibley has volunteered to be your first contributor, I will pledge to be your second contributor. But I think you must first find out how much building the school will cost. Then you will have a better idea on how much you will be trying to collect."

"She is right! She is right!" boomed the squire. "Let us remove to our antechamber, and we can discuss the idea in more detail."

Her head spinning with delight, Selena rose with the others and followed them into the Nibleys' antechamber, or withdrawing room, more comfortable and less formal than the parlor. Red brocaded, tufted armchairs, centered around a table displaying a lovely multicolored rug, offered them comfortable seating. A small Maplewood table stood next to each armchair. Candles on the mantle shelf were already lit and glowing brightly, but due to the warmth of the day, no fire had been lit in the hearth. Instead, a lovely screen with the scene of the woods and a blue sky shielded the red brick hearth from view.

Never had Selena believed persuading Mistress Nibley to become involved in collecting money to build the school would be so easy. 'Twas the squire's doing. Mayhap he realized how beneficial it would be for his wife. Give her a good reason to call on all the upper societal families in the community. And, if Lady Rotherby was promoting the project, no one would snub the squire's wife, not even Lady Edgerton.

Settling comfortably on her chair, Selena watched as her aunt and the squire and his wife began a fruitful discussion on the first steps required in the process. The squire volunteered to contact the craftsmen who had helped with the remodeling of his house. He believed they could well be the workmen needed for the job. The original church had been stone, but the brick mason and his apprentice, who had added on to the squire's house, had been most competent. Did Lady Rotherby not object, he could see no reason not to build the school in brick instead of stone.

"Would save having to quarry the stone," Squire Nibley said. "And stone masons cost more. Brick is the way to go, I am thinking."

Aunt Rowena agreed with him. By the time Selena and Aunt Rowena took their leave, multiple plans were in the works. The squire was in charge of finding the workmen and getting the best prices. Mistress Nibley was in charge of spreading the word among the gentry and asking for donations. Aunt Rowena was to see about securing them a schoolmaster, determining his wage, and arranging a fund to see he was paid.

Selena was to spread the word among the yeomen, laborers, and their families. She was so excited. That morning, when she had ridden through Whimbrel with Jimmy to take a closer look at the remains of the church, she had encountered the owner of the granary that sat next to the church. A jovial man, he had applauded her plans and had said he wished her luck in achieving them. She hoped he meant what he said, because she meant to have him help her promote the idea among the Whimbrel villagers.

On the morrow, she would tell Calder. She hoped he would be pleased. She wanted to see approval of her plans in his vibrant blue eyes. But for the time being, as a footman helped her into the coach, she hoped she would not be in for a long lecture by her aunt.

Once settled on the cushioned coach seat, Aunt Rowena said, "I cannot think whether I should be angry with you, or if I should compliment you."

Selena giggled. "Oh, then by all means, can you not decide, let us go with the compliment, dear Aunt."

Aunt Rowena joined in Selena's laughter. "Naughty child. Very well. Compliment you, I will. Other than your falsehood concerning my opinion of Mistress Nibley's abilities, I would say your manners could not have been more appropriate. Never did you bring up any objectionable or offensive subjects, and the way you redirected Mistress Nibley's conversation each time she started to go off on one of her tangents was remarkable. I could not have done near so well. That is, could I have done it at all.

"Now that Mistress Nibley has accepted the responsibility of securing the funding for this school you have for some reason decided Whimbrel needs, I think you were right. I do believe she will work diligently at the project. Does it give her something else to talk about besides her gowns or hats, it can only be a blessing."

Selena took her aunt's hand and held it warmly for a moment. "Thank you, Aunt Rowena. Thank you for being so willing to help. As to why I want the school, I want it for the servants' and laborers' sons, who have to walk so many miles to attend school in Rotherby. Do we go to Rotherby, we ride in a coach. Does it rain, it matters not to us. Does the sun beat down, no mind to us, we are shaded. But 'tis a long walk for many of the children. We know how much difference an education can make in a young man's future. Look what a difference it made for Reynard."

In the dim light of the coach, Selena saw her aunt smiling at her. "You have a good heart, Selena. You may not always be the perfect lady in your actions, but in your heart, you are a true lady. I may never succeed in teaching you all you should know in the proper management of a home, but I will never need teach you to love or to be generous to those of lesser ranks."

Selena kissed her aunt's cheek. "Never could I ask for a dearer or more understanding aunt." At last, the two of them seemed to have reached a communion.

❈ ❈ ❈

Leaning back in his chair next to the hearth, Calder lit his pipe. He took a couple of puffs, watched the smoke float up toward the ceiling, and let his mind drift back over his day. First, his visit to Buxton's, then his stopover at White Acres. Ware Huddleston, White Acres steward and Calder's cousin, had thought the acquisition of Buxton's land a fine idea. His blue eyes squinting against the midday sun, Ware rubbed his stubbled cheek. "Aye, Calder. Fact is, I would feel better, did you have the lease of those acres rather than Buxton. When I let him renew his lease, I questioned whether 'twas wise to do so. Him getting old like he is. But he always paid his rent, so I went ahead and renewed the lease. Lord Penhaligon gave his approval."

Ware shrugged. "To be honest, his lordship cares little what I do, as long as his park is kept well stocked, and his hunting lodge is ready and waiting for him whenever he might choose to visit. Mayhap I have told you this before, the previous Lord Penhaligon, him being the fifth Earl, having sided with neither the Royalist nor the Roundheads, never lost any of his lands to the Puritans." When Calder looked at him questioningly, he continued. "Penhaligon the fifth took his two sons and traveled around Europe until the fighting ended. Came back to nary a loss of property or fortune, so the present lord, Penhaligon the sixth, has nary a care about his finances."

Frowning, Calder said, "I thought Lord Penhaligon fought with Charles II in fifty-one."

Nodding, Ware said, "Aye. That was Penhaligon the sixth. He fought with Charles II, was captured, spent time in prison, but his father got him out. The Puritans could not penalize Lord Penhaligon the fifth for his son's actions. After all, the fifth Earl had not sided with nor financed Charles I or II. So again, Penhaligon the fifth lost no property. Suffered no financial losses. When Charles II returned to the throne, the King had no wish to penalize the Whitakers for not siding with his father, because the future heir, then Viscount Tunbridge, but now the present Lord Penhaligon, had fought for Charles II in fifty-one."

Calder chuckled. "Luck was with the Whitakers, but seems it has always been so from the time White Acres changed from the English thegn's hands to the Norman's. I am but glad, that over the centuries, my forefathers saw no reason to take sides in the various conflicts, and my property is still intact six hundred years after the Norman Conquest."

Ware agreed. "Aye, the Huddlestons have profited by the Whitakers always choosing the winning side. But look, here come the milkmaids, 'tis time to go into dinner."

Following Ware up the steps to the first floor of the ancient block-house, dating back to the eleven hundreds, that Ware and his family called home, Calder swiped off his cap and brushed the sweat from his brow with his shirt sleeve. It was a warm day, and he was more than a little ready for some cider or ale to quench his thirst.

The first floor was one large hall. Originally the hearth had been in the center of the stone floor, but sometime in the early fifteen hundreds, a chimney had been added to each end of the hall. Putting in the chimneys allowed for a second floor to be added because a vaulted ceiling with vents allowing the smoke to escape from the central hearth was no longer needed. The second floor housed bedchambers and a parlor for the Huddleston family.

A long trestle table in the center of the room was set with wooden platters and noggins, and a serving girl was filling the noggins with cider when Ware, Calder, the milk maids, and two laborers poured into the room. Ware's two older sons came in with the laborers. Sturdy boys, both Tom and Will, ages eleven and nine, had been working in the fields beside the laborers. Ware's five-year-old son, Derwin, and daughter, Molly, had been weeding the family vegetable garden. One-year-old Tacy, the newest member of the Huddleston family, toddled about after one of the family dogs, pulling at its ears and tail.

Ware's wife gave Calder a bright greeting, and he answered in kind. "Avis, how you manage with this crowd to still look so young is beyond my understanding," he said.

Her face red from the heat, her blond hair with wisps of gray poking out from under her cap and curling in damp ringlets around her ears, she gave him a slap on the arm. "Go on with you, Calder Grantham. You need not pile on the flattery just to get some dinner. Sit you down, and tell me what brings you here today. We have not seen you in many a long month, though your man, Jared, we see often enough," she said, sitting down beside Calder after setting a large platter of rye bread on the table.

The sturdy, large-breasted cook was dishing a porridge thick with chicken, carrots, and beans onto each plate, and a slim, youthful serving girl, following behind her, doled out a sprinkle of salt onto each plate. The bread platter was passed around the table, and soon little but the sound of hunger being assuaged could be heard. Between spoonsful of porridge, Calder explained to Ware's wife his errand. She, too, applauded his ambition.

"We have hopes to continue both Tom's and Will's education," she said, "but naturally, Tom will someday take over here as steward, as the family has done all through the centuries. But Will, we have hopes he may find a place as a clerk in Ware's brother's shop in Leicester."

"Oh, aye," Calder said, nodding and savoring a chunk of bread sopped in the porridge. "Beorn has done well in the city."

"Marrying the grocer's daughter helped him do well," Ware said with a chuckle.

"Beorn," Calder said, a grin stretching his face, "always had the looks the lasses liked."

"Still does, I guess," Ware said, "though we have not seen him in near three years. I have had no call to go to Leicester. Beorn has no call to come here, unless he comes to visit."

"But are you not sending some of your cheeses to him?" Calder asked.

"Aye, but I only cart it as far as Rotherby. From there, it is transported with cheeses from other farms to Leicester. All the same, Beorn's shop, or his wife's father's shop, is prospering. I am thinking, could Will someday clerk there, he could learn enough to move on to maybe clerk for a woolen merchant. Then, does he learn the business, he could move up in the world."

Calder looked down the table at Ware's son. The boy's blond head was bent over his plate as he shoveled in his dinner. So hard to provide a decent future for all one's children. Assuming the children made it into adulthood. Ware was lucky. He had lost none of his children, but they were not yet grown. Too easy for accidents and illnesses to take young people away from their parents. Did anything happen to Pascal, Calder wondered how he would cope.

Chasing that fearful thought away, he turned back to Avis and asked after her parents.

"They are mostly well, though Father often suffers with the gout. When Mother can make him follow the physician's orders and eat and drink less, he mends, but as soon as he feels better, he goes back to his old habits." She sighed and shrugged, then smiled. "But my sisters and brother are well, and my brother's wife just gave birth to yet another baby boy. That makes four boys and no girls. Oh, but she does want a little girl she can dress in pretty gowns."

Ware chuckled. "Avis's brother, Bruce, says he is happy to have just boys. Boys he can send off to school, and they can then make their own way in the world. Girls need dowries. I think he still resents having three sisters, and all needing dowries, which lessened his future income. I will say this for Avis's father – Squire Greene provided well for all his daughters, no matter how much Bruce might begrudge them their dowries."

"That is enough, Ware. You will have Calder thinking Bruce a regular miser," Avis said.

"True. Bruce is a good sort. Does he someday have a daughter, no doubt he will provide her with a substantial dowry."

The conversation had next turned to the constant needs of farm and manor. Thinking of those many demands pushed thoughts of the Huddlestons from Calder's mind and brought him back to the present. Sighing, he drew another puff on his pipe. Hannah was finishing meal preparations for the next day. She would again have many mouths to feed. He would need to ride over to Buxton's and tell him he would take the deal, and they would make arrangements to go to Rotherby to have the contract drawn up. More things to take him away from his work, but hopefully, it would prove worth it.

He could not help but wonder if Selena would come by for a visit. She had been most helpful each time she visited. He knew he should not be spending so much time thinking about her, but he could not stop thinking of her and had given up trying. He could never hope to marry her, but thoughts of her aroused feelings in him that had long been dead.

Sitting forward in his chair, he said, "You have worked hard today, Hannah. Are you near done with your cleaning and preparations?"

She turned around and smiled. "Aye, Calder. I am near done. I have my dough rising overnight. It will be ready to bake come morning. I have had no time to make up the buns Lady Selena likes, but does she visit on the morrow, I can toast her some bread and put some fresh honey on it. There be plenty of buttermilk keeping cool in the stream."

"Are you thinking Lady Selena will visit tomorrow?" He tried to keep any excitement from his voice.

Hannah had turned back to her worktable for another swipe at her dough, but she answered over her shoulder, "I am thinking she will come on the morrow. She loves the freedom she is allowed here. I would guess when she is at Whimbrel, she must ever be the upright lady."

Calder snorted. "Aye. When I think of how she was down on the ground with the sheep, or how she had no fear of that frightened cow, I wonder how she will fare when she must live her life as an upright lady, as you do term it."

Hannah looked back around and cocked her head to one side. "Ah, but mayhap she will find a way to avoid that fate. She is a resourceful young woman."

"What are you meaning by that?" Calder demanded, his voice more intense than he meant it to be.

Hannah smiled and shrugged. "Just what I said, nothing more." Wiping her hands on a towel, she added, "I am off to my cot now. Good-night to you, Calder."

Calder stared after his housekeeper. What could she have meant? He dared not even let himself think for even a moment that Selena would choose to marry him. That could never happen. Her family would never permit it. Besides, what would make her even want to marry him. Foolish, foolish thoughts.

# Chapter 18

Doing her best to push thoughts of her plans for the Whimbrel school, and thoughts of Calder from her mind, Selena tried to concentrate on how to keep the house stocked with proper provisions, including how to have on hand items that could be served if unexpected guests arrived. She wanted to continue the growing communion between her and her aunt. That she had won her aunt's praise was a milestone, and she hoped to continue in her good graces. Not just for herself, but to insure her aunt would continue to support the building of the grammar school. And at some point, she would need her aunt to support her in her decision to marry Calder Grantham.

"You have done well today," Aunt Rowena said as they came out of the buttery. "Let us dine. Then, I know you are eager to spread the news of your plans for the school."

"I am, Aunt Rowena. I mentioned the idea to the granary owner, Mister Hall, yesterday. He seemed to think it a fine idea. I wish to speak with him again today and ask him if he would organize a meeting where I might speak to the whole village."

"A fine idea, dear. 'Tis best, before we get too involved in all this, to determine whether the Whimbrel villagers would like having a school in the village."

Selena had never doubted but what the villagers would be delighted. Why would they not? It would save their sons the long walk into Rotherby. Mayhap more of the village boys would be able to continue their education. She smiled at her aunt. "They will want it."

❧ ❧ ❧

Returning from Buxton's, Calder could not help but be pleased. On the morrow, he would drive his cart over to Buxton's, then the two of them would go into Rotherby to have their contract made out. Jared was eager to move into Buxton's house, and no doubt would soon be taking a bride. Did all go as discussed, Abner's older son Billy would take Jared's place, and his younger son Lyell would take Billy's place at Buxton's. The boy could see to the old man's needs when Jared and his future wife were working, and he could tend the animals and see to the vegetable garden. Yes, all the pieces were falling into place.

Calder returned to his farm in time to sit down to dinner. Pascal was helping Hannah serve, and the table was crowded with platters of cheese, sausage, bread, a couple of jams, dishes of butter, a dandelion salad with hard-cooked eggs and a vinegar and honey dressing, and a veal rump pie with carrots and onions. Noggins of cider or ale were quickly consumed by the thirsty workers. Hannah had set pitchers of both drinks on the table, so noggins were easily refilled.

The lively chatter ended when everyone delved into their dinner, but after initial hungers were assuaged, some bantering resumed. Jared and Abner were eager to know if Calder and Buxton had come to an agreement, and broad grins spread across their faces when they learned an agreement had been reached. Jared eagerly agreed to move into Buxton's house and to assume the responsibility of caring for the slightly more than one hundred acres. Abner was pleased Billy would be coming to work on Calder's farm, and that Lyell would have a live-in position at Buxton's. Both his sons seemed pleased as well. Joseph was the only one not overjoyed by the news. His friend, who had worked beside him for more than fifteen years, was stepping up in the world, while he was still in the same position. Plus, he would have young Billy to train.

Slapping the thin, bright-eyed youth on the back, he said, "Not that I mind trainin' ye, Billy, 'tis just I will be missin' Jared. Though I guess I will not be missin' his snoring."

"My snoring!" Jared took immediate umbrage. "'Tis you who snores."

"Wait until ye marry Rachel. Then I will ask her, who does the snoring."

"Mayhap you both snore," Hannah said. The three Whimbrel girls giggled, and one with limp brown hair and a wayward eye, glanced shyly at Joseph. Calder knew the girl, Hermia, to be a good worker. He had been pleased when she returned to help with the hemp. But was she casting her eye on Joseph? Might she see him as a possible mate? He was not sure Joseph had noticed the girl, but when the meal ended, Joseph managed to exit the door at the same time as the girl. Hermia was more a woman than a girl, Calder thought. She could easily be on the lookout for a husband. Though no great beauty, she had a bright smile and a sweet voice.

Calder supposed if Joseph should wish to take a wife, he could let him build a cottage and give him four acres to see to his family's needs. He had a piece of land bordering on Squire Nibley's manor that he had used for naught but grazing for any number of years, so the soil should be fertile. With Jared moving to his new position and soon taking a wife, Calder would not be surprised if Joseph, too, wanted to start a family. Men and women had needs beyond just being provided their daily bread.

He was again feeling those needs himself. With that thought, he wondered if Selena would be coming by. He hoped she would. He needed to start harrowing his fallow fields, but the thought of being off in a distant field when she came to visit kept him near the house. The sheep had been culled, and those to be sold were being fattened for sale on the hay stubble. The cows and calves also needed to be separated, but that, too, he would let wait for a couple more days. Though feeling guilty about neglecting his farm on the chance that Selena might visit, he, all the same, sent Joseph and Billy to do the harrowing, and he set to chopping into hearth size logs, the trees he and Joseph had drug down the hill from the woods the previous evening. Chopping wood was not a job he normally chose to do, but it would keep him close to home. He sent Pascal and Lyell to weed the wheat field, and Abner and Jared were to continue spreading the marl and manure on the plowed fields. Wally, having milked the ewes and not needing to milk them again until closer to evening, could help the girls working on the hemp.

Squinting his pale blue eyes, Wally nodded, his unruly hair dancing about his shoulders. "Aye, Calder, I have worked hemp often enough, I know what needs be done." His soft melodic voice was a contrast to his shabby appearance. Calder wondered that Wally's brother, Laban, failed to see that his brother had a proper pair of breeches and a shirt that was not so worn it had patches over the patches. Disheveled or not, Wally was ever willing to do whatever chore was asked of him. Trouble was, he was often caught day dreaming. Ever good natured, Wally would apologize and resume his work with a vengeance. At least he always got the milking done, and he was gentle with the sheep. And, at night, after supper, they would all gather round to hear his stories. Wally was a master story teller.

Calder hated chopping wood. He usually gave the job to Jared or Joseph, and he had no doubt they were curious as to why he assumed the job this day. Bending to gather up the logs to stack in the shed behind the house, he heard hoof beats. Rising with the load in his arms, he saw Selena, followed by her footman, Jimmy, reining up in front of the house. Spotting him, Selena gave him a wave. His arms full, he could do naught but bob his head in greeting, but his heart began thundering in his chest. She had come. Somehow, he had known she would.

Leaving Jimmy to see to the horses, Selena hurried over to greet him. "Oh, Calder, I have exciting news. I am so glad you are to home and not in a field."

Stacking the wood, then rising, Calder smiled at Selena's brightness. "What has you so excited, Lady Selena?"

"We are to have a grammar school built in Whimbrel. The boys, including Pascal, will no longer have to walk all the way to Rotherby to attend the Rotherby grammar school."

Tilting his head, Calder asked, "Who is the we? Your uncle?"

"Well, he will help, of course, but … Oh, might we go inside and have something to drink? I am parched, as is Jimmy, no doubt. Then I can tell you and Hannah all about it."

"Please, forgive me, Lady Selena. I should have offered you refreshment."

"There is naught to forgive. I gave you no chance to offer me anything. I was so excited to see you and tell you about the school."

"Let us go now and get you and Jimmy some ale. I am eager to hear about this school. I would be pleased did Pascal not have to walk all the way to Rotherby. I know Hannah will also want to hear about it." That Selena was excited to see him sent a thrilling tingle racing up his spine as he followed her into the house.

Once Hannah served Selena and Jimmy noggins of ale and toast with honey, and they were all seated at the table, Selena explained her new mission. Hannah thought the idea wonderful and promised to spread the word, and Calder offered to walk Selena over to White Acres that she might meet the Huddlestons. He believed they would favor the idea and could be a big help to her. It would give him some time to be alone with Selena.

"But would I be taking you from your work?" Selena asked, concern in her voice. That was one more thing he liked about her, her concern for others before herself.

"The wood will still be here on the morrow. It will eventually get done. Besides, I have news of my own to report. I can tell you about it while we walk."

Her blue-green eyes bright, she said, "I cannot wait to hear your news, and I would dearly love a good walk. You say 'tis little less than a mile? It seems farther than that."

"Do you go by the road, it is, but we will cut across the pastures."

"Splendid," she said, jumping up.

"What would you like me to do, Lady Selena?" Jimmy asked. "Could I be of help here, I would do so. I saw several workers by the pond. Mayhap they are cleaning hemp. I could help."

"Oh, Jimmy, you are in your livery. 'Twould not do to dirty it."

"They are cleaning hemp, Jimmy, but I would not task you with it. However, do you wish to bear them company, that might be a way to amuse yourself. Plus, Wally Shandy is helping, and he is always good for a story or two. But mind he keeps working while telling his tale."

"Wally Shandy is here?" Selena asked.

"Aye." Calder looked at her curiously. "You know Wally?"

"No, but his sister Alice is my maid. She has told me he tells wonderful stories, and I told Alice I would like to hear a couple. Could be a friend of my brother might publish them."

Calder snorted. "That would be something. One of Wally's stories being published."

"Mayhap when we return, you might spare him long enough that he might tell me a couple of his stories?" Selena asked.

"Aye. Jimmy, tell Wally that when I return, I would like him to come to the house."

"That I will do," Jimmy said.

"Are you able to walk in your riding boots?" Calder asked, looking down at Selena's feet.

"Oh, yes, my boots are comfortable enough. They have a good sturdy heel to them. I spend time in the stables, and I must have boots that give me a solid footing."

"So be it. Let us be on our way."

# Chapter 19

Selena could hardly contain her excitement. She was to have Calder all to herself on the walk to and from White Acres. She had meant to ride over to White Acres and introduce herself, but 'twas so much better to have Calder introduce her to the Huddlestons. His support for her project, she hoped, would encourage the Huddlestons to support it as well.

"Tell me your news, Calder," she said, falling in beside him and matching her pace to his.

Looking down at her, he smiled and nodded. "Tomorrow, I ride into Rotherby with Goodman Buxton, and we sign a contract conveying his land and leases to me. In return, I will see to his care and maintenance. 'Tis a hundred more acres I will be adding to what I now have."

"How many acres do you have at present?" The more he had, the more likely she was to win her family's approval of her marriage to Calder. After all, many a country gentleman owned fewer than a thousand acres.

"Five hundred," Calder said. "Three hundred are freehold. Since before the Conqueror, my ancestors owned this land. They were freemen, not thegns to my knowledge, but as free as any thegn, though owing taxes and allegiance to the King. When the Normans conquered England, because none of my ancestors fought against William, the males being too old or too young, so the family fable claims, they were allowed to keep their land. They held the land direct from the crown. We were never tenants of some lord. When White Acres was granted to Lord Penhaligon's knighted ancestor, it too was held direct from the crown."

"How do you know all this?" Selena knew that her own distant D'Arcy ancestor had come over with William I, had fought for William and had been granted a small fiefdom on the Wirral Peninsula. It was still the D'Arcy family's primary seat, though her uncle, the Earl of Tyneford, held other manors throughout England and Wales accumulated over the years by various ancestors. But the family seemed to know nothing of their ancestor's background before he came to England. Because of his surname, they knew he came from Arcy in France, and he married the daughter of the defeated thegn who had previously owned the manor. That was it.

Calder paused. His eyes grew thoughtful. "'Tis mostly by word of mouth, handed down from one generation to the next. Finally, my great-grandfather had enough education to be able to write it down. But we also were given proof by the previous Lord Penhaligon. He wanted to learn more about his family's heritage. He actually saw William's Domesday book – not that Lord Penhaligon could read it. He needed a scholar able to understand the abbreviated Latin used at that time. The scholar read him the notations. After learning about his family and land, he was kind enough to make note of my family as well. You see, the knight, Sir Piers le Beau, who was the founder of the Whitaker family, married the daughter of my ancient ancestor."

Delighted, Selena laughed and clapped her hands. Calder's ancestry might not be noble, but it was ancient, and the same blood ran in his veins as ran in the Whitakers'. Surely that would count for something with her parents.

"Anyway," Calder continued. "I lease two hundred acres from the White Acres manor. I admit, I am leery of taking on the added responsibility of Buxton's holdings. Especially as the acreage is not bordering the rest of my land. But I must think of Pascal's future. His education."

Selena was fascinated by Calder's knowledge of his past. She needed to learn as much as she could about Calder's assets to win over her father. Hoping she would not appear overly nosy, she pressed on. "Is the new acreage a great distance?"

"'Tis but a little north of White Acres. Thirty acres are freehold. The rest are leased from White Acres. Jared has agreed to move in with Buxton and see to his care. I believe Jared plans to marry. The house will need a woman to see it is run properly. Abner's younger son Lyell will also live there. He will tend Buxton's needs and see to the farm animals and vegetable garden. There is a cottager on the land. Though aging, he is still fit enough to be an aid to Jared come time to plow and harrow the fields, or to see to the sheep."

"It sounds like you have your plans well organized."

He again gave her that smile that set her heart skittering about in her chest. "I hope you may be right. I admit to being a bit frightened. Sometimes it seems I can barely manage to get all done that needs doing on my five hundred acres." He shook his head. "Now, I am adding another hundred." Stopping, he pointed to a fence of thorns and brambles. "Look there. That fence needs mending. When the sheep have eaten the stubble from the hay field, I will move them into this clover field. Though the rent is small now, it could grow and allow the sheep to escape."

"I feel certain all will go well for you," she said, falling into step when he set off again. "I do to some extent understand your trepidation. I felt some fear when I decided to undertake gaining support to build the school. Still, do I fail, it will have no impact on my pocket."

Calder stopped, for they had reached the stream that wound down from the hill and wove its way across his pasture. Standing beside him, she looked down at the flat stones placed strategically in the stream bed to make a sort of bridge for crossing the clear running water.

"You are all right to cross on the stones?" Calder asked.

"I shall have no trouble crossing, but do you go first."

He nodded and hopped from one stone to another until he reached the opposite side of the stream. Turning, he held out a hand toward her. "The stones have baked in the sun, so they are not slippery. All the same, be careful."

"I will," she said, starting across. Nearing the other side, though she had no need of Calder's hand, she readily accepted it. The feel of his hand encircling hers set her whole body to tingling. It was such a luscious tingling. He made certain she was secure in her footing before he released her hand. Was he just being courteous, or was he also affected by their touch? She wished she knew.

Calder nodded toward a well-worn path trailing up a low grassy hill. "Now, we head up to the top of this rise."

The hill was not high, so Selena was surprised by how far she could see when they reached the top. "Oh, my, you have quite the view up here."

He chuckled. "It is a nice view. We are now on the White Acres manor. As the stream divides my land from your uncle's manor, so does it divide my land from White Acres." He pointed off to the south. "You can see the forest where you enjoy hiking. The hill above my back pasture is higher than this hill, but it slopes so gently to the east, that from Whimbrel Hall, the incline is scarce discernible. The stream meanders down the hill with nary a rapid until the low falls. There, I can open a dam and fill my pond." He pointed to the east. "Off in the distance, emerging from the woods is the trek leading to Whimbrel and on to Rotherby. 'Twould be the way you come when you ride over here rather than when you walk."

"Oh, yes. The land on the other side of the road is Uncle Nate's game park. He told me it is three hundred acres. He likes to hunt, but besides the hunting being an entertainment, it provides variety to the meals, and it allows Uncle Nate to give gifts to his friends."

Turning, Calder pointed northeast. "There you can see the blockhouse that the Huddlestons have called home for many a generation."

The stone house with its slate roof was weathered and so dark it looked almost black. She marveled at its age. She believed it to be the oldest building she had ever seen, and she was eager to see inside it. A field of white clover spread out before the house, but behind it, a thick stand of woods stretched as far as she could see.

Calder set off on the well-worn path winding down the grass-covered, gently sloping hill. She followed after him on the narrow trek, and nearly bumped into him when he suddenly stopped. He pointed to a muddy looking area of scraggy grass and moss off to one side of the trail. "'Tis a morass," he said. "Spring water seeps up there. Do you ever take this trail, keep clear of that muck. It could easily suck you right under, do you fall into it."

She frowned. "Indeed, I will be careful."

He nodded and resumed his trek along the path. As the hill melded into the clover field, he slowed his pace, that she might again walk by his side. His blue eyes twinkling, he said, "When I was a boy, my dearest friend was Ware's younger brother, Beorn. He was a year older, but no bigger than I was. We had many a fun time on this field – running races, playing ball, fighting duels with sticks for swords. Oh, we had our duties, but our parents always gave us time to just be boys." Stopping, he pursed his lips and looked off at the largest stone barn Selena had ever seen. "I fear I am not giving Pascal the same amount of playtime. I always seem to need him to help with one chore or another. He is so willing…" He shook his head. "I hope I am not adding an even greater load on his young shoulders, as I take on extra acreage."

"From what I have seen of Pascal, he wants to help. But you are correct, he needs time just to be a little boy and to play. Especially during the summer when there is no school to attend. Yet, this is your busiest time. Could you not keep Wally on for the summer? Alice says he needs work."

Calder grimaced, and Selena worried she had overstepped her bounds. What right had she to be telling Calder how to raise his son, or that he should hire Wally? Here Calder was trying to raise the money to send Pascal off to a good school. She held her breath and waited for him to say something, anything.

Finally, he said, "Wally, when not dreaming, is a good worker. He works for a moderate sum, does it include bed and board. But I already have hired him to milk the ewes, and when not milking, he is helping with whatever chore I may need him to do. Could be he could take over some of the chores I give to Pascal. I would like Pascal to have time to play."

"Are there children his age he may play with?"

"Aye, he is close to the Huddlestons' children. While you speak with Avis Huddleston, I may talk to Ware today about time for the younger children to play. I cannot remember all that many times I ever saw Ware out playing. Not like his brother and I played."

They were near the house, and Selena was surprised by the numerous outbuildings. Besides the huge stone dairy barn, she saw several chicken runs, dove cotes, a pig sty, stables, a smoke house, what appeared to be a laundry house, and a couple of other buildings she could not name. The Huddlestons were the stewards of a very prosperous manor.

A blond-haired woman, looking to be in her late thirties, came down the flight of stairs leading to the Huddleston living quarters and welcomed her guests. Calder introduced Selena to Avis Huddleston, and Selena took an instant liking to the woman. While Calder went to find Ware, Avis led Selena upstairs, offered her a seat at the long trestle table, and served her a cool noggin of cider.

"I keep the cider on the ground floor. One half the floor is a dormitory for the milkmaids. We have made it comfortable for them, cool in the summer. Warm in the winter, for those who stay with us year round. The other half is our buttery and storage. It has stone flooring, and thick stone walls. Everything keeps cool, including cheeses, milk, and butter for our own use."

"I suppose the walls are so thick because this was once almost like a castle," Selena said.

"Yes, the Scots were known to raid even this far south, but turmoil between the rulers also kept things stirred up, or so Ware tells me. He is a font of information on his family's past. And he is happy to spout about it to anyone who will listen."

Selena laughed, and the baby, Tacy, looked up at her and laughed. The stocky cook, busily kneading dough, turned around and smiled. Avis also smiled, and said, "You have a delightful laugh, Lady Selena. Almost tinkling sounding. You have certainly intrigued Tacy."

The little blond girl, toddling around and holding onto the ear of a patient dog, let go of the dog to stand before Selena. Her blue eyes wide, she laughed the laugh that only babies can laugh, showing off her two upper and two lower teeth. The child's laughter made Selena laugh again, and that set the baby off once more.

The dog was nuzzling Selena's hand, and the cook's slim, youthful assistant, brushing straggly, brown hair off her sweating forehead, said, "Would you be looking at Woof. See how he tikes to Lady Selena."

Avis started to shoo the dog away, but Selena said, "Oh, he is no bother," and she scratched the dog's ears.

"Woof is old," Avis said. "He has put up with all my children mauling him at one time or another, but he is ever so gentle. Still, Lucy is right. He does seem to take to you."

"I like animals, so mayhap that is why they like me," Selena said, continuing to pet the dog. Its bushy tail was wagging, and Tacy seemed to find the swishing back and forth irresistible. Grabbing for the tail, she missed a couple of times, caught it, but then landed on the floor on her buttocks, pulling the tail down with her. Woof looked around at his tormentor for but an instant before returning his attention to Selena.

"Lucy," Avis said, "do you take Tacy and Woof outside and watch them that I might have a chance to talk with Lady Selena."

"Yes, Mistress Huddleston," the skinny girl said, sticking the large wooden spoon into the pot she had been stirring, and with the hem of her apron, she pushed the large pot away from the low glowing fire in the hearth.

The cook looked over her shoulder. "You want me to continue stirring that jam?"

"Nay, Mildred, you go ahead with your bread making. The jam will keep."

"I hope I am not here at a bad time for you," Selena said. "Seems you are quite busy."

Avis laughed. "We are always busy, but it makes no never mind. 'Tis an honor for us that you would pay us a visit."

"I hope you will think so once I have told you my mission." Selena half-frowned.

"What would that be?" Avis asked, her blue eyes curious.

Avis remained silent until Selena finished telling about her project, then she said, "I think 'tis a wondrous idea."

"So do I," chimed in Mildred.

Giving Mildred but a glance, Avis continued, "There are times, especially in the winter, when 'tis hard to make myself bundle up the children and send them off to the Whimbrel petty school, let alone send the boys to Rotherby. When we go to Sunday services, we ride in the wagon that we use to cart the cheeses and butter to market. Mildred and Lucy, and Hannah and Pascal ride with us, but the milkmaids and other laborers must walk, do they choose to attend services. Where school is concerned, the boys have no choice. No matter the weather, Ware says they go to school. We let Tom take the small cart, is the weather too dismal. But was there a grammar school in Whimbrel, 'twould be less than a two-mile walk."

"'Tis more than three for Squire Nibley's tenants' sons," Selena said. "Matters not whether they take the road from Nibley Hall, or the back trek past Calder's farm. But 'tis much nearer than walking to Rotherby."

"Again, I say, I think it a splendid idea," Avis said. "Sunday, I will talk to some of the women from the hamlet north of here, and to tenants from other farms and the smaller manors to the east, whose boys must go all the way to Rotherby. They, in turn, can talk to their friends and neighbors. You say you plan to speak to the tenants in Whimbrel?"

"Yes. I have arranged with the granary owner to hold a meeting at his home. He is spreading the word, and Saturday next, after dinner, is when we plan to gather. Mistress Nibley is to arrange a meeting with her tenants for me, and I have hopes I can get Lord Edgerton to allow me to meet with his people."

Tilting her head and gazing sightlessly at the hearth embers, Selena said, "In the past, every manor had a church or chapel, and the vicar taught the boys. Of course, in the past, roads were near nonexistent, and there were no coaches, so each small village and manor had to have their own churches. But this modern life with all its conveniences, which we would not want to do without, from chimneys, to glass for our windows, to brick to build homes and businesses, also creates hardships for some people. Can I help alleviate a hardship, I want to do so."

Shaking her head, Selena laughed, and brought her gaze back to Avis. "Now that I have told you of my plans, and you have graciously volunteered your aid, before Calder comes to fetch me, do tell me more about your home. Its history is fascinating. My family's home is newly built, as is Uncle Nate's. They have all the modern conveniences, but no history. Calder told me that your husband's ancestry and his are intermingled with the Whitaker ancestry, and that this house dates from the twelfth century."

Avis chuckled. "Ware could tell you much more. He loves to tell all who will listen of the history of the old place. Myself, I could wish we had a more modern home, as has your uncle. However, this serves us.

As to its history, my understanding is, it was built in eleven thirty by Piers le Beau's heir, Alain of White Acres, but I believe he spent little time here. He was always off fighting in France. His wife was French, and she and her children lived in France. Their eldest son and heir, do I remember correctly, was Emile le Corbet. There is much more to his story, but I cannot remember it all."

"He almost lost this manor because he chose to fight on Queen Maud's side instead of King Stephen's," Mildred said, her hands busy rounding and whacking a mound of dough. "Have I not heard Mister Huddleston tell his tales often enough, I know them all by heart. Had Thurbert's son, Ector, not held out against Stephen's men, right here in this blockhouse, White Acres could well have been lost to the Whitaker family."

Smiling and shaking her head, Avis said, "Sounds right to me. Mildred has been with the family long enough to have heard the tales, not only from Ware, but from his father. Anyway, when Henry II came over here and became King in eleven fifty-four, Alain's son Emile came with him.

"It is believed he spent little time here at White Acres. Mayhap he came here with King Henry to go hunting, but basically, he just took his rent. Thurbert's son, Ector, and then Ector's son, Remy, continued on as stewards. Ware could name you every generation of White Acres stewards from Remy on to himself. He could name every Whitaker from Emile on through today's Lord Penhaligon the sixth."

Selena was impressed, but Avis gave a little twist to her mouth and said, "Let me get back to the house. 'Twas sometime in the late fourteen hundreds that the first Earl of Penhaligon remodeled the tower. He was into hunting and wanted more comfort than what was offered in this centuries-old blockhouse. But in fifteen thirty, the second Lord Penhaligon had a hunting lodge built. You cannot see it from here. It is located just outside his park. Ware claims he built it to please King Henry VIII, who loved to hunt. Leicestershire being known for good hunting."

"Oh, yes," Selena said, "my father has come here to hunt with my uncle. But do tell me how the house has changed. Obviously the chimneys were added. What else?"

Avis went on to describe the changes from the adding of the second floor, to bringing the kitchen area inside the house instead of having it in a separate building behind the blockhouse.

"I would guess the food got mighty cold coming from an outdoor kitchen, then up the stairs before finally reaching the table," Mildred threw in.

Chuckling, Avis agreed. "I would say that was one reason the first Lord Penhaligon remodeled the house. Probably was not happy with his cold dinners." She next described the structures added to the grounds as the manor changed from farming to herding and dairying.

"The rest of the manor, that is not used for the cows or for growing oats or turnips to feed the cows over winter, is leased out. Calder leases a couple hundred acres. Other lesser leases are held by various tenants and freemen. This manor is small compared to other Whitaker manors. Only fourteen hundred acres, and four of those are Lord Penhaligon's park. Ware is heedful of everything that concerns the acreage, even the acres that are under lease. He must make sure the land is not being abused. Crop rotation is important to keep the soil productive. Then, with all the cows, what manure is not needed for the demesne is sold to the leaseholders. There is much to managing the manor."

"There would seem to be," Selena said, enjoying learning more about the lifestyle she hoped she would soon be a part of. She could see the Huddlestons lived well, if not frivolously, and as Ware Huddleston was the manor steward, he and his wife were addressed as Mister and Mistress Huddleston. They might not be considered upper gentry, despite Ware's ancient ancestry, but they were well respected by their neighbors.

Turning at the sound of footsteps, Selena smiled as Calder, followed by a man she guessed was Ware Huddleston, entered the hall. Like Calder, Ware's eyes were blue, but they were a lighter blue, not the brilliant blue of Calder's eyes. He was about Calder's height, but a tad slimmer, and his shoulders were not as broad. He looked to be older than Calder, and his face showed the ravages of too much time in the sun. Still, he was a good-looking man.

"So, have you convinced Mistress Huddleston you need a grammar school in Whimbrel?" Calder asked after introducing Ware.

"She has," Avis answered for Selena. "Convinced me and Mildred. We intend to do our part to encourage the community to support the project."

"Splendid," Ware said, looking at Selena. "Calder has told me of your plan, Lady Selena, and I am in favor of it. The trek to Rotherby for my sons is dreary, come winter."

"I hope others will as readily agree with you," Selena said, then looked at Calder. "If I am to hear one or two of Wally's stories and still get back for supper, I think we had best be off."

Calder nodded. "Indeed, I have my cows to milk, so Abner can bring the milk over." He glanced at Ware. "Saturday afternoon, we give the young ones a respite from their chores?"

"We do," Ware said. He glanced at his wife. "I will explain after we see our guests off."

Good-byes were made, and Selena and Calder were soon headed back to Calder's farm.

# Chapter 20

"You enjoyed your chat with Avis?" Calder asked, slowing his pace as Selena adjusted her stride to his.

"I did indeed. She is a delightful woman, and so full of information, not only about White Acres Tower, but about her husband's and the Whitaker's family history. Though she says her husband knows much more. She says he knows the names of every steward that served at White Acres. They are all his ancestors. He also knows the names of all the White Acres lords."

"I have no doubt Ware knows them all by heart."

"Were you aware that my aunt's first born son is married to a Whitaker? Not a Whitaker of the main branch. Fonda, Lady Crossly, is the daughter of a younger son."

Calder's eyes narrowed, and after pursing his lips, he at last said, "I believe when your aunt and uncle first moved here, I did hear something about that. Gossip will make the rounds. Until you now mentioned it, I had forgotten about it. Ware has told me, when Lord Penhaligon visits his lodge, he always pays a call on your uncle and aunt, and your uncle is invited to join him in a hunt or two. I thought it no more than one peer favoring the company of another."

"I would think you are right. Aunt Rowena has not mentioned Lord or Lady Penhaligon, even in passing."

"I am thinking Lady Penhaligon has not been to White Acres more than once, and that was years ago. I understand she cares little for hunting."

"You know a lot about the comings and goings of White Acres," Selena said.

"That would be because Ware and I are close. We grew up together with our lands bordering as they do. We are cousins. His grandfather was my great-grandmother's sibling."

"So besides your distant ancestors having married, your more recent ancestors were siblings? No wonder you are close. 'Tis nice for Pascal to have family close by. Especially, him being an only child."

"After my wife died, Pascal lived with the Huddlestons for near a year. In my grief, I fear I could do little but think about keeping the farm going. Hannah stood by me. I saw Pascal as often as I could, but I could not give him the care he needed. I will ever have a special spot in my heart reserved for Avis, for the loving care she gave my son. Because Pascal spent a year with his cousins, he is very close with the two younger ones, Molly and Derwin."

"You loved your wife very deeply," Selena said, her voice soft. It was a statement not a question. She admired his devotion to his wife, though she hoped he could find love with her. "That is the only kind of love to have," she continued. "It is a love worth giving and receiving. 'Tis the kind of love my parents have, and that Aunt Rowena and Uncle Nate have. I would say that my brother, Reggie, and his new wife have that wondrous kind of love. By the looks of them, I would venture Mister and Mistress Huddleston know that kind of love."

Calder nodded when she stated that he had loved his wife deeply. He nodded again when she said the Huddlestons bore that same kind of love. "Ware was a lucky man when he convinced Avis to marry him," he said. "She was being courted by several youths, but she once told me she had eyes only for Ware. She is the younger daughter of a squire over to the next parish. Ware met her at a fair and lost his heart to her. Ware being a steward with a good income, Avis's father gave his consent to the marriage."

"How romantic," Selena said. "They met at a fair and fell instantly in love." She sighed.

Calder chuckled. "Are you a romantic, Lady Selena?"

She half-smiled and glanced sideways at him. "I think I must be, though I cannot say I have ever given it much thought. I do think love is important in a marriage. I know many people marry for various reasons other than love – be it for fortune or to rise socially or because a parent forces them into a marriage. Some marry because they are desperate and have no other means of support. But a marriage built on love – that is the kind of marriage to have."

144

Calder slowly nodded. "Aye. That is the kind of marriage that is most rewarding."

Selena liked the word he used. Rewarding. Yes, a marriage brimming with love would be rewarding. Her heart was brimming with love for the man beside her. But how to make him love her was proving difficult. Before she knew it, her cousins would be arriving, and her time with Calder might be harder to fit into a bustling schedule.

"Ah," Calder said, interrupting her thoughts. "Here come Wally and your footman. You shall have your stories."

※ ※ ※

Selena sat at Calder's table with a noggin of buttermilk in front of her and listened to Wally's melodic voice as he told one story after another. His stories were short and amusing, but wise, almost like fables. His pale blue eyes dreamy, his first story was about a rooster that night after night began crowing when all should be sleeping. His crowing would start the dog to barking. The husbandman would go out with his lantern but could find nothing amiss. Near every night the crowing resumed. People in the neighboring crofts started complaining. The husbandman feared he would have to kill the rooster, but he was a good rooster and he hated to kill him.

As a last resort, the husbandman decided he would stay outside near the barn and see if he could find out what was making the rooster crow in the middle of the night. Eventually, he dozed, but the rooster's crowing woke him. The dog beside him started barking and took off toward the hen coop. Just enough moonlight filtered through a thin layer of clouds for the husbandman to see the dog chase away a shadowy form the farmer believed was a fox. The rooster issued a few more crows, the dog returned to the husbandman and issued a couple more barks to say he had done his duty, then all was again quiet.

The next day, the husbandman went around to his neighbors and discovered most of them had suffered the loss of a chicken or two. The neighbors suspected the marauder to be of the two-legged variety. Their hen coops, being a ways above ground to protect the hens from vermin, had been found with their hatch covers open. Feathers scattered about the ground gave evidence a hen was missing. But the husbandman was certain he had seen a fox. He decided to set a trap and catch the fox. For two nights he kept watch, but the fox failed to appear. On the third night, the rooster began his crowing. The husbandman had left his dog in the house so he would not run the fox off. He wanted to see how the fox got to the chickens.

The moon was bright, and the husbandman watched in amazement as the fox scaled the ladder to the hen coop enclosure. Digging his claws into the ladder rails, the fox climbed right up to the door of the hen coop. He thrust his nose against the latch, and after several attempts, he nudged the latch lose and leaped to the ground as the door flopped open. A couple of hens peeked out. One, thinking it must be morning, fluttered down to the ground.

The rooster continued to crow from his perch atop the barn, but the hen paid him no heed. She started pecking about on the ground, looking for a beetle or some left over seeds. The fox, his sight on his dinner, failed to notice the husbandman sneaking up on him. As the fox lunged for the unsuspecting hen, the husbandman threw a fish net over the fox. Fox and hen were both trapped. The hen set up a-squawking, the fox a-hissing, and the husbandman chuckled. He had caught the most crafty fox ever to be encountered in his parish.

He managed to free the hen and wrap the squiggling fox up in the net. The following morning, he put the fox in a cage and invited all the neighbors to come see the crafty fox. The husbandman was made a hero. He had outsmarted the fox. But the husbandman knew he owed the respect his neighbors paid him to his rooster. He then and there promised his rooster he would live into old age and would never become the prime ingredient in a Sunday porridge.

Each of Wally's stories involved animals and usually the humbler class of people. Selena would have liked to stay and listen to Wally's stories all evening, but she knew she had to return to Whimbrel. She asked Wally to write his stories down that she might send them to her brother's publishing friend, but Wally said, first, he could not afford the paper. Second, his ability to write was not great.

"That is a shame," Selena said, her brow furrowed. "I had hopes I might get you a job with the publisher, did he like your stories, which I cannot imagine he would not. Still, I will give Alice a day off, and you can tell her the stories, at least a couple of them. She can write them down for you. I will supply the paper, and, once written, I will send them to the publisher."

She looked at Calder. "You must tell me when you can spare Wally for a few hours that Alice might write down his stories."

Calder frowned. "I need Wally to milk the ewes twice a day, and I can use him on numerous other chores once his milking is done." He brightened. "I would say I can give him time in between his milking to tell his stories to his sister. They can sit here at the table. Hannah will not mind, I cannot think."

"Indeed, I will not mind," Hannah said. "I love Wally's stories."

"Then, might I send Alice over tomorrow. The sooner the better, I would say."

"Best make it the following day, Lady Selena," Wally said, scratching behind an ear. "I am thinking I will yet be helping with the hemp. One more day, and it should be finished."

Selena nodded. "Very well. Will that be all right with you, Calder."

"'Twill be fine. Alice can come mid-morning to work with Wally. She can then have dinner with us. Are she and Wally not finished, they can continue after they have eaten."

Smiling, Selena said, "Thank you. I am excited about the stories. We need more good cheer in our lives. People need to smile. 'Tis good for the soul, to my way of thinking. Plus, we need more stories about ordinary people. Stories about people and animals the children in school can relate to. Wally's stories are not only perfect, they are a delight."

"Thank you, Lady Selena," Wally said, blushing a bright red.

Pleased with her day, Selena let Calder help her onto her horse. She loved the feel of his hands on her hips when he boosted her onto her saddle. She liked the way his eyes held hers. She liked the way for an infinitesimal moment their lips were but inches apart. She loved his smile when he promised her she was always welcome.

She thanked him again for taking her to meet the Huddlestons and for letting Wally tell her his stories. "I think he has a bright future ahead, though I do wish he could be more like his brother, who is a teacher. Being able to read and write would help him immensely."

"I hope you are correct, and that the publisher likes his stories." Calder said. "Wally has a good soul. I would like to see him better himself."

"Indeed," Selena answered, and, cocking her head, added, "I missed seeing Pascal today. Tell him I will hunt him down next time I visit, is he not near to hand."

"I will tell him," Calder said, as she waved to him and set off for Whimbrel with Jimmy following in her wake.

For a while, Selena rode in silence. She would not see Calder on the morrow, for he was going into Rotherby to conclude his purchase of Goodman Buxton's land. She liked that. The more land he had, the more chance she had of claiming him to be a member of the gentry. She wanted her parents' approval of her marriage, but whether they approved or not, she intended to marry Calder Grantham. That is, did he ever get around to asking her to marry him.

A horrid thought struck her. What if he failed to ask her because he believed himself too inferior a match for her. She would somehow have to let him know their ranks in society made no never mind to her. How to do that was a puzzle? She would think of a way. Turning to Jimmy, she said, "Tomorrow, I plan to visit the granary owner again and maybe Mistress Forester. Many of the villagers stop in her ale house. She can encourage them to come to the meeting at the granary on Saturday. After that, I want to ride over to the Nibleys'. I want to see what Mistress Nibley has accomplished."

"Whatever you say, Lady Selena," Jimmy answered, riding up beside her.

She smiled at him. "I appreciate your company, Jimmy. You are good with the horses. As I am a tad late today, I will ask you to give Brigantia her rub down. I know you will see she is well tended."

"Indeed, Lady Selena. She will have a most thorough rub down, and a good brushing so she is ready for your busy afternoon tomorrow."

Pleased, Selena said, "Thank you," and patted her horse's neck. Brigantia was in good hands with Jimmy.

# Chapter 21

The day after her visit with Calder and the Huddlestons, Selena set about visiting Mister Hall, the granary owner. According to him and Widow Forester, Whimbrel villagers were pledging to come to Selena's meeting on Saturday. She next had a fruitful visit with the Nibleys, learning Mistress Nibley had arranged for her to speak to the Nibley tenants the following week. Mistress Nibley had also sent notes to several local gentry families asking to meet with them to tell them of the project. Pleased with her afternoon accomplishments, Selena returned home to be greeted by her aunt with the news a missive had arrived from Carola Mead, Aunt Rowena's bland, but accommodating, cousin, saying Flavia and Ewen and their friends were to arrive the following day. Aunt Rowena expected Selena to be on hand to greet her cousins.

Selena spent the evening and into the night wondering how she could escape the house for long enough to tell Calder her visits might be less frequent. When she finally drifted into sleep, no plan had come to mind. But the following morning, Aunt Rowena gave her the excuse she needed. Her aunt canceled their lessons.

"I have too much to do to insure that all is ready for their arrival," Aunt Rowena said.

Begging she be allowed to exercise Brigantia, Selena promised she would give her horse a good run and would return before her cousins arrived. Distracted and busy with a multitude of details, Aunt Rowena gave in to Selena's pleas, though she was already annoyed that Selena had given her maid, Alice, the day off.

"What could you have been thinking, Selena?" Aunt Rowena said. "You know all help is needed to ready the house for not only your cousins, but also their guests."

"I am sorry, Aunt Rowena, but I promised Alice she could help her brother. I could not break my promise."

Her aunt might not have agreed that Selena had to keep her promise, but she allowed Selena to leave for her ride after admonishing her to keep her ride short and not to be giving her maid a day off without first consulting her aunt about it. Selena promised she would do as bid and hurried off. She wanted to see how Alice and Wally were doing at Calder's, but more importantly, she wanted to see Calder. She wanted to tell him that her plans for the school were moving forward. She hoped Calder would pass the information on to Avis Huddleston. She believed Mistress Huddleston would have sway over many of the locals in the surrounding areas.

Emotionally torn, Selena nudged her heels into Brigantia's flanks and set the mare to galloping. She had no idea what her cousins' arrival would portend. She was excited to see them, yet fearful their arrival would interfere with her visits to Calder's farm.

At the crossing that would have led to White Acres or eastward toward the Edgerton manor, she heard a shout. Glancing over her shoulder, she saw a rider wave to her. She returned the wave, but continued on her way to Calder's. Urging his horse forward, Jimmy hollered, "'Tis Mister Darnell calling to you."

"I have much to do and will not be slowed," Selena said with a glance back at Jimmy. "Am I not home when my cousins arrive, Aunt Rowena will be greatly offended." Flapping Brigantia's reins to get the horse to lengthen her stride to a run, she gave Brigantia her head and the mare raced down the road. They splashed through the stream marking the boundary between Calder's land and White Acres and were soon drawing up in front of Calder's house.

Hopping from his mount, Jimmy took the reins of both horses as Selena, sliding off her saddle, landed lightly on her toes. Jimmy was leading the horses off to the well for a drink, and Selena was looking about to see if she could spot Calder when Darnell rode up.

"Gramercy, Lady Selena, did you not hear me call to you?"

Frowning, Selena said, "Aye, Mister Darnell, but my time is limited today. I have an errand to dispatch, then must return to Whimbrel Hall. My cousins are to return this afternoon."

"Are they! Zounds, that is good news," Darnell said. "I have missed Ewen. 'Twill be good to see him."

Selena but nodded, her gaze still searching the grounds. She had decided she would go inside the house to ask after Calder, when Calder, his arms filled with a squiggling lamb, emerged from the barn. Rollo exited behind him. Upon sighting Selena, the dog set up a mad yapping and raced toward her. Then everything turned into a mound of confusion. Darnell, pulling his sword from his sheath, yelped, "Lady Selena, beware!" Thrusting his arm out in front of her, he pushed her back.

Calder, seeing Darnell with sword raised, started yelling, "No! No!" and came running after Rollo.

Not knowing what to do, but fearing for the dog and for Calder, Selena stuck out her foot, and as Darnell stepped forward, bringing his sword down in a swipe, she tripped him. He fell forward, the blade of his sword missing the tip of Rollo's nose by a fraction. He landed with a thud and a harsh cry on the hard packed dirt before the house.

Rollo gave Darnell but a cursory glance before greeting Selena with excited yelps. Calder set down his lamb and reached Darnell as Selena squatted to see if Darnell was badly injured. She looked up into Calder's eyes. "I do believe he is hurt," she said.

A groan from Darnell advanced her theory, and a puddle of blood seeping onto the ground confirmed it. Darnell groaned again and Calder turned him over as the door to the house opened, and Hannah, followed by Wally and Alice, came out.

"Whatever has happened here?" Hannah demanded.

"He damn near killed me!" Darnell exclaimed, looking up at Calder.

"What!" Hannah cried.

"No," Selena said. "Calder was nowhere near Mister Darnell. I tripped Darnell because he meant to hurt Rollo."

Darnell turned his head to look at Selena. "The dog was attacking you."

"Nay, he was but running to greet me. Oh, Mister Darnell, you are bleeding." She looked up at Hannah. "We must stop his bleeding."

"Indeed," Hannah said. "Wally, you help Calder carry him up to the spare room. Alice, run ahead and turn back the bedding. 'Tis the first door off the stairs."

"Yes, Hannah," Alice said and hurried off to do the older woman's bidding.

Calder and Wally gingerly picked Darnell up, but he groaned all the same. Jimmy, returning from the well, gave them a hand. Darnell was protesting and insisting he was not badly injured, but Selena could see blood blotching his chest and his arm, and he was starting to lose color and slur his speech.

Following everyone into the house, she asked, "What can I do, Hannah?"

"I mean to make up a bread and herb poultice, but do I need to stitch up his wounds, he will need some laudanum. You will find some in the cupboard. Mix it in with some of the cider and a glop of honey. You will find both on the table. I was just serving Wally and Alice a treat."

Selena followed Hannah's directions, and while Hannah mixed up a poultice, she poured cider into a noggin and added honey and a few drops of the laudanum. With the poultice prepared, Hannah, grabbing her sewing basket, said, "Let us go see how much damage is done."

Selena followed Hannah up the stairs to the spare room. Wally and Calder had stripped off Darnell's coat, waistcoat, and shirt, and he lay bare-chested on the clean linen sheets. Jimmy was holding a large cloth to Darnell's chest to stop the flow of blood, and Alice was holding another cloth to his arm while Calder tied a tourniquet around the arm just under the shoulder. Eyes closed, Darnell moaned softly.

"Mister Darnell, do you hurt terribly? I am so sorry," Selena said, clutching the noggin with the laudanum concoction. She had only been trying to save the dog. She had never dreamed she would injure Darnell. What if he should die. He seemed to be losing so much blood.

Darnell's eyes blinked open, but they seemed to be having trouble focusing until they finally rested on Selena. "My father and mother," he said, "you will tell them I was but … protecting you."

"You have no need to be worrying about your parents, Mister Darnell," Hannah said. "I will stitch you up, and you will be just fine. These wounds are not that bad. Lady Selena, give him that draught to drink, then you and Alice best leave the room. Neither of you being married, and you both being young, you have no business to be seeing a man with his shirt off."

Selena protested that she had seen her brothers numerous times over the years, but Hannah said, "Mister Darnell is not your brother. Now give me the noggin and out with you."

Frowning, Selena handed the noggin to Hannah, and she and Alice left the room. For a moment, she stood in the doorway until Hannah bade Jimmy close the door. Frowning, Selena paced the corridor for a few moments until Alice said, "Would you like to see the stories I have written down?"

Vigorously nodding, Selena said, "Oh, yes, I do need a diversion. Should he die, I could not live with myself. I just acted so quickly. I could not think what to do but to stop him from using his sword on Rollo."

"Hannah says he will not die, but who is Rollo?" Alice asked as they started downstairs.

"He is Calder's dog. He was but coming to greet me, and for some reason, I cannot fathom, Mister Darnell thought the dog was attacking me."

"I am certain Mister Darnell will be fine. Hannah says so. I am wondering, though, should you not tell Lady Rotherby what has happened. As is, you will be late returning home."

Selena slapped her hand to her forehead. "Oh, my. How will I ever tell Aunt Rowena about this? But, yes, you are right, Alice, I must send word to her. She no doubt will need to inform his parents. I best send Jimmy with the message. Do give me a sheet of the paper, and I will write her a note."

She had just finished the missive when Jimmy came down the stairs. "Calder said I had best see to Mister Darnell's horse."

"Yes, Jimmy, then you must ride back to Whimbrel Hall and give my aunt this note. I have written to tell her about the accident, and to tell her I will not be home as soon as I had promised." She had also asked her aunt what she should do, stay with Darnell or return home.

Jimmy nodded. "As soon as I have seen to Mister Darnell's horse, I will head out."

"Thank you, Jimmy," Selena said, sinking down onto a bench at the table. How would she ever explain this to her aunt? And what would Lady Edgerton think of her now? She would probably never want to help with the Whimbrel Village school after this debacle.

"Do you wish to look at a story, Lady Selena," Alice asked, holding out a sheet of paper.

Numbly, Selena took the paper, and once Alice moved the table lantern close to hand, she started to read. It was a sweet story about a little girl who found a tiny cloud caught in the branches of a small tree. The little girl did all she could to free the cloud so it might join the larger clouds floating slowly by in the sky. She begged the cloud not to cry, and with all her might, she shook and shook the tree until finally the tiny cloud was free and could float away into the bright blue sky.

Selena finished the story shortly before Wally came downstairs. "Hannah said I was to tell you Mister Darnell will be fine. She has stitched him up. He has such long hair, she used his own hair for the thread. He is sleeping peacefully. Fact is, once she gave him the potion you made for him, he was soon feeling no pain. She will stay with him for a bit to make certain he is not restless, which might reopen a wound. Then I will sit with him while she prepares dinner."

Clasping her hands to her heart, Selena cried, "Thank goodness Mister Darnell will be all right." Feeling like a weight had been lifted from her shoulders, she smiled at Wally. "I am so looking forward to reading more of your stories. I cannot believe this accident had to happen." Holding the paper out to Wally, she said, "I love how you describe the tiny cloud's raindrops as teardrops."

Taking the paper and squinting, Wally held it close to his nose. He shook his head. "I am sorry, Lady Selena, but I cannot make this out."

"Why, Wally," Selena said. "'I do believe you need some spectacles. Could be you could write your own work if you could but see to do so."

Wally shrugged. "'Tis true. When younger, and my eyes were a tad better, I learned my letters and could read fairly well, did I hold the book close to my nose, but each year, my eyes have failed me more and more. I can see at a distance well enough, but small things, like print, I cannot see. Though I may be needing spectacles, I cannot afford them."

"Oh," Selena said. She paused but a moment before adding, "Well. I shall buy them for you, and you may repay me from the profits from your books. Do you know if there might be a spectacle peddler in Rotherby? Or must you go to Leicester to one of those optical experts?"

Ignoring Selena's offer to purchase spectacles for him, Wally asked, "Lady Selena, do you truly think my stories will sell?"

He looked so hopeful and earnest, Selena had to smile. "I do, Wally. Fact is, I intend to send these stories off to my brother's friend the first chance I get. He may want to meet you. And, are you to go to London, you must first have spectacles."

"Go to London! I could never afford to do that." Wally sounded aghast.

"Of course you can. Fact is, Mister Postgate might even take you on in his shop. Never fear the cost of a ticket. That can be worked out. But first, we need get you some spectacles."

Wally slowly shook his head. "I cannot think why you would want to do this for me."

"I choose to help you because I like good stories. Happy stories. Stories about ordinary people leading ordinary lives. I like your humor. I have hopes your stories might encourage more people of the working class to read. Not just to better themselves. But to make life more interesting, more enjoyable. So many people have such hard lives. Adding a little fun and flavor to their lives seems like a good thing to do. Do you not agree?"

Wally was numbly rubbing his chin with his knuckles. "Aye, but this is all a bit bewildering, Lady Selena. Yet, I cannot but hope you may be right, and that my stories might entertain people enough they would care to buy them."

"I have no doubts they will be loved. But you must look into obtaining some spectacles. If you must go to Leicester, I think I will be able to persuade my cousin, Ewen, Lord Sutherlin, to take you there and to see you are not cheated."

"My lady, why would Lord Sutherlin do such a thing for me?" Wally asked in surprise.

Narrowing her eyes and cocking her head, Selena said, "Because I know things." She had been in London with her father and her brother, Reggie, when Ewen had skipped away from Oxford for a spree in London with some friends. He and his friends had ended up spending too much, and gambling too much, and had been unable to pay for their rooms. She and Reggie had come up with enough funds to bail them out, and Ewen's father was never made the wiser. Ewen owed her. He would not disappoint her.

As Wally still looked confused, she patted his arm. "Never you mind. Just find out what you can about the spectacles, and I will see to their cost."

"You are most kind, Lady Selena."

"Indeed you are," Alice added.

"I must agree with both of you," Calder said from the foot of the stairs.

Selena had not heard him coming down, but at the sound of his voice, she quickly turned to him. He wore a soft smile, and was looking at her in a way that made her heart turn flips.

"Calder," she said, "how is Mister Darnell?"

"Sleeping soundly, a smile on his face. He is feeling no pain."

Selena put her hand to her heart. "I am so relieved. When I saw how he was bleeding, I feared I had killed him."

"Nay, the cuts are not deep. He will be left with minor scars is all. You must not blame yourself. You but did what you did to save Rollo. Speaking of the dog, I must see to him and the lamb. I was bringing the lamb in because its bobbed tail is not healing properly, and I need Hannah to work her miracle with her potions and poultices."

"Might I help in any way?" Selena asked.

"You and Alice may cuddle the lamb when I bring her in. She is a sweet little thing. I must go to the pond and see how the girls are doing with the hemp. Wally, do you please relieve Hannah that she may finish preparing dinner."

"That I will do," Wally said, rising, but as Calder exited the hall, Wally turned back to Selena. "I thank you, again, Lady Selena. I will look into finding spectacles. Mayhap my brother, John, who is the grammar school teacher in Rotherby, can help me. I will ask Alice to write to him for me."

"Yes," Selena said, looking at Wally's sister. "Alice, do you write the letter now, and I will see it is posted on the morrow."

Alice sat down and started to write as Wally headed up the stairs to relieve Hannah. Calder came back inside, the lamb in his arms. Rollo, his tail wagging furiously, followed Calder in and immediately went to Selena. She laughed at him and patted his head. "Have you been minding the lamb," she asked.

"Indeed he has," Calder said, setting the lamb down at Selena's feet. "He herded the little thing over to a shady bush, and the two of them were having a nap. If you will mind the little miss, and tell Hannah the problem when she comes down, I will be off to the pond. I am hoping the girls can finish up by evening."

Selena sank onto a bench and took the lamb's head between her hands. The lamb went baa and blinked its eyes at her. She laughed. "I will see to her and to Rollo," she said, scratching the lamb under its chin while ruffling Rollo's neck hair before scratching behind his ears.

"Thank you, Lady Selena," Calder said and headed out the door.

Selena had not yet had a chance to tell him about her cousins' imminent arrival. Thinking of their arrival took her thoughts back to the trouble she was going to be in with her aunt. She had no idea what she should do. Wait for her aunt to send her word? Head for home and leave Darnell in Hannah's care? Why had Darnell followed after her? The entire debacle was his fault. All the same, she felt terrible that she had caused his injuries.

Sighing, she hoped Calder would soon return. She then turned her attention to the animals.

# Chapter 22

Glancing out the window of her coach, Rowena sighed. She could not believe she was having to leave her home when her children and guests would soon be arriving. Whatever had Selena done now! She thanked God she would only have to deal with Lord Edgerton, as Lady Edgerton was visiting her sister and would not be returning for a week.

When the footman, Jimmy, had arrived with the message from Selena, Rowena had wanted to scream and pull at her hair. Oh! That girl! Instead, she told Jimmy to find the housekeeper and send her to her immediately. He was then to tell the coachman to ready the coach. "You are certain Mister Darnell can be moved?" she had asked.

"Aye," Jimmy said. "He will be groggy, having lost some blood, and because Hannah gave him a potion to drink, but Calder and Wally can easily get him out to the coach."

According to Jimmy, Darnell was not badly injured. That was a blessing. While Jimmy attended to her instructions, she went to her writing desk, drew out pen and paper, and wrote a note to Lord Edgerton. When Jimmy returned she sent him to deliver the message.

"But first ride back to the Grantham farm and tell them I will be coming with the coach to fetch Mister Darnell."

"Aye, Lady Rotherby," Jimmy said before hurrying off on his errands.

Rowena bade the housekeeper prepare Ewen's room for Darnell, and to prepare the cot in Ewen's closet for Ewen. Having only seven bedchambers in addition to her own, and with Selena occupying one room, and the three guests plus her daughter and cousin Carola Mead arriving, she had no choice but to give the seventh room to Darnell. Fine homecoming for her son. Fortunately, Ewen and Darnell were close friends, so Ewen should not be terribly upset at losing his bed.

Ewen's move to the cot meant Ewen's aging manservant would have to move into the men's dormitory in the basement. The old fellow would not like that, but he would not complain, though his old bones would miss the comfort of his thickly padded cot. Melvin had been Rowena's husband's manservant in her husband's youth, before Nate had gone off to fight for Charles I and then Charles II and had then taken to the road as a highwayman, robbing from the Puritans and sending his gains to Charles II in Europe. When the Puritan hold on England ended, and Charles was restored to the throne, Charles rewarded Nate with the Rotherby earldom. Nate settled into his new lifestyle, and Melvin resumed his duties as manservant to Nate. But Nate, after so many years of caring for his own needs, found that, unless he needed to prepare for some special occasion, he preferred not to be waited upon.

Consequently, when Ewen turned four, Melvin became the young Viscount's manservant. Melvin had served his young master loyally ever since. However, like his father, when Ewen took to the road, he never took Melvin with him. For one thing, Melvin was getting too old. For another, Ewen, wanting to earn his father's respect, had learned to see to his own basic needs. Having met Ansel Yardley at her oldest son's home, Rowena knew that youth traveled with no servant, but she had no knowledge of whether the other two young men accompanying Ewen would have servants. Well, Melvin would see to them and get them settled in their rooms. The housekeeper would see to Flavia and Carola. Dear Cousin Carola would be exhausted after making the lengthy trip to and from Lancashire. She had volunteered to retrieve Flavia and serve as Flavia's chaperone until they arrived home. For that, Carola deserved to be pampered, and Rowena gave the housekeeper strict orders to see to Carola's every wish, and to have a hot bath waiting for both Carola and Flavia.

Her stomach rumbling as she was having to miss her dinner, Rowena knew she could trust the butler to see the preparations for supper progressed according to plan. She could count on her staff to see arrangements ran smoothly even if she had to be absent. Even if she could not be there to welcome her children home.

Having known her young guests' fathers and mothers, Rowena was looking forward to meeting the youths. Over the years, what with building a home and raising a family, she had lost touch with the LaBrees and the Yardleys, but she had continued to correspond with Arcadia, Lady Preston, though she had not seen her friend in many a year. Nate had recently invited the Prestons and the Yardleys to attend the next D'Arcy family reunion. She hoped both families would attend.

Her coach splashing through a stream brought Rowena back to the present. In a matter of moments, the coach was pulling up in front of the Grantham residence. She had been there but once, to offer her condolences to Goodman Grantham when his wife died. It was a handsome stone house, well-built, and with two chimneys and a goodly number of windows. When her footman opened the door to the coach, Calder Grantham was there to welcome her and to assist her from the coach.

My, she thought, he is a good-looking man. Incredible blue eyes. Good features, sun-bronzed skin and broad shoulders. The shoulders and body of a man used to heavy labor, yet his touch on her hand was light as he helped her descend her coach steps. Selena stood behind him, her eyes wary, her mouth twisted in a worried frown.

"Lady Rotherby, I welcome you to my home, though I am sorry for the circumstances that bring you here," Grantham said.

Clasping her hands together, Selena stepped forward. "Oh, Aunt Rowena, I cannot begin to tell you how terrible I feel. Hannah assures me Mister Darnell will be fine, but I fear his injury is my doing, though I was but trying to protect Rollo, Calder's dog. Darnell would have killed Rollo had I not tripped him."

Rowena had no doubt she looked as confused as she felt after Selena's disjointed speech, for Grantham said, "Lady Rotherby, do come inside out of the sun and have a seat." He extended an arm, urging her to enter the open door. "Hannah has a nice cool cider drink for you, and once you are settled, we will tell you all that has transpired."

Nodding, Rowena accepted Grantham's invitation and entered the semi-dark hall. The stone walls were hung with colorful woven rugs and a tapestry depicting a wooded scene with a stream flowing through it. Rowena guessed the tapestry to be quite old as the colors were fading and portions looked a little frayed. A lantern on the long trestle table, and one hanging over the cooking area, plus the daylight streaming in the diamond-paned windows cast part of the room in light, part in shadows. A couple of woven reed mats were strewn on the clean stone floor, and the cooking area was neat and orderly.

A strongly built woman, her graying hair tucked in a bun, greeted Rowena with a curtsy and said, "Lady Rotherby, please do have a seat." She indicated one of the two chairs with sturdy slatted backs. The chair had a thick cushion on it to aid in its comfort. "Let me get you a cool glass of cider."

"Mayhap I should see Mister Darnell first," Rowena said, wanting to see for herself that Edgerton's son was not seriously injured.

"If you wish," Grantham said, "but he is sleeping peacefully. Do you follow me, I will take you up to see him."

Following Grantham up the narrow staircase, Rowena was pleased to note she had no need to worry the hem of her skirts would be soiled by dust or dirt. She was impressed with the room Grantham escorted her into. A colorful patchwork counterpane rested on a maple chest at the foot of the four-poster bed. Cream-colored curtains like the ones on the downstairs windows were pushed back and the diamond-paned single window had been opened to allow fresh air into the room. A heavy oak cabinet below a framed looking glass held a white crockery washbowl, and brightly colored rag rugs adorned the walls.

A young man with squinting eyes, and clothing so patched he looked like a ragamuffin, jumped up from a stool at the side of the bed. "Lady Rotherby," he said, making an awkward bow that sent his disheveled, straw-colored hair floating about his shoulders.

"This is Wally Shandy, Alice's brother," Grantham said. "He has been sitting with Mister Darnell while Hannah readies our dinner."

Giving Wally a nod, Rowena stepped over to the bed and looked down at Darnell. The youth looked pain free. He actually seemed to have a slight smile on his pale lips. Grantham pulled back the sheet covering him to show the bandages on his chest and arm.

Nodding, Rowena said, "I see I can do nothing here. Let us go back downstairs, and you can tell me what happened."

Upon returning to the hall, Rowena took the seat she had previously been offered and accepted a gold-colored goblet of cider. She guessed the goblet was seldom used, for she saw naught but wooden noggins lining a cupboard shelf. "Thank you, Hannah Burbage. I see you regularly at Sunday services with Goodman Grantham's young son. I applaud your devotion."

"'Tis kind you would notice me and know my name, milady. And yes, Pascal and I attend services as regularly as we can. 'Tis often hard in the winter."

Rowena had taken a sip of the cider while Hannah addressed her. "Oh, my, this is very good," she said and took another sip.

"I sweeten it a bit with honey," Hannah said proudly, "but it must be blended carefully or the honey will simply sink to the bottom."

Raising her eyebrows, Rowena said, "You have blended it well. But now, I would know all you did for Mister Darnell that I may tend his needs."

Hannah smiled. "First I gave him a wee dose of laudanum, and he went right to sleep. Never felt the stitches I put in his arm or his chest."

"I was confused by Selena's note. She said she tripped him, and he fell on his sword." Rowena looked from Hannah to Selena, who was standing beside the table.

"Allow me to explain, Lady Rotherby," Grantham said, with a slight bow at the waist. "To start, seems Lady Selena has a way with the animals."

"Of that, I am well aware," Rowena said.

"Yes, well, when I came out of the barn, a lamb that needed some attention in my arms, my dog Rollo was with me. When he spotted Lady Selena, he made a bee line for her, yapping and his tail swishing. I cannot think why, but Mister Darnell took the dog's eagerness to greet Lady Selena as a threat. He drew his sword, and made to swipe my dog. Had I not had my arms full with the lamb, I might have arrived soon enough to stop him, but my running was hampered. Lady Selena did what she believed she must to prevent Rollo, my dog, from being struck by Mister Darnell. She tripped Mister Darnell, and he fell on his sword. She meant not to hurt Mister Darnell, she meant but to protect Rollo."

Rowena's gaze had traveled back and forth between Grantham and Selena. "Yes, I can see, 'twas an unfortunate event."

"I swear I could not know, Aunt Rowena, that he would fall on his sword. I never meant to harm him. Just, everything happened so fast."

"So it would seem." She looked again at Hannah. "Would you say Mister Darnell is well enough to travel? I would like to take him in my coach back to my house. Not that I in any way think you have not cared for him in the best possible way, but I am certain you have better things to do than wait upon an invalid. Plus, I believe it would be best, did his father visit him at Whimbrel Hall."

"He is plenty fit to travel. I have Wally up there watching him, that I might finish getting dinner. Soon the laborers and the girls working the hemp will be coming in for their dinner, and it not near to ready. So, indeed, 'twould be best does Mister Darnell go home with you. Better for his comfort, is he with people he knows. He will likely sleep all the way back to your house. You but need check no bleeding starts up, then change the bandages come morning. For my poultice, I used bread crumbs and honey, some crushed alder bark, and mashed dandelion leaves. Should keep the inflammation down. Neither wound is deep, but does the poison set in, that is what needs be watched for. Do you have some laudanum, another potion would be good. Keep him quiet through the night so he will not thrash about and reopen a wound."

Rowena smiled at Hannah. "You are very knowledgeable. Indeed, you did what I would have done. I thank you for taking such good care of Lord Edgerton's son. I would guess Lord Edgerton, too, will wish to thank you." Noting Hannah's blush before turning back to Grantham, she said, "Goodman Grantham, I wonder might you, and what was his name, oh, yes, Wally. Might you bring Mister Darnell down. Do you need help, my footman can help you."

"I think we will have no trouble getting him down," Grantham said. "Lady Selena, do you please open the door, and then ask the footman to have the coach door open."

"I will, Calder," Selena said and hurried to do his bidding.

"Might I help in some way," Selena's maid, Alice, asked.

Rowena had not noticed the girl sitting quietly at the opposite end of the table until she spoke. "Alice, yes, you can ride back to Whimbrel Hall with me and help keep Mister Darnell comfortable. Such a day this was for you not to have been about to help ready the house."

"I am sorry, Lady Rotherby," the pretty blond girl said, her blue eyes looking contrite. "I did ask Lady Selena should I not stay and help, but she insisted she wanted Wally's stories written out that she might send them to a publisher in London."

Rowena noted the girl sat with a neat stack of papers, a couple of quill pens, a small knife for sharpening the pens, and a font of ink in front of her. Rowena nodded at the papers. "Those are the stories there in front of you?"

"Yes, milady. Wally, my brother, tells interesting and funny stories, and Lady Selena believes the publisher in London will like his stories."

"Ah, yes," Rowena said, "Goodman Grantham mentioned that Wally, who has been watching Mister Darnell, is your brother?"

"Yes, milady. Wally does whatever work he can find. Right now he is working for Goodman Grantham, but he has worked at harvest times on the Whimbrel manor. Once he helped round up geese for Lord Rotherby that my brother-in-law might take them to market."

Raising her eyebrows, Rowena said, "But my niece thinks he should be writing stories?"

Alice tilted her head to one side then shrugged. "She thinks his stories are good."

"Hmmm. Well, mayhap I may find time to read one tonight. Hard to say with my children returning and with the number of guests arriving today."

Alice dimpled. "That would be kind, Lady Rotherby. Wally would be proud did he know you had read one of his stories."

Rowena returned Alice's smile, then rose when she saw Grantham and Wally carrying a sleeping Darnell down the stairs. Grantham had Darnell's shoulders, Wally his feet. Darnell looked pale, but he appeared to be in no pain and seemed totally unaware he was being transported out to the coach. The footman helped ease him inside and prop him in a corner. Alice, her supplies and Wally's stories tucked in a basket, was handed in and then Rowena.

Selena would follow on her horse and would lead Darnell's. Rowena noted that Selena, before mounting, stopped to talk to Grantham. He smiled at her, then boosted her up onto her saddle. Oh, the way he looked at Selena, and the way Selena looked at him – this was not good. Not good at all. Sighing and settling back into her seat, she knew ere long she would need to pay a visit to Calder Grantham. Good thing these other young men were arriving. A very good thing.

# Chapter 23

Ewen burst into laughter. Seated at the end of the table in his father's stead, he pointed to Selena. "What did I tell the lot of you. Poor Orland has known her little more than a month, and already he is laid up."

Flavia frowned at her brother, and Lord Edgerton, from his seat next to Flavia's mother at the opposite end of the table said, "I hardly find it amusing, Sutherlin. My son could have been much more seriously injured."

"Indeed he could have been," Ewen agreed, "which is just what I have been telling these three dunderheads since we left Lord Tuftwick's. Any man fool enough to think to take Selena to wife, better make a pact with the devil, does he think he can survive the marriage."

"Ewen! That will be enough!" his mother said, her voice like cold steel.

Ewen looked down the table at his mother, saw the look she directed at him and sobered. Raising his goblet of wine he said, "I offer a toast to Orland. May he soon be recovered and in complete control of his senses."

Everyone raised their goblets to Orland, but Flavia saw her mother was still frowning, the toast offering little to mitigate Ewen's previous statements. Flavia looked across the table at her cousin. Seated between Algernon LaBree and Ansel Yardley, Selena should have been blushing a bright red, but instead, she bore an amused smile on her lightly flushing face. Her lively blue-green eyes darting daggers at Ewen, Selena said, "Ah, ha, so you have been singing my praises have you, Cousin." She turned to Yardley. "Has he convinced you that you take your life in your hands do you converse, walk, or ride with me, Ansel?" Raising her eyebrows, she slanted her eyes. "He could well be right."

Ever merry, his dark brown eyes twinkling, Yardley chuckled. "Nay, Selena, I spent a fortnight with you at Crossly Oaks and came to no harm. Fact is, we had a jolly good time. You are good company."

At his comments, Selena's tinkling laugh floated about the table. Her laughter always made others laugh, and Flavia could not help but join in the merriment. She was at first surprised that Yardley and Selena were on a first-name basis, but as they had spent time together at Crossly Oaks, she supposed she should not be surprised. That would be Selena, ever informal. No doubt, Selena would soon be on a first-name basis with LaBree and Preston. Flavia frowned. LaBree, Preston, and Yardley still addressed her as Lady Flavia. She was not sure if that was preferable or not. Certainly it seemed more respectful.

Glancing sideways at Silvester Preston, seated beside her, Flavia noted his amused look as he surveyed the table. She could not help but wonder what he might be thinking. He seemed amused by any number of things in which she could find no humor. Algernon LaBree, on the other hand, was a consummate flirt, and from the moment he was introduced to Selena, he had been plying her with compliments and sallies. Selena had responded with her usual lighthearted laughter that charmed all who heard it, but was she enamored of either LaBree or Preston, or even Yardley, for that matter, she gave no such indication.

Flavia's mother and Selena, having missed their dinner due to Orland's accident, devoured their supper. Flavia noted her mother at least apologized for her intemperance, but Selena, ever a hearty eater, made no excuses for her gluttony. Somehow, none of her three new admirers seemed to take note. Not a one looked askance at her when she took a third helping of the rum-poached peaches.

Despite Ewen's numerous warnings, all three of his friends seemed enthralled by Selena. But then, she could talk of horses, anything and everything concerning horses, from their care and breeding, to the best saddles or bridles for riding or for hunting. Selena knew all about dogs, be they hunters, pointers, or herders, or even just pets. She could converse about hunting, though she abhorred fox hunting, despite acknowledging the animals were a pest to farmers. Even Lord Edgerton, recovered from the shock of seeing his heir injured and lying abed, entered into the various discussions. Selena could even comment on London plays. Her father had taken her to several, and she adored them. Flavia found it unfair. She had never even been to London, let alone to see a play.

With supper ended, Flavia was not surprised her mother suggested they all remove to the parlor. Lord Edgerton made his excuses that he needed to be starting home, but he wanted to see his son once more before he left. Flavia's mother, smiling brightly, escorted him upstairs, while Ewen directed everyone else into the parlor. Tables had been set up, and cards and games set out. Brandy was made available for the men, sherry for the women, but Flavia wanted no more to drink. She wanted her bed.

Cousin Carola had taken her supper in her room and then planned to go right to bed. Flavia wished she could have done the same. She was tired, but she was also leery of her cousin. Selena had caused Orland's injury. What might she do next? And was Orland infatuated with Selena? She prayed he was not. Ewen had been allowed to check in on Orland, but Flavia had been told Orland was sleeping, and 'twas best not to disturb him. One of the footmen would be sitting up with Orland all night in case he should wake and need something or be confused by his surroundings.

That Lord Edgerton seemed to think Orland was in no great danger of dying was a relief to Flavia. She would feel more relieved could she see him for herself. She had not seen Orland in nearly two years. Not since her last sojourn at home before returning to her Aunt Phillida's, where she had been fostered on and off since she was eight. Ewen had been fostered with Aunt Phillida, too, until at sixteen he was sent off to Oxford. Flavia knew her mother had not wanted to foster her and Ewen with their aunt, but her father had insisted. He had been fostered and had learned much from his uncle and aunt that, he believed, he could not have learned from his own parents. Normally, Flavia was fostered for but eight months at a time, but going to and returning from her aunt's involved the long, tedious coach ride from Cheshire to Leicestershire.

Her cousin, Elizabeth, two years her senior, had also been fostered with their Aunt Phillida, but Elizabeth's journey home was short. Elizabeth's home on the Wirral Peninsula was not two days by coach from her aunt's, or one day if traveled by horseback, which Elizabeth often did. Flavia had not been surprised to learn Elizabeth would soon be getting married. Elizabeth was so beautiful, and she had a substantial dowry. No doubt she had had any number of suitors. Over the years, she and Elizabeth had grown close, and Flavia was more than a little disappointed she would not be able to attend her cousin's wedding. But no, she had to stay home and help show Selena how to be a proper lady, that Selena might find a husband. From what Flavia could see this evening, Selena was having no trouble attracting male attention. Mayhap, 'twas as Ewen often said, Selena makes a good comrade but would not make a good wife. LaBree, Preston, and Yardley might be enjoying her company and her bright conversation, but would they become romantically interested in Selena once they knew her better?

Selena's father had chosen to keep Selena and her four brothers at home. He had not wanted them fostered. But had Selena been fostered with Aunt Phillida, mayhap she would not be such a hoyden. Flavia could not imagine Aunt Phillida would have allowed Selena the unrestrained freedom that Selena's father had allowed her.

Sinking back in a corner chair, Flavia watched her vibrant cousin. She and Preston were engaged in a game of backgammon while Ewen, Yardley, and LaBree took up a game of cards. Flavia would not allow herself to be annoyed that no one seemed to notice she had not joined in the entertainment. That was simply normal when Selena was around. The smile on Preston's face told Flavia he found her cousin amusing, but she could not think he was at all interested in Selena in a romantic sense. Selena was no different than Flavia had ever known her to be. She was lively, friendly, and both thoughtful and thoughtless. One could never know what Selena might say next, though she never deliberately meant to offend anyone.

When Flavia's mother joined them, after seeing Lord Edgerton off with his pronouncement he would return early on the morrow, Flavia asked if she might be excused.

"Of course, my dear child," her mother said, pulling Flavia into her arms. "How I have missed you. That you were away from home for near two years this time was entirely too long. However, last year, with that deadly fever sweeping through the shire, we dared not bring you home. Thank God the fever died out and never reached Cheshire."

Returning her mother's hug, Flavia said, "I understand, Mother. I missed you and Father terribly, but Aunt Phillida is such a dear. She and Elizabeth managed to keep me constantly engaged, leaving me little time to be homesick."

Frowning, Flavia tried again to convince her mother to let her go to London for her cousin's wedding. "Mother, is there no way I may attend Elizabeth's wedding. To think she is getting married so far from home, and her mother and father cannot be with her. Surely she would want me to be with her on her special day."

Her mother patted her shoulder. "Flavia, dear, Elizabeth will be much too busy to spend time with you. Not only is she planning her wedding, but she must also furnish and staff the house your father has helped her find. Your Aunt Phillida will be busy helping her, and she will not have the time to be watching over you as well."

"But Father will be there."

"Yes, but he, too, is taken up with Elizabeth's needs. They need a coach and horses and any number of other things. You could not expect your father to entertain you. Besides, he is currently staying in your Uncle Ranulf's apartment, but he must vacate it when Ranulf's family arrives. He will then be staying with a friend." Her mother patted Flavia's face. "Sweetheart, I am sorry, but you will meet Elizabeth's husband in the fall at Selena's brother Giles's wedding, and then Elizabeth will have much more time to spend with you."

Flavia sighed. "Well, I will say goodnight, Mother."

Her mother smiled sweetly. "Goodnight, dear."

Goodnights from Selena, Ewen, and the others followed her out the door. She wearily dragged herself up the stairs and started down the corridor to her room, but as she passed her brother's room, she stopped. Why should she not stop in to see Orland? He was her friend as well as Ewen's. Had she not known him all her life?

Quietly opening the door, she peered into the room. A candle burned on a table next to the bed, and the footman sat half-dozing in a chair not far from the bed. Jerking awake when Flavia entered the room, the footman straightened. "Lady Flavia, do you check on Mister Darnell?"

She smiled. "Aye. How does he?"

"So far he does little but sleep. He woke enough to know his father visited him, but was again asleep before Lord Edgerton was out the door."

Stepping over to the bed, Flavia looked down at Orland. How sweet he looked with a half-smile on his lips, and his dark eyelashes resting on his cheeks. She brushed a lock of hair off his forehead, and his eyes drifted open but seemed not to focus on anything. "Lady Selena," he said. "So good of you to visit me."

"I am not Selena," Flavia said, hearing her disappointment in her voice. "'Tis Flavia. Your longtime friend."

He made no answer. He but drifted back off to sleep.

"Lady Rotherby gave him another dose of laudanum," the footman says. "He would not know who is here or not. 'Tis best that he feels no pain and gets a good night's sleep."

Flavia nodded. "Yes." She looked over at the footman. "He will need his sleep to rebuild his strength. I understand he lost a lot of blood."

"He was bandaged by the time I first saw him, milady, but 'tis so I heard."

She nodded again. "Watch him well."

"I will, milady."

She left the room as quietly as she had entered and slowly trudged down the corridor. When she entered her room, her maid, Gertrude, who had been dozing on the gold tufted daybed, sprang up. "Oh, Lady Flavia, be you ready for your bed?"

"More than ready, Gertrude. Do hurry and help me out of this gown and petticoats and into my nightshift, or I fear I will fall asleep on my feet."

Gertrude had already turned down the bed and laid out the nightshift, so getting Flavia readied for bed took little effort. Climbing into her four poster bed with its pink and gold flowered curtains, Flavia said, "Gertrude, we will not worry about braiding my hair tonight. Just put out the candles and go on to your bed. You may wait until the morrow to put my clothes in the wardrobe. Leave them on the daybed for now. I know you, too, must be exhausted."

"Aye, milady. I am tired." The maid went around blowing out the candles, then with one in her hand to light her way to her cot in the closet off Flavia's room, she said goodnight.

Lying in her bed, her bed that she had not slept in for almost two years, Flavia stared out at the darkness that engulfed her pretty pink and gold room. It felt so good to be home. It was wonderful to see her mother. And her mother told her she was through being fostered. She would not have to leave her home again. She was, after all, eighteen. Old enough to marry. After seeing Orland again, she knew her love for him had not faded. Her only problem was how to win him away from Selena. He seemed besotted.

The good thing was, she doubted Selena had any interest in Orland. If she could but manage not to be trapped into doing something foolish at Selena's suggestion, she believed she could win Orland's love. She was no longer the child he had teased. She but had to make him see her in a different light. And she would. She knew she would.

# Chapter 24

"She has to be a witch, I tell you. Look at the stitches she put in me. Yet I never felt even a prick. Was she not a witch, did she not cast a spell on me, why did I not feel any pain?"

"Probably because I dosed you with too much laudanum, you dunderhead." Selena said. She was standing on one side of Darnell's bed beside her aunt. Darnell's father, Lord Edgerton, was on the other side, looking down at his son.

"Selena! That is no way to speak to Mister Darnell," Aunt Rowena said.

"Oh, he is talking nonsense. He says Calder tried to kill him when Calder was nowhere near him, then he claims Rollo was a wild dog trying to attack me. He knows not what he says!"

Lord Edgerton was chuckling. "Lady Selena, do recall my son has been drugged. He is yet delirious."

"Nay, Father," Darnell said. "I am not delirious. I want Calder Grantham and his witch housekeeper arrested, and that wild dog destroyed. I tell you, I do."

"Orland, I think you forget who is constable," his father said. "Lady Rotherby's son-in-law, Bardwith. He is not apt to arrest Grantham when Lady Selena says Grantham is innocent."

Darnell turned anguished eyes on Selena. "Why do you defend him so?"

"Because he caused you no harm. I am the one who tripped you. I am the one who drugged your drink, that you would feel no pain. Do you wish someone to be arrested, you should be asking to have me arrested."

He shook his head slowly back and forth on his pillow. "Everything is so blurred. I remember the ferocious dog charging you. Grantham carrying something and running …"

"The dog is not ferocious. He was coming to greet me. He likes me, and I like him. And Calder was carrying a lamb and crying out to you not to hurt his dog. I am ever so sorry I tripped you, but you had your sword out and were making to strike the dog. I had to stop you."

"I do believe that is pretty much how it happened," Lord Edgerton said. "I went by to see Grantham this morning to thank him and his housekeeper for taking such good care of you. Grantham described the event in the same manner as Lady Selena. Blamed himself for not dropping the lamb that he could run faster and mayhap stop your sword display. I told him he should not fault himself. I am pleased with the report Lady Rotherby has given me on your wounds. No inflammation is flaring up, and, already, both wounds appear to be healing. Lady Rotherby believes I can safely take you home tomorrow. With your mother away from home, Lady Rotherby wants to keep you here another day to monitor your mending."

Darnell sighed, his slim nose flaring, but his gray eyes showed no luster as he looked from his father to Selena. Selena could not help but feel sorry for him. He wanted to blame someone for the mishap but was having trouble blaming her or faulting himself. Had she been able to reach across the wide, four-poster bed, she would have patted his hand reassuringly. Instead, she softened her voice and said, "You need to stop worrying and rest. Aunt Rowena says your wounds should heal quickly, and you will soon be up and about. Do you wish, this afternoon, after dinner, I will come back and read to you."

His eyes brightened. "Would you? I would like that."

"Then so I shall." She glanced at the door and saw her cousin standing in the entrance. "Oh, look, here is Flavia come to see you. I know she will have much to tell you of her adventures with our aunt in Cheshire, as well as her journey home." She beckoned to her cousin. "Do come in Flavia and see how well Mister Darnell fares."

Flavia entered, and Lord Edgerton stepped aside for Flavia to move next to the bed. She looked lovely, Selena thought. Rested. The dark circles that had been under her eyes the previous evening were gone. Her freshly washed brown hair glowed like a halo on her head, and her soft brown eyes were luminous. She wore a pale yellow bodice and overskirt with the hem of the skirt turned up to reveal a much darker yellow petticoat.

Placing her small hand over one of Darnell's that rested outside the summer quilt, she said, "Poor Orland. You were so brave, I hear. So gallant. How could you have known the dog was not attacking Selena. Certainly, I am glad the dog was not slain, but you must be applauded for your readiness to defend my cousin."

Selena believed Flavia's little speech should have been balm to Darnell's bruised ego, but he was staring at Flavia as though he had no idea who she might be. Finally he said, "Flavia? Gramercy, is that you?"

Giggling, Flavia nodded. "Why, yes, Orland. You cannot say you fail to know me."

"Indeed, you have changed greatly."

"Have I?"

"You look most fetching."

"That she does," Lord Edgerton said. "I believe you will be in good hands with her to entertain you until Lady Selena returns from her ride. Now, I have things I must attend, but Lady Rotherby has invited me to supper again this evening, so I will check on you then, son. I want to hear no more talk of having anyone arrested. Hear me."

Darnell lowered his eyes. "Very well, Father."

Relief flooded Selena. Thank goodness Lord Edgerton had not believed his son's foolish accusations. Hopefully, once the drugs wore off, Darnell would no longer be so confused and would not continue blaming Calder for his injuries.

"So are you riding with us or not, Selena?"

Looking to the doorway, Selena saw Ewen, dressed to ride, his boots newly polished by his manservant, Melvin, his fingers drumming his leg. He had been in earlier, before his breakfast, to check on his old friend, and, Selena guessed, to laugh at him. Ewen was not one to offer sympathy or pity unless he believed it deserved. She had a suspicion, Ewen found Darnell's injuries of his own making.

"I am coming, Ewen. Sorry. Have I kept you waiting?"

"Aye. Do we not leave now, we will be late returning for dinner." He glanced past Selena to his mother and added. "Mother would not like that."

Selena agreed, and said she was ready. She was eager to go riding with Ewen and his friends. Ewen had promised to take them to visit a horse breeding farm in the next parish. The farm also had a straight stretch to race the horses, and after a conversation with Silvester Preston, she was desirous of matching Brigantia against his gelding. That her aunt had no problem letting her go off with Ewen and his friends, relieved her. Especially after the incident with Darnell. She had feared a long lecture, but thus far had not received one. She guessed her aunt had been too busy with Ewen's guests, with Darnell and his father, and with the welcome return of her children. With luck, mayhap the lecture could be avoided altogether.

✿ ✿ ✿

Leaving Flavia to spend time with Orland, Rowena went to her room to change into her riding habit. She was pleased with how pretty and demure Flavia looked. Flavia moved with a fluid grace, her voice was sweet and cultured, she was every bit a lady. The epitome of gracious, young womanhood. Nate's sister, Phillida, could not be faulted in her foster rearing of Flavia.

That Flavia was attracted to Orland was apparent. Rowena liked that. She would be pleased did her daughter marry Orland Darnell and remain close to home. She had no worry Orland's infatuation with Selena was lasting. He would soon tire of Selena's headstrong ways. But Calder Grantham – that was a different matter. Selena must have been seeing much more of Grantham than Rowena had any knowledge of for the two to have exchanged the look she saw pass between them. She had to make certain Grantham knew any alliance with Selena was out of the question.

Rowena still enjoyed riding, and once the footman boosted her into her saddle, she felt a rush of exhilaration race through her. With the footman following behind her, she set off for Grantham's farm. She took her time, letting herself savor the ride, the fresh air, the beauty of the world surrounding her. Luck was with her. Grantham, a tree switch in his hand, was herding a group of calves into a fenced area behind his barn. He saw her ride up, gave her a wave of acknowledgement. With the aid of his dog, he finished herding the calves into the enclosure before joining her.

The footman, having helped Rowena down, led the horses over to the well. Tapping her riding whip into her palm, Rowena awaited Grantham.

"Lady Rotherby," he said, when he joined her, "I have been expecting you."

"Have you Goodman Grantham. Then you know why I am here."

"I think I must. Would you care to come inside?" He looked toward his house.

"No. Thank you. I believe our conversation must be private. Between us alone."

He nodded. "Yes, no doubt you are correct." After wiping his brow on his sleeve, he indicated a large oak tree with a bench under it. "Let us go under the shade. This has been a warm summer."

"Mayhap it seems warmer because you have been working hard," Rowena said, turning and heading for the shade, but she ignored the bench and remained standing. "Are those calves for the market?"

"Aye. I grow a goodly number of turnips now for winter feed, but I can still overwinter a limited number of cows besides my dairy cows. Of course, I also have my horses. Those calves, I will fatten up, and either take to market, or sell them to Guy Hamon."

"You look to have a prosperous farm here, Goodman Grantham."

"Thank you," he said, but made no additional brag.

She liked that. She liked him. Gads, but he was a handsome man. 'Twas no wonder Selena had formed an attachment to him. But that was going to have to end.

"It would seem my niece has become quite familiar with you and your farm."

"She has visited us. Yes."

"I fear she may have formed a fondness for you, Goodman Grantham. You must know that will never do. There could never be an alliance between you and my niece."

Slowly nodding, he said, "Aye. That I know. Lady Selena is bright and lively, and my son adores her, as does my dog. Of that, you are well aware. But I know I am not of her social status. I have thought to but enjoy her company while I might."

"I fear I must ask you to discourage her visits. Do I try to dissuade her from visiting you, she will rebel and be the more determined to see you. Selena is a very unique young woman. She sees things others of her status never see, never notice. She has a heart brimming with love for her fellow man. She is ever wanting to help anyone who looks like they might need saving. Now, she has involved herself in getting a school built in Whimbrel." She shrugged. "That is Selena.

"You have a large farm here. I would think, you could find enough things to busy you, that you would not be to hand, should Selena pay a visit."

His direct gaze met hers. She could easily see how Selena could get lost in his incredible blue eyes. Eyes she had seen dance with life, but now looked sad and dull. "I know what you ask is for the best, Lady Rotherby. I knew it from the beginning. I have been foolish to let it go on. I have much to do in my far fields. They will occupy me for a good many days, I should think."

Rowena half-smiled and patted his arm. "Good. I thank you."

She left him standing under the tree. The footman brought her horse and boosted her onto her saddle. She laid the riding crop gently across her horse's rump, and the horse started off at a trot. Riding past Grantham, she looked down at him. He stood with his back to her, his head slightly bowed. She pitied him. He had obviously fallen in love with Selena. She hoped Selena had not fallen too deeply in love with Grantham.

Thank goodness Ewen had brought his new friends home. They were all handsome, personable, young men. Selena was already on familiar terms with Ansel Yardley. Could be the young men would keep her too occupied for her to mope over Grantham.

She wished her heart was not feeling so heavy.

# Chapter 25

Selena had definitely enjoyed herself, and she was in high spirits because Brigantia had finished in a tie in a race with Preston's gelding. Mares seldom had the stamina of the male horses, but Brigantia had such heart, and she loved to run. Selena had liked the horse breeder they visited and his farm. She had seen a colt she liked exceedingly well. The little fellow, full of frolic, had been chasing about the field, kicking up bits of turf, and annoying his mother, who took a nip at him when he darted past her. Dark brown with black mane and tail, he was beautiful. Just the kind of horse Calder should have, so he and she might go riding together.

She wondered if Calder might need riding lessons, if he was to handle a horse of the young colt's caliber. No doubt he would find such an animal of little use on a farm, but once they were married, income from her dowry property could pay for the maintenance of the colt as well as Brigantia. Of course, a proper stable would have to be built for them, and she would need a groom to see to them and exercise them when she and Calder could not. She was hoping she would be able to get Aunt Rowena's footman, Jimmy.

Jimmy wanted to be a coachman, and Selena supposed she would have to have a coach. It, and the horses to pull it, would have to be housed. She prayed Calder would not find the additions to his farm too upsetting. She smiled inwardly. Did his love for her match hers for him, and from the look he gave her the last time she saw him, she believed it did, she knew he would not object. She had no wish to play the great lady. She wanted the simpler life. She could not give up Brigantia or her rides, but she could easily give up formal dinners and grand entertainments.

"You are lagging, Selena," Ewen said, breaking in on her reverie. "Do we not hurry, we will have no time to freshen ourselves and change for dinner."

Laughing, Selena looked past Ewen to his friends a short distance ahead. "I was woolgathering, Ewen. I was thinking of that colt racing about in the field."

"Aye, he is a fine one, but put your heels to your mare and let us make haste."

Selena did as Ewen advised, and dashed down the road leading back to Whimbrel. She had no wish to be late for dinner and earn a scold from her aunt. At least she could count on her maid, Alice, to have warm water for washing awaiting her, and a clean gown and petticoats laid out on the bed. She wished she could visit Calder in the afternoon, but she had promised she would read to Darnell. Hopefully he would fall asleep, and she could at least get in a walk about the lake before time for supper.

✻ ✻ ✻

Flavia was sorely disappointed in her morning with Orland. She had tried telling him about life at Harp's Ridge with her aunt and about the tiresome journey back to Whimbrel. She had talked about Tuft-wick Hall and how royally Lady Tuftwick had treated her, but Orland had continually interrupted her, asking questions about Selena. She believed he had scarcely heard a word of anything she said unless she was answering one of his questions.

Why he could not see Selena had no interest in him was beyond her. But no, he wanted to know about Selena's family. Wanted to know about her likes and dislikes. What amused her. What made her angry. What made her sad. Flavia was able to answer few of his questions. "Really, Orland, I have not seen Selena in three years. As is, I only see her when our families gather for a reunion at Uncle Kenrick's Walling House near Wallingford in Oxfordshire. I know she likes to ride. She likes to take walks. Animals follow her wherever she goes, does she let them, and small children adore her. I think 'tis her laugh attracts them, and then she will play any manner of game with them. She hates wearing anything pink, she prefers plain hair styles, and she always seems to have a voracious appetite."

After her aggravated speech, he had smiled dreamily, and said, "Oh, she is unique, is she not? I have never known any woman to know so much about horses and dogs."

Flavia frowned. "Yes, well, I will leave you now, Orland, that you may rest before your dinner is brought up to you." Rising, she started to turn from him, but he caught her hand.

"Thank you, Flavia. Thank you for sitting with me."

At his touch, her heart did a little flip. "You are most welcome, Orland."

Then her heart plummeted when he said, "You will remind Selena, she said she would read to me this afternoon."

Eyes narrowed, lower lip pouting, she said, "Yes, Orland, I will remind her." Jerking free from his grip, she turned and flounced out of the room.

Once in the corridor and out of his sight, she leaned against the wall and put her face in her hands. Her cheeks burned, and unshed tears stung her eyes. Oh! The fool! The fool! She straightened and firmed her chin. Well, he could just have Selena. And Selena would make his life miserable. That would serve him right.

With anger filling her heart, she marched to her room to dress for dinner. She would put on a bright cheerful face and would flirt with all three of Ewen's friends. Would serve Orland right did one of them ask her to marry him. By golly, did one of them offer for her hand, she would accept.

❈ ❈ ❈

Calder did his best to hide his misery, but he felt certain Hannah noted his silence at the dinner table. He should be in a good mood. The contract with Buxton was completed. Jared and Abner's son, Lyell, had moved into Buxton's home and would begin work on the sorely neglected property. The hemp was cleaned, beaten to separate the fibers, and hung up to dry. Soon, other than what he kept for himself to make rope, it would be ready for sale. The cows and sheep had been culled, the bee hives were prospering, the manure was spread, and a good start was made on the wood supply needed for cooking and for winter heating. Billy was proving to be a good replacement for Jared, and Pascal was looking forward to having Saturday afternoon free to play with Derwin and Molly.

All was well, yet he could remember no time since his wife died that he had felt more miserable. More lost and dejected. He had not meant to fall in love with Selena. He had but been enjoying her company, her brightness, and then his feelings for her began to deepen. He had known from the start that she was far above him. Never had the thought of marriage entered his mind – at least not until recently, when, in watching her, he began to realize, she had feelings for him. Her aunt had made note of their growing relationship. He had expected Lady Rotherby to object to Selena's visits to the farm.

Lady Rotherby told him plainly, he would not suit. He could never hope to marry Selena. To save them both from pain, he should make himself scarce, avoid any contact with Selena. Oh, but God, that would be hard to do.

❧ ❧ ❧

While half listening to the conversation floating around her, Rowena watched her daughter. Flavia was laughing too gaily. Her face was too flushed, her eyes too bright. She had spent part of the morning with Orland. Apparently, that had not gone well. Orland seemed to fancy himself in love with Selena, and Flavia must have discerned that fact.

Selena did have a way of charming the young men. Older men, too, if Lord Edgerton was any example. Yet, what they found charming about her would not make for a good wife. Selena would ever be more interested in horses, dogs, the outdoors, and fighting injustices wherever she might perceive them to be than she would be in the proper running of a home. The young men might find her entertaining, but Selena would forever be offending their mothers.

Mayhap Arcadia Preston, Silvester's mother, might be accepting of Selena's hoydenish ways. Arcadia had enjoyed her days of formality abandonment when she had dressed as a male youth to help Nate's highwaymen. Arcadia still enjoyed recounting the tales of those adventures. But she no longer rode astride or dressed as a male. She was the wife of a baronet, and she behaved accordingly. She would want Silvester's wife to behave accordingly.

However, despite the fact Silvester seemed to be enjoying Selena, Rowena could see nothing lover-like in his attentions to her. Silvester, as a possible prospect for Selena, seemed highly unlikely. Ansel Yardley seemed taken with Selena, but did he offer for her, how would his parents respond. Rowena was not well acquainted with Ansel's mother, but she understood his mother preferred not to dwell upon her husband's past antics. Rowena knew Ansel's father well, but Ansel's father, too, was a baronet. Would Sir Cyril not want his son's wife to compliment his son's station?

Rowena believed Selena had learned enough that she could run a household. She could direct the servants. She could, mayhap, with the help of a good steward or housekeeper, set a proper table, serve an elegant meal, and seat her guests appropriately by their status, but Rowena doubted Selena would ever be happy doing such mundane tasks. She would want to be riding, or taking walks, or breeding horses or dogs, or any number of other things. What Selena could do, and what Selena would rather do, were two very different things.

On the other hand, Rowena had no doubt Flavia would excel at wifely duties. She would enjoy being the hostess, setting a fine table, and entertaining guests. Any man would be proud to call Flavia his wife. She was pretty. She was accomplished on the pianoforte. Her voice was pleasant, her smile sweet, and thanks to her Aunt Phillida, she was well read. She would be able to discuss numerous authors with her husband – a sure way to while away a winter evening, and to keep a husband at home rather than out carousing. Rowena was a firm believer in a woman's intellectual capacities. After the first bloom of marriage, she believed nothing would drive a husband from his home faster than an insipid wife.

Before she knew it, dinner was ended. Ewen said he was taking his friends on an outing to Rotherby, Selena said she intended to spend the afternoon reading to Orland, but she hoped she could later get a walk around the lake before supper. Flavia said she had letters to write. She needed to thank Lady Tuftwick for her many kindnesses. She needed to thank her sister-in-law, Fonda, for the lovely respite in her home. Carola Mead, feeling rested enough to have joined them for dinner, said she, too, needed to write to her endearing and charming hostesses. So Rowena was left to her own diversion. She decided she, too, would write some letters.

Her first letter would be to her husband. Lord how she missed him. Her bed was so empty without him. Every night, she would curl up beneath the quilts, and clutching his pillow to her breasts, she would let her imagination drift. She would touch herself, dreamily imagining his touch on her skin, his kisses and caresses. Her fingers would ache to feel the hard muscles of his arms and legs and those across his back. After all their years together, she still marveled at his strength. In her musings, his love would surround her, and when they united and became one, they would explode in a galaxy of stars as they soared heavenward together.

The night before he left to return to London that he might aid his niece Elizabeth, their lovemaking had been resplendent. Sitting at her writing desk, her chin resting on her hand, Rowena clasped that night to her heart. It offered some comfort, but not nearly enough. In all the years of their marriage – in all the years since they had first met, this was the longest they had been separated. Once Elizabeth was married, Nate would travel with her and her new husband to Cheshire, first to visit Elizabeth's husband's father, who, coincidentally, was a former member of Nate's highwayman gang. They would then go on to Wealdburh, Nate's family home that dated back not just to the Conqueror, but to the days of Saxon might.

Rowena could not blame Nate for wanting to help Elizabeth. Elizabeth's mother was dying of consumption, and her father, Kendrick, the Earl of Tyneford, would not leave his beloved wife. That was why Nate felt obligated to be at Elizabeth's side, and when necessary, to guide her decisions. He proclaimed, 'twas the least he could do for his brother. But Rowena wondered if her husband knew what hardship it was causing her. She missed him so much, she had considered changing her mind and going to London for Elizabeth's wedding, but reason had prevailed. The trip was long and arduous, she would have little time to actually be with Nate, and they would have the expense of finding rooms, not just for them, but for Flavia and Selena, and Ewen and his guests. She could hardly go off and leave Ewen and his guests at Whimbrel.

Ewen and Ansel, Elizabeth's future husband's cousin, had discussed Elizabeth's wedding. They had given some thought to going to London for the wedding, but Ewen knew he had his other guests to entertain. He had brought them all the way to Whimbrel. Ansel, having ridden with Ewen to collect Flavia in Lancashire, was not that eager to ride to London for a few short days. He would rather see his cousin William when he could actually spend some time in his company.

Rowena was proud of her son. And pleased with Ansel. Both youths showed a good deal of common sense. She approved of Ewen's new choice of friends. Some of Ewen's comrades at Oxford, she had not found to her liking. They had been too rebellious, too reckless. Ewen had once come close to being expelled for a ribald prank. Only his father's intervention, and the payment of a substantial donation to the college library, had kept Ewen in his college. Ewen had completed his four years and earned his BA. Unlike Orland, he would not go on to one of the Inns of Court or Chancery. Nate believed Ewen could learn more of what he would need to know in the management of the manors from his sister Cecily's husband. Come autumn, Ewen would begin his studies with Reynard.

With everyone departed on their missions, Rowena settled down to write her letters. She had much to tell her husband, but mostly, she would tell him how much she missed him. How much she loved him. And how much she looked forward to his return.

# Chapter 26

"Marry you! Good heavens no! Mister Darnell, whatever can you be thinking?" Selena stared down at Darnell who was clutching her hand between both of his. She had finished reading to him and, in preparing to leave, had put aside the book. Looking forward to a brisk walk before supper, she started to rise, but Darnell reached out, grabbed her hand, and made his foolish proposal.

"I love you, Lady Selena. I have never known any woman like you. I believe you have feelings for me as well." His slim nose flared, his round gray eyes, wide and unblinking, he looked trustingly up at her.

She wished he was not looking so vulnerable. Sighing, she attempted to speak gently but firmly. "Mister Darnell, I scarcely know you, nor you me. I have enjoyed your company. You sit a horse well and play a good game of backgammon, and you have a ready laugh, but that is hardly grounds for contemplating marriage."

Hearing a footstep, she glanced over her shoulder and, in considerable relief, saw Darnell's manservant had arrived. "Ah, here is your valet to give you a shave and ready you to join us this evening for supper, now you are feeling more the thing. Soon your father will be arriving, and after supper he will be taking you home with him. Once in your own home, your own bed, you will no doubt come to your senses, and we will hear no more of this foolish idea of yours." Jerking her hand free, she hastily rose.

When he started to protest, she waved her hands. "Nay! No more." Turning, she hurried to the door and stepped aside that a footman might enter. He had a basin of water in his hands and several towels draped over an arm. Ewen's manservant, carrying an armload of clothes, entered behind the footman. With nary a backward glance, Selena scurried out the door.

She hoped Darnell, once fully recovered, would realize he was not really in love with her. 'Twas but the injury talking. No doubt, he would be embarrassed by his foolish proposal. Seeing the door to her cousin's room slightly ajar, she stopped and tapped lightly.

"Come in," Flavia said.

Upon entering, Selena found Flavia reclining on her daybed and gazing out her window. "If you are not a pretty picture," Selena said. "I have come to ask you, if you would like to take a walk around the lake with me."

Looking around, Flavia said, "I thought you were my maid, Gertrude. She was to see if Carola had mended the rent in the flounce on my favorite petticoat. Carola is so handy with a needle. I could have done it, for I am quite good with a needle, too, but I have a blister on my finger from touching the curling iron." She held up her hand to show Selena her injury.

"Oh, when did you do that?"

"This morning. I was wanting to try something new with my hair. I thought if Gertrude could curl the front of my hair and catch it up into the frill on my lawn cap … Ah, but we failed. All I did was burn my finger."

Selena smiled. "At least it is not a bad burn. Did you put balm on it?"

"Of course. I have a salve Carola gave me."

"Good. Did you finish your letters despite the burn?"

"I did." Flavia cocked her head. "Why do you ask?"

"Because if your letters are written, then a mere blister on the finger should not prevent you from coming on a walk with me. It will do you good. You have hardly been out since you returned home."

Flavia shrugged, then brightened. "Mayhap a walk will do me some good. Elizabeth and I used to walk any day the weather was not too inclement." She pouted. "I cannot believe we are not to go to Elizabeth's wedding."

"Hmmm. I know. I would so love to see her again. But we shall have to wait until Giles's wedding, I suppose. You and Elizabeth must have grown very close over the years."

Flavia nodded, her lower lip still in a pout. "We were very close. 'Tis hard to think she is getting married and will be living in London, and I will seldom see her anymore."

"That is sad," Selena said, turning as Flavia's maid entered. "Here is Gertrude. Change your gown and get your walking shoes on. I will do the same and be back here in a thrice."

❦ ❦ ❦

Selena laughed as she and Flavia raced to the far side of the lake. Though Selena won the race, both she and Flavia were panting and giggling. They fell into each other's arms and gasped for air. "Oh, I have not run like that since I left Aunt Phillida's. Elspeth and I used to race after some tedious lesson Aunt Phillida expected us to learn. We needed to run to feel alive again. We particularly abhorred learning to balance the household account."

Selena giggled. "Oh, yes. 'Tis boring, but as I studied with my brothers' tutor, I had no trouble with the sums. 'Twas learning to make beds, and take mincing steps with a book on my head, and learning which earl sits next to which baron that bored me."

Flavia vigorously nodded. "Oh, yes, yes. Indeed, very trying. What Elspeth and I liked best was reading aloud. Aunt Phillida has a good library. As good as Mother and Father's. Elspeth liked any story that revolved around a different time or different part of the world. She envied Ewen being allowed to attend the boy's grammar school in Frodsham. There he learned Latin and arithmetic and some geography. But Uncle Berold taught him to ride, to shoot and to hunt, to use a sword, and to speak clearly with good pronunciation. He said Ewen must be prepared to someday make speeches in the House of Lords. He was forever telling Ewen that to be a good lord and a good neighbor, he should do acts of bounty and charity."

They had started walking as they talked, but Selena stopped when she noted a path on the hillside leading into the woods. She was surprised she had not seen the path before, but when passing the lake, she was either admiring the shimmering water or in a hurry on her way to Calder's. "Where does that path lead?" she asked Flavia.

Flavia frowned. "It slopes down the hill through the woods, but 'tis very steep. Ewen and Orland used to take it when they wanted to stop me from following them around. 'Twas too steep for me to manage. It ends up on the road that leads past White Acres and goes to the Grantham farm." She blushed. "Some of the male servants have been known to use it when they want to take a short cut to White Acres to court one of the milk maids. The path on the other side of the road rambles up a grassy hill and leads right to White Acres."

Selena could picture the hill. She had taken that hillside path with Calder. "So you used to follow Ewen and Mister Darnell about, did you?" she teased Flavia.

Giggling, Flavia said, "Aye, they would put up with me for a while. I had no one else to play with, and I think they felt sorry for me. But sooner or later, they were ready to be rid of me. And this is where they always came. Did no good, did I whine. They would tell me I could come with them, did I want, but they knew, and I knew, I could not navigate that slope. Not in a gown. Mayhap did I wear breeches as they did, but that could not be."

Selena nodded. "We women often have our movements and freedom hindered by our dress. I often wonder if men would fight so many wars did they have to wear gowns and petticoats as do we."

Flavia burst into a fit of laughter. When she regained control of herself, she said, "Oh! I was just picturing Ewen and Orland dressed in gowns. What a funny thought."

Selena joined in her cousin's laughter. "Indeed. They would never be able to manage the flounces. And certainly not these form fitting bodices." She patted her sides, feeling the boned stays. She never laced hers tightly, preferring to breathe properly, but she had seen ladies at court with waists too tiny to be natural. She could not help but pity them. She had been pleased to note, at least for their walk, Flavia was not laced tightly either.

Both she and Flavia laughed some more as they worked their way around the lake. "Do you go with me tomorrow, when I go to Whimbrel Village to talk to the tenants about building the school," she asked.

"Do you ride over?"

"Yes."

"Then, no. I will not go. You know I hate to ride."

"Just because you got thrown that one time?" Selena frowned. "That should not keep you from riding ever again."

"But it does. I could have been killed. I was never so scared in my life. I was sore and bruised for days afterward. Nay. I will not ride."

"I could walk. 'Tis not but little over a mile, but Ewen and his friends plan to ride over, and I mean to ride with them. I wonder, will Ewen be more support or hindrance to me. He has not said does he think my plan is good or not."

"I doubt he cares one way or the other. But you know, Mother seems to approve."

"Yes. I think your mother understands how the school will help more boys get their education. 'Twill be much nicer for the students, come winter."

Flavia nodded. "Yes, I can see it would be. Sometimes it gets quite cold here." She shivered. "It can get cold at Harp's Ridge, too. Sometimes, even huddled close to the hearth, I thought I would near freeze to death. I think winter is my least favorite time of year."

"Mine, too. Except I do enjoy the yuletide celebrations. I am glad the Puritans are not still running the country. So I am told, they abhorred Christmas celebrations."

"Yes, I find that strange," Flavia answered, a thoughtful look on her face. "Why would anyone object to celebrating Christ's birthday? Mayhap it was not the exact day he was born, but I would think everyone, especially the Lord, has the right to a celebration of their birth. Even if not on the exact date."

"I agree. The merrier the celebration, the better. Hmmm. I suppose we should speed our steps. We will need to change for supper."

"Yes." Flavia grabbed Selena's hand. "Thank you for getting me out. This has been lovely. I had forgotten how beautiful my home is."

Selena gave Flavia's hand a squeeze. "Yes, it is lovely. We will walk again soon. I promise."

❧ ❧ ❧

Rowena was pleased Selena had gotten Flavia out for a walk. Her daughter looked much more herself. Normally a cheerful child, 'twas not like Flavia to sulk or pine in her room. The brisk walk had brought a glow to Flavia's cheeks and a sparkle to her eyes. She had dressed carefully, and looked positively radiant. Seated between LaBree and Preston, she flirted prettily, but not immoderately, with both. She was polite to Orland, but otherwise paid him little heed.

Seated across from his father and on Rowena's left, Orland seemed not to notice Flavia's lack of attention. His entire focus was on Selena. How the boy could have formed a tender for Selena, Rowena could not imagine, but she had little doubt Selena would soon disabuse him of his affection. Selena, in a rather unladylike fashion, had plopped herself down in a chair to the right of Ewen before anyone else reached the table. She had then beckoned to Ansel Yardley to sit beside her. He had, of course, readily accepted her invitation. Rowena guessed Selena's actions had been devised as a maneuver to avoid sitting near Orland. Never once did she cast a glance in Orland's direction, unless Orland or his father said something that caught the entire table's attention. She then was forced to look in his direction.

If Orland noticed Selena was avoiding him, he gave no indication. He just stared starry eyed at her and smiled whenever her lively chatter reached his end of the table. Poor boy. Why he could not see Flavia was the girl for him? Well, mayhap, with time he would.

# Chapter 27

Selena was vastly pleased with the reception she received from the Whimbrel villagers and tenants. They all favored building the school. The men even offering to do the labor for free. At least what unskilled labor they could do. All they needed was the materials. The miller's wife said she would be happy to house the schoolmaster. An ample-sized woman, she hated that her young son had to go into Rotherby for his schooling, especially in inclement weather. Her husband, a robust fellow with bright red cheeks, firmed his lips and nodded when his wife made the offer. If it created any kind of a hardship for him, he was not making it known. Selena guessed he had long since given up arguing with his stalwart wife.

The villagers decided the monthly fee the students paid could be used to help pay the miller for the schoolmaster's room and board, and one of the more substantial farmers said he would donate two acres of his land to the schoolmaster, that he could farm and make a little profit on his efforts. The villagers liked the idea of building in brick and were pleased to learn Squire Nibley would engage the masons who had worked on his house to build the school.

Ewen must have been feeling generous, for he swept off his hat, placed it on the floor and threw three shillings into it. "First donation," he said.

His friends, even though they would not benefit from the school, each cheerily tossed in a couple of shillings each. Soon others made penny donations, and Selena headed home with the promise of the new school jingling in her pocket.

On the ride home, she asked Ewen if he would take Wally to Leicester to buy him some spectacles. She had learned from Alice that morning, that Alice's brother in Rotherby had written telling her the spectacle trader had passed through Rotherby several months earlier and was not expected to return in the near future. Was Wally to get spectacles, he would have to go to Leicester. Never having been any farther from home than Rotherby, and being unfamiliar with city shops, Selena believed Wally would need help finding his way around.

Ewen had laughed uproariously at her request. "You want me and my friends to go to Leicester. For shame, for shame, Selena," he joked, then sobered. "Truth be told, we are getting bored, and I was thinking we needed a trip into Leicester. This gives us the perfect excuse, and Mother cannot complain. Who would not want to help Wally. His stories are a delight."

"I was not aware you knew Wally."

"Gramercy, Selena. This is my home. How would I not know the people who live here. Besides, everyone knows Wally. He is not the best worker, but no one cares does he but tell his stories. I cannot think why I never thought of having his stories published. 'Tis a splendid idea. Never thought of getting him spectacles either. I suppose, is he to go to London, we will have to get him some new clothes as well. Cannot send him off in the rags he usually wears."

"Oh, Ewen, you are wonderful! Thank you. I knew I could count on you."

He shrugged. "'Tis nothing, Selena. What I would have done that time in London had you and Reggie not been there to come to my aid… Well, I know not what I would have done."

"Tell us more about this Wally," Ansel said. "He sounds a character."

"Oh, he will regale us with stories all the way to Leicester," Ewen said with a chuckle. "Though I am not sure he has ever been on a horse, I suppose we will have to find him a mount. Hope he can stay on the horse all the way to Leicester."

When they arrived back at Whimbrel Hall, Flavia and her mother were waiting to discover the outcome of the meeting. "Could not have been better," Selena declared, and pulling the coins from her pocket, she held them out to her aunt. "Look, we have already collected our first donations."

"I must find you a strong box for your donations, and a ledger book" Aunt Rowena said. "You will need keep a good accounting of all you collect and all you spend. 'Twill be a good lesson for you. Come up to my room, and I will see can I find a box for your collections."

Selena followed her aunt upstairs as Flavia ordered ale for her brother and his friends and then followed them into the parlor. They would no doubt engage in a game of cards or some such until time to change for supper. Selena enjoyed sharing laughs with her cousin and his friends, but she was sorely missing Calder.

The following day being Sunday, she knew the routine – church then dinner with Cecily and her family. 'Twould be Monday before she could see Calder. She had never guessed love could be so wonderfully beautiful and yet so exquisitely painful. She could better understand how her Aunt Rowena must feel having Uncle Nate gone for such a long time. It must be how her mother felt when her father had to go to London at the King's request or to attend parliament. Smiling inwardly, Selena was glad Calder would never be obliged to go off to London to attend Parliament. Indeed, there were many benefits to not being a member of the peerage.

❧ ❧ ❧

Selena knew that by helping Wally go to Leicester with Ewen to purchase spectacles, she would be taking Wally away from Calder, and Calder needed Wally to milk his sheep. She hated to hurt Calder in any way. Having completed setting up her ledger book, she discussed her dilemma with Alice, and Alice came up with a solution Selena felt certain would work. One of the young women from Whimbrel village, who had helped work the hemp for Calder, had experience milking sheep. Alice believed the young woman, Hermia, would be pleased to get the extra work. It would give her more toward her dowry.

Buoyed, Selena wrote a note to Hermia asking would she be willing to do the work until Wally could return, and she wrote a note to Calder asking if he would be willing to have Hermia fill in until Wally could return. Giving a note to each of her aunt's footmen, she bid them return as soon as possible with the answers. Ewen was set to go to Leicester on Monday.

Aunt Rowena graciously agreed to allow Wally to ride one of their older, more docile horses and was furnishing the saddle. Like Ewen, Aunt Rowena hoped Wally, unused to horses, would be capable of riding all the way to Leicester without causing numerous delays. Ewen and his friends would be staying in Leicester, enjoying its entertainments for a couple of days, so Wally would stay with them. Selena reasoned it would be a good experience for him, especially should he secure employment in London with the publisher.

Selena had sent two of Wally's stories to Giles's friend in London but had yet to hear back from the publisher. She hoped the stories would be accepted, otherwise, she was putting everyone to a lot of trouble. Even worse, she was raising Wally's hopes. She would hate for his hopes to be dashed. But if the publisher did want the stories, and wanted more stories, he could, in fact, want to meet Wally. How Wally could go off to London on his own worried Selena, but she decided that possibility would have to be handled, did the need arise.

Pushing her speculative worries to the back of her mind, she finished dressing for supper, and hurried downstairs to the parlor. She found everyone awaiting her. Apologizing for her tardiness, she took Ansel's arm and let him lead her into the dining parlor.

❦ ❦ ❦

Calder had returned from plowing a far field when Jimmy arrived with Selena's note. Abner, being near to hand, agreed to put the horses away so Calder could attend to the missive, as Jimmy had assured Calder, he was expected to await an answer. Calder was thrilled to receive a note from Selena. It might not have been a love missive, but it was written in her hand, and it had started out with a Dear Calder. He thought her plan to have Hermia milk the sheep until Wally returned was suitable, but in his return note to her, he told her even could Hermia not take Wally's place, he would find someone to do the milking. What was most important was to get Wally the spectacles.

Never having been further from home than Rotherby, Wally, hearing of his proposed expedition, was fearful yet excited about going to Leicester. As directed in the note, he was to be at Whimbrel Hall by ten of the morning on Monday to set out with Lord Sutherlin for Leicester. Though he had seldom been on a horse, he hoped he would manage the ride without causing undo delay to his companions.

For Calder, the best thing about the note was Selena's assurance she planned to visit come Monday afternoon. He knew Lady Rotherby would expect him to absent himself, but that he would not do. He had to see Selena at least one more time before he cut off contact with her.

Pascal, too, was missing Selena, and at the supper table, news that Selena planned to visit Monday brought a pleading request he be assigned chores closer to the house that he might enjoy her visit. "Oh, please, Father, I have missed hearing Lady Selena's laugh. Today I was telling Molly and Derwin about her laugh. How it sounds like bells tinkling, and no one can help but join in her laughter. They want to meet her."

"No doubt one day they will," Calder said, ruffling his son's hair. "Did you enjoy your afternoon with Molly and Derwin?"

"Oh, yes, Father. We played tag and blind man's bluff, and then two of the Huddleston tenants' children completed their chores and were allowed to join us. We made Molly the princess queen, and we had to kill the dragon who kept her in his castle. Oh, it was great fun."

"'Tis only right at his young age he be allowed to play a bit," Joseph said. "I can remember times my father would give me a pat on me buttocks and say, 'Go take the dogs for a run, or 'tis hot, go cool off in the pond. Then off me brother and I would go." Chuckling, Joseph shook his head. "Come the next day, we always worked that much the harder. Sort of a thank you for the respite, I suppose."

"Aye," Hannah said. "Never hurts the young folk to have a little freedom. But Pascal, we will be off to church tomorrow, so you best be finishing your supper. 'Tis early to bed for you."

Pascal frowned, then brightened. "Oh, aye. We are like to see Lady Selena, are we not?"

"Most like we will," Hannah said, "but you are not to be pestering her. She will be with her family. I understand Lady Flavia has returned home. They have any number of gentlemen guests as well."

Pascal frowned, but Calder said, "Hannah is right. You are not to pester Lady Selena. You may work near to the house come Monday. Soon enough to get to see her."

"Yes, Father," Pascal said, then asked, "Might Wally give us a story ere I go to bed?"

"Oh, that would be great," Billy said. "'Tis good fun to hear Wally's stories."

Calder smiled at Abner's son. He looked like his father, thin and wiry, but without his father's stooped shoulders or tired eyes. The boy was still full of life and vigor. "On the morrow, Billy, your father is borrowing the cart and will take your mother and sister to services in Rotherby. He asked could you go with them. I told him both you and Lyell could go. From here on out, I see no reason you cannot spend part of Sunday with your family. Just get the feeding done early so you can clean up before your father arrives."

"Thank you, Calder," Billy said, a wide smile stretching across his sun-bronzed face. "I cannot say I care that much for the services, but 'twill be good to see my mother."

"Did you pay heed to the preaching," Hannah said, "and not be looking about, you would get more out of it."

Abashed, the boy ducked his head and nodded. "Aye, but there be some right pretty girls to be looking at. And I am not seeing pretty girls all that often."

Calder joined Joseph and Wally in their laughter, and Joseph said, "Aye, and all dressed up in their best finery. When I was a lad, and my mother made me go to church with her, I thought looking at the girls was the best part of the services."

Wally agreed with Joseph, and Hannah told them all to hush. They were being disrespectful to the Lord and supplying Pascal with very poor examples.

Calder agreed. "Hannah is correct." He looked at his son. "You had best not be repeating this nonsense to Molly and Derwin tomorrow. You would be embarrassing Hannah."

Pascal shook his head. "No, Father, I will not say a word."

"Good boy," Calder said. He would not want Avis Huddleston to think he was putting disrespectful ideas into Pascal's head. He was grateful to the Huddlestons that they took Hannah and Pascal to church with them in their large wagon. It allowed him to loan his cart to Abner, and it saved him having to make the trip into Rotherby. Saved him from attending services, too.

With the meal ended, Pascal helped Hannah clear the table, and Joseph and Billy filled three large buckets full of water, ready to be heated for the morning ablutions. Calder settled back with his pipe, the one smoke he allowed himself each day, and with Hannah washing up the dishes and readying meal preparations for the morning, Wally began telling one of his stories.

Calder liked Wally's stories, but this evening his mind was not on the story. It was on Selena. He had not seen her since Orland Darnell's accident. He had heard Darnell mended fine, but he had also learned that when Ewen D'Arcy, Lord Sutherlin, returned to Whimbrel Hall, he brought three handsome, fun-loving gentlemen with him. Calder was jealous. He knew he was, and he wished he could push such foolishness from his mind. But he could not help but wonder if Selena was attracted to any of the gentlemen. He would picture her laughing with them, mayhap playing cards or some game with them, sitting next to them at the table as she had sat next to him at his table. Such thoughts sent pangs through his heart, but he could not keep them at bay, try as he would.

Come Monday, he would see her again. Would that soft gleam he was certain he had seen in her eyes when she looked at him still be there? Or had he imagined that gleam because he knew that gleam shone in his eyes when he looked at Selena. Lady Rotherby had seen the way he looked at Selena and had reminded him of his place. He could never hope to marry Selena, but he could love her from afar. That he could do, and he feared he would not soon recover from the love that twisted his heart with such sublime pain. No, he would not soon recover.

# Chapter 28

With services ended, Selena, following behind her aunt and cousin, stopped at the church door to praise the vicar. She talked to him about the progress she was making on the school for Whimbrel Village. She next greeted and talked to the Nibleys and several other local gentry families. She talked to Avis Huddleston and to Hannah and gave Pascal a little hug and told him how much she had missed seeing him. That brought a bright grin to his face. She received a boisterous greeting from Lord Edgerton who proclaimed his son now fit as rain. Lord Edgerton then engaged Aunt Rowena in a dialogue while a pretty girl with blond curls and blue eyes dragged Flavia off for a chat.

Seeing Cecily waiting by Aunt Rowena's coach, Cecily's own coach with her brood inside already headed for home, Selena started to join Aunt Rowena's older daughter, but she was halted by Darnell stepping in front of her. Annoyed, but putting on a pleasant smile, she said, "Mister Darnell, indeed, you are looking as fit as your father declared. I believe, did Ewen know you would be here, he might have left his friends sleeping or idling about and come with us to services. As is, I imagine they are only now crawling out of bed. They stayed up late last night. Long after Aunt Rowena and Flavia and I went to bed. I heard a lot of laughing and carousing before I fell asleep. But as Cecily expects Ewen to bring his friends and join us for dinner, they must be up by now."

Selena was chattering away, hoping to forestall any more declarations from Darnell, but he grabbed her hand and said, "Lady Selena, would you do me the honor of going riding with me tomorrow afternoon?"

She shook her head. "Nay, Mister Darnell. I have plans for tomorrow. Ewen and his friends are leaving for Leicester for a brief stay, and I mean to see them off. I have my lessons with Aunt Rowena, and then I have some letters I must write ere my mother and my new sister-in-law think I have forgotten them. After dinner, I mean to walk to the Nibleys, stopping by the Grantham farm on the way. I have much to attend, am I to get construction on the school in Whimbrel Village underway." Pulling her hand away, she said, "I have a splendid idea. You should go with Ewen and his friends to Leicester. Do you wish, I will tell him you would like to join them." She smiled brightly, pleased with her idea of ridding herself of Darnell.

"No. I have no wish to go to Leicester. Lady Selena, I must speak with you again. In private. I feel I bungled my proposal, and I know …"

Selena was not about to allow him to continue. "That is enough, Mister Darnell. I see my aunt beckoning to me. I must go. Good day to you." Before he could protest or again clasp her hand, she darted around him and joined her aunt at her coach.

Flavia arrived at the same time, and Cecily gave her sister a big hug. "Dear Flavia," she said. "'Tis grand to have you home. We will not be letting you go off again any time soon."

Flavia smiled and said, "Mother says I am not to return to Aunt Phillida's. She believes I have learned enough to be capable of managing a home and a family."

"Indeed, I have no doubt but Mother is right," Cecily agreed, before she and Flavia were handed into the coach behind Selena and Aunt Rowena. Once they were all four settled with their skirts squashed about them, the coach lurched forward, and they were on their way to Cecily's house for dinner and no doubt games afterward.

"Who was the girl you were talking with?" Selena asked Flavia when a bump in the road momentarily interrupted conversation.

"Suzanne Sizer. We have long been friends. She is a year older than I am."

"Doctor Sizer is the local physician," Cecily said. "His wife died a year ago, and Suzanne is only now coming out of mourning. It was a sad time for her and her father and younger siblings. Suzanne, as the eldest, has had to shoulder much of the running of the home. Fortunately, they have a competent housekeeper. Am I not mistaken, Reynard told me Doctor Sizer told him that his sister, who recently lost her husband, is going to come stay with them. Though 'tis sad Doctor Sizer's sister lost her husband, her presence will allow Suzanne to resume a more normal life."

"Poor dear," Aunt Rowena said. "Her mother was not well known to me, but we always spoke, did we encounter one another in a shop."

"I told Suzanne, once I was settled, I would invite her for dinner," Flavia said. "Mayhap while Ewen's friends are still visiting, Mother, is that convenient to you."

"Yes," Selena interrupted. "That sounds lovely. It will give Algernon …" She shook her head and rolled her eyes. "Yes, Aunt Rowena, I know I am too informal. Forgive me. I should say, it will give Mister LaBree another girl to flirt with." She giggled. "He does manage to say the prettiest things, does he not, Flavia. He looks up with those bright blue eyes and pretends he means every word."

Cecily joined in Selena's laughter. "You are saying he is only pretending?"

"She is right," Flavia said. "Mister LaBree is delightful, but he flirts with every woman he encounters. He is ever so sweet and considerate, but he seems to love to flirt."

"He is charming, I will agree to that," Aunt Rowena said. "And I see no reason we should not invite Mistress Sizer to dinner once the gentlemen have returned from Leicester."

Flavia clapped her hands, and Selena said, "Did we invite Cecily and Reynard, and mayhap the Edgertons and Nibleys, we could have a party to truly welcome Flavia home. I would think Brilliana is old enough to join us. We could even have dancing." She looked pleadingly at her aunt. "What do you think, Aunt Rowena?"

Aunt Rowena cocked her head to one side and eyed Selena warily. "Have you a reason other than welcoming Flavia home that you are wanting this party, Selena?"

Selena giggled. "Yes, but I would as soon not confess the reason."

Cecily issued an unladylike guffaw. "Selena, you do slay me. Who else would dare admit to a hidden agenda. Not be willing to confess it. Yet still expect to get your wish."

"Well," Flavia said, "I think even if Selena does have a hidden agenda, that her idea is lovely. I would enjoy a party."

"Then you shall have one, my daughter," Aunt Rowena said. "I had meant to have a party for you anyway. You and Selena may make out your guest list, but I want no more than ten extra guests besides Ewen's friends for dinner. Do you wish to invite others to come later in the afternoon for games and dance, that will be fine. Once we decide on a date, I will have to see about hiring some musicians."

Selena was pleased her aunt had so easily acquiesced to her plan. She believed the surest way to turn Darnell's attentions away from her and toward Flavia was for Darnell to see Flavia at her loveliest. She had not a doubt but what Flavia was in love with Darnell. Why Darnell could not see Flavia would be the perfect wife for him, Selena could not comprehend, but she was determined to do all in her power to point the fact out to him.

She would ask Ansel to pay particular attention to Flavia. Ansel was a good sort. He would enjoy helping make Darnell see Flavia as the young woman she now was, not the little girl that had tagged around after him and Ewen. Yes, a dinner, then a party afterwards with music and dancing, should be just the thing to open Darnell's eyes.

❦ ❦ ❦

Rowena sat back in the plush, high-backed chair and enjoyed the laughter floating around her. Cecily had outdone herself with the dinner she served, and Ewen's three guests had been eloquent in their myriad compliments. After dinner, everyone retired to the parlor, and the young people were engaged in several different games, some playing cards, some backgammon. Selena was enmeshed in a game of chess with Cecily's husband. The girl had a calculating mind, Rowena thought with a silent chuckle. No wonder she liked chess, and was good at it.

Reynard was a good challenge for her. Having a lawyer's mind, he too could be calculating. That Reynard came from yeoman stock had never troubled Rowena. He had gone to Oxford and then attended Lincoln's Inn and had been called to the bar. He had chosen to return to Rotherby, though much of his practice was based in Leicester and Melton Mowbray, and he had to make occasional trips to London. When Reynard and Cecily met, soon after he returned to Rotherby, love had quickly blossomed. Being a barrister, he was a member of the gentry, even if his father was naught but a farmer. Reynard inherited his father's freehold, which meant he had property in the country as well as a home in town. So despite his background, Rowena had had no trouble giving her consent when Reynard asked for her daughter's hand.

But Calder Grantham was different. He was not a member of the gentry. He was naught but a farmer, had never gone beyond grammar school. He had never been exposed to the social etiquette expected in the homes of the gentry. His education being limited, his conversation would be limited. His world revolved around his farm. That he was a good man, Rowena had no doubt, but that he was not suitable for Selena, she knew, too.

She wished Selena would show some interest in one of Ewen's friends. Selena was enjoying their company, but if she was attracted to any of them, she gave no indication. That Ansel Yardley and Selena had formed a friendship was obvious, and given some encouragement, Ansel might become more romantically inclined toward Selena, but Selena offered him no such enticement. Hopefully, as Selena became more involved in getting her school built, she would forget about Grantham. Surely he had been but a brief diversion, a means of alleviating the boredom of her lessons.

Was Nate home, Rowena believed he would know better how to handle the situation. But near two months would pass before her husband returned to her. Her last letter from him told her of the house Elizabeth and her soon-to-be husband William had selected. Nate had also helped William choose a coach and horses. That Elizabeth had been in yet another mishap had Rowena concerned, but Nate assured her all was well, and he would relate all to her when he returned. In an earlier accident, Elizabeth had almost drowned, but the circumstances surrounding the incident had been kept quiet so not to harm Elizabeth's reputation. Apparently this new mishap would also be kept secret.

Considering these developments revolving around Elizabeth, Rowena was all the more glad she had not allowed Flavia to go with her Aunt Phillida and Elizabeth to London. Rowena had never liked London and never liked going there. She went on occasion with Nate when he was needed by the King in the House of Lords, but more often, when Parliament was in session and Nate had to attend, she had stayed at Nate's older brother's Walling House in Oxfordshire. Before her illness, Kenrick's wife, Blanch, had also stayed there. Wallingford, not being but a two day journey from London, Nate and Kenrick had been able to join their wives at every opportunity, so their separations had never been of long duration.

Rowena knew Blanch was dying. She would never see her friend again. Never share laughs and stories about their children. Hopefully Blanch would live long enough that Elizabeth would have one last chance to see her and present her husband to her mother. What a sad but sweet final meeting between mother and daughter that would be.

Giving her head a little shake, she chased the morose thoughts away. Better she should enjoy the gaiety of the young people. As their laughter and chatter bubbled up around her, she basked in her own good fortune. A wonderful husband, five healthy children, and eight delightful grandchildren. She could hardly ask for more.

Well, she could ask that Selena bring no more calamities down on her house. With her desire for the party to celebrate Flavia's homecoming, Selena was up to something. Rowena could but pray it would not lead to another harmful incident. Pray it should not involve the Edgertons.

# Chapter 29

After seeing Ewen and his friends and Wally off on their visit to Leicester, Selena and Flavia sat down together in the family parlor to make out their list of guests for the party. Their dinner guests had already been determined, but Selena convinced her aunt they should invite the vicar and his wife. Aunt Rowena complained it would crowd the table, but she at last relented. After all, they did need the vicar's help in promoting donations for the school.

Flavia, knowing most of the gentry families in the parish and surrounding area made out most of the list. "I suppose you intend to talk to them about this school you want built," Flavia said with a slight frown.

"I will, and Mistress Nibley will, and if the local gentry see the vicar approves, that should encourage them to be generous in their donations. I would think, they would want a school closer to hand for their tenants' children."

"I suppose you could be right. Myself, I just mean to enjoy myself. Mother says, as the weather has been so warm, we may set up tables and chairs outside, and have the parlor doors open so the music floats outside, do couples choose to dance on the terrace. I do love to dance."

Selena laughed and agreed dancing was fun. She but hoped her plan to make Darnell see how suited Flavia was for him would be a success. She determined she would make certain she did nothing to show herself off to advantage. She would pull her hair starkly back from her face. She would wear her least flattering gown. Did she dance with Darnell, she would make certain she stepped on his feet as often as she could. She also intended to make certain that, at dinner, Flavia was seated between Darnell and Ansel Yardley.

Their list completed and initial plans made, they sat down to dinner. Aunt Rowena praised them for their industry. "You two have done a good job. I will go over your list and plans, and we can discuss them at supper this evening. If I find no fault with anything, you may start writing the invitations tomorrow."

"Thank you, Aunt Rowena," Selena said.

"Yes, thank you, Mother," Flavia added. "Do you realize, Mother, this will be my first dance in my own home?"

"Yes, dear. I know. 'Tis sad to think your father will not be here for you, but it cannot be helped. However, when he returns, we will have another party. Another dance. But, we must visit the seamstress in Rotherby. You both shall have new gowns for the party."

"Oh, no, Aunt Rowena," Selena said. "I prefer to wear one of the gowns I already have. Mother had so many gowns made for me before I came here. I need not have a new one. I stood for enough fittings. You saw all the trunks I brought."

Aunt Rowena laughed. "Well, yes, you did come with quite a wardrobe. Very well, if you have no wish for a new gown, that will be fine. Mistress Sloan will need only make one for you, Flavia. Mayhap, we shall have her make a couple of day gowns for you as well. And you will need a new cloak for this winter. We should get her started on these things."

Flavia was beaming with the thought of the new gowns, but Selena could only be happy she was not again having to endure fittings for gowns she had no desire to wear.

When dinner ended, she convinced Flavia to join her in her visit to the Nibleys and to Calder's. Aunt Rowena encouraged Flavia, telling her the walk would be good for her. "I would like to ask after Maris Nibley," Flavia said. "She was ever a quiet girl, but I liked her."

"Presently she is living in London with her grandparents – her mother's parents," Aunt Rowena said. "But do ask after her. 'Twould be nice to know how she fares. Sadly, I failed to ask after her, as I should have when we dined with the Nibleys."

"Let us change and be on our way," Selena said, rising, and Flavia followed suit. Soon they were out the door and striking off across the meadow leading to the woods. Stopping to pick up the walking stick Calder had given her, Selena said, "'Twas given me by my friend Calder Grantham. We will visit his farm after we visit the Nibleys."

"I know Calder Grantham," Flavia said. "Or at least, I know who he is. My maid, Gertrude, thinks he is the most handsome man she has ever seen. I will say, though I have but seen him from a distance, he seems agreeable."

Selena laughed. "He is, yes, he most certainly is." Before Flavia could comment on Selena's enthusiasm, Selena said, "We best walk in single file here as the trail is more narrow."

"You seem to know this path well," Flavia said, falling in behind Selena.

"Yes, I like to walk it. The trees are young, your father having replanted after selling off a good portion of this section of the woods, so he told me. But the new trees have leafed out beautifully, and they cast pretty dancing shadows over the path."

"Aye, it is lovely in here," Flavia agreed. "The trees have truly grown a lot since I was last home. I can remember when many of these trees were but tiny saplings. Father's steward was ever being so caring of them. Once he gave Ewen a good scolding for pulling on one when he and Orland were racing around."

"I have yet to meet your father's steward," Selena said. "Uncle Nate said he sent him, as he does twice a year, to check on his other two manors. The ones left to him by his mother, our grandmother, whom we never met because she died when I was but two, and you may not even have been born yet."

"Yes," Flavia said, "those manors are so far away. Sutherlin Castle is in Yorkshire and Medford Crossing is in Northumberland. I have never been to either manor, but Father has taken Ewen to both, as he will one day inherit them. Ewen said Sutherlin Castle is a cold and uncomfortable place, but at least it is not desolate like Medford Crossing. He said there is nothing at Medford Crossing but an ancient blockhouse and

a multitude of sheep. I shiver just thinking of either place. I am glad
Father never took me to visit them. Mother has seen both, but she never
visits them anymore."

Selena shrugged. "My mother can never visit any of her manors anymore. Before the accident, we went a couple of times to her house in
Bath, and several times to the tiny but lovely manor in Buckingham-
shire. The house and gardens there are like a fairyland. Reggie and I
stopped there one night on our trip here. I have been to the Lincolnshire
manor I will inherit but once. I cannot say I found it appealing in the
least."

"At least your dowry is fixed. Father has not yet determined mine. Or
if he has, he has not told me about it."

"Never fear, your father will see you have a suitable dowry."

"Yes, I know you are right. I but wish I knew what it will entail."

Selena glanced over her shoulder and pointed ahead. "We are almost
to the bower. That is midpoint on the trail before we go down the hill.
'Tis a good place to rest if you are tired."

"Nay. I am not tired. It feels good to be walking again. I walked
some when at my brother Milo's house, but Fonda was so busy with
upcoming plans for some remodeling Milo and she are to have done,
that I wanted not to press her. And Godwin and Mary's baby, Emil, is
already cutting his front teeth. He was so cranky, and Mary was worrying about him. I could not expect her to take long walks. I did walk
some with my maid, Gertrude, but 'tis not the same."

"Aye" Selena agreed. "From what I have seen of Gertrude, she is
quite sweet, and she does lovely things with your hair, but I cannot
think her the best at conversation."

"You are right. Gertrude is a dear, but she has had little education.
Not her fault, of course. Her family did the best they could by her,
and she is skilled in caring for my needs, but she can talk of little but
the weather, or the pretty birds she so loves, or the gossip of the other
servants. Aunt Phillida said I should never encourage the servants to
gossip."

"Oh," Selena said with a laugh, "then I would be in trouble with Aunt
Phillida. I love to hear any little on-dits from the servants."

Flavia giggled and flushed. "Oh, Selena, I do, also. And I am always so ashamed for letting Gertrude go on. But I let her, and then pretend to chastise her. I am horrid."

Stopping as they entered the small clearing with the sunlight drifting through the overhanging trees, Selena turned and hugged her cousin. "Flavia, you are always so delightful. I love you. I will bet you Elizabeth listens to her maid's gossip as much as you and I do."

Flavia returned the hug then pulled away and giggled again. "I know she does, because she and I used to discuss what our maids told us."

Laughing in unison, Selena and Flavia crossed the bower side by side, then Selena set out in the lead again. Selena was pleased Flavia had no trouble keeping up with her, and soon they had hopped across the stream and were headed down the hill toward Calder's farm and the path that led to the Nibleys'. Selena pointed out Calder's neat stone house and outbuildings to Flavia, then turned west toward the Nibleys' manor.

By the time they reached the Nibleys' property, and passed the fields and tenants' homes, both were feeling thirsty and looking forward to their visit with Mistress Nibley. As they grew close to the house, the dogs in the kennel set up a sorrowful howl, and Selena knew she would have to visit the animals.

"I do wish you were not so appealing to animals," Flavia said, following Selena to the kennel. "Every time I go out of the house, a couple of dogs, that barn cat, and a pesky rooster are under foot. I nearly tripped over the cat today."

"I love the dear creatures," Selena said as they neared the kennel, and the dogs' jubilance became even louder. The dogs bounced around their pen, their tails spinning in circles. Leaning over the fence to scratch the ears of one of the dogs, Selena said, "This is really too much. You need to calm down. I am but visiting your mistress, and you are all being much too exuberant."

The kennel man, Deaver, arrived, and tugging off his cap said, "Lady Selena, I see these cur have noted your arrival."

"They have, and I have given each of them a pat and bade them calm down. My cousin, Lady Flavia, and I are here to see Mistress Nibley, but the dogs were so boisterous, I had no choice but to greet them." She was pleased the dogs had stopped their howling and seemed content with having their ears scratched and heads given a pat.

"I apologize for their behavior," Deaver said, but Flavia sniffed. "You need not apologize. 'Twas nothing you could have done to prevent it. My cousin is a magnet to animals." Grabbing Selena's hand, she said, "Come. Let us go inside. I am thirsty."

The dogs set up a whine when Selena left but did not resume the loud sorrowful howling. Hurrying around to the front door, they were greeted by a footman who took them immediately into the parlor where Claudia Nibley graciously welcomed them. "I am so glad you came today, Lady Selena," Mistress Nibley said, her expressive brown eyes sparkling. "I have arranged for you to address the tenants this Wednesday after their dinner. I thought, did you have dinner with us, you could then go out to speak to the tenants. They are to gather in the courtyard after they have eaten. They know the speech is concerning the school in Whimbrel."

"That is wonderful," Selena said, accepting a glass of ale from the footman.

Flavia had already received her glass and was thirstily, if daintily, sipping the creamy liquid. Her thirst quenched, she asked after Mistress Nibley's step-daughter, Maris.

"We receive a dutiful letter from her once a month," Mistress Nibley said, "but the squire wishes she would come home for a visit. I know he misses her. His son, Giffard, who has been at school in Eton, should have come home a month ago, but he instead asked to visit his grandparents and sister in London. My husband felt he could not refuse the request."

"Well, Mistress Nibley," Flavia said, "do you give me Maris's address, I will write to her and tell her I hope she will come back for a visit. I would enjoy seeing her. I have not seen her in any number of years, and I always enjoyed her company. And I will tell her how gracious and helpful you have been to Selena and her school project."

Mistress Nibley beamed. "Oh, Lady Flavia, that would be lovely of you. I fear I have not done enough to encourage her to return."

"'Tis not always easy to come in as a second wife, I am guessing," Selena said with a soft smile. She was proud of Flavia. Offering to write Maris and to stress her approval of Maris's step-mother was most kind. Mistress Nibley's appreciation of Flavia's offer was palpable.

"On to other news," Mistress Nibley said, "I am guessing that, even as we speak, my husband is talking with Lady Rotherby. He intended to take the head mason to meet her, and to get her permission to show the mason the site of the Whimbrel church, or rather future school."

Selena clapped her hands. "How splendid! I am sorry I have missed meeting the mason, but once we have the funds raised, and he starts work, I would guess I would see him often."

Almost bouncing on her chair, Mistress Nibley said proudly, "I have secured pledges for funding from the Elliotts, the Adkins, the Meyers, and the Brenners."

"Have you truly!" Selena said, giving her own bounce on her chair.

Nodding vigorously, Mistress Nibley added, "And, they have all agreed to spread the word to their tenants. I told them even a single penny from each and every tenant would add up."

"So right you are," Selena agreed. She had known, she made the right choice in picking Mistress Nibley to head up the drive. She recognized the names of the families Mistress Nibley had contacted. They were all members of the local gentry and were on the list of guests for Flavia's welcome home party.

"I finished the book you loaned me," Mistress Nibley said, "and I have started another. 'Tis one from Florian's library – by Shakespeare. 'Tis called *Hamlet*. I find the language a bit hard to follow. Florian says they spoke differently in Shakespeare's day. All the same, I am determined to make my way through it. Then I mean to read *Macbeth*. Florian says it is his favorite. After I have read these, I plan to invite several women, including Lady Rotherby, over for a discussion." She looked from Selena to Flavia. "Of course, both of you will be invited."

"I think that a splendid idea," Selena said. "I love Shakespeare."

"I do, too," Flavia said, "but I prefer his romances. I enjoy discussing the books I have read. I had several delightful discussions with Lady Venetia, Algernon LaBree's mother, when I was staying with her. She is such a gracious and lovely lady."

"Must be why Algernon is ever so gallant," Selena said with a laugh. "You will meet Mister LaBree, Mistress Nibley, at Flavia's welcome home party. We have not yet set the date, but it is to be a grand affair. You and Squire Nibley will be our guests at dinner along with a few specially chosen friends, then the other guests will start arriving around mid-afternoon. We will have dancing and games, and then a supper as evening approaches."

Mistress Nibley's eyes glowed with pleasure, and she clasped her hands to her breast. She looked at Flavia. "We will be your dinner guests at your welcome home party?"

"Indeed you will," Flavia said, flashing a pretty smile. "Mother must approve the rest of our list, then we will determine a date, and Selena and I will start writing invitations."

Mistress Nibley sighed audibly. "How lovely. The squire will be so pleased."

"I suppose we should be going now," Selena said. "We must need stop by the Grantham farm, yet."

"I am so glad you came by," Mistress Nibley gushed, rising. "Would you like me to return the book now? Or mayhap, you have no wish to carry it as you are walking. I could have the footman return it to Whimbrel Hall."

"Yes, that would be best," Selena said, also rising. "As it is Aunt Rowena's book, I would not want anything to happen to it."

"Indeed," Mistress Nibley agreed. "I will wrap it and have the footman hand deliver it. I thank you for loaning it to me. I did so enjoy it."

Selena smiled. "I made certain you would. So, then, until Wednesday when I shall arrive for dinner and afterward, I will address your tenants."

"Yes," Mistress Nibley said, bouncing a little on her toes. She put her hands to her cheeks, and then her stomach, and finally blurted out, "Oh, I simply must tell someone, or I shall burst! Dear Lady Selena and Lady Flavia, oh, I must tell."

Selena laughed. "Then yes, Mistress Nibley, do tell. We would not wish you to burst."

Her round eyes brilliant, she proclaimed, "I am with child. Florian said we should not tell anyone until the quickening, not even my father, but I felt the first kick this morning."

"How grand!" Selena cried, and Flavia seconded her.

Her eyes dreamy, Mistress Nibley said, "Florian and I had given up on having children. 'Tis such a surprise to us both. My father will be so pleased. He, of course, will hope for a boy."

"I cannot think why," Flavia said, and Selena and Mistress Nibley both looked at her. "Well, think, Mistress Nibley. Squire Nibley already has a son, an heir, who will inherit Nibley Hall and this manor. A second son, even if he inherits wealth, will not inherit a title. But a daughter … Well, with the squire's ancient birthright, and with your father's wealth for a dowry … Why, your daughter could marry almost anyone, a baronet, a baron, mayhap even an earl. Your father could have a great grandson who might someday be an earl."

Mistress Nibley stood with her mouth open, her eyes wide, and Selena patted her shoulder. "Flavia is right. Do you have a daughter, who knows whom she might marry."

"Yes, yes!" Mistress Nibley exclaimed. "Who knows! Oh, Lady Flavia, how bright of you. I had not given such an idea a thought." She put her hands to her stomach. "My daughter might marry an earl."

# Chapter 30

"You were very kind to Mistress Nibley," Selena said, once she and Flavia were headed back toward the Grantham farm.

"Why should I not be?" Flavia asked. "I like her. She is sweet and jolly and so eager to please. And she serves a very nice ale."

Selena chuckled. "Yes, and I was very thirsty. I am hoping at Calder's we may have some buttermilk fresh from the stream, cool and rich."

"At Calder's?" Flavia questioned. "Not Goodman Grantham?"

"From the first I met him, Calder asked me to call him by his given name. As do his servant, Hannah, and his laborers. I know them all, and call them all by their given names."

"Yes, but Goodman Grantham is a prosperous land owner, not a laborer."

Selena glanced sideways at her cousin. "He says he is a yeoman farmer. He works his land, and enjoys working it. No doubt, he will tell you to call him Calder. He is not formal."

Flavia shrugged. "I should not be surprised. You call all Ewen's friends by their given names when Mother is not around."

Laughing, Selena admitted to her informality. "When one is on friendly terms with another, why be formal. It detracts from the friendship."

"I know there will be no changing you. Much as Mother hopes she may teach you to behave as a lady, I doubt she ever will."

"Would you have me change? Be that perfect lady, dear cousin?" Selena asked, stopping and clasping Flavia's hand to halt her.

For a moment, Flavia stared deep into Selena's eyes. Slowly shaking her head, she said, "I am not certain. You have pulled me into more scrapes than I care to remember, but would I have you change? Honestly, Selena, I cannot say. You always are an awful lot of fun."

Starting to walk again, but still holding Flavia's hand as her cousin fell into step beside her, Selena said, "I am torn, also. For my mother's sake, because she wishes it, I would like to oblige her, and be that lady she wants me to be." Stopping again and releasing Flavia's hand to put both her own hands on either side of her head while waggling it from side to side, she sighed. "The things that seem important to a lady, seem so unimportant to me. I find I must choose between pleasing my mother or pleasing me. I fear my mother will not be the one to be pleased. Through no fault of your mother's," Selena added, before resuming the walk.

Matching her steps to Selena's, Flavia said, "Ewen says he pities the man who marries you, but he says, all the same, he would not change you."

"I always appreciate Ewen's honesty."

Their conversation turned from Ewen to his friends and soon they were skirting Calder's lower sheep meadow and heading up to the house. Did she not know better, Selena would have suspected Calder had been watching for her, for he came from the barn as they neared the house.

"Welcome, Lady Selena. We have not had the pleasure of your company in several days. I must ask after Mister Darnell. He has recovered?"

Selena's heart did its usual flip upon first seeing him, then settled into a gentle hammering as she answered, "Mister Darnell is well. You need have no fear there." Turning to her cousin, she said, "Flavia, may I present Goodman Calder Grantham." She then looked at Calder. "May I present my cousin, Lady Flavia D'Arcy."

Calder had already swept off his hat at first greeting them, but he bowed courteously to Flavia and welcomed her to his home. "I hope you mean to come inside and rest yourselves. Have some buttermilk and some of Hannah's cakes."

"We do indeed," Selena said. "I have been telling Flavia about the buttermilk."

"Splendid. Let us go inside. Pascal and Hermia have been helping Hannah today. Hermia is mending sheets, and we had a large harvest of strawberries, so Pascal has been put in charge of stirring the jam. He told me you would be coming by today, and he wanted to be on hand to see you. The last few times you were here, he was out helping in the fields."

"Yes, I have missed seeing him," Selena said as Calder opened the door, and she and Flavia passed inside.

"Lady Selena!" Pascal cried, dropping his spoon on a saucer near the hearth. "I knew you would come today."

Selena stooped to give Pascal a hug, then upon rising, she introduced Pascal, Hannah, and Hermia to Flavia. "This is my dear cousin Lady Flavia," she told them, and they all made their bows, then Hannah said, "Do have a seat at the table. Pascal, you run to the stream and bring up a crock of the buttermilk."

"Yes, Hannah," Pascal said and hurried to do her bidding. Hermia resumed her seat in a chair under the window where the light was best for the mending she was doing.

"Lady Selena, I do thank you for recommending me to fill in for Wally while he is away," Hermia said. "I am to have a cot next to Hannah's so I have not the walk back to Whimbrel every night, and I can be here to milk the sheep bright and early. Then the rest of the day, I am able to help Hannah with things she needs doing."

"She has been a big help, already" Hannah said. "She has been doing the weeding in the vegetable garden this morning, and she is handy enough with a needle to do the mending. Tomorrow, she will help me with the wash."

"I am so glad all has gone well," Selena said, pulling out a stool and urging Flavia to sit down beside her.

"It is going very well," Calder said, sitting down across the table from them. "I but hope all will go as well for Wally."

Selena felt her heart soar as she gazed into Calder's eyes. Lord how she had missed him. She knew the conversation ebbed and flowed around her, but she could concentrate on little but the fact that she was again in Calder's presence. She drank the buttermilk when Pascal returned with it and nibbled on Hannah's cakes, but she feasted on Calder's face, his smile, his laughter, and his mesmerizing eyes.

When Flavia nudged her and reminded her they needed to be heading home, she rose as in a dream, but managed to thank Hannah and Calder for their hospitality. She gave Pascal another hug and promised to return at her first opportunity. Still floating on air, she and Flavia headed back to Whimbrel Hall.

Before starting the gentle climb up to the woods, Selena turned. Calder and Pascal stood near the house. Both waved, and she returned their wave. Flavia had been chattering away about the refreshments they had been served, but when they reached the top of the hill, she stopped and blurted out, "Selena D'Arcy, you are in love with that man. With Calder Grantham. You need not try to deny it."

Selena let a smile drift across her face. "Nay, Flavia, I cannot deny it. I am in love with Calder Grantham, and I intend to marry him."

"Selena! You cannot think to marry him. He is but a yeoman, a farmer. True. He is exceptionally handsome, and his eyes are arresting. But you are the daughter of an earl."

"You think I care for that. It matters not to me. Calder is kind and fair and hardworking. He is honest and caring and good to his servants and his laborers. He cares no more than do I whether Baron Swagger or the Earl of Prideful are seated at the correct spot at the table. Nor would he mind do I ride astride, or do I have a pack of dogs following at my heels. Do I wish to tie my hair back in a queue and wear a serviceable gown that allows me to move freely, he will find no fault in me." She clasped Flavia's hands. "Do you not see, he will love me for who I am."

"You cannot think your father will let you marry him."

Selena raised her chin. "I will be twenty-one this October. At that time, Father cannot tell me whom I can or cannot marry. I hope he will approve my choice, but does he not..." She raised her chin even higher. "Well, I intend to marry Calder anyway."

"Has he asked you to marry him?"

Releasing Flavia's hands, Selena turned from her. "Not yet."

"Has he declared his love for you?"

She turned back. "No. But I can see it in his eyes. I know he loves me. Just like you could tell that I love him."

Flavia stuck out her lower lip and shrugged. "He may well be in love with you. But he also knows his place. I think he knows he is not good enough to offer for you."

"Oh! He is good enough! Because he was not born to gentry has no bearing. He is as good and better than many who make up the gentry but have not a gentle bone in their bodies."

"'Twas not what I meant. I am sure he is the same in God's eyes as the richest Duke or the poorest cotter. What I mean is, he may know your father will never approve. He may doubt that marrying you would be fair to you. The daughter of an earl. You are used to being waited on. Used to fine food and clothing and furnishings. He cannot offer you those things."

"I have thought of that, but I care not about those things. Well, I do to some extent because I am accustomed to them. But did I have to give them all up to marry Calder, I would. And must I ask him to marry me, then so I will."

"I can see you love him very much. I think I understand how you feel. Especially when it can seem so hopeless."

Touching Flavia's shoulder, Selena said, "You are thinking of Darnell?"

Flavia frowned. "I suppose it shows."

"Only to me, dear one. You have hidden it well. But you must not give up hope."

"I feared Orland to be in love with you, and mayhap you with him. I am happy to learn, at least, you are not in love with him."

"I cannot for the life of me think why Darnell believes he is in love with me. I have done all in my power to discourage him. But I have a plan for your welcome home party that I think will help open his eyes."

Flavia slanted her eyes and glared at Selena. "What are you planning?"

Selena laughed. "Nothing that will cause you any distress. That I promise you. Now come. We must hurry or your mother will start to worry about us."

With Flavia at her heels, Selena set off down the path at a brisk pace. Not breaking her stride, she hopped over the brook as did Flavia and in no time, they were back at the bower. Neither of them being winded, she had not planned to stop, but she thought she heard voices.

Halting, she looked around. "Did you hear something, Flavia?"

Flavia shook her head. But her answer, "Nay," was scarcely out of her mouth, than three men sprang up from behind some bushes.

"Run, Flavia!" Selena cried, raising her stick to whack the first man approaching her.

Flavia took off across the bower and down the path toward Whimbrel as Selena's walking stick connected with the front man's shoulder. She then used the stick to punch him in the stomach. "Get the other one!" she heard one of the men yell, and out of the corner of her eye, she saw one of the men take off after Flavia. Facing the two men and swinging her stick at her predators, she prayed Flavia could outrun her pursuer and make it to Whimbrel Hall.

# Chapter 31

With one man trying to circle behind her, Selena backed up and swung at him, but the man she had whacked on the shoulder was advancing on her, and she had to ward him off. She connected with his head, knocking his hat off. He yelped, but at the same instant, the other man worked his way behind her, and before she could turn, he threw a bag over her head. The bag reached down to her waist, hindering her movements. The next thing she knew, he had pinned her arms to her side. She kicked backwards, striking his shin, and though he hollered, he still held her and called to the other man to loop the rope around her arms.

Between the two of them, despite her struggles, they bound her arms to her side. She could not see and was having some trouble breathing as the sack wanted to slip into her panting mouth. Her walking stick was torn from her hand, and a harsh voice growled, "Calm down, we mean you no harm. But damn, if you have not raised a welt on my head. Tom, sling her up over your shoulder." Before Selena knew what was happening, one of the men did as he was bid, and she found herself lifted and slung across a shoulder.

She immediately started squiggling, but the man tightened his grip. "You best stop your struggles, or you will be bumpin' your head or scratchin' yourself on the branches," the man said. "Besides, have we not already told you that you will come to no harm."

Why she was being abducted, Selena could fathom, but she knew she could injure herself if she continued her struggles while being carted through the woods. Better to be whole when she reached whatever her destination might be. She had no idea the direction the men were taking her, but she knew they were pushing their way through the woods, not traveling down a worn path. Then they were out of the woods, and she heard horses snorting, heard hooves stomping. They were on the road.

"She gave us a right smart fight, sir," the man with the harsh voice said. "What you want Tom should do with her."

"Put her in the coach. But gently, gently."

Selena heard concern in the new voice, and she thought the voice sounded familiar.

"Where is Jimson?" the familiar voice asked as Selena felt herself being deposited on a seat inside a coach.

"Chasin' down t'other one," the harsh voice said. "There bein' two, we knew not which one you was wantin', so I sent Jimson after the other one."

"The other one! What other one?"

Now Selena knew the voice. "Darnell!" she demanded, the best she could, her voice being muffled by the bag over her head. "Darnell, I know that is you. Release me now!"

"How did you know? Oh, never mind. Lady Selena, you must forgive me that you have been handled in this manner," his voice sounded apologetic. "I could not think what else to do."

"Release me!" she demanded as harshly as she could, but she feared she sounded more amused than angry.

"I will release you do you promise you will not try to run away."

"Why would I run away? I want some answers from you."

"Very well. But you promise."

"Yes. I promise. Now get this sack off me. I can hardly breathe."

Fingers fumbled at the rope binding her, then the rope was loosened and pulled away, and she pulled the sack up and over her head. She threw it at Darnell, and he caught it, then dropped it. Holding a hand out to her, he said, "Do let me explain."

"Let me out of this coach first," she snapped, slapping his hand away, and hopping out before he could lower the steps.

Once out of the coach, she glared at the two men who had abducted her. Both stood with their floppy brim hats in their hands, and both had rather sheepish looks on their grizzled faces. "We was told was a lark, mistress, a joke. We meant you no harm."

"Good lord!" a voice from overhead said, and Selena looked up at the coachman. "Mister Darnell, you ne'er told me you were abducting Lady Selena. Oh, dear, what will your father say." He looked down at

222

Selena. "Honest, milady, I had no idea 'twas you the master was abducting." With his head, he gestured toward the two men. "I give you my word. Nor did Silas nor Tom nor Jimson either, we none of us knew Mister Darnell was set on abducting you."

"I am pleased to hear that, but I cannot think anyone would like being abducted. Whether 'twas but a lark or not. 'Twas quite terrifying." The coachmen, Silas, and Tom all looked contrite so Selena turned her gaze on Darnell.

"Well, Mister Darnell," she said, hands on her hips. "Do you plan to explain this to me?"

He looked cowed and glanced at the two men. "Come over here with me, please, Lady Selena," he said attempting to take her arm, but she pulled away. "Please," he begged.

Relenting, she followed him over to the edge of the road and out of earshot of the other men. "'Tis I wanted to talk to you, but you have been avoiding me. I want to marry you, but you seem to think I am not serious. You but joke with me. I thought, did I take you to my father's hunting lodge, 'tis but a little north of here, and did we spend the night together at the lodge..." He waved his hands in front of his chest. "Oh, not that I meant we should do anything improper. But did we spend the night together in the same lodging with no chaperones, then my parents and your aunt would insist we must marry.

"I told the coachman I meant to abduct a friend as a joke. He was leery, but I offered him two shillings, so he agreed to help. Having not had much to do while mother has been gone, he said the horses could use the exercise. The three men I sent to collect you, I hired in Rotherby. They, too, believed 'twas as I told them, a lark with a friend. A tryst."

"Humph! A tryst. Was I not a lady, I suppose no one would be feeling contrite. It would be just a lark to cart off a serving girl." She looked over her shoulder and glared at the men standing beside the coach.

She turned back to Darnell. "Can you imagine how your mother would respond did you come home with me as your wife. Good heavens, you could well kill her."

"Lady Selena!"

"You could. You know well she considers me highly unacceptable. Your father might be accepting, but your mother would be aghast. And what of my feelings. I have no wish to marry you. At this point, I am not sure I even like you."

Before he could answer her, the third man burst out of the woods with Flavia over his shoulder. "Darn near failed to catch her," the man said, setting a tearful Flavia down on the road. "She is fast. Had she not tripped over a root and sprained her ankle, I would never have caught her." He at first looked proud of himself, then as he looked at his cohorts and Darnell, and then at Selena, he started shaking his head. "Somethin' here amiss?"

"I should say it is," Selena said, gathering Flavia into her arms, as the third man ducked his head and slunk over next to his friends. "Are you badly hurt, dear?" Selena asked, brushing Flavia's hair away from her tear-stained face.

"Selena what is happening? Has Orland saved us?"

"Saved us! Humph! Mister Darnell has been a very foolish young man, Flavia," Selena said, looking over her shoulder at Darnell. "He thought 'twould be a lark to abduct me. But he had no way of knowing you would be with me."

"Flavia, I am so sorry," Darnell said, reaching out toward her. "Yesterday, Lady Selena told me she would be walking over to the Nibleys. I wanted to talk to her." He flushed, but kept his gaze on Flavia. "I fear I wanted to force Lady Selena into a position where she would have to marry me. I know these woods as well as you and Ewen from all our years playing here. I hired those men to wait at the bower, and to grab Lady Selena and bring her to me. As Lady Selena said, I had no way of knowing you would be with her. I would not have you hurt for anything."

"You wanted to force Selena to marry you?" Flavia said in a quaking voice.

Vigorously shaking his head, Darnell said, "I know, I know. 'Twas cruel and foolish."

"You are a fool, Mister Darnell," Selena said. "Why you even think you want to marry me is beyond me. Did you have a brain in your head, you would be paying court to Flavia. She is far prettier than I am." At that moment, Flavia did look beautiful – her dark eyes brilliant with misty tears, her cheeks rosy from her exertions, her lips full and luscious, and her dark curls loose and softly framing her face. "Your mother will adore her manners. Flavia will never say or do the wrong thing. She is the daughter of an earl and a member of a very old and distinguished family, and no doubt her father will provide her with a very good dowry. Besides the fact, she is a sweet and loving person."

Darnell glanced at Selena as she spoke, but his eyes went back to Flavia. Was Selena not mistaken, he was seeing his longtime friend in a new light. Mayhap this misadventure would have a happy ending.

"Mister Darnell," the man with the harsh voice called. "What should we be doin' now?"

Darnell looked at them with a confused look on his face, and Selena caught his arm. "Pay them off and let them walk back to Rotherby. 'Tis not that far. Best pay them well, do you wish them to keep this adventure to themselves. I would give them warning, they would not like Lord Rotherby to hear about this."

Darnell was nodding and started to dig out his purse, but Selena caught his arm again. "Then, you had best take Flavia home in your coach." He nodded again.

"Flavia, you must tell your mother you tripped and sprained your ankle. Tell her I went to the road for help, and what luck, Mister Darnell was driving past. He came and got you, and carried you back to his coach."

Flavia, too, nodded. "Yes, I think that would be best. Did mother think we had been attacked in the woods, she would be fearful of letting us take walks on our own. I know you would hate that, dear Selena."

Selena smiled at her cousin and gave her another hug, while Darnell paid off his henchmen and sent them on their way. "You are the dearest cousin I could ever have," Selena said. "I hope your ankle will not pain you too much. You are due to be fitted for some new gowns on the morrow."

Flavia smiled, if a tad weakly. "Nothing is going to interfere with my new gowns."

"Good," Selena said, turning to find the three men lingering with hats in hand in the middle of the road.

"We mean to apologize again, Lady Selena. And Lady Flavia. We have given Mister Darnell our word we will breathe not a word of this to a soul. And he said you would not be pressing charges on us."

Selena laughed, and the men brightened. "Mister Darnell is correct. Lady Flavia and I will not be pressing charges, does no word get out. Now, be on your way back to Rotherby."

"Yes, milady, and thank you," they each said, then slapping their hats on their heads, they set off down the road.

"Now," Darnell said. "May I help each of you into the coach?"

"You may help Flavia into the coach, but I have something I must retrieve in the woods. I will walk home. You just take good care of my cousin, Mister Darnell."

"I will, I will," Darnell promised, and giving Flavia his arm to lean on as she limped across the road, he escorted her to his coach.

"Mind your tale to Lady Rotherby, you two. No doubt she will be suspicious, but I am guessing she will not want to press you or trip you up." So saying, Selena headed back into the woods. She had a prized walking stick to collect.

# Chapter 32

Rowena knew when Orland arrived with Flavia in his arms, and Flavia was in such disarray, that something had happened beyond Flavia tripping and spraining her ankle. But as Orland was being so solicitous and seemed intent on seeing to Flavia's care, she decided not to question them too closely. That Orland just happened to be passing on the road because his coachman was exercising the coach horses was too ludicrous to believe, but if Orland was now paying such devoted attention to Flavia rather than to Selena, that was good.

Consequently, she was not surprised to see Selena was also a disheveled mess when she returned from her walk. That Selena more than likely had something to do with Orland's change of heart, Rowena had little doubt, but she reasoned she would better serve all concerned, did she not interfere in their little fabrication. She instead let Flavia's and Selena's maids flutter around Flavia, making sure the pail of well water Flavia had her foot in was still cool. She let the maids coo and sympathize with Flavia, and let them bring cups of ale to the three young people.

When Rowena finally suggested the girls should go up to their rooms and rest before supper, Orland, behaving like a besotted lover, insisted he carry Flavia up to her room. He then repeatedly said his good-byes to Flavia until Rowena shooed him out. She noted that Selena, watching the display, was beaming, and Orland, standing in the doorway, promised he would call on the morrow to see how Flavia fared. When informed, despite Flavia's ankle sprain, they would be going to Rotherby to the mantua maker after dinner, he promised he would call early enough so he would not interfere with their plans.

With Gertrude working to settle her mistress on her bed, Orland finally took his leave. Selena laughed merrily, hugged Flavia and said. "I know you are needing a nice rest so I will leave you for now." She turned with a satisfied smile to Rowena. A smile that offered a thank you for not questioning us. "We must tell you of our visit with Mistress Nibley when we sit down to supper," she said.

"Yes, so you must, and after supper, we will finalize your guest list. But now, go to your room and rest. You look exhausted." She fluttered her hand. "Go, go."

With Alice hurrying off to the kitchen to fetch water to Selena's room, Selena did as she was bid and, with a wave to Flavia, exited. Rowena doubted she would ever know what truly transpired on this sunny afternoon, but whatever it was, she was satisfied with the result. Did Orland's courtship of Flavia progress, she and Nate would be pleased. Rowena could ask for nothing better than to have her daughter marry a neighbor and stay close to home.

※　※　※

Flavia knew she should try to nap, but she was too excited. She had experienced one of the most terrifying events in her life – being abducted to face she knew not what – only to have it turn into the most wonderful day of her life. She was certain. Oh, she could not be wrong, Orland was seeing her in an entirely new light. He was looking at her the way he had been looking at Selena. Did she but build on his emotions, she believed he would offer for her hand. He had been so caring of her in the coach, worrying about her ankle, insisting she lean against him, brushing her hair off her face. And she was certain he had planted a soft kiss on her head when she rested her head on his shoulder.

She had known some calamity would befall her, was she in Selena's company. That was a given, but in this case, it was for once, all for the good. She had been in love with Orland forever, but he had treated her as, at best, an annoying pest. But he was not now seeing her as a pest. He was seeing her as a woman. A woman he found attractive. At last her dreams were coming true. Funny to think, she owed Orland's change of heart to Selena. Had she not let Selena persuade her to join her in her visit to the Nibleys and to Calder Grantham's, she would not be basking in the knowledge that Orland was now paying her court. Life was sweet. So very sweet.

❉ ❉ ❉

Calder had numerous chores to attend ere he went into supper, but he was happier than he had been in days. Just seeing Selena brightened his day. Yes, he knew he could never hope to marry her, but he had no intention of obeying Lady Rotherby's request to busy himself in his far fields that he should not be around when Selena visited his farm. Nay. He would enjoy each moment he could have with Selena. They would be memories to warm his bed on cold winter nights. Selena's smile, her light, ready laughter, her thoughtfulness, her ability to charm the animals, and the look in her eyes when she looked at him would be his forever.

Sadly, he knew he needed to spend time in his back fields. He had to finish his mid-summer plowing and harrowing so his fields would be ready for the autumn sowing. So whether he liked it or not, he more than likely could be absent when Selena visited. For the first time in his life, he envied his laborers, Jared and Joseph. They could marry the women they loved. Jared was settling in at Buxton's house, and he and Rachel were making plans to get married. Jared said the sooner the better. The house needed a woman's touch, not to mention a woman's cooking, but the Buxton acreage needed so much work, that Jared and the cottager, Olly Keat, and Abner's young son Lyell were kept busy from morning light to evening dark ploughing and harrowing the fields. Jared was hoping, once the fields were ready for the autumn sowing, he and Rachel could be married. Not only did she have her dowry, a chest of sheets and toweling and blankets, but she would keep her position as a milkmaid and add to their revenue.

Calder could also see a romance awakening between Joseph and Hermia. They would walk out in the evenings after supper. Though a bright and cheerful young woman, Hermia was no great beauty, but then, Joseph, despite his wide blue eyes and big toothy grin, was not what Calder could call handsome. He had told Joseph that did he mean to take a wife, he could have four acres of meadow land, and he could cut what trees he might need to build his house from the woods on the hillside. Joseph had been pleased with the offer, and Calder had little doubt Joseph would be asking Hermia to marry him.

Yes, Jared and Joseph were lucky. They might never be wealthy, might never own their own land, but at least they could marry the women they loved.

❧ ❧ ❧

Curled up in the window seat, Selena stared out at the glorious summer sunset. Full and content, she let her thoughts wander. Supper had been later than usual because Aunt Rowena had wanted Flavia to rest, but when Flavia came down to supper, with the aid of Gertrude and a footman, she had not looked rested, she looked excited. And beautiful. Her eyes glowed and her supple mouth was curved in a ravishing smile. Selena had never seen her look so alive. Could Darnell have seen her at that moment, his heart would have been lost for certain. Not that it was not already lost. Selena could not be happier for Flavia and for Darnell. She was ever so pleased Darnell had finally awakened to Flavia's many merits, from her beauty, to her sweet nature, to her ability to be a true lady in every respect.

Aunt Rowena had looked pleased with Flavia's appearance. That Aunt Rowena had not tried to delve more deeply into the events of the day was a blessing Selena greatly appreciated. With everyone in a happy mood, supper had been a lively affair. Aunt Rowena had informed them they would be adding Suzanne Sizer's father to their dinner guests. They were short one man and needed someone to escort Carola Mead into dinner. Doctor Sizer, being a widower, would be the perfect choice.

Carola had blushed and said, "How kind you are, dear Cousin Rowena."

"Every lady must have an escort," Aunt Rowena said, before turning to her daughter. "Flavia, in what order will you have your guests proceed into the dining room?"

Flavia at first looked surprised at her mother's question but then answered, "The Edgertons, being our highest ranking guests, Ewen will of course escort Lady Edgerton, and you, Mother, being the highest ranking lady present, plus being the hostess, will be escorted by Lord Edgerton." She turned to Selena. "You will be next, you being the daughter of an Earl. I should come after you, as I, too, am the daughter of an earl, but you have precedence as you are older. I think 'twould be best did Algernon LaBree escort you, as he is the son of a Baron." Blushing, Flavia looked at her mother. "Then Orland will escort me. We will be followed by the Nibleys, the vicar and his wife, Reynard and Cecily, Suzanne Sizer and Silvester Preston, then Brilliana and Ansel Yardley, and finishing with Doctor Sizer and Carola."

Aunt Rowena smiled. "Well done."

Flavia, smiling broadly, said, "Thank you," then asked, "Have you set a date, Mother?"

"Yes, I believe two weeks from tomorrow should give us sufficient time to accomplish all we must do to have a successful event." She looked at Selena. "Dear niece, let us see what you have learned. We are planning a gala festivity, with music and dancing, and after dinner we will have many more guests arriving. What all will we be needing?"

Raising her chin and smiling brightly, Selena had not hesitated. "Food. We must decide not only on our dinner menu, but what we will have for refreshments and for supper. We will need extra servers. I would assume we might hire some from Whimbrel and, if needed, additional staff from Rotherby. The cook will need extra help in the kitchen. Several days in advance, I would think. The day of our party, we will need to accommodate our guests' coaches and horses, so we will need someone in charge of directing the coachmen where to go after the guests have alighted. I would think we should have some kind of meal and refreshments for the coachmen and footmen as well."

"A good thought," Aunt Rowena said, with a nod of her head.

"We will need musicians. And we will need to go over with the additional staff, where they are to set up tables, chairs, games, and the refreshments, both inside and outside of the house. They must know what needs doing as quickly and quietly as possible. Oh, and we will need a room for both the men and the women to refresh themselves, especially as they may be drinking heavily."

Flavia burst out laughing. "Oh, Selena, I would not have thought of that. Indeed, Mother has taught you well."

Aunt Rowena laughed, too, then asked, "Anything else?"

Selena frowned, then brightened. "I would guess we should have the house cleaned especially well. The silver should be polished from spoons to goblets. I think we must commission the baker in Whimbrel to do some of our baking so the cook may concentrate on other items. We will need to select what wines we mean to serve at dinner, and which ones with supper. I am thinking we will need some kind of punch for the dance. I am not certain whether we should have some kind of decorations other than flowers, but 'tis Flavia's party, so she should decide on that. Of course, the footmen's livery should all be laundered in advance, and plenty of clean, starched aprons should be on hand for the extra maids helping our staff.

"I suppose after dinner, when the other guests arrive, we should have someone greeting them at the door. Could be, we should have someone announce them."

"You have done wondrously well," Aunt Rowena said with a smile. "Tomorrow morning, you and Flavia and Carola may write your invitations. The footmen can deliver them the following day." She chuckled. "Some of our guests may decide they want a new gown for the party. They will wish to see the seamstress, Mistress Sloan, but we shall have her already engaged making Flavia's gown first."

"Oh, Mother," Flavia said with a giggle. "You are so wise."

"Yes, well, she will also be making a gown for Brilliana. It will be Brilliana's first grown-up party gown."

"Oh, she will be so excited," Flavia said.

"Yes," Aunt Rowena answered. "I sent a message to Cecily this morning that she and Brilliana should join us at Mistress Sloan's tomorrow afternoon." She looked at Selena. "You said you have no need of a new gown, but you mentioned some other purchases you would like to make."

"I need new gloves and a new hat band for my black hat. I also need new heavy stockings for my walks as mine were ripped today." Selena hated bringing up her trek through the brush, so she rushed on. "Plus, I want to visit the vicar and tell him what we have accomplished thus far toward the school." She frowned. "I think 'tis not fair grammar schools are just for boys. I think girls should be able to have a more advanced education, also. I was lucky to be allowed to learn from my brothers' tutor, but many girls are not so lucky."

Aunt Rowena sighed. "We can go round and round endlessly, Selena, about what boys may do and girls may not, but at present we are unlikely to change anything. Mayhap someday men will realize we women have minds capable of many things, but that day is not now. So be content that you are offering boys a school closer to their home, so more of them will be able to get an education. The more education they receive, the better the future they will have, and the better life they will be able to provide for their future wives and children."

Knowing her aunt was right, Selena nodded. "I would like to ride Brigantia into Rotherby tomorrow, if I may," she said. "I have not ridden her in two days, and I know she misses me."

"I can see no reason you may not ride your horse to Rotherby." Her aunt smiled and looked from Selena to Flavia and back to Selena. "Now, I have been saving some good news for you. I have had a letter from Nate today. He says your cousin Elizabeth's wedding was lovely, and he said Elizabeth looked beautiful."

"No one could doubt that," Flavia said, interrupting her mother.

Agreeing, Aunt Rowena continued, "He said he is looking forward to seeing his brother and to visiting the home of his youth. He also is eager to see his old highwayman friend, Elizabeth's new father-in-law, Caleb Hayward. Due to a back injury, Sir Caleb could not attend his son's and Elizabeth's wedding. However, Sir Caleb's land borders on the Yardley's, so Nate will again see Sir Cyril. He says, as he has asked the Yardleys to join our next family reunion, he will also invite William's father. I am guessing we will be having an even larger than usual gathering next year."

"That should be great fun," Selena said. "I love getting to see all our family. 'Tis a long distance for some of the family to come, especially for cousin Timandra, coming all the way from Newcastle, yet she never fails. It gives her a chance to see her parents and siblings."

With a nod, Aunt Rowena agreed with Selena. Smiling, she said, "Selena, I am happy to tell you that your uncle thinks your idea to have a school built in Whimbrel is a wonderful idea. He wishes he had thought of it himself. He says he has no problem with Squire Nibley selecting the contractor and getting the work started. He says he will not only help pay for the building, he will make certain the teacher is paid a high enough wage so that we may be certain to have a really good teacher for the boys attending the school."

"Oh! Aunt Rowena! Uncle Nate is the best uncle ever!" Selena cried, clapping her hands. "Wednesday, when Flavia and I have dinner with the Nibleys, I will tell the squire the news. Mayhap the contractor will soon be able to start the work. We already have several pledges."

Aunt Rowena nodded. "Yes, I approved of the master mason Squire Nibley brought by to meet me. He has seen what is left of the church foundation, and has said he will soon be able to give us an estimate on what it will cost to build a two-room school. I see no reason the petty school cannot be housed in the same building. I told the mason we must have at least three windows on each side of the school, and a door at the front and one at the rear, and a hearth large enough to keep both rooms warm, come winter."

"'Tis a lovely plan," Flavia said. "Gertrude is excited about it. She says her sister was dreading sending her little son, Claud, all the way to Rotherby. He turned seven this summer and is ready to start grammar school."

"I hope the school may be completed by the end of the harvest season," Selena said. "But I had no idea Gertrude had family here. I thought she was from Cheshire."

"Oh, no. Gertrude's family are long time tenants," Aunt Rowena said. "Most likely her ancestors were here when a portion of this manor belonged to the nunnery. Her father is the Whimbrel village reeve as well as our butcher. Gertrude trained under my maid to be Flavia's maid. One of her brothers is our shepherd. The older brother will no doubt someday be the reeve, as his grandfather was reeve before his father. But enough of Gertrude's family. We must continue with our plans for the party."

Turning to Carola, Aunt Rowena said, "I would be pleased would you work with Selena on the dinner and the supper menus. Of course, you will need to consult with the cook as well. Flavia and I will decide on the refreshments to serve during the dance, and where we want to set up the game tables, and what decorations we will want. I believe I will consult with Cecily on the musicians. She will know more about who is dependable."

And so the conversation had gone on until supper was ended, and they all retired to the parlor. Staring sightlessly at a book of poetry, Flavia sat with her foot propped up on a stool. Carola sat in a corner doing her knitting, and Aunt Rowena sat near a brightly glowing oil lamp with an open book on her lap, though she appeared to be thinking rather than reading.

Very pleased with her day, Selena turned back to the sunset. Everything seemed to be falling into place. Darnell and Flavia were falling in love. Preparations for the party were coming together. Uncle Nate approved of the school, so construction could soon begin. All she needed now was to receive a proposal from Calder, and her world would be perfect.

# Chapter 33

Selena had never known days to fly by so quickly. The previous two weeks had been a flurry of events. That the dinner guests would soon be arriving for Flavia's welcome home party seemed impossible, yet the day had arrived. And it was a glorious summer day. The table was set, the servants were dressed in their finest with scrubbed hands and clean fingernails. The coachman was waiting to direct the guests' coaches to the meadow between the woods and the lake. Tables with food and drink would await the coachmen, and grass for the horses to graze was plentiful. All was in readiness for the first guests. At least, so it seemed when Selena hurried to her room to ready herself for the party.

Sitting before the looking glass as Alice combed her hair straight back from her face, Selena tried to recall all the bustle that had kept the household on the run. They had made several trips to Rotherby for fittings for Flavia's new gowns. Flavia was thrilled with her party gown. A dark rose-colored creation with a scoop-neck décolletage, puff sleeves that ended with a bow at the elbow, and an overskirt that was hitched up at the sides to reveal a slightly lighter rose petticoat embroidered with tiny roses. The gown set off to perfection Flavia's light brown hair and radiant brown eyes. Darnell, who had been calling on Flavia almost every day, would today be mesmerized. Of that, Selena was certain.

Her thoughts turned from Flavia to the Nibleys. Mistress Nibley would no doubt be dressed in the latest fashion. Her short plump frame would be gowned in silk and satin, and her expressive round eyes would be sparkling. The Nibleys were elated at being invited to the dinner. Selena had hand-carried their invitation to them when she and Flavia dined with the Nibleys before Selena addressed the Nibleys' tenants about the school. Tears had sprung to Mistress Nibley's eyes, and she had given Selena a hug. Mistress Nibley really was a dear woman, and she was making a valiant effort at becoming better read. And, the work she was doing to promote the school could not be underestimated. Certainly the Nibley tenants had been receptive to the idea of the school being built in Whimbrel. Most seemed to recognize the value of an education. One of the tenants, a carpenter, said he would be happy to help make the tables and stools for the children.

Selena had collected some monetary donations that day, as well as promises of future contributions from the tenants. She met Alice's oldest brother, Laban Shandy, and could not say she found him as winsome as Alice or Wally. His direct gaze offered no warmth, and his thin lips looked like they seldom knew a smile. All the same, he said he was pleased about the promise of a school in Whimbrel, and handing over a sixpence, promised more would be forthcoming. Selena also met Calder's deceased wife's brother, Jonah Hadrian, and his wife, Elsa. They made a handsome couple, and Selena guessed Calder's wife must have been very pretty, as her brother was quite handsome with his lively, steel gray eyes and a ready smile that brightened his whole face. His dark-haired wife, just as merry, cheerily introduced the elder Goodman Hadrian.

The old man's eyes, identical to his son's, danced when he shook his walking cane at her and demanded, "Why could you not have been here when my boys were young. I do think 'twas what my dear wife, may she rest in peace, hated most about winter was sending Jonah and Ely all the way to Rotherby to grammar school. 'Twas why she finally insisted we board the boys at the school in Leicester. Then she wept because she could not see them on a daily basis." He shook his head, and his daughter-in-law patted his arm.

"But think, Father," Jonah said, "how good it is that Edward and Dale will not be having to go all the way to Rotherby or to Leicester. And," he stressed, "Lady Selena says Lord Rotherby intends to help pay the schoolmaster's wages, so our boys will have as good a teacher as they would have did they go to Leicester, as did Ely and I."

"Aye, that is good," the old man said with a nod. "I but wish their grandmother was here to share in this new good fortune." He looked up at Selena. "I thank you, Lady Selena. I thank you from the depths of my old, withered heart."

She took his knobby, workworn hand in hers, and said, "I appreciate such thanks. But you must give credit to Mistress Nibley. She has been working to get pledges from all the gentry in the area. She arranged this meeting that I might explain the school and the funding needed to all the tenants. She is working diligently on behalf of the Nibley tenants."

Jonah said, "We must remember to thank Mistress Nibley as well." He looked over his shoulder at Mistress Nibley, who stood with Flavia awaiting Selena. "I had not recognized such qualities in the Squire's new wife. 'Tis a pleasure to know she is as caring as his previous wife."

As thrilled as Selena was with the advancement of the school – Aunt Rowena had approved the master mason's plans, and bricks had been ordered – she was equally delighted to have received a letter from her brother Giles's friend, Malcolm Postgate. The letter not only stated Postgate wanted to publish the stories Selena sent him, he wanted to meet the author. He had hopes Wally would write more stories. When Ewen and his friends and Wally returned from Leicester, Selena had another surprise. Not only had Ewen helped Wally find appropriate spectacles, he had changed Wally's whole appearance. New haircut and shave, new clothes, consisting of a slim-cut yellowish tan coat, darker yellow waistcoat, brown breeches and brown stockings, black shoes, and a white cravat at his throat, had turned the raggedy laborer into a man of distinction.

Tears flooded Alice's eyes and dribbled down her cheeks when she gazed upon her brother. "Oh, Wally, would you be lookin' at you. You are so handsome."

Indeed, he was. His square jaw, clear skin, golden hair, and pale blue eyes were a winning combination, and when he learned his stories were to be published, his expressive face fairly glowed. "I am to go to London, you say?" he asked Selena.

"You are. I have arranged for your brother, John, to accompany you, he having more experience with larger cities than you. Mister Postgate says he has a room for you, do you choose to stay in London and work for him. You are, mayhap, a tad old to apprentice at printing, but with your winning smile and easy manner, you could well be a salesman for the publishing company. You could sell not only your books, but other books."

Ewen had slapped Wally on the back. "See. I told you that you would have no trouble refunding us the money for your clothing. Not that you need to. The four of us had great fun turning you into a gentleman."

Wally, looking dazed, slowly shook his head. "When do I leave?"

"Tomorrow would be good," Selena said. "Mister Postgate is eager to meet you, and we are set to return to Rotherby tomorrow for another of Flavia's fittings. We can send word to your brother to be ready to catch the stage with you on the morrow. I would suggest you go home and make your good-byes, then return here for the night. You can sleep above the stable with the coachman and footmen. That way, you may be here and ready, when we set out in the morning."

"What am I to tell Calder? I was to be milking his sheep?"

"Hermia is doing a fine job and has need of the income," Selena said. "She will be happy to continue the work. Besides, another week, and they will stop milking the sheep to fatten up the ones for sale and ready the ones Calder means to keep for breeding. So you should not worry on that score. Go by and tell him of your plans. He will be happy for you." She laughed. "I but wish I could see Calder's and Hannah's faces when they see you."

Wally looked down at his clothes and the two packages he held in his arms. He handed one package to Alice. "These are two extra shirts Lord Sutherlin said I should have. Bless him and his friends. This other package is my old work clothing. Lord Sutherlin said I should give them to a beggar, but I feared I would yet need them." A small smile touched his lips. "I guess I will be leaving them with Laban. He may use them as he pleases."

"Wally!" Selena said, "you have not yet shown us your spectacles."

"Ah, yes," Wally answered, pulling a pair of wire rimmed spectacles from his pocket and setting them on his nose. "I am to wear them when I need to read or see things up close."

"Very distinguished looking, I would say," piped up Ansel Yardley.

Wally turned to Yardley, then let his gaze rest on Preston and LaBree. "You have all been more than kind to me. How I can ever thank you or repay you …"

"Nonsense," Preston interrupted in his lazy drawl. "We but left you at the tailor's and told him to outfit you. The tailor and his apprentices did the work. Fitting you out like they did in but two days' time was exemplary. Seeing you now as you are, 'twas worth every shilling."

"Aye." Both LaBree and Yardley agreed, and Ewen slapped Wally on the back. "Be off with you. You have thanked us enough. We will look to see you off on the stage to London on the morrow."

Wally set off with Alice at his side. She would accompany him a short way before returning to her duties.

"You four were so kind to outfit Wally as you did," Selena said.

"What else could we do," Ewen joked. "We could hardly expect to be seen in his company, him looking as he did. Gads, but the man had the shabbiest clothing I have near ever seen, even on a beggar."

"I felt sorry for the poor man's rump," Yardley said with a chuckle. "He had never ridden any distance on a horse before. By the time we reached Leicester, he scarce could walk or sit."

"Brave fellow, I would say," LaBree said. "He would cling to that poor horse's mane, and did we gallop or trot, he managed to keep up with us. I have to say, I respect him."

"Add to that, we did enjoy his stories," Preston said. "As did a number of patrons in the tavern we frequented in the evenings. Wally would start telling a story, and everyone would stand around listening. The man not only has good stories, he is a master storyteller."

Selena liked that Ewen and his friends had been impressed with Wally. That could bode well for Wally when he met Postgate. She hoped he would be able to find employment with Postgate and would never again have to be dependent upon his older brother.

The following morning, before Wally and his brother boarded the stage, Flavia gave Wally a letter to deliver to Maris Nibley. The letter told Maris that Flavia would love to renew their acquaintance. It also told Maris of how much they enjoyed Mistress Nibley's company, and how much Mistress Nibley was doing to get the new school started. Selena applauded Flavia in her effort to reunite Maris with her family.

"Well, what would you be thinking, milady?" Alice asked, bringing Selena back to the present. "I have not softened your look, but I would say your hair is still festive."

"It is. You are a marvel, Alice." Selena was pleased with the hair creation. Though she believed Darnell was now thoroughly in love with Flavia, just to be certain, she had decided she would do nothing to turn his gaze in her direction. She had directed Alice to pull her hair starkly back from her face and to put it in braids. That was exactly what Alice had done, only she had woven emerald green ribbons in among the braids and then piled the braids atop Selena's head. No curls, no frills, and yet no one could say Selena had not taken pains with her appearance.

"Well, let us get me dressed. I want to be downstairs before the guests begin arriving. It would not do to have the responsibility left entirely to Aunt Rowena."

Alice helped Selena slip her petticoats and then the skirt of her silky, emerald green gown over her head. The bodice was fitted over her chemise, and little green ties held the paler green stomacher in place. The sides of the gown were hitched up to reveal a petticoat embroidered with tiny pink flowers with bright green leaves. The green of the gown made the green in Selena's blue-green eyes more pronounced, and set off the golden hue of her skin that had returned once her aunt allowed her the freedom to roam when she completed her lessons.

Satisfied with her appearance, Selena gave her maid a well-deserved thanks, and hurried off to await the guests in the main parlor.

# Chapter 34

When Rowena entered the parlor, she found Ewen and his friends already there. Each was dressed impeccably, and each graciously greeted her. Selena appeared moments after Rowena finished complimenting the young men, and Rowena was pleased with how the girl looked. A different hairstyle might have complimented her face more, but in this instance, with the form fitting gown she was wearing, the coif worked perfectly. Gave her a distinguished look.

Rowena believed, should Selena so choose, she could play the role of a lady in even the grandest of homes. Problem was, she doubted Selena would ever want such a role. But she had done a perfect job selecting the food for the dinner. Carola had worked with her, but Carola said she had let Selena make all the selections and had not felt she needed to do more than agree with Selena's decisions. Carola said Selena had also worked well with the cook and with the baker and the butcher. She could in no way fault her.

The preparations for Flavia's welcome home party were as good a test as any to determine what Selena had gleaned from her lessons. Besides her selected dinner menu, Selena had superintended the setting of the table, had seen hers and Flavia's bed chambers were set up for the ladies to use to refresh themselves, and she had come up with the idea of setting up a tented area outside, a little ways from the festivities, for the men to use. She had seen the footmen's livery was clean and starched, and that the maids had clean aprons and caps. The punch table was set up on the terrace, and the hall had been cleared of furnishings except for chairs lining the walls, so the dancing could take place in the center of the room. The musicians would be near the terrace doors so their music could float outside.

Selena had helped Flavia decide where to set up game tables down from the terrace and had helped her decide which flowers she wanted in arrangements for both indoors and out. The two girls had decided other decorations were not necessary. A beautiful summer day being the best adornment. Fortunately, they were having a beautiful summer day.

The Nibleys were the first guests to arrive. The butler showed them into the parlor, where they were introduced to Ewen's friends. Rowena had to admit Mistress Nibley was a changed woman. Instead of rambling on about the newest fashions or complaints about her staff, she was enthusiastically talking about the school funding she had raised, or about the newest book she was devouring. In Rowena's mind, Selena had worked a miracle with the woman.

For that matter, getting the school project going was another miracle. Rowena had never known the Whimbrel tenants to be so enthusiastic about anything. They were all ready to pitch in to do whatever might be needed to complete the school and make the project a success. Why Selena had decided to help Wally Shandy, Rowena had no idea, but certainly, with Ewen's help, that young man now had a bright future ahead of him. What project Selena would take up next, Rowena could not guess, but she believed the girl would find some person or undertaking that she believed she could help or further along.

Shortly after the Nibleys' arrival, Flavia joined the group in the parlor. When she entered the room, all conversation stopped. Flavia looked absolutely gorgeous. Her brown hair, in soft curls atop her head and framing her face, looked like a golden halo under the gleam of the sunlight pouring in through the parlor windows. Her shapely lips spread in a sweet smile revealing small glistening teeth, Flavia blushed, and her cheeks glowed a rosy pink. The dark rose gown made her pale skin appear pearly white, and the cut of her décolletage exposed the upper mounds of her pale breasts.

Selena was the first to greet her, but Ewen's friends were soon surrounding her. It was at that moment that the Edgertons and Orland arrived. Orland greeted not a single soul but made a bee line for Flavia. Chuckling, Lord Edgerton edged up next to Rowena. "Just so you know," he said, "Orland has told us as soon as Lord Rotherby returns, he means to ask for Lady Flavia's hand. Lady Edgerton and I could not be happier. Hope it also meets with your approval."

Rowena gave him a bright smile. "Indeed it does, Lord Edgerton. Indeed it does."

Other guests were arriving, and Rowena greeted them but allowed Flavia and Selena to introduce the various guests to Ewen's friends. Dressed in her first grownup party gown, Brilliana, a good head taller than her petite mother, looked excited, but though her blue eyes danced, she carried herself with controlled dignity. Her mother, lovely as always, tiptoed to give Rowena a peck on the cheek. Cecily's handsome, dark-haired, dark-eyed husband also gave Rowena a kiss, then stepped back to be heartily greeted by Lord Edgerton.

Soon the other guests arrived and the butler announced the dinner was ready to be served. Selena and Flavia had arranged the members of the party in the order they should enter the dining chamber, and the procession began with Ewen escorting Lady Edgerton, and Lord Edgerton escorting Rowena. Pleased that Carola seemed comfortable talking with Doctor Sizer, Rowena took her place at one end of the table with a satisfaction she would not have expected she would feel two months earlier when Selena had arrived at her home.

❦ ❦ ❦

Seated between Orland and LaBree, Flavia gazed about the table at the bright, happy faces. That Orland intended to monopolize her attention was evident, but then LaBree seemed not to mind. How could he mind when he had Selena on his other side. Selena, seated between Ewen and LaBree, was more than capable of entertaining both men. Ewen would of course have to devote some of his attention to Lady Edgerton on his right, but she would also be conversing with Squire Nibley on her right. Flavia believed they had selected their guests wisely. It was a good mix of young and old. She was pleased Brilliana seemed perfectly comfortable with Ansel Yardley, but then, the girl had met him before at her uncle's home in Derbyshire. Yardley was such a jolly soul, he would never treat Brilliana like a child.

Flavia enjoyed renewing her friendship with Suzanne Sizer, and she was happy to see Suzanne seemed to be enjoying Preston's languid flirtation. Preston was the least animated of Ewen's new friends, but he did have his own charm, even if he often seemed to be amused when Flavia had no idea what might have amused him. Still, she liked all Ewen's friends, and, though she had enjoyed flirting with them, she knew her heart had always belonged to Orland. That Orland now seemed to feel the same way about her was her dream come true.

She could not help but smile when remembering her brother's words, "I cannot say I am surprised Orland finally awoke to your charms, little sister. You have turned into a real beauty. Orland tells me he must have been blind not to have noticed sooner how you have grown into the most beautiful woman he has ever seen. He does naught but rave about your poise and grace." At that point Ewen chuckled. "He seems to have completely forgotten how we used to tease you and call you a skinny ninny or a frothy moppet and then run off and leave you stomping your foot in anger. Now, he has become a bore, as he can talk of nothing but you." He harrumphed. "I knew when he seemed to be drawn to Selena that would never last. He may be a foolish oaf at times, but he is no dunderhead."

"You look so lovely, Flavia," Orland said, drawing her attention back to him. "What puts that beatific smile on your face?"

Widening her smile and her eyes, she said, "I was thinking of you. Of the poem you wrote me. 'Tis so lovely. I think I will save it always."

"You truly like it?"

"Indeed I do." It was not the best poem Flavia had ever read, but it was certainly a flattering poem.

"I meant every word. You are indeed an angel come down to earth. Why I failed to see that sooner is beyond my comprehension."

"Well, Selena had you entranced. She can do that. She is so alive, so vivacious."

He shook his head solemnly. "Spirited, I agree. Still, I cannot think what attracted me to her. Mayhap 'twas her laugh." At that moment, Selena's tinkling laughter floated over the table, and Orland looked in her direction then back at Flavia. "Yes, it could well have been her laugh. It is so light and gay, it makes one think she is the same." Frowning and again shaking his head, he said, "But she is not like her laughter. She is stubborn and, and…," he lowered his voice, and leaning closer to Flavia, whispered, "hoydenish. Not to mention bossy."

Flavia raised her chin and narrowed her eyes. "Orland, you are speaking of my cousin."

Looking apologetic, he prayed, "Do forgive me, Flavia. I mean not to disparage Lady Selena. As Ewen says, she has her merits. Indeed, she has many good qualities. They are just not what a man may look for in a wife."

Though Orland's apology could scarcely be called an apology, Flavia nodded in understanding. Selena would never behave the way most men would want a wife to behave, but the image of Calder Grantham rose up in Flavia's mind's eye. Selena would be perfect for him. He would not find her hoydenish or bossy. He would appreciate the qualities that would daunt most gentlemen. But what chance did he and Selena ever have of marrying?

Shaking off such hopeless thoughts, she turned a bright smile on Orland as the footman dished an oxtail soup into her bowl. This was her welcome home party, and she meant to enjoy every moment of it.

The meal, from the soup to the breads to the main dishes to the wines, was all perfect in Flavia's opinion, and she knew her mother was very pleased with Selena and the progress Selena had made in her attempt to become the lady her mother wanted her to be. Flavia could not say whether she had helped Selena, but she knew Selena had helped her win Orland.

With dinner ended, the women left the men to their port and went upstairs to Selena's and Flavia's chambers to refresh themselves before the other guests arrived for the dance and the welcome home celebration. Flavia could hardly wait to dance with Orland. Amidst the chatter of the other women, Flavia let her heart soar. Never had she been so happy. She heard the musicians tuning up their instruments, and after a quick glance in the looking glass to see that her curls were still in place, she was ready to exit.

Her mother and Ewen would receive the guests as they arrived. "You and Selena have done enough," her mother said. "The two of you should enjoy the party." And so Flavia had eagerly accepted Orland's hand when the musicians started to play. They were joined on the floor by Selena and LaBree, Brilliana and Yardley, Suzanne Sizer and Preston, Cecily and Reynard, and the Nibleys. The first dance was a quick-paced, country dance, and by the time it ended, all the dancers were laughing. Recent arrivals joined them in the next dance, and the floor became more crowded. After the third dance, Orland had to relinquish Flavia, and he turned to Brilliana, not Selena. Inwardly, Flavia smiled. Orland was now hers. His imagined love affair with Selena was over.

With the crowd increasing, some of the guests drifted out to the game tables in the garden. Some danced on the terrace, and when Orland again claimed a dance with Flavia, he urged her outside. When the dance ended, Orland grabbed her by the hand and led her down the steps. Happily following her lover, Flavia let him lead her out into the garden. A few other couples were rambling down the pebbled paths, admiring the various blooming flowers and shrubs, but Orland led Flavia toward a trellis thick with dark red climbing roses. The roses' scent perfumed the late afternoon air, and a cooling breeze rustled the vines' vibrant green leaves.

The location of the trellis and its dense covering offered Flavia and Orland a modicum of privacy, and Orland captured both Flavia's hands in his and pulled her close. "Flavia, I had to have this moment with you. I must tell you, with your permission, when your father returns, I mean to ask him for your hand." His grip tightened slightly. "Do tell me I have your permission. I have already told my mother and father of my intentions, and they are most pleased."

His eyes glued to hers, searching hers, she smiled. With her heart hammering so loudly in her ears, she could hardly hear her own voice, she answered, "Oh, yes, Orland. You do have my permission to speak to Father."

"My darling!" he exclaimed, pulling her into his arms. Before she knew what was happening, his lips found hers, and she knew she had to be floating on air. His kiss, at first, was ever so gentle, but as she responded to his need, he drew her even closer. Her breasts pressed tight against his chest, she managed to sneak her arms up around his neck, and he emitted a low moan. Then his tongue was tasting her lips and urging her to part her lips. She did, a little at first, and then she tentatively let the tip of her tongue meet his. He moaned again, but this time pulled away from her. Looking down at her he whispered, "Oh, my sweet, sweet Flavia. How am I to survive until your father returns? I find I am desperate to be with you. I hope you will not mind if I push for a wedding before the first frost?"

Still awed by her first kiss, Flavia gazed up at the man she had loved since he was but a boy, and said, "As soon as we may make arrangements is fine with me."

"Ah! You are so wonderful." Glancing down at himself, he blushed and said, "I think mayhap we should walk a little before we return to the party. Do you mind?"

Noting a bulge in his breeches that his flared coat tails failed to hide, she said, "I would enjoy the walk, Orland. I enjoy having my hand in yours."

He inhaled deeply, and his chest puffed out. Then his eyes widened, and he gasped, "Flavia! I have not yet told you that I love you. What a clodpoll you must think me."

"Oh, never, Orland, never would I think such."

"I should have told you of my love, first thing. What a muddle I have made of my proposal."

She took his hand and gave it a kiss. "No, Orland. 'Twas a beautiful proposal. But I do like to hear you say you love me, for I love you so very much."

He pulled her into his arms. "My darling, my sweet darling. My love." Again he kissed her, but he quickly pulled away from her. "I think we had best take our walk. Indeed, I think 'tis best do we make a circle of the garden." Taking her hand, he tucked it into the crook of his arm, and they set off.

Dreams can and do come true, Flavia thought happily. Oh, yes they do.

<h1 style="text-align:center">Chapter 35</h1>

Dressed in her riding costume, Selena answered her aunt's summons. Entering the parlor, she recognized the petty school usher, Herbert Osgood. "Why Mister Osgood, how good to see you. I hope naught is amiss at the school sight."

The thin, middle-aged, slightly balding man jumped up from the seat he had been barely perched upon. Clutching his hat in his hands, he said, "Ah, Lady Selena, no, all is well. I have been speaking with Lady Rotherby about the plans for the classes."

Looking ever so regal, Aunt Rowena, from her seat on a floral-print, straight-backed chair, said, "Mister Osgood has hopes to take some classes himself from the schoolmaster, once we have one hired. He hopes someday to be able to teach grammar school himself."

"That is nice," Selena answered hesitantly. What did Osgood's ambition have to do with her? She was eager to go on her ride. Having risen later than usual after the previous day and evening's festivities, she felt a need to gallop into the wind.

"He believes the new schoolmaster is like to have a very large class and may upon occasion need Mister Osgood's help."

"That is understandable," Selena said, looking from her aunt to Osgood. She had to pity the man. Ushers, or petty school teachers, were generally poorly paid, and she guessed Osgood was no exception. On his modest wage, he had no option but to live with his brother. Selena had learned from Alice that Osgood was sweet on a widow in Whimbrel Village, but he could not afford to court her.

"Mister Osgood was thinking, was he to take on more responsibility, he might merit a slightly higher wage. He tells me he now makes eight pounds a year. Having started, he reminds me, at five pounds a year."

"That is correct," Osgood said, vigorously nodding his head. "Near all my wages go to my brother, who gives me bed and board and allows his parlor to function as the classroom."

"Yes, that is very kind of your brother," Selena said. "My maid Alice tells me you have been teaching there for many a year now. Alice says you taught her to read and to write."

"Indeed," Osgood interrupted, stating, "I have been teaching the petty school for seventeen years now."

"That is remarkable. You must be very dedicated. However, I cannot say I think eight pounds a year sufficient pay after all your years of teaching." She looked at her aunt. "What say you, Aunt Rowena?"

"No, I would say eight pounds is a tad low. That is one reason Mister Osgood is here. He is hoping his wage might be increased to twelve pounds a year. That is, does he take on more responsibility."

"That sounds reasonable to me," Selena said, still uncertain why her aunt was consulting her on raising the usher's wage. He would be paid partially by the village funds, and partially by Uncle Nate. She really had no say in the matter. "I know the Whimbrel villagers, as well as villagers from other manors, are doing a wonderful job of raising the funds, not only to build the school, but to buy books and slates and to help pay the teachers."

"Correct," Aunt Rowena said. "But Mister Osgood feels, if he is at times obliged to be helping the schoolmaster, he will need some help in his classroom."

"Yes, I can see he might," Selena said, tilting her head questioningly.

"He would like to have Will Huddleston assist him. He tells me Will is exceptionally bright. While still in petty school, he always completed his work quickly and was able to help other students who might be struggling. He believes, if the boy does help, he should receive some token wage." Holding up her hand to stop Selena from eagerly endorsing an approval of the plan, Aunt Rowena continued, "Mister Osgood would like you to suggest the matter to the villagers. He would also like you to broach the issue with Will Huddleston's parents. You have worked closely with Mistress Huddleston, and she has been a big supporter of the school project, so I have been told. So, as you seem to approve of Mister Osgood's proposal, I ask if you are willing to oblige his requests?"

Looking from her aunt to Osgood, Selena said, "Indeed I will. That is a wonderful idea. I think the Huddlestons would be proud, did Will assist Mister Osgood. And get paid for doing so. As I am off for a ride, I will visit the Huddlestons today and put the proposal to them. Do they, and of course, Will, approve, then Saturday, when I am to again meet with the Whimbrel villagers, I will present the idea to them. I shall ask them to pass the word around to the other manor villagers. I cannot think anyone would object." She finished with a broad smile.

"I thank you, Lady Selena. I knew I could count on you. You have already done so much. Just getting a school started in Whimbrel is wonderful. Everyone I talk with is so pleased they will not have to send their sons to Rotherby. I must tell you, too, the area around the old church has been cleaned, and the stone foundation leveled off and ready for the masons to begin laying the bricks as soon as the bricks are delivered. The miller's wife says she has a room all readied for the schoolmaster when he comes. Goodman Smite, who is donating the two acres for the schoolmaster's use, says he will see the two acres are plowed and ready for planting."

"My goodness," Selena said. "I have been so busy the last few days with helping prepare for Lady Flavia's welcome home party, that I had no idea so much was going on in the village. I must make a point to get over there to see what all has been done."

"Well," Osgood said, nodding his head and fumbling with his hat. "I best be getting back. My brother is expecting me to help with the harrowing. I told him I must need speak with you, but I promised I would return as quickly as I could. So, again I thank you." He looked at Aunt Rowena. "I thank you for your time, Lady Rotherby. So good of you to see me."

"You are welcome, Mister Osgood. Good day to you."

Bowing himself from the room, he was met by a footman who showed him out of the house. Selena watched him depart, then turned to her aunt. "Much good news today on top of a most successful party. I am to tell you that Flavia has risen and will be down shortly. Today she was as much a sleepyhead as I was. Ewen and his friends are only now breaking their fast. But, as I have broken my fast with a piece of toast and butter, I think I will take my ride."

Aunt Rowena laughed. "Yes, dear, take your ride. You deserve it. You surpassed all my most ambitious hopes. I can write your mother that she can be very proud of you."

Selena grinned. "Thank you, Aunt Rowena. That will make Mother happy." With a little wave, she near bounced out of the room. Such praise was greatly appreciated. Few things could bring her more happiness than to have her mother pleased with her.

Upon arriving at the stable, though, she was met with disappointment. "I fear Brigantia has thrown a shoe," Jimmy told her, and holding up the horse's hoof, he showed Selena the bare hoof. "I think it must have happened yesterday morning. I gave her but a quick run, as I was needed to help with the party, and I thought when we were returning, her gait was off, but being in a hurry, I fear I failed to check her out. My apologies, Lady Selena."

Selena frowned, but said, "You have naught to apologize for, Jimmy. That you even gave her a run with all your other duties was most kind of you."

"I will take her into Whimbrel to the farrier," Jimmy said. "Should not take him too long to have her shod. But I will have him check her other shoes as well, to be sure no others need replacing. I would think, did you wish a ride this afternoon, she would be ready for you."

"Yes, I suppose that is what you will have to do. You will walk her slowly, will you not? She will be wanting a run, but you must hold her back."

"Yes, milady. I will put a strong lead rope on her and keep it tight. And I shall ride the old cob that pulls the manure cart. He is slow and will not be tempted by Brigantia to run."

Selena laughed. "Good thinking, Jimmy. I did want to go see the Huddlestons today. Mayhap I will change clothes and walk over." She gave Brigantia a pat on the neck. "You be good, and we shall have us a fine gallop this afternoon. Could be Ewen and his comrades will want to go for a race or some such."

Deciding she would not let the morning's disappointment disrupt her plans to visit the Huddlestons, she quickly changed out of her riding costume and into a walking gown and her sturdy walking shoes. The day being warm, she grabbed up a wide-brimmed hat with a jaunty plume and set off. Walking around by the road would take extra time. She decided she would take the trail the other side of the lake that went down the hillside. Flavia thought the trail too steep, but Selena believed she could navigate it. Over the years, she had traipsed up and down many a hill with her brothers, Reginald and Artemas.

After giving pats and scratches to the animals that as usual followed her about whenever she was outside, Selena bid them stay and set off at a good pace. She found the path with no trouble and started making her way down the hill. It was steeper than she had expected, but bushes and trees gave her firm branches to grip for support, and before she knew it, she was down the hill. She decided she would not try to climb back up the hill. Instead, as she had made such good time descending the hill, after she visited at the Huddlestons', she would go by Calder's farm and see him, was he to home. She could still be back at Whimbrel Hall in time for dinner. With everyone rising late, dinner was to be served an hour later than usual.

She had not seen Calder in over two weeks, and she missed him terribly. She had been so busy with the school and with preparations for Flavia's party, that she had been able to visit the Grantham farm but twice when she took her rides on Brigantia. Both times, Calder had been absent. Busy plowing and harrowing more distant fields, Hannah told her. She had shared a chat with Hannah. Had learned Hermia was not only doing a fine job milking the sheep, but in between milkings, she was helping weed the pea and bean fields. She also learned Joseph and Hermia had been walking out together, and Hannah was expecting any day to hear they had decided to wed. Selena envied the couple. She wished she could go walking out with Calder.

Traipsing up the rise between Calder's land and White Acres, Selena heard a pitiful bleating. Looking down the hill she spied a lamb stuck in the scraggly grassy morass Calder had warned her about when he first took her to visit the Huddlestons. "Oh, you poor little thing," she cried. "You must be stuck. Well, there is naught to do but to get you out."

Carefully working her way down the hillside, and taking care not to slip, she reached the edge of the murky bog. "Oh, dear, you are a bit far out. How did you get that far? Did you think those muddy grasses looked more tasty than the grass on dry land? Foolish lamb."

The lamb starting bleating more loudly and struggling harder, and Selena could see the movements were making the lamb sink more rapidly. Sighing, and wondering what her aunt would say when she came home covered in muck, Selena took off her walking shoes and hose, and, hoisting her gown and petticoats up around her waist and tying them in a large knot, she waded into the mire. The muck squished between her toes, and she was sunk up to her knees before she reached the lamb. The lamb, being several months old, was large enough to be heavy for her to lift, especially as it continued to bleat and squiggle, but finally she had it freed. Lifting it up in her arms, she struggled to turn and start back to the bank, but she found herself sinking deeper with the weight of the animal. Holding it out from her, she tossed the lamb toward the edge of the mire. The lamb's back feet hit her on the chest, but the lamb flew through the air and landed in the shallow area. It managed to scamper out of the mire, but in the process, its little feet trampled on Selena's hose and shoes and flung them into the mire.

"Oh, great," Selena said. "I hope I can find them. I have no wish to walk home barefoot." The lamb, paying no attention to Selena's scolding, cavorted around, jumping and kicking up its little feet.

"At least you are happy," Selena said, before trying to take a step forward. For a moment, panic seized her. She could not move her legs, and she was sunk near up to her hips. Be calm, she told herself. Just move slowly forward. Push your leg forward. She moved a little, but she was sinking faster than she was moving. Her heart began pounding in her chest, and her throat went dry. She started calling for help. Surely someone would hear her. Again she tried to move one leg forward. She was now sunk to her waist, her skirt and petticoats clumping around her. "Help! Someone help!" she cried at the top of lungs, but all she heard in response was the lamb's bleating, then it too left her, scampering up and over the hill.

Never in her life had she been so terrified. How could she have been so foolish. Calder had warned her not to go near the morass, but she had let her heart overrule her common sense. She had been so confident she could save the lamb, that she had given no thought to her own safety. Surely she was not going to die. Surely she would not die in this terrible muck. She would never see her family again. She would never see Calder again. Never feel his arms around her or feel his lips on hers. "Oh, God," she cried. "Help! Help!" But again she received no answer.

No one would know what had happened to her. They would not even find her shoes. Her hat! She would toss her hat over to the edge. They would find her hat and at least would know how she had died. Raising her muddy hands to her head, she pulled the hat off. Feeling a gust of wind, she gave the hat a toss with a prayer it would reach the edge of the mire. The wind gust, catching the hat like it was a kite, carried it up into the air, let it momentarily dip, then floated it up and over the hillside.

"No!" Selena cried. Now, how would anyone finding the hat know she had disappeared into the morass. She could not move out of the morass, but did she remain still, she was not sucked downward quite as rapidly. She would try calling and calling for help. Someone might yet hear her. Filling her lungs, she called out until she was too hoarse to make much more than a low squawk, and she was near up to her armpits in the mire.

Tears filled her eyes and trickled down her cheeks. What a horrid way to die. She wondered how long she would suffer once she was sucked under. She wanted to kick out, to fight, to struggle, but something told her she had to remain still. Then she heard a voice.

# Chapter 36

"Why look at you, you naughty lamb. What are you doing out here. Here you are all muddy. How did you get so muddy?"

Pascal! Selena recognized Pascal's voice. He was the other side of the hill, talking to the lamb. "Pascal!" she cried, but it came out as naught but a croak. Oh, God! How was she to make him hear her?

"What is that you are chewing on?" she heard Pascal scold. "Why, looks like a lady's hat. Where did you find that hat? Look how you have chewed it up. It looks like a hat I have seen Lady Selena wear. If 'tis hers, and you have chewed it up, Father will be most angry at you."

"Pascal!" Selena cried again, but she could barely hear her own voice.

"I best get you back in the field and remind Father that bramble fence needs patching. Gramercy. You are just covered in mud. Were you in the mire?"

Then Selena heard him cry, "Rollo! Come back here! Where do you go?" An instant later the black and white dog came bounding over the hillside and scooted to a stop at the edge of the morass. Shrill yips interspersed with barks, he bounced on his front paws and danced back and forth along the edge of the morass. The next instant, Pascal was at the top of the hill.

"Begad! Lady Selena!" He started to come down the hill, but stopped. "Lady Selena, I will get Father. But you must remain still. Very still!" With that, the boy turned and ran off.

Hope filled Selena's heart. Maybe she would not die. But she was still sinking. Could Pascal find his father and get him here in time to save her? Did he not, at least they would know how she died. She was glad to have Rollo for company. The dog had the good sense not to try to come to her. He continued to yip and bounce along the edge of the mire, but whenever he got his front paws too far into the muck, he backed out.

Stretching her arms out as far as she could to her sides, she hoisted her chin and tilted her head back into the muck. They had best hurry. Oh, dear God, hurry! Hurry! Did she hear pounding footsteps? Yes! She started to cry as Calder appeared over the hillside. He was down the hill in an instant and tossed her one end of a rope.

"Tie it under your arms around your chest," were his first words to her. "Make the knot secure, Selena. You can do it." He started wading into the mire as he spoke.

"No," she croaked. "Be careful."

"Never mind me, just do as I say."

His steady voice was helping to calm her desperate fears as she struggled to get the rope around her when that part of her body was buried in the muck. Absurdly, considering the desperate situation she was in, she was buoyed by his use of just her given name, Selena. Not Lady Selena. Strange she thought as she pulled the knot tight, that she could notice that little slip when she was so near to death. But notice it she had.

Panting and near breathless, Pascal arrived, but like Rollo, he bounced at the edge of the morass. His eyes darted from her to his father and back to her.

Calder was now into the mire up to his mid-calf, but he paid no heed to her worried croaks and commanded, "Grab that rope and hold on tight. I am going to pull you out."

She did as she was bid. Clinging to the rope, she at first seemed not to move, but then she realized her torso was being dragged forward. She had to fight to keep her head above the muck, but she was moving. As she was inched forward, Calder began slowly backing up. Then with one large step backward, he had one foot on dry land. Then both feet were on secure footing. Bending slightly forward, he tugged steadily, one hand over the other. He backed up more, took another firm stance, gave a hefty tug, then dropped the rope, stepped into the mire and pulled her up and out.

Dropping onto the ground in a sitting position, he pulled her into his arms, and cradling her on his lap, he rocked her while murmuring, "Oh, my dear one, my dear, dear girl. Thank the Lord I have not lost you."

She was alive! She was not going to die! And she was in Calder's arms with him cooing endearments. Her heart hammered in her breast. Calder was in love with her. Whimpering and nestling against his chest, she felt Rollo licking her face and Pascal patting her head. "You will be all right now, Lady Selena," Pascal said. "You are safe. And we will get you all cleaned up. Will we not, Father?"

Calder nodded his head. "Yes, we will get you all cleaned up," he told her, and though he stopped rocking, he still held her tightly. Looking up at Pascal, he said, "Run ahead and tell Hannah what has happened. Tell her to start heating what water she has on hand."

"Aye, Father."

Before Pascal could dart off, Calder continued with a series of instructions. "Find Billy and tell him to cart the bathing tub up to my room. Then he is to get a fire going in the hearth. Next he is to start filling buckets of water for Hannah to heat. Hermia is in the bean field. Get her and send her to fetch Mistress Huddleston. Can you do all that, son?"

"Aye, Father."

"Good boy," Calder said, and Pascal took off on the run.

Calder heaved a deep sigh, and Selena raised her head to look into his eyes. "I believe you cannot deny your love for me, Calder Grantham. You should not even try."

With a shallow snort, he said, "No, my dear girl, I cannot deny my love for you. But where does that leave me?"

"I would hope it would lead you to ask me to marry you," she answered, her voice still little more than a croak.

His arms tightened around her. Placing his head on hers, he said, "God, if I only could."

"Prithee, why can you not?"

"My sweet child, you are a lady of the realm. Your father is an Earl. I am naught but a yeoman. Your father would never permit such a match." As he spoke, he surprised her by scooting her off his lap. But after rising to his feet, he pulled her to her feet and helped her free her petticoat and skirt from the slimy knot at her waist. Once her muddy legs and bare feet were decently covered, he scooped her up in his arms.

Gads he is strong, she thought, loving his strength and the gentle way he held her. She wrapped her muddy arms around his neck and brought his mouth to hers. She would have her kiss. She had dreamed of kissing her yeoman for too many nights. Knowing he loved her, and she loved him, she would no longer be denied.

His lips met hers hungrily. The kiss was better than she could have imagined. Lightning flashed, bells chimed, choirs sang, and a heavenly light beamed down from above. Her head spinning, her pulse racing, she clung to Calder and willed the kiss never to end. But it did. Though she could feel his heart pummeling, he pulled away from her.

"Selena, I love you more than I have words to tell you. But I cannot take advantage of you. You feel grateful that I saved you, but on the morrow…"

"I love you, Calder!" she cried, interrupting his speech. She wished her voice sounded sweeter and less like a frog, but she would proclaim her love anyway. "On the morrow, I will love you even more. I have loved you from the first moment I met you. If you think I will let my father stop me from marrying you, you must think again. I will be twenty-one this fall. I may then marry whomever I please. Does my father not approve, it will sadden me, but it will not stop me from marrying you. You have professed your love, and we will be married."

He gazed into her eyes, then kissed the tip of her nose. "That is near the only part of you that is not covered in mud," he said, cocking his head and smiling. "Do you say we will be wed, then I can tell you now, there could be no happier man on the face of this planet. But I must get you to the house and get you into a tub of water. It will not do to have this slime cake on you."

Smiling, she heaved a happy sigh. "Yes, my love, take me home." After all, his home would soon be her home.

# Chapter 37

With Rollo bouncing along at their side, Calder set off for his house. He splashed through the stream, not bothering to traipse over the foot stones. If she was a heavy load to carry, he gave no indication. Halfway back to the house, they met Hermia. She exclaimed over Selena, but then went scurrying off to get Avis Huddleston. Hannah was waiting at the door for them when they arrived. She had two full buckets of water at her feet. After fussing over Selena and assuring herself that Selena was all right, she said, "Before you enter the house, I mean to dunk these pails of water over you. Calder, you go to the pond and wash. I will get Lady Selena up to your bedchamber. The tub is half full with warm water, a fire is crackling in the hearth, and here come Billy and Pascal with more water. They can put it to heating. It may take some scrubbing, Lady Selena, but we will get you all cleaned up and then into bed."

Selena submitted to having the water dumped over her, but she failed to see where it did much good. All the same, Hannah seemed satisfied, and she bustled her up the stairs and down the corridor to Calder's bedchamber. Dripping muddy water and slime all along the way, Selena apologized for the mess she was causing, but Hannah just clucked at her and told her not to be minding it. She had Hermia to help her clean things up.

Selena hated being parted from Calder, especially, as in her mind, they were now betrothed, but she knew he could not help her with her bath, much as the idea sent a tingle up her spine. Something to remember for the future, she thought. Entering the bedchamber, it was as she remembered it from the day she had secretly peeked inside it. A bright room, warmed by the glowing fire in the hearth and the sun beating in through the windows. The blue window curtains and coverlet on the four-poster bed gave the room a cheery feel.

Catching a glimpse of herself in the looking glass above the stand holding a pitcher and wash basin, Selena gasped. Her hair hung in muddy strings, her face was blotched with mud, and her favorite walking gown was solid mud with a few water streamlets running down it. Hannah closed the door to the bedchamber and said, "Turn away from that looking glass. You are not one to be vain, that I know. You need worry about naught but thanking the Lord that Calder reached you in time. Now, let us get those clothes off you."

Selena forced herself to turn from the mirror. Hannah was right. She might look a fright, but she was alive, and she had not yet thanked the Lord for that miracle. She had never come so close to dying, and she hoped she never would again. At least not until she was old and gray and had enjoyed a long life with Calder. As terrified as she had been, her spirit was now soaring. Calder had admitted his love for her. Now, all she had to do was tell her parents she had at last found the man she would marry. They might balk at first, claiming he was not of her status, but she was confident, she and Calder would eventually win them over.

With Hannah's help, she managed to struggle out of her mud-covered clothing. She hated leaving the clothes in a slimy puddle on Calder's clean floor, but Hannah poo pooed her and shepherded her into the tub. The water turned murky the moment she stepped into it, but Hannah bid her sink down into it anyway. A tap at the door, and she heard Pascal call, "Hannah, we have two more buckets of water. They be but middlin' warm, but we thought you might be needing them quick."

"That is good, just leave them at the door, and go get more," Hannah said.

"Aye, Hannah," Pascal answered, and Selena heard footsteps retreating.

Hannah opened the door and retrieved the two pails. "Good thing we have no shortage of pails and buckets," she declared. "These be a couple of the milk pails. Of course the water must be heated in the kitchen hearth's iron caldron, then dumped back into these wooden pails. One could hardly lug the caldron upstairs. Most times, when we bathe, we bathe in front of the kitchen hearth, so there be no need to be carting the water upstairs." She chattered on as she dumped a portion of one pail of water over Selena's head. Clumping a glob of soft soap into Selena's hair and starting to scrub, she continued, "Calder always lets me bathe first. When I am all done and dressed, I let the men back in the house, and I go to my room until they have all had their turns in the tub." She chuckled. "'Tis funny to hear them splashing and making cracks to one another. Jared and Joseph were ever chaffing one another. 'Twill be different now I suppose, with Jared over to the Buxton farm. In the summer, the men folk all bathe in the pond near the falls that trickle down from the hillside. Come Saturday evening, after all the men are retired, I just use the foot tub to clean up for Sunday services."

Selena began to relax under Hannah's gentle scrubbing and genial, if trifling, chatter. She liked hearing about the workings of Calder's household. Soon she would be a part of the household, and she too would bathe before the kitchen hearth rather than have the water carted upstairs. She had never paid heed to how much work was involved in getting the bath water in and out of her bedchamber whenever she had wanted a bath. It had just always been something she accepted. Certainly, she had never shared her bathwater with anyone. That thought rather repelled her. She decided she could easily bathe in the kitchen, but she had to have her own bath water, did she have to haul it from the well herself.

A tap on the door sounded, then a voice called, "Hannah, 'tis Avis Huddleston. I came as quickly as I could."

"Come in," Hannah said. "The door is not latched."

Avis entered, followed by Hermia. "Oh, Lady Selena," Avis said, "Hermia has told me what happened. I thank the Lord you are safe." As she spoke, she and Hermia came closer to the tub. Looking at Hannah, Avis asked, "How may I help?"

"I have not had time to pull towels from the linen chest," Hannah said. "The chest is downstairs in the far corner. Bring up as many as you can carry. Then, in the chest at the foot of Eloisa's bed, you will find a night shift and robe. Do you fetch them, please."

Avis glanced down at the water Selena sat in, and her blue eyes filled with empathy. "You poor dear," she said, shaking her head before hurrying off.

"What of me, Hannah?" Hermia asked. "What would you have me do?"

"Bring up one of the larger buckets and bundle Lady Selena's clothing into it." Hannah nodded to the puddle of clothes on the floor. "Take them to the falls and see can you get most of the muck washed off afore it dries and cakes. I have some hope the gown may be saved."

"Oh, that would be grand," Selena croaked. "'Tis my favorite walking dress. I have already lost my shoes in the morass."

"How came you to be stuck in the mire, Lady Selena?" Hermia asked.

Selena noted Hermia was the first one to ask her that question. Not even Calder had asked her. "I was on my way to the Huddlestons', and I saw a lamb stuck in the mire. It was bleating so pitifully, I had to try to save it. I wadded out too far, and though I saved the lamb, I was stuck. Fortunately for me, Rollo sensed I was there, and thanks to that wonderful dog, I am alive. Pascal was able to bring Calder to my rescue just when I was near to going under."

Hermia grabbed both her hands to her breast. "Oh, Lady Selena! How frightful!"

"At least I will know never to try my luck at such a venture again."

"I should say, you had best know better," Hannah said with a snort.

"I will get the bucket and see to the clothes," Hermia said.

Avis returned with the towels, laid them on the bed, and looked again at the water. "Should we not get her into some cleaner water, Hannah?"

Hannah nodded. "Aye. There is a foot tub in my bedchamber. If Calder is clean, ask him to bring it up."

Avis chuckled. "He is clean, but he is ringing wet. He went down to the pond and jumped in clothes and all. He wants not to disturb Lady Selena's bath, but he is in need of some dry clothing."

"Ah," Hannah said, "look in the chest at the foot of his bed. You will find a couple of pair of breeches and shirts. Take him whatever you please. He can change in my room and then bring up the foot tub."

Avis did as Hannah directed, but Selena could not help feeling guilty that Calder was being kept out of his own room, and that he was standing around in wet clothing. She would never forgive herself, were he to catch a cold.

Hermia returned with a large empty bucket and began stuffing Selena's clothing into it. "Billy says the water in the caldron be pipin' hot, Hannah," she said.

"Then tell him and Pascal to bring it up. 'Twill cool enough to use by the time they haul it up here. Tell them to set the buckets outside the door as they did before."

"I will," Hermia said and exited.

"I believe I have a goodly portion of the mud out of your hair now," Hannah said. "I mean to pour the rest of that water over you. 'Twill be a tad on the cool side, but we will soon have some hot water up here for you."

"It matters not, Hannah. I simply cannot thank you enough for all you are doing for me."

"Nonsense. 'Tis little enough for what you have done for Pascal and Calder. Little enough I tell you. Saving Pascal from those dogs, and getting the squire to pay what he owed for the dogs killing the lamb. Helping with the shearing. Saving Rollo from Mister Darnell. Good thing you did save Rollo, so he could be saving you."

"Indeed. That dog deserves a special treat," Selena said with a laugh. Her first laugh since she had been pulled from the mire.

"'Tis good to hear your laugh again," Hannah said, as a tap sounded at the door, and Pascal called in that the water was delivered.

Hannah dumped the remainder of one pail over Selena's hair, then scrubbed her fingers through the tangled mass. "I fear your hair will need another scrubbing, Lady Selena, but let us see about the rest of you." She handed Selena a cloth. "You scrub on your front, I will work on your back. When Calder gets the foot tub up here, we will get you out of this mucky water and get you rinsed off with some nice clean water."

Selena began scrubbing. She would be only too happy to get out of the dark colored water that surrounded her. It reminded her too much of the mire she had barely escaped.

❦ ❦ ❦

Calder sat at the table attempting to compose a message to Lady Rotherby. He was having trouble concentrating with his heart continuing to run rampant in his chest. His fear for Selena had near overwhelmed him. But her avowal of her love for him, and then her kiss, had his head in a whirl. He could not seem to arrange his thoughts in any order.

Twice in the past fortnight, Selena had come by the farm. Both times, he had been plowing a distant field. He had known she would be busy planning the party for Lady Flavia, as well as organizing funding for the school, so he had not expected her to visit. But this morning, he had determined he would stay near the house. He would continue his wood chopping, much as he hated it. For whatever the reason, he believed she would come by, and he desperately wanted to see her. To just hear her laugh, see her eyes dance, listen to her voice.

When a breathless Pascal raced up to him and panted out the heart-stopping tidings, Selena was stuck in the morass, he wondered that he had retained the capacity to think clearly enough to grab a rope from the barn. Racing toward the morass, his lungs burning and near to burst, his vision blurred with his fear, he had no thought but to reach Selena in time. God, but he would trade his own life for hers.

But now she was safe, safe upstairs in his bedchamber with Hannah and Avis ministering to her. Avis told him they meant to tuck Selena into his bed once they had her thoroughly clean and her hair dry. The thought that Selena would be in his bed stirred feelings in him that he knew he should not be feeling. That Selena loved him, had told him she loved him, brought him more joy than he had known in many a year, if ever. He almost chuckled at her adamant declaration that she would wed him. He knew that to be impossible, but at least he would always have that shared kiss with her. That, he would always hold to his heart.

Many a time he had imagined Selena as his wife, living in his home, sharing his life. He knew such thoughts to be but foolish dreams. He could not expect Selena to be content as a farmer's wife. She was used to having people serve her. She was used to fine food and clothes. Used to fine homes with paintings on the walls and costly furnishings. No, as proud as he was of his home, he knew he could never expect Selena to be happy in such an abode. Besides, her parents, despite Selena's claims, would never allow such a marriage.

Forcing his thoughts back to the sheet of paper before him, he began to write. After informing Lady Rotherby that Selena was well and unharmed, he explained how Selena had been stuck in the mire, but she was being cared for by Hannah and Avis Huddleston, and her spirits were good. Selena would need clothes and shoes, though. With the message completed, he gave it to Billy to take to Whimbrel Hall.

Hermia returned, saying she had cleaned Lady Selena's gown and other garments as best she could and had hung them to dry beside his clothes across the fence outside the horse barn. "I think once they are truly laundered, they can be saved," Hermia said. "'Twill take some scrubbing though, I am thinking."

"I thank you, Hermia," he said. "Hannah asked if you might start getting the mud from the floor. Billy wiped up a good portion of it, but I believe there may be a puddle up in my bedchamber."

"I will get right to it, Calder, but is it not time to be taking dinner out to Abner and Joseph? Sun is nigh directly above the house."

He ran a hand through his hair. "With all that has been going on, I forgot about Abner and Joseph. They can have no idea what has happened and will be wondering about the delay of their mid-day meal." The field was too distant for the men to come back to the house for their dinner. "Best you cut up some bread and cheese and some of that ham hock, and pour up a jug of ale, then you and Pascal can take it out to them. The mud on the floor in my room can wait."

"Yes, sir," Hermia answered, turning to the work table. "Here, Pascal, you break off the bread while I see to the cheese and ham."

Absently watching Hermia and Pascal ready his laborers' mid-day meal, Calder again turned his thoughts to Selena. She was like no woman he had ever known. Her gaiety, her love of animals and their love for her was more than a little unique. Her eagerness to help others was inspiring. What she had done for Wally Shandy was unparalleled. He had not even recognized his former laborer when he came by to share his news and apologize for not fulfilling his obligation to milk the ewes. Hannah and Pascal had both stood with their mouths open.

Wally promised once his first book was printed, he would send Calder a copy. Despite Wally's protestations, Calder had insisted paying him the wages he had earned.

"Give you some spending money until you get paid by your new boss," he told Wally, and Wally, after thanking him graciously, had shown them his new spectacles. He had praised Lord Sutherlin and his friends for taking him to Leicester and seeing him outfitted, but he gave the real credit for his good fortune to Lady Selena.

"Indeed, she is a marvel," Hannah had declared before Wally set off to bid his goodbyes to his family. Calder had wished he could see Laban Shandy's face. No doubt Laban would be relieved to have his brother out of his house, but he could well be jealous of Wally's new eminence. The two brothers had never been close.

What changes Selena was making in so many lives. The school in Whimbrel would mean so many more boys would be able to attend school. Pascal would not have to go all the way to Rotherby to continue his schooling. And by helping Wally, Selena had helped bring Hermia and Joseph together. Calder had no doubt Joseph would soon be asking Hermia for her hand. He liked the idea of permanently employing Hermia. Hannah was showing her age. Rightfully, she should have help with her numerous responsibilities.

What life would be like once Selena was no longer in their lives was too dreary to think about. But someday she would return to her home and marry someone in her own class. That thought was too mind numbing to consider. Fortunately, Hannah came downstairs at that moment and brightened his thoughts by telling him she and Avis had Selena tucked into his bed, and Selena was resting peacefully.

"To think," Hannah said, "Lady Selena was on her way to visit the Huddlestons to tell them the petty school usher wants young Will to help him teach the petty school. Lady Selena says the boy is to receive a wage for his help. Is that not something. Avis has always said that Will has a bright mind. This proves it. Avis has hope this may help Will get a scholarship to continue his schooling beyond even Leicester. Mayhap go on to one of the Inns of Court or even Oxford. Now, that would be something."

"One more thing Lady Selena has made possible," Calder said, speaking more to himself than to Hannah.

"True enough," Hannah answered.

Hermia, arms burdened with the meal for the laborers, told Hannah, "Calder said Pascal and I should take the mid-day meal to Joseph and Abner."

"Good," Hannah said with a bob of her head. "I had forgotten all about them, but I mean to get dinner for the rest of us and a nice broth with some lamb chucks and peas for Lady Selena. You and Pascal hurry on but scurry back. I am not wanting to hold up dinner for you."

"Yes, Hannah," Hermia answered, and with Pascal lugging the jug of ale, they set off for the far field.

Calder doubted they would return as quickly as Hannah might wish. They would have to tell Abner and Joseph about Selena's mishap and rescue.

"Might I see Lady Selena?" Calder asked. "Think you, it would be improper? Her being in bed?"

"Humph! Considering you carried her home in your arms like you did, I am thinking with Avis there in the room, and Lady Selena with the sheets pulled up to her chin, there can be naught improper in you visiting her. Go on up. No doubt, she will be happy to see you." Hannah, a grin on her face, turned from the work table to look at him. "Especially as she says you and she are now betrothed."

# Chapter 38

"What!" Calder jumped to his feet. Could he have heard Hannah correctly?

"She said she wanted me and Avis to be some of the first to know. She intends to tell her aunt today, she said, and she means to write her father and mother on the morrow."

"My God!" He started laughing and shaking his head. "She is beyond comprehension."

"You cannot claim you are not in love with her, Calder Grantham. I have eyes in my head, and I have seen how you look at her and how she looks at you. If ever two people were more in love than you two, I have not seen it."

"Yes, I love her. How could I not love her? But what have I to offer her. Besides, her father will never permit her to marry me."

"She says she has no need of her father's permission. She will be of age in two months. Then she can marry whom she pleases. Did I not tell you before that Lady Selena is a resourceful young woman. Does she mean to marry you, that she will do, Calder. Now, go up and see her."

For a moment Calder just stared at Hannah, then a hope like he had never known leapt into his heart. Maybe somehow he would be able to marry Selena. Maybe somehow he would be able to make her happy here in his humble home. She was so different from other ladies of the higher social status. As Hannah said in the past, Selena loved the freedom she had here on his farm. That, he would never take away from her. Was he truly able to marry her, her license to be the free soul she wanted to be would be his gift to her.

As he slowly climbed the stairs, he tried not to let his excitement overtake him. They had yet to confront Lady Rotherby and then Selena's father, but maybe, maybe …

Rowena could not believe she was again on the way to the Grantham farm in her coach, this time to bring home her niece. When she had received the message from Grantham, she had come as close as she ever had to fainting. Fear had gripped her heart. Selena, her beloved niece, stuck in a morass. Unharmed, Grantham wrote. But the very fact that he wrote "unharmed" meant Selena must have been close to dire circumstances.

The boy delivering the note had been shown into the parlor where Rowena, Flavia, Ewen, and his friends were gathered, lounging and re-living the previous day's successful party. Still panting, the boy handed Rowena the folded paper. Having read it, Rowena had clasped it to her heart. That she was near to collapsing must have been obvious, for Ewen and Flavia both rushed to her side. Flavia fanned her, and Ewen asked Yardley to pour a brandy for his mother.

Gently taking the note from his mother, Ewen scanned it and passed it to Flavia. She read it and gasped.

"What is amiss," Yardley demanded, handing Ewen the brandy for his mother.

"Seems my cousin, as per usual, has had another calamity. Got stuck in a bog. Mother will have to retrieve her. Seems she needs clothes and shoes. Oh, she will have a story to tell."

"This is nothing to be trite about, Ewen," Rowena snapped, annoyed Ewen could not recognize the seriousness of Selena's misadventure.

Ewen handed his mother the brandy and smiled at her. "Feeling better, Mother?"

Taking the brandy, she sipped it and nodded. Her son had been bait-ing her to revive her spirits. It had worked. She rallied enough to send the footman for Alice, Selena's maid. After finding her, he should order the coach brought around.

"I will go with you, Mother," Flavia said. "Poor Selena."

"Thank you, dear." Rowena patted her daughter's hand, then looked over at the thin, wiry youth who brought the note. "You look exhausted. Did you run all the way here."

"Aye, Lady Rotherby." His eyes wide and round, he held his cap in his hands and was twisting it anxiously.

Rowena guessed he had never been inside a grand home before. She looked up at her son. "Ewen, will you please take this youth by the kitchen and tell cook to give him something to drink." She looked back at the boy. "When you are refreshed, go round to the front of the house and wait for the coach. You may ride back on the coach."

"Oh, aye, Lady Rotherby. Thank you, thank you." He started backing out, then turned as Ewen slapped him on the shoulder and said, "Come with me, young fellow."

At the door, Ewen turned back to his mother. "I believe I will ride over to Grantham's, Mother." He looked at his three friends. "Care to join me? After we see Selena is safe and sound, we can ride over to Nibley's and try out that port he invited us to taste. Claims it is outstanding."

"What of your dinner?" Rowena asked.

"Ah, no doubt Nibley will see we are well fed."

"We are with you," Preston said. "Got to be a good story on how Lady Selena ended up in a morass."

"Aye," Yardley and LaBree agreed, and they all traipsed out of the parlor to go get their horses, as Alice entered.

"Best tell Cook dinner will not only be delayed, but you will not be eating," Rowena called after her son.

"Aye," Ewen called back to her.

Told of Selena's dire mishap, Alice hurried to gather up clothes and shoes and hose for Selena. She was back down to the parlor by the time the coach rolled up to the front door. The boy, Rowena learned his name was Billy, eagerly joined the coachman atop the coach, and Rowena, Flavia, and Alice settled into the coach. The coach set off with Ewen and his friends following far enough behind not to be eating the summer dust kicked up by the coach wheels.

Rowena knew Selena's father was used to Selena's numerous mishaps and accidents, but Rowena was glad none of her children had ever been drawn to such misadventures. She doubted her heart would have been able to stand the constant shocks. That she herself had joined Nate and his highwaymen as they sought riches to send to the King in his exile seemed like a long distant memory. More myth than reality. Still, danger to oneself was somehow different than danger to one's beloved children. That she had borne five children, and they all survived into adulthood made her a fortunate woman. But she would never have been able to face her brother-in-law's wife if, under her watch, something dreadful had happened to Selena.

Selena was not her child, but she loved her. Who would not love Selena? But, indeed, Rowena would be relieved when Selena returned to her home.

❀ ❀ ❀

Calder heard the arrival of the coach, and rose from the chair next to the bed. He and Selena had been quietly talking. He had kept the conversation light and on inconsequential matters. Things concerning the farm and Pascal and the school. He dare not let himself hope that he really would be able to marry Selena. Not yet. And he would not let her discuss the possibility with him. She had a way of making things seem so reasonable.

Avis had busied herself cleaning up the mess made from the mud and slime, but she never left the room. She knew Selena believed she was betrothed, but Avis knew better than to allow any impropriety. Calder had been able to hold Selena's hand, but he had not been able to kiss her, much as he would have given near anything for that privilege.

"I believe your aunt has arrived, Lady Selena," he said. "I must go down and greet her."

"You must call me Selena," she said, her voice having resumed some of its lightness. "We are betrothed. You must call me Selena, as you did when you pulled me from the mire."

He smiled at her. "When either your father has consented to our marriage, or you are of age, I will address you more personally. Until then, you are Lady Selena."

When Selena started to protest, Avis, coming over to the bed, said, "That is as it should be, Lady Selena."

Grateful to Avis for intervening, Calder blew Selena a kiss before hurrying downstairs, arriving in time to greet not only Lady Rotherby, but Lady Flavia and her brother Lord Sutherlin, his three friends, and Selena's maid Alice. The three women immediately hurried upstairs to see Selena, leaving Calder to entertain the four gentlemen. Hannah soon had noggins filled with ale on the table. She next placed platters of cheese, chunks of ham, slivers of lamb, and toasted bread with butter on the table.

The four men seemed to be ravenous, devouring the spread before them, while listening to Calder tell what he knew of how Selena ended up in the morass.

"That would be Selena," Lord Sutherlin said, after learning Selena had been rescuing a lamb stuck in the bog. He looked at each one of his friends. "Did I not tell you she was naught but trouble. Been that way all her life. Always into something. Great fun. As good a horsewoman as you will find anywhere, but not the woman I would wish on any of my friends."

A young man who had been introduced as Yardley, said, "I fear I am beginning to agree with you, Sutherlin. Lady Selena dances divinely, she is a great companion at the table, and she plays a good game of pall mall, but I can see how, as a wife, she could be a tad eccentric."

Calder was torn between wanting to defend Selena and being glad the three handsome young gentlemen considered Selena's behavior erratic. That would mean they would not be tempted to woo her or win her hand. Certainly, socially, any of them would be a more suitable choice for Selena than he was, but what they found eccentric, he found charming and endearing. As he listened to the young men, he came to the realization that he would be by far the best husband for Selena. She was a treasure, and by God, he would fight for the right to marry her. He could make her happy, and that was all that mattered.

Surprised by his decision, he smiled at his unexpected guests. A joyful group they were, and becoming more so as Hannah refilled their noggins. Billy had come in and was lingering near the door, watching the four carefree gentlemen. Calling to the boy, Hannah bid him take noggins of ale out to the men with the coach. The boy obeyed, and Hannah, turning to the cauldron simmering over a low flame in the hearth, dished up a bowl of broth.

"'Tis a good lamb broth with some slivers of lamb in it," she told Calder. "Be just what Lady Selena needs to help bring her voice back. I will take it on up to her."

As Hannah went up the stairs, Lord Sutherlin asked, "What ails Selena's voice."

"She did a lot of hollering for help," Calder said.

"Oh, gads," Sutherlin said, frowning and scrunching his nose. "I hate to think what she went through. No one, especially a woman, should have to endure that. I tell you, Grantham, we could never be more grateful to you, and that is a fact."

"Aye," Yardley seconded. "Mighty lucky she is that you were able to save her in time."

Bursting through the door before Calder could respond, Pascal cried, "Father, Billy said he rode back from Whimbrel Hall atop the Rotherby coach."

"That he did son. But make your bow to Lord Sutherlin and his friends."

Pascal's eyes wide, he made a quick bow and advancing on the group around the table said, "Those are fine horses you have. The coachman let me pet each one of them."

The young men all chuckled, and Sutherlin said, "For one so young, you have a good eye for horses."

"Oh, aye," Pascal said with a proud grin. "I mean to have me a fine horse someday."

"Do you keep that as a goal, no doubt you will," Sutherlin answered. "Tell me, are you the one who found my cousin in the bog and went racing for help?"

"Aye, sir. Well, Rollo first found her. He stayed with her until Father and I came."

Cocking his head, Sutherlin asked, "Who is Rollo?"

"Our dog," Pascal said proudly. "As good a dog as can be found anywhere."

"I will agree with that," Yardley said, joining the conversation. "Your Father told us how the dog sensed Lady Selena was stuck in the mire. He is a good dog."

"The best," Pascal said with a firm nod to his head, as Hermia and Billy entered, Hermia burdened with the empty food hamper and ale jug.

"You left the jug sitting on the ground, Pascal. One of the horses could have stomped on it," Hermia said, eyeing the young men at the table while making her way over to the work table.

"I am sorry," Pascal said, looking contrite.

Hermia shrugged and turned to Calder, "Abner and Joseph said t' tell you they made good progress on the plowing this morning. Ground should be ready for harrowing tomorrow. They also asked you t' tell Lady Selena, they are most sorry about her dire mishap."

Calder nodded. "I will tell her. You and Billy and Pascal must be hungry. Hannah has set food on the table. Grab you some plates and sit down and eat. I cannot think Lord Sutherlin and his companions will mind, do you join them at the table."

"Nay," the jovial Yardley said, and another man Calder believed had been introduced as Preston, raised sleepy-looking eyes and said, "Do join us. The more the merrier."

Hermia poured Pascal a noggin of buttermilk and noggins of ale for herself and Billy, took wooden trenchers from the open cupboard above the work table, and she, Billy, and Pascal joined the young gentlemen. They were all having a merry time, when Lady Rotherby, her daughter, and Avis came downstairs.

"Hannah is feeding Lady Selena the broth," Avis said, "and I, thinking Lady Rotherby, after hearing Lady Selena's tale, was looking a bit pale. I thought it best she come down and have something to drink. After Lady Selena has finished her broth, Alice will help her dress. Lady Selena is looking much more herself, I am pleased to say."

Calder had risen and pulled forward a chair for Lady Rotherby. The chair he used in the evenings when the others had retired for the night. The chair he sat in and dreamed of Selena. After Lady Rotherby was seated, he offered her a glass of brandy. "'Twas a gift from Beorn Huddleston last time he visited the area. Near three years ago," he said.

He brought the bottle out from a chest at the far side of the smaller hearth at the back of the hall. The bottle was still almost full. He had little taste for the fiery drink. From the cupboard where Hannah kept the pewter plates and mugs, he took a small decorative glass and poured a small amount of the brandy into the glass. Handing it to Lady Rotherby, he said, "'Tis a shade on the powerful side. Best take a tiny sip."

She gave him a weak smile. "Yes, brandy can have a bite. Thank you."

"Lady Flavia, would you like some ale?" Calder asked.

"Do you have any buttermilk? I would enjoy that," she said.

"Oh, aye," Hermia said, jumping up. "I will get you a noggin. Do have a seat, milady." She looked at Avis. "What would you be having, Mistress Huddleston?"

"Ale would be fine, thank you, Hermia," Avis answered. Taking a seat beside Lady Flavia at the table, Flavia introduced her to all the young men.

Chuckling, Avis said, "I know Lord Sutherlin well." She smiled at Flavia. "Many a time has your brother come to hunt with his father in Lord Penhaligon's park."

"'Tis good to see you again, Mistress Huddleston," Sutherlin said. "Do you know, is Lord Penhaligon due to come for a hunt any time soon?"

Tilting her head, Avis glanced at Calder before addressing Sutherlin. "I am thinking, 'tis a good possibility. Seems my husband has complained of a boar that has grown overly large and is terrorizing other animals in the park. He could well be writing his lordship about the problem."

"On one of our rides," Preston said, "Sutherlin pointed out Lord Penhaligon's park and his lodge. The lodge looks substantial. Good hunting in his park, is it?"

"The lodge is most comfortable," Avis said. "Sleeps a goodly number, when Lord Penhaligon has a party with him, and he keeps his park well stocked. So 'tis good hunting."

"I can vouch for that," Sutherlin said. "Better stocked than our park, eh, Mother?"

"Your father has not had as many years to build up his herd, Ewen. The Whitakers have owned White Acres since the days of the Conqueror. That is a good many years to insure a good-sized herd. But enough of deer and hunting." She looked from her son to Calder. "I cannot begin to thank you enough, Goodman Grantham. Selena told me how you put your own life at risk by wading into the mire to save her." She shook her head, then asked, "A reward of some sort…?"

"Nay!" Calder said adamantly. "Nay!" he could not keep the hurt from his voice. He felt insulted, but she was immediately apologizing. "I am sorry. That was wrong of me. I only meant to somehow show you how grateful I am."

"We are all grateful," broke in Sutherlin. "Selena may be a bane, but she is our bane, and we love her."

Angered by the affront to Selena's character, Calder was tempted right then and there to tell them he intended to marry Selena. But no. Selena needed to tell her aunt herself. It would not do to let his temper cause any bad blood between him and the family he would soon be related to by marriage. Better to have them on his side.

"Well, here she is," Hannah announced from the staircase, and Calder whirled around to see the woman he loved descending behind Hannah.

She looked beautiful. Her hair, pulled back from her face and pinned in a bun atop her head, glistened in the sunlight streaming in from a nearby window. Hannah had done a terrific job of getting the mud and slime from Selena's lush dark hair. Wearing a bright red gown with a cream-colored petticoat peeking out under the folds of the skirt hiked up on the sides, Selena smiled brightly. A white lawn scarf was tucked into the red bodice laced with creamed colored ties, and as Selena skipped down the stairs, Calder noted her neat little black shoes and white hose. He had never seen her so gowned. Ever she had worn a riding costume or a sturdy walking gown when visiting the farm. Oh, but she was a vision for his eyes.

His gaze met hers, and his smile mirrored hers. Yes, he would marry Lady Selena D'Arcy. He might not be of her social class, but he was the right man for her, that he knew.

# Chapter 39

With everyone departed but Avis and Hannah, Calder joined them at the table to eat his dinner. Lord Sutherlin and his friends had eaten a major portion of the spread Hannah had placed on the table and had gone through several rounds of ale. Now, they were off to Nibley's to indulge in some of the squire's port. They could end up a riotous foursome by the time they returned to Whimbrel Hall, but they were genial young men, and Calder doubted they would cause anyone any trouble.

Selena had given him her hands before departing and had gazed up into his eyes. She whispered low, "I will tell my aunt this evening. We will be wed."

Having determined he would wed Selena whether her family approved or not, he nodded and smiled down at her. "Good," was all he said, but the light that shone in her eyes when he said that one word was all he needed to read her love for him. He had no doubt she could see his love for her.

Once the coach rolled away, Calder sent Billy and Pascal to mend the bramble fence near the stream. Had that lamb not wormed its way out, Selena would never have been in danger. He was beginning to think he should hire another laborer. There seemed to be too much to do and not enough time to get everything done that needed doing. Once he married Selena, he would have even more cares.

Hermia was seeing to tiding his room and to the tedious task of carting away the water that had been carted up for Selena's bath. She was a good girl, a good worker. This very evening, he would offer her a permanent position on his farm. That should please Joseph.

"So," Avis said, interrupting his thoughts, "are you going to marry the girl? She is in love with you. 'Tis easy to see. And you love her."

After taking a sip of ale, Calder set the noggin on the table. His eyes met Avis's. "'Twill not be easy. I am not of her social status. No doubt her family will object. They could well cart her back to Surrey. She says when she comes of age in two months, she may do as she pleases, but a lot can happen, does she return to her own home."

"Humph!" Hannah said. "Getting Lady Selena to go somewhere she is not wanting to go would take some doing."

"That is true," Avis said. "I have met her father, Lord Rygate. He seems a caring man. I cannot see him carting Selena off against her will. He may balk at first, but once he gets to know you, Calder, I believe he will relent. After all, you are a substantial farmer. You have three hundred acres in freehold and three hundred rented from White Acres. That gives you six hundred acres. I believe Squire Nibley has no more than nine hundred. 'Tis his wife, makes him so prosperous. His home was a bit of a ram-shamble before he married the new Mistress Nibley.

"You have a good size flock of sheep ready for market," Avis continued before Calder could interrupt her, "and a nice herd of cows. I have been told, you had a good yield from your crops this summer, and your fall wheat is looking good. You have a sturdy, well-apportioned stone home, and well-kept outbuildings. You also have cousins of some merit. The Cardingtons, the Lintons. Families of considerable wealth and standing, even if they are not peers of the realm. Your land tenure dates to before the Conqueror. You have much you can be proud of. When you meet Lord Rygate, and I have no doubt he will commit to meeting you, you have no reason to be meek or humble."

"Avis is right," Hannah said. "You have much to be proud of."

Calder chuckled. "I hope you may both be right, because does Lady Selena continue to claim she will marry me, then by God, I mean to marry her."

"Good for you, Calder, good for you," Avis said. "Now, I suppose I should head back home. I left Mildred and Lucy to take care of dinner, but I best see what we shall have for supper. These summer days, with all the work, everyone comes in hungry."

"Indeed they do," Hannah said, "indeed they do. I best get this table cleaned so I can be setting it for supper," she added with a chuckle.

"I should get back to my wood chopping," Calder said, thinking again, as he headed out the door, how lucky fate was that he had stayed near to home on this of all days. For a day that had brought him a greater terror than he had ever known, it had also brought him great happiness. He would marry Selena D'Arcy. Indeed he would.

❋ ❋ ❋

"You cannot be serious," Rowena said, setting her spoon into her soup bowl. "Naturally you feel drawn to Goodman Grantham after he saved your life, but …"

"No, Aunt Rowena," Selena said, "that has nothing to do with it." She looked at Flavia. "Ask Flavia. More than a fortnight ago, I told her I intended to marry Calder. Did I not, Flavia?"

Flavia nodded. "She did, Mother. The fact is, I could see how much they were in love, so I confronted Selena with it. She said she was but waiting for him to declare his love."

"And so he did today," Selena said, her eyes glistening, her smile as bright as Rowena had ever seen it. That her niece was in love was very evident, but oh, it would never do. What was she going to tell Selena's parents.

Rowena slowly shook her head. The young men had returned from Nibley's long enough to tell Rowena they were headed into Rotherby for the evening, so she, Flavia, and Selena were enjoying a quiet supper in the parlor, when Selena broke the news of her intention to marry Calder Grantham.

Frowning, Rowena tried again. "Mayhap 'twould be best did you go home for a while, give you time to think this over."

"No, Aunt Rowena." Selena narrowed her eyes. "When you knew you were in love with Uncle Nate, do you think your love for him would have faded were you parted?" Again she looked to Flavia. "Would Flavia fall out of love with Darnell if they were parted?"

"Oh, no," Flavia said. "I have always loved Orland. I always will. And I have been parted from him for two years."

Rowena frowned at her daughter. "I can see you are on Selena's side."

"I am. Goodman Grantham is perfect for Selena. He will allow her the freedom she craves. She will not need to be the perfect lady. She can just be who she is."

"Flavia is right, Aunt Rowena. I have tried, but what you and Mother want for me is not what I want for me. I love Calder, and I will marry him. If not now, then when I come of age. I would much sooner have my family's blessing." She looked appealingly at Rowena. "But it matters not, for marry him I will."

Looking down and again shaking her head, Rowena said, "Oh, beloved child, what am I to do with you? You are ever so willful, but ever so dear. I suppose you want me to support you in this with your father?" She looked up and saw Selena smiling at her.

"I have hopes you will, dear Aunt. I pray you will."

Rowena heaved a sigh. "I must write your father on the morrow. This will mean another trip up here for him."

"Another trip?"

"Yes. He asked me not to tell you he was visiting Reggie and his new wife. He feared if he came by here to see you, you would convince him to take you home. Oh, that he had."

"Nay, Aunt Rowena. I was already in love with Calder. I would not have asked to go home. Much as, no doubt, that would have surprised everyone," she said with her tinkling laugh.

"I have yet to meet Reggie's new wife," Flavia said, changing the subject with a glance at her mother that said she was giving her mother time to think. Rowena needed the time. Selena's arguments were hard to resist.

Smiling, Flavia added, "Ewen says Reggie's wife is absolutely lovely and very sweet."

"So she is," Selena said. "She is the dearest. You will love her." Turning back to Rowena, Selena said, "Aunt Rowena, do allow me to write Father and Mother. I intend to tell them I want to be married as soon as possible. As Flavia and Darnell wish to be married before the first frost, mayhap Flavia and I could have our weddings together. That way, those who are coming to the weddings will not have to make extra trips."

Flavia clapped her hands. "Oh, that is a splendid idea. Think, Mother, how much less work that will be for you."

Rowena sighed. "I can see you have both decided I am to acquiesce and give up arguing against Selena's marriage to Goodman Grantham." The girls both smiled, but she continued, "It would appear, Selena, that you plan to have your wedding here, rather than at your home, so your mother could be present."

Selena frowned. "I would dearly love for Mother to be present, but we know Mother cannot travel all the way here. Just going to London is a strain for her. But I will not be parted from Calder to return to Rygate Park and plan my wedding without Calder at my side. Calder will be busy with his harvest. He cannot long be gone from his farm. Besides, all my new friends, the Nibleys, the Huddlestons, all the lovely people at Flavia's party, and all the wonderful Whimbrel villagers would be unable to attend the wedding in Surrey.

"Aunt Rowena, you know how much I love my mother. Only my love for her could have brought me here to be trained to be a lady. You have been the best teacher. I do think I could pass any test at this time, but, as Flavia says, was I to be that lady Mother wants me to be, I would not be me. I would not be happy. Calder accepts who I am. He loves the person I am. He has no wish to change me. Nor do I have any wish to change him. So, as much as I love Mother, I will not be parted from Calder to return to Surrey without him."

Rowena slowly nodded her head. "Yes, sadly, Elizabeth had to make the same decision as you now have to make. Her mother is too ill to travel anywhere, and Elizabeth had to choose to have her wedding in London, far from her mother. However, I will assume, that, as Elizabeth and her husband have gone to visit Elizabeth's mother, you will go to visit yours and introduce your husband."

Selena smiled broadly. "Not only will Calder and I go, but Pascal will go with us. But the visit must wait until autumn is in recline and the harvesting, threshing, sowing of the rye seed, and butchering of the hogs, not to mention any number of other things that I have little knowledge of are attended to. We will go in December before the snows set in." She wrinkled her nose. "Of course, I must discuss all this with Calder. He only today declared his love for me, so we have not yet had a chance to talk of any of these things that you and I now speak on."

Rowena rolled her eyes. She had little doubt that whatever Selena decided she wanted, Grantham would accede to. She could understand Selena's wish to be married in the community that would be her new home, surrounded by her new friends. Rowena could not help but pity Selena's mother, though. Angelica had not only missed her son Reginald's wedding, she was now to miss her only daughter's. Rowena wished she could write as raving a letter to Angelica about Calder Grantham as she had been able to write about Reginald's wife, Amaryllis, but though she believed Grantham to be a good man, an upstanding member of the community, he was not a gentleman. Or, at least, not as would be recognized by the Heralds' College.

Selena was right. Did she so choose, she could be the perfect lady, but that was not Selena's choice. What many a woman might well sell her soul to claim, Selena had no use for. Well, she would let Selena write her letter first, and then she would write her letter to Angelica. She but prayed she would be able to find the right words to assure Angelica that Selena would be happy. What else could a mother wish for a child, but that her child should be happy.

# Chapter 40

Stalking from her chair to the hearth, Selena whirled around and confronted her father. "Unless you mean to drag me from Aunt Rowena's with my feet and hands bound and a gag in my mouth, I will not be leaving. You have not even met Calder. You think he is not good enough for me. Just because he is not of the gentry, and because I am a D'Arcy. You claim he is not suitable. Well, he is suitable."

Selena had written her father but little more than a week earlier, and he had already arrived at Whimbrel. He arrived the previous evening shortly before supper. Exhausted from his ride, his attire and hair dust covered, his green eyes blurry, he had given Selena an embrace and a kiss on the cheek from her mother but had told her he would discuss nothing with her until the morning. So supper had been a lively affair with Ewen and his friends asking questions about London, and Flavia and Aunt Rowena asking about Elizabeth's wedding and her new husband. With her father's good cheer, Selena had been hopeful all would bode well on the morrow.

That had not been the case. Her father had breakfasted early, then closeted himself with Aunt Rowena in the parlor. Selena and Flavia had paced the grand entry outside the parlor until, finally, Aunt Rowena had called Selena inside. Flavia had not been allowed to join them, but she had given Selena's hands a squeeze and had whispered, "All will be well."

Selena had been told to sit, and her father had spent considerable time talking about her mother and how she was faring. He had talked about Reggie and Amaryllis, and spoke of how pleased he was with Reggie's choice. Amaryllis was every bit the lovely and charming lady. Selena had agreed with him, though her nerves were becoming more frayed by the moment.

Finally, he broached the subject he had been avoiding. "Selena, your mother and I have discussed your letter. Rather, your surprise announcement, I should say. Though we cannot say we approve of your decision to marry this farmer, we are not ready to completely condemn it."

Selena's hopes had risen with his words, but then were dashed when he continued.

"We believe, 'tis best, do you come home with me. Hasty decisions are never good." He held up a hand when she started to protest. "Now wait, Selena. You must understand how very concerned your mother is. She is worried you are rushing into something you will come to regret. You want to marry a man who is not your social equal. You have been raised with servants to do your bidding. You have been given a good education. You are a D'Arcy, and whether you like it or not, you have your family to think of. Your brother, Giles, is soon to marry a lady of standing, a lady of the realm. You want to marry a farmer who has little education and no social upbringing. Is that fair to him or you?

"I tell you, Selena, we cannot think this man is suitable for you. You will come home with me. Given time, do you persist in this frame of mind, we will reconsider the notion. That is final. You will tell your maid to start packing …"

Selena had not allowed him to finish speaking. She was off her chair in an instant. Taking her stance before the hearth, she had let lose her tirade.

"Selena! That is no way to speak to your father," her aunt declared.

Raising her chin, Selena stared at her still handsome father. He was in his early fifties, but few gray hairs streaked his flame-gold hair. He was still trim and his shoulders were erect. She was proud of her father. He was a good father, a loving father. Indeed, he had ever spoiled her. Aunt Rowena was right. She needed to better control her tongue.

"You are right, Aunt Rowena. I spoke in haste. My tone was unkind, but I do mean what I say. I will not go home with you, Father, and I will marry Calder."

Her father had not risen from his chair but his steady gaze met hers. "You mean then to defy me, to defy your mother, who could not come here herself to talk with you."

"You cannot doubt my love for Mother. I am here at Whimbrel because of the great love I bear her. You know that. I had no wish to leave Rygate Park. But I obeyed Mother's wish for me. I became the lady she wanted me to become, but I cannot like being that lady."

Before her father could answer, a knock on the door sounded, and the footman, Plocket, poked his head inside the room. "I know you said you were not to be disturbed, Lady Rotherby, but Lord Penhaligon and his cousin, Mister Cardington are calling."

"Oh, my," Aunt Rowena said, rising. "Do show them in and get glasses for some port to serve them."

"Yes, milady," the footman answered. Opening the door wide and standing back, he announced, "Lord Penhaligon and Mister Cardington."

Selena's father also rose, ready to greet the sixth Lord Penhaligon that Avis Huddleston had told Selena about. The earl looked to be near Selena's father in age. He was trim like her father but a tad taller, and when he whipped off his wide-brimmed, side-cocked hat, to reveal a mane of golden blond hair, Selena noted his hazel eyes were twinkling. Despite his quality riding apparel, he had not the appearance of a dandy. He moved with an easy grace, and gave Selena the impression, that, if called upon, he could spring to action as effortlessly as a cat.

"Lady Rotherby, I hope I am not disturbing you, calling unexpectedly as I am."

"Nonsense, Lord Penhaligon, you must know you are always welcome. How is Lady Penhaligon, and your mother?"

He shook his head. "Cymbeline is busily translating some ancient Saxon writing. The woman amazes me. I cannot think how many languages she knows. She is in a constant communication with a Mistress Aphra Behn, a woman playwright my mother told her about some years back. Quite amusing plays, I understand. As for Mother, she is in London. She has always loved London and thinks there could be no better place to live. My sister, Serretta, and her husband also make their home in London, so Mother is not alone there."

While he spoke, he grasped Selena's father's hand in friendly greeting. "Cymbeline hates London as much as Mother loves London," he continued, looking again at Aunt Rowena. "Mother hated any time she

288

had to spend in Essex. Cymbeline loves it." He chuckled and looked back at Selena's father. "Consequently, I never get to London unless the King calls Parliament, which he is not apt to do, so I hear."

"I think not," Selena's father said.

"Will you not have a seat Lord Penhaligon, and you, Mister Cardington," Aunt Rowena said, looking pointedly at the man accompanying the earl.

"Ah, forgive my manners, Lady Rotherby. Rygate," he added, glancing at Selena's father. "Allow me to present my cousin, Mister Arnold Cardington."

Cardington's round genial face brightened with a cheery smile. A man of medium height and weight with nondescript brown hair, he would not be memorable but for his lively brown eyes. "I forcibly pulled him away from his observation of the stars," Penhaligon said, clamping a hand on his cousin's back. "Told him his report to the Royal Society could wait. He needed to get out in nature. His wife agreed with me. So here he is, and that brings me to why I am here."

"Before you get into the reason for your most welcome visit," Aunt Rowena interrupted. With a smile and a nod to her second guest, she said, "'Tis a pleasure to meet you, Mister Cardington. Please, have a seat? Here is Plocket with some glasses. Might we pour you both some port?"

Both men heartedly agreed, and Aunt Rowena indicated the two chairs across from her and Selena's father. She then realized one of the chairs had been vacated by Selena, and after a quick glance at Selena, she put her hand to her forehead and said, "You must forgive me, Lord Penhaligon and Mister Cardington. Allow me to present my niece, Lady Selena D'Arcy." She nodded toward Selena's father. "My brother's only daughter."

Selena dropped a curtsy, and both men bowed. Taking a seat on the tufted footstool near her aunt, Selena left the cushioned chairs to her aunt's unexpected guests. The two men seated themselves and accepted the promised glasses of port from the footman. Selena's father and aunt also took glasses, but Selena declined the offer. She wanted her head clear when her discussion with her father resumed.

"So, Lord Penhaligon, you have come on an errand?" Aunt Rowena asked, after they all had a sip of the port.

"I have," Penhaligon answered. He looked at Selena's father. "I came to White Acres at the request of my steward, Ware Huddleston. You remember him from times you have hunted here, eh, Rygate?"

"I do. Fine fellow."

"Yes, well, he wrote to tell me a boar in my park has grown too large and is tearing up the park. He felt I might like to deal with the beast myself. Naturally, I would. Plus, as long as I am here, I thought I could do some deer hunting." He looked at Aunt Rowena. "You could do with some fresh venison, could you not, Lady Rotherby?"

She smiled. "Venison is always a welcome treat."

"Splendid. Rygate, I plan to hunt tomorrow. Huddleston is organizing things, as I sit here. He will have some beaters set to drive the deer out of hiding, and I am hoping to bag a couple of bucks. What say you, do you care to join Arnold and me tomorrow?"

"I would normally be delighted, but I had planned but a short visit to Whimbrel."

"Ah, extend it if you can. My cousin Arnold is not particularly skilled in the hunt. I could use a man of experience to help me chase down that boar."

"That is a tempting offer."

"Good, now we cannot take up too much of your morning. Arnold has his cousins to visit. He has been neglectful of late. When were you last here, Arnie?"

The same cheery grin brightened Cardington's face, and he scratched his neck. "Sad to say, it must be three years now. The Huddlestons had a grand affair when Ware's sister, Troth, returned from Europe with her new husband, Garin Wistow." Cardington looked from Selena's aunt to her father as he spoke. "Fine fellow with a bright future in the foreign service."

Aunt Rowena nodded her head, "Yes, yes, I remember something about that." She looked at Selena's father. "Am I not mistaken, I believe the affair took place when we were at the D'Arcy family reunion in seventy-eight."

"Wistow is clerk to my wife's brother," Penhaligon said. "The one time my wife came to White Acres, she met Troth and took to her. The girl is bright. Learned Latin on her own. Not but a little help from Ware. Cymbeline started sending Troth books. Girl devoured them. When Cymbeline's brother, Byram, wanted a companion for his wife to accompany them, when Byram was sent to Spain, Cymbeline recommended Troth. Great experience for the girl."

"I can imagine so," Aunt Rowena said. "I would think seeing some of Europe would be a marvelous thing for anyone, young or old."

With her aunt's statement, Selena wondered if her aunt regretted she had never had the opportunity to tour some of Europe.

"So," Penhaligon said. "We should be heading back so not to hold up dinner. I know Ware's laborers and dairymaids are used to dining when the sun is straight up in the sky." He chuckled. "'Tis always a treat to sit down to table with the people who keep White Acres profitably functioning. Ware's wife, Avis, sets a good table. Arnie and I are staying at the lodge, but we are not eating there. Last night we supped with Arnie's cousin, Eloisa Tusket, in Rotherby." He looked at Aunt Rowena. "Her husband is a vintner. Served a fine wine at supper." He licked his lips. "Mayhap you know the Tuskets."

Aunt Rowena nodded. "I nod to Mistress Tusket at church, or when we meet in town." She looked at Cardington. "You say she is your cousin, Mister Cardington. I believe she is Calder Grantham's sister, is she not?"

Selena perked up. Lord Penhaligon's cousin was Calder's cousin? Oh, that had to be helpful. She glanced at her father, but his eyes were on Cardington.

"Aye, she is." Penhaligon answered for Cardington. "My Aunt Cordelia, Father's half-sister, was Arnie's grandmother. Ware Huddleston's grandfather was Arnie's grandmother's half-brother, and her half-sister was Calder Grantham's great grandmother."

This was getting better and better, Selena thought, squiggling on her seat.

"When Grandmother was alive," Cardington said, "we had near annual visits to White Acres. It was Grandmother's home, where she grew up, and it meant a lot to her. "I fear I am not a good correspondent with my various cousins," he continued, "but my younger sister, Jacquetta, is ever in communication with Eloisa, both having children of the same age."

"We are to sup with Grantham this evening," Penhaligon again interposed. "His servant Hannah is a marvelous cook and makes the best cross buns I have ever tasted."

"Oh, yes," Selena broke in, "her buns are wondrously delicious." In listening to Penhaligon and Cardington, she had come to the conclusion they had come to convince her father that Calder was a worthy match for her. Calder was, after all, Cardington's cousin, and Cardington was Lord Penhaligon's cousin. Why they had come to promote Calder, she had no idea, but she could hardly be more grateful.

When she spoke, everyone turned to look at her, and Penhaligon chuckled. "A lady who knows when something is good and worthy of savoring, eh?" With that he rose and said, "We really must be going. Rygate, look forward to a good hunt with you on the morrow. Come to the lodge to break your fast. I will have some of Hannah's buns, no doubt, and Ware's cook has promised us a meal of duck eggs and sausage. Ware's cook, Mildred, may not be as good a cook as Hannah, but she is good. Is she not, Arnie?"

"Aye," Cardington acknowledged, rising as Selena's father and aunt also stood. "A pleasure to have met you, Lady Rotherby, and you, Lord Rygate." He looked at Selena and nodded to her. "Charmed, Lady Selena."

Selena came forward to join her aunt and father in seeing the two men out, and Lord Penhaligon took her hands, pulled her close and whispered in her ear, "I look forward to welcoming you into the family."

Overjoyed by his remark, she looked up at him and said, "Thank you."

When the guests had been escorted out, Selena's father looked at her and said, "I suppose you will not be telling me how you arranged for Penhaligon to make his visit."

Shaking her head, Selena said, "I give you my word, Father, I have no idea how he came to be here. How he came to visit."

He looked into her eyes for a moment, then said, "Hmmm, would seem you are an innocent in this." He sighed. "However, it came about, I will go meet Grantham after dinner. Send him word."

Unable to control her joy, Selena threw her arms around her father's neck. "Oh, thank you, Father. You will find Calder much to your liking. I promise you, you will."

Returning her embrace, he held her close for a moment, then said, "I have not yet given my consent."

Smiling up at him, she said, "Yes, but once you have met Calder, you will, Father. You will understand why I love him. You will see how he is the only man for me." She looked to her aunt. "Is he not, Aunt Rowena?"

Her aunt shook her head. "I will not interfere in this. It is between you and your Father."

Selena was disappointed her aunt would not give her approval, but she could understand that her aunt would not wish to come between Selena and her father. Aunt Rowena had been responsible for Selena's conduct. That Selena had met and formed an attachment to a man her father might not find suitable put her aunt in an awkward situation. But her aunt's approval was not of major importance. What mattered was getting a message to Calder that her father would meet with him. Hurrying from the room, she went to find the footman, Jimmy. She could trust him to find Calder wherever he might be and get him the message.

She had no doubt that once her father met Calder, he would approve of him. Yes, soon, she could start planning her wedding.

# Chapter 41

Ranulf D'Arcy, Lord Rygate, had to admit to not only being impressed with Calder Grantham, but also with the neatness and prosperous appearance of his home and farm. He could also understand why Selena believed herself to be in love with Grantham. No question Grantham was a handsome man. His smile and his sky blue eyes were riveting. No doubt he could capture any woman's heart. Dressed in what must be his Sunday best apparel, close-fitting, gold-colored coat with skirts flaring out to mid-thigh, unbuttoned enough to reveal a linen shirt tucked into full breeches ending below the knees and tied with matching gold bands, Grantham looked the thriving farmer. A linen cravat was at his throat and buckled shoes, that looked as though they had seldom or never been worn, adorned his feet and completed his raiment. If not for his short, shoulder-length hair, Grantham could pass for a well-to-do merchant on any street in London.

Grantham's son and housekeeper were also dressed in their best. The young son had bowed deeply at the waist when introduced, and the housekeeper had dropped a low curtsy. The hall was spotless, the long table covered with a clean, white cloth, and a heavenly scent wafted about the room.

"What would I be smelling that sets my mouth to watering, though I have not that long since dined?" Ranulf asked.

"'Twould be my cross buns," my lord, the housekeeper answered. "I be baking them for Lord Penhaligon. He sups with us tonight, and I make enough for him to have when he breaks his fast on the morrow. Should be some ready afore long, would you be wanting a taste."

"I thank you. I believe I will give them a try. Lord Penhaligon recommends them."

The housekeeper blushed and bobbed her head. "Aye, my lord. That he does."

Turning back to Grantham, Ranulf said, "Come, Grantham, and show me about your farm. From what I have seen, you seem to have good sturdy buildings, and I saw a number of healthy-looking sheep in a pasture near the stream on my ride over here."

Grantham beckoned to the door. "This way, Lord Rygate. I would be pleased to show you about. There is never an end to all that needs doing, but I try to keep up with any mending or repairs. Sometimes, though I know things need mending, they fail to achieve the repairs as soon as would be best, I fear."

Once they were outside and walking toward the stone barn, Ranulf said, "I have yet to thank you for saving my daughter's life. She told me in great detail how she near drowned in the mire. 'Twas good fortune you were to hand and able to reach her in time."

Grantham stopped and faced Ranulf. "Much of the thanks must go to my son and our dog. 'Twas Lady Selena's way with animals that saved her. Rollo sensed her plight and led my son to her. My son ran to get me." His blue eyes clouded. "I have never known such fear in my life, Lord Rygate. But 'twas not good fortune that had me near to hand. Lady Rotherby had bid me keep my distance from Lady Selena. At first I tried, but I found I could not abide by Lady Rotherby's wishes. My love for Lady Selena was too great. I knew I was not of her social status, and I believed she would at some point leave and return to her home. But I decided I could at least enjoy being with her for as long as it lasted. That day she was stuck in the mire, I was to hand because I had hopes she would come to visit. I had not seen her in many a day. For some reason, I became certain she meant to call." He looked away. "I needed just to see her, to hear her voice and her laughter. They would give me memories to tuck away."

He looked back. "I never dreamed, never thought I could win Lady Selena's love. Though I believed she had some feelings for me, I dared not hope anything could come of it." He half-smiled. "But Lady Selena has a mind of her own. She says she loves me, and she says we will be wed. Lord Rygate, I know I am but a humble farmer, but I tell you honestly, I believe I can make your daughter happier than can any other man. I love who she is, and I would change nothing about her. With me, she can forever be the person she wants to be. Lady Selena and I both hope for your blessing and approval, but does she mean to marry me, then indeed, I mean to take her to wife."

Ranulf pursed his lips, and slowly nodding his head, said, "I, too, hope I may give you my blessing." That Grantham loved Selena deeply was undeniable. The love he bore Selena was the only reason Selena was alive. Had Grantham not longed to see Selena, he would not have been near enough to hand to save her. He was right. Selena would be happier being a farmer's wife than the wife of a baron or an earl. That was undeniable. "As you say, Selena has a mind of her own," he admitted. "She will soon be turning of age, and short of locking her in her room, I cannot prevent her from marrying you."

He started walking again toward the barn, and Grantham fell into step beside him. "I received a visit this morning from Lord Penhaligon and his cousin, Mister Cardington," Rygate threw out, not knowing whether to expect any particular reaction from Grantham. "I understand Cardington is also your cousin."

"He is, Lord Rygate. His grandmother and my great grandmother were half-sisters. I have but the vaguest memory of Arnie's grandmother. She died when I was quite young. My main memory is that every year, she brought her family together at White Acres, and some of the family stayed with us. It was always great fun."

"I am curious, Grantham. How well do you know Lord Penhaligon?"

Stopping before the barn door, Grantham shrugged. "I cannot say well. He is a lord. I have not kept company with him. He has, from time to time, asked to lodge extra hunters in my home when he has many guests. He loves Hannah's cross buns. Insists he must have some each time he visits his lodge. He sups with us this evening because my cousin, Arnie, is with him. Otherwise, I cannot say I have had much contact with him. Though I believe my father was close with him. But they were more of an age."

"You would not know why he is suddenly visiting White Acres?"

Grantham cocked his head. "Ware told me he has come to rid his park of a boar."

Ranulf slowly nodded his head. "So Penhaligon told me. I am to join him in the hunt on the morrow."

"I wish you good hunting, Lord Rygate," Grantham said, extending his arm to invite Ranulf to enter the barn.

By the time the tour of the barns and other outbuildings was concluded, and Ranulf returned with Grantham to his house, Hannah had her cross buns cooling. Placing a couple on a plate, she presented them along with a mug of creamy buttermilk to Ranulf.

"Lady Selena likes the buns with the buttermilk rather than ale, my lord," Hannah said, "but do you prefer ale, we have a soft one just made yesterday by Widow Forester in Whimbrel. No one makes a creamier ale."

"The buttermilk will be fine, Hannah. I have not had any in many a year. 'Twill be a treat." He found the buns and the buttermilk much to his liking. He could see why Penhaligon asked for the buns any time he visited White Acres. That Penhaligon was on familiar enough terms with Grantham and his housekeeper to make the request meant he was well enough acquainted with them to pay regular, if not lengthy, visits. Penhaligon was obviously accepting of Grantham, at least as a respected member of his family's family.

When he rose to leave, he took Grantham's hand. "I am impressed with your farm and your home, as well as your manners. Mid-morning, day after tomorrow, come see me."

"I will, Lord Rygate. Thank you for coming to meet me and to see my home."

Upon returning to Whimbrel, Ranulf was pleased and surprised to find his brother, Nathaniel, had returned from his visit to family and friends. What with helping Elizabeth with her wedding plans and her husband with the purchase of their house, and then accompanying Elizabeth and her new husband to see William's father and Elizabeth's parents, finishing with visits to additional friends and family, Nathaniel had been absent from Whimbrel for near three months. Ranulf knew Rowena had missed her husband terribly, and the fact that she clung to his side gave evidence of her joy at his return.

Seated next to his wife on the parlor's tufted couch, Nate joked, "I return to find my daughter means to marry. The sooner the better, she says, though I have not yet given my approval." His genial smile made his blue-green eyes twinkle. "Flavia knows I will consent. Could not be more pleased with her choice. But I also learn your daughter means to marry a neighbor and respected farmer, Calder Grantham. Rowena tells me you have been to visit him." He cocked his head. "He met with your approval?"

From his seat across from his brother and Rowena, Ranulf looked to the door. He had half expected Selena to be awaiting him, but Rowena told him Flavia had dragged Selena off to the village to talk to some of the girls and youths about helping serve at their weddings. Plans were already moving forward, and he had yet to give his consent. He should be angry, but it would serve no purpose.

"Yes, I liked Grantham," he said. "But 'tis hard to consent to him marrying Selena. Her mother and I expected a much different match for her."

"You are an earl, so you expected your daughter to marry a member of the peerage," his brother said with a knowing nod of his head.

"If not a peer, at least a gentleman, a man of some standing."

Nate chuckled. "The question becomes, Ranulf, is that what your daughter wanted? Rowena tells me Selena worked hard and can now grace any table, manage any household, but that is not what she wants to do."

"Sadly, I know that. Selena has ever been different from other girls. The way she is with animals. How animals respond to her." He shook his head. "Mayhap, had Angelica not been injured when the coach overturned, she might have been able to turn Selena in another direction than the one I allowed her to travel. Trouble is, Selena always seemed to have a good reason for anything she wanted to do, and, I fear, I could seldom resist her."

"I know the feeling," Rowena said.

"Ranulf," Nate said, "you know well, had King Charles not rewarded us by making us earls and bestowing upon us our manors, we would be but humble commoners, mayhap knights, but not members of the peerage. With your marriage to Angelica, you would still be well off, but I am not certain where Rowena and I would be if not for Charles's generosity. True, you and I are members of an ancient family. One that dates back to the conqueror, so we would still be gentlemen, but, unless knighted, we would not even bear a coat of arms of our own."

Ranulf frowned. "I know that, Nate. But the thing is ..."

Nate held up his hand. "Hear me out, Ranulf. Grantham, as I said, is highly respected, as is his cousin, Ware Huddleston, Penhaligon's steward. Both Grantham's and Huddleston's lineage date back to before the Conqueror. Fact is, do you look back to the first Penhaligon, you will find they are all related."

"Yes, Selena has informed me in detail of their long family history."

Again chuckling, Nate said, "That would be Selena. You know you could convince Charles to make Grantham a baronet as he did Elizabeth's husband. Then, with Selena's dowry, and a bit of remodeling, Grantham's farm could be a fitting home for Selena."

"Nate is right," Rowena said, leaning forward, excitement bubbling in her eyes. "Grantham has a lovely home, but it will need to be expanded. It will need a parlor, a private dining chamber for special guests, a nursery, more guest sleeping quarters, and quarters for the servants. Selena will have to have her maid. No doubt she will want to take Alice with her. The two have grown quite close. Plus, they will need a suitable coach house and stable for riding horses and the coach horses. And a coach. With the added income from her Lincolnshire manor, Grantham could hire a couple more laborers and become more the gentleman farmer."

Nodding his head, Ranulf said, "That might work. Grantham's schooling may be limited, but I think he would not be shamed in his manners. Besides, Selena could teach him any table manners he might need to know for more formal dining." He smiled. "Yes, I am beginning to believe Grantham will do. Selena will receive an initial two thousand pounds upon her marriage from her Lincolnshire estate. That should cover the cost of renovating the house, and she will receive four hundred pounds a year, which should cover other expenses. I can set the estate up so her issue will inherit. The manor would go to the eldest male son, or, if no sons, it will be divided equally among any daughters." He frowned. "Should she fail to have any children…"

"Which would be doubtful," interrupted Nate.

Ranulf nodded and agreed. "But should she bear no children, upon her death the estate would go to her oldest brother, Giles, as he is heir to my earldom."

"I think you have made a wise decision," Rowena said, sitting back in her seat and leaning closer to her husband.

"Yes, I believe you are right," Ranulf said, but at the same time, he knew he had no choice. He loved Selena too dearly to lose her, and lose her he would, did he not consent to her marriage to Grantham. Who knows, he thought, Selena could one day be entertaining Grantham's Cardington cousins as well as Lord Penhaligon.

# Chapter 42

Selena believed she had never known such joy in her life. She had returned from Whimbrel village with Flavia to learn her father would consent to her marriage to Calder. Certain conditions would have to be agreed upon, but Selena believed they would prove no problem, though her father chose not to talk of them until he had her and Calder together. Since her father was hunting with Lord Penhaligon on the morrow, she would have to wait two days before Calder would present himself at Whimbrel and officially offer for her hand. Then she and Calder and Flavia and Darnell could set the date for their weddings, and the plans she and Flavia had already been formulating could be put into action. Invitations would need to be written. Housing for all the guests Aunt Rowena said they could expect would have to be arranged.

Aunt Rowena believed many of the D'Arcy family members would come, as they would be attending Giles's wedding in November. As they would need to be making the trek to London anyway, why not come first to Whimbrel, then move on to London. The Edgertons would also have family coming for such a prestigious affair as the wedding of their only son and heir to the daughter of an earl of an ancient family heritage.

Uncle Nate, having given his whole-hearted consent to Orland Darnell when he asked for Flavia's hand, promised he would soon get with Baron Edgerton and discuss the marriage settlement. Selena and Flavia were both giddy. They had but little more than two months to plan their weddings. Having decided they would save their parents considerable expense did they have their weddings and celebration on the same day, did their grooms consent, they chose Wednesday of the second week of October. Harvesting should be completed, sowing of the winter grains should be accomplished. Threshing and winnowing and storage of fodder for the winter should be finished.

Selena had learned much from Calder of the needs of his land. Sheep and cattle, that were not sold and herded off to market, would be fattened in the stubble of the harvested fields. Hogs would be turned lose in the woods to scavenge for acorns and beech nuts. Come the first of November, or the first cold frost, hogs, sheep, and cattle, not to be over wintered, would be butchered, and their meat salted, smoked, or stored in barrels of brine.

Calder's two laborers, Jared and Joseph, each had marriage plans being formulated. The house on the Buxton property, that Jared had moved into with Buxton and Abner's younger son, Lyell, needed major repairs before it would be fit for Jared's future wife to move into. Joseph, though he had managed to cut down several trees, had yet to find time to build a cottage for his future bride, Hermia, who was residing at Calder's and sleeping on a small cot in the pantry. Calder had hired Hermia as a permanent laborer. She would help Hannah in numerous ways, from picking the apples and pears, to assisting Hannah in making the cider and perry. She had been put in charge of the herb and vegetable garden and had taken over the care of the various fowl. Hannah heartily approved of the girl and was grateful to have the help.

With so much work needing to be done on the farm, Selena knew she could not expect to see Calder as often as she would like. But just knowing they would soon be wed, and she would then be able to see him every day and every night made the next two months survivable. She, too, would be busy. She had the wedding to plan. The future Whimbrel school needed her attention. Tables and chairs for the students were still being made, and she needed to raise more funding for them. Wood or coal for the winter heating needed to be bought and stored. The two-room school was to have one large hearth and several braziers to be strategically placed to keep the students warm enough to concentrate on their lessons. Slates and books would need to be provided for the students, and with school due to start by mid-October, they had yet to employ a teacher. Uncle Nate said he would pay for a good teacher. Now he was home, she needed him to advertise for one and to let his many connections know he was in search of a suitable teacher.

In talking with the master brick mason, she had learned he meant to have the school completed by the end of September. The master's assurance had given her an idea. The new school sat on the foundation of a previous chapel. It was on consecrated ground, like the cemetery next to it. Instead of having to go into Rotherby to be married, why could she and Calder and Flavia and Darnell not be married in Whimbrel? The school could serve as a chapel one last time before it became a school. That way all the Whimbrel villagers and tenants could witness the ceremony. When she broached the subject with Flavia and Aunt Rowena, both thought the idea excellent.

"I will call upon the vicar myself and suggest the matter," Aunt Rowena said. "'Twill make it much easier for all the guests." She cocked her head to one side and smiled. "Mayhap I will take Carola with me. She enjoys the trips into town. I have noted of late, that since Flavia's party, Doctor Sizer has paid particular attention to Carola after service on Sundays. Last week when we went into Rotherby, Carola had a book she wanted to loan the doctor. While I visited the dressmaker, she stopped in at the Sizers'. She is also developing a friendship with the doctor's sister, who arrived to help manage the household and relieve Suzanne of the burden."

Flavia clapped her hands. "Might Doctor Sizer be developing a tender for Carola?"

Aunt Rowena shrugged. "'Tis possible."

Selena hoped the doctor might be thinking of Carola Mead in a romantic fashion. She had always pitied the woman. Though treated well by Aunt Rowena, Carola was still a poor relation dependent upon the generosity of her cousin. Carola was ever eager to help in any manner she could, and, though knowing how long and tiring was the coach trip from Lancashire to Leicestershire, she had readily volunteered to bring Flavia home. Could the dear little dove-like woman make a match and have a home of her own, she would well deserve it.

Selena was also excited to receive a second book of short stories from Wally Shandy, his first book having been an immediate success. Wally was writing his stories and working in sales for Giles's friend, Postgate. And, ever since delivering Flavia's letter to Nibley's daughter Maris, he had apparently been paying calls on her. He wrote that he would be escorting Maris and her brother Giffard home. He claimed Maris was eager to see Flavia, and meant to stay for a nice visit, though Giffard would need to return to Eton come September.

Wally would return to London after escorting the Nibleys home, but Selena guessed Maris and Wally could be courting. Maris might be wanting her father to see Wally in his new position. Though Wally would hardly be an acceptable match for Maris, his family being Nibley's tenants, Wally was now employed in a respectable profession and was earning a respectable income. Add to that fact, he was a handsome lad with a sweet and winning way about him, and Selena could see why Maris would be attracted to him. Was a romance blooming between Wally and Maris, Selena hoped the fact that he convinced Maris to come home would make him more acceptable to Squire Nibley.

'Twas a summer for romance, Selena thought. If rumors were correct, the petty school teacher, Osgood, was making progress in his courtship of a particular Whimbrel widow with a small cottage and a couple of acres of land. With the increased wages Osgood would be receiving once the new school opened and the session started, he might feel encouraged enough to ask for her hand. Love was in the air, and Selena wanted everyone to be as happy as she was.

She was also pleased for the Huddlestons. They were so proud that Osgood wanted their son, Will, to help with the petty schoolers at times when Osgood was needed to help with the grammar school students. Not only would Will be earning a small wage, he would be getting experience that could bode well for him when he left grammar school and went on to university. The Huddleston's older son, Tom, would eventually take his father's place as the steward of White Acres, but Will and their youngest son, Derwin, would have to make their own way in the world. The better the education they could receive, the better their chances of living fruitful lives.

Her heart beating happily, Selena looked forward to the morrow, when she could visit Calder. She longed to feel his arms around her, to taste his lips, and to see his love for her shining in his heavenly eyes. She envied Flavia. Darnell, being a longtime family friend, came for dinner or supper almost every day, and after dining, he and Flavia would wander in the garden. Selena knew they shared a kiss or two, because whenever they returned, Flavia would be glowing, and Darnell would be gazing at her with abject longing.

Ewen and his friends, were they to home, would bait and bedevil Darnell, but he took their chafing in good humor and, taking Flavia's hand, would promise to see her on the morrow. Ewen and his friends were courting several of the girls in the parish, including Suzanne Sizer, but Selena doubted any of the four youths were doing anything more than amusing themselves. They were beginning to get bored, and Selena wondered how much longer before they were seeking more exciting entertainments than could be found in Rotherby. She would miss them when they decided to move on. They definitely made dinners and suppers entertaining. Oftentimes, she went on more distant rides with them. Rides she would not be allowed to go on, was she not accompanied by her cousin, Ewen.

She and Calder had talked about her love of riding, and he assured her, he wanted her to continue with her rides. She knew they would have to add to the stable to make it suitable for Brigantia, and she hoped to get horses for Calder and Pascal to ride. Not that either one would have that much time to ride. Pascal would be attending school, and Calder would be busy with his farm, but, maybe on Sunday afternoons, they could find time to ride together. She had hopes of taking Alice and the footman, Jimmy, with her when she married Calder and moved into his home. Alice had already said she would like to go with her. Jimmy could share the loft with Joseph and Billy. Once Joseph built his cottage and married Hermia, Jimmy and Billy would have plenty of room. Alice could have Calder's sister's former room. Oh, she knew they could work things out. The main thing was, she and Calder would be together.

❧ ❧ ❧

Calder had been pleasantly surprised by Selena's father. He had expected the earl to be more high-handed, more aloof, but Lord Rygate had been as congenial as Lord Penhaligon or Lord Rotherby. He found him knowledgeable about the needs of running a farm, from the raising of sheep and cattle, to the fodder needed to overwinter them, to crops needed to support a family or to sell on the market. He obviously took an interest in the management of his manors. With being told to call on him in two days, Calder was more than a little hopeful.

But many things needed tending, and no sooner had Rygate ridden away, than Calder had changed into his work clothes, and was off to saddle old Cob. He had to ride over to Buxton's and arrange for the harvesting of the few acres Buxton had planted. Olly Keat and Abner's son Lyell could harvest the wheat on those acres. Calder needed Jared to help with the harvest on his main farm. Calder had asked Abner to arrange with his wife and daughter, and any other laborers in the hamlet where he lived, to help. Harvesting was a big job, and it needed to be done quickly and neatly. Everyone would have to help, including Hermia, and even Hannah, though Hannah's duty would be to supply food and ale to the laborers. Nibley had a number of tenants, and often, after they were done with their harvesting, they were eager to earn a little extra and help with his harvesting. It was a good year, and did the weather hold and no heavy rain come, Calder believed he could look forward to a substantial harvest.

He knew he had little to offer in a marriage settlement, especially as his farm would someday go to Pascal, but his farm was prosperous, and he hoped Rygate would consider him an eligible match for Selena. Of course, Selena had a dowry of a manor in Lincolnshire. That could go to any children he and she were to have. With his hopes high, he set off to Buxton's. It would all work out. It had to.

# Chapter 43

"No, Father. We will agree to everything else you want, but I will not have Calder made a baronet." Selena was up off her seat on the parlor couch and pacing the floor. "I love the man Calder is now. I have no need for him to be Sir Calder."

Carefully keeping her voice under control despite her agitation, she continued, "I say, yes, we will add on to the house. I understand we will need a parlor and dining chamber and more guest rooms for when my siblings visit. I cannot expect Aunt Rowena to house them. 'Twould not be fair. And yes, we will need a nursery and more servants' quarters. A coach, a coach house, and better stables will also be nice, but we have no need for Calder to be knighted." She stopped her pacing and looked from her father to Calder and back to her father.

"What say you, Grantham?" Selena's father asked.

"I say will Selena be happier if I am not knighted, I prefer to make her happy. I have no wish to be knighted, however …" He looked up at Selena, then back at her father. "Whatever we must do to gain your consent to wed, we will do, Lord Rygate."

Her father chuckled, and Selena twisted her mouth to one side. 'Twas down to her will against her father's. Looking up at her, her father said, "Do sit, Selena. I have no wish to be craning my neck. Are you set against having Grantham knighted, so be it. However, you may some-day have a son who might wish you had thought more about his future."

Selena sat. "Do we have a son." She looked at Calder. "And does he wish to be a baronet, he may purchase it for himself. From what you say, Father, he will have adequate income to do so. You are very gener-ous in my dowry, Father. Two thousand pounds to do the construction needed, plus a yearly income of four hundred pounds, is more than we could wish for."

Indeed, Lord Rygate," Calder said. "I fear I have little to offer in way of a settlement."

"The settlement from you is your acceptance that the changes are to be made to your home and property. The added income will allow you to hire more laborers so you may entertain guests in your expanded capacity as a gentleman farmer, and you will be able to accompany your wife to social events near to home, or to our family events, weddings, reunions, and such. Which means you will be coming to my eldest son's wedding in November, and you will be introduced to Selena's mother."

"Oh, but, Father," Selena interjected. "I shall come to Giles's wedding, of course, but Calder will have the butchering to see to. We will come to visit you and Mother at Rygate in December, when the needs of the farm are not so great."

"No, Selena," Calder said, taking her hand and patting it. "Your father is right. 'Tis only right I accompany you to your brother's wedding. Abner has worked for me long enough, he knows what needs doing. He can take charge of the butchering. We will do our culling early. As your father says, with your dowry, we will have the funds to hire an additional laborer or two."

"Good," Selena's father said, nodding and pursing his lips. "Now, a couple more things. Selena's dowry will go to her children. Does she have no children, or do they not survive her, it will go to her brother, Giles, or his descendants."

"As it should be," Calder agreed.

"Once a year, you are to accompany her to her manor in Lincolnshire and begin, using funds that will be made available to her, to renovate the manor. The manor house is centuries old. Built in the early fourteen hundreds when Henry V was king. It has seen little renovating. Fell into my wife's family's hands after Henry Tudor became king. It is a cold and dark place. Selena has always hated it, but do you and she have a son, it will someday be his home. It needs to be a presentable place to live by the time he reaches his majority. I would expect you to spend at least two to three weeks there each year, more if needed."

"Agreed, sir," Calder said.

"Currently, there is a bailiff, a housekeeper, a stableman, and a grounds keeper living at the manor. Most of the house is shuttered and closed up. I normally go there once a year to insure all is as it should be. My bailiff is trustworthy. Has long been with the family, but he is getting old and will soon need to retire. He wishes to stay on the property. He has always lived in the gatehouse. I see no reason to turn him out. When a new bailiff is hired, he may take a room in the manor."

Looking intently at Calder, Selena's father said, "I will expect you to work closely with the new bailiff. Go over the accounts. Compare them to previous years. Do you feel you are competent enough in your accounting to do that?"

"I would hope so, Lord Rygate. I fear I would have lost my land by now was I not."

Selena smiled. Her future husband was no uneducated oaf.

Her father smiled, too. "I thought as much. That is good. One final thing. Any children you may have will be raised on your farm. No doubt they will love their home. I want your guarantee that home will always welcome them. Should any of them want to live there, they will have that option. Consequently, I would recommend at some future date, you build a Dower house." He looked at Selena. "Might well be something you would have need of."

Selena took Calder's hand and held it to her cheek. "Pray God I never will, but as we begin having children, we will build one."

Her father placed his hands on his knees. "I think we have settled things. I will see Reynard Bardwith and have the settlement drawn up. I know your mother will be disappointed she will not be able to attend your wedding, Selena, but I also understand, after talking with your aunt, why you feel you must have the wedding here. This parish will be your home, and your future husband has much to attend to insure his farm is profitable. So, once the settlement has been signed, I will go back to Rygate and explain all to your mother."

Selena hopped up and hugged her father. "You have made me so happy, Father. I, too, am saddened Mother cannot be here, but not only will we come to Giles's wedding, but we will come for a visit to Rygate as soon as we have all settled on the farm."

Smiling and returning Selena's hug, her father looked around her at Calder. "I have a few things to discuss with Nate concerning the cost of the weddings and celebration." He looked at Calder. "I will give you two a few moments alone, but remember, until the settlement is signed, you are not truly betrothed." With that he left the room, closing the door behind him.

Selena stepped immediately into Calder's arms. He clutched her tightly to his chest, and called her, "My dear one. Can this be true? Are you really to be mine?"

Pulling away to look up into Calder's eyes, Selena said, "Aye, my love. In but two months, we will never again need be parted."

At that point Calder brought his lips down to hers. His kiss was so soft, almost feathery, then the kiss intensified, yet he was still so gentle. His tongue urged her lips to part, and she responded to him with an urgent craving, tongues tasting, hearts beating as one, longings finally being satisfied. They pulled apart when a light tap sounded at the door, and Flavia poked her head inside the room.

"All is well? I may congratulate you?" she asked.

"Come in, Flavia," Selena said slowly withdrawing from Calder's embrace. "Yes, come in and congratulate us. We are betrothed."

Flavia hurried to Selena's side and gave her a hug. "I am so happy for you. Love can conquer any stumbling blocks after all." She looked up at Calder. "When Selena first told me of her love for you, I feared she would never convince her father to allow the match." She looked back at Selena. "But you did it, dear cousin, you did it. We can start writing our invitations and see to having our gowns made."

Selena laughed. Her cousin was fairly dancing on her toes in her excitement and joy. That Flavia would be so happy for her made Selena grab her cousin and give her another hug.

"I think I must leave you two to your plans" Calder said. "I have much work that needs doing, and I need to stop by Whimbrel and see can I line up some laborers to help harvest my grain. 'Tis near time to begin the harvesting. It would seem I must hire a couple more perma-nent laborers. Mayhap I should speak with the brick mason working on the school. If we are to add on to the house, 'twould be good to get the plans formulated."

Selena again went into his arms. "You have so much to attend, but I must have one more kiss before you depart, my true love. I plan to see you on the morrow, if you are close to home."

"Not until late afternoon. I must check my fields. The wheat must be monitored daily, and I must see if the fields for the winter grains need additional harrowing."

Still in his arms, she asked, "You will tell Pascal and Hannah and the others this evening of our betrothal?"

"Aye, my dear one, that I will. And with such great joy in my heart."

With his words setting her heart to skittering about in her chest, she reveled in the feel of his lips on hers. When he at last released her, she could scarcely bear to let him go. "I do hope these next two months fly by," she told Flavia as her love exited with a little wave at the door. Flavia readily agreed with her.

"I know how you feel, Selena. I have loved Orland for so long. Now, to know that he is to be mine, sometimes I must pinch myself to know I am awake, and that I am truly to marry him. Father has spoken with Lord Edgerton." She grabbed Selena's hand. "Father is to give as my dowry a section of the manor that borders between the two manors, and Lord Edgerton has said as his portion of the settlement, he will build us a house on that land."

"That is wonderful," Selena said.

Flavia nodded. "It will not be a large house, just a pretty house that can someday serve as a Dower house or guest house. I suppose between the enlarging of your future home, and the building of our house, the brick mason will be kept very busy."

"Where are you to live until the house is built?" Selena asked. She would not want the renovating of Calder's house to interfere with Flavia getting her own home.

"We will live in the hunting lodge. The one on the far side of the manor that Orland had thought to take you to before he realized 'twas me he truly loved. Lord Edgerton said he will make the lodge comfortable enough to serve us until our house is built."

"That is good. But come, let us find your mother," Selena said, taking Flavia's hand. "She must help us with our guest list." Stopping, she put her hand to her head. "I wonder if Calder will know all his cousins who should be invited. I will get a list from him, and then, I do think, I will need to consult Avis Huddleston."

"Yes, I will have to consult Lady Edgerton on their guest list. She may want to do some of their family invitations herself. At least I hope so. We must start planning where we will lodge all these people."

"I understand from Avis, that the Huddleston and Grantham extended family is rather large. Avis says most family members will eagerly attend. Best we start with the D'Arcy side. After that, we will go to our mothers' families. That may be more difficult with my mother. Mayhap she will have to write those invitations. I really have not met but one of her cousins, and that was in London a number of years ago."

"I believe our fingers will be little more than nubs by the time we finish the invitations," Flavia said with a rippling laugh.

"I cannot suppose we could consider having the invitations engraved? I remember last year, besides an announcement in the newspaper, and at church, the Reigate butcher's daughter sent our engraved invitations. I thought they were most pleasing," Selena said.

Flavia shook her head. "Nay, Mother would never condone it. But I would guess she and Carola, and mayhap Cecily, will help us write them."

"That would be good. What we need is our list. Let us see if your mother is in her room."

They found Flavia's mother in her chamber getting dressed for dinner. "Yes, girls, I will help you with your list after dinner. Now, run on with you."

"Shall we at least start on the list, Flavia?" Selena asked. "We are already dressed and have no need to change for dinner. I am curious how many extended family members we will remember from the last reunion."

"'Twill be a challenge. We can work in my room until time for dinner."

"Agreed," Selena said, and soon both she and Flavia had pens and paper and were settled on Flavia's day bed with their writing desks on their laps. Their chore would be both fun and intimidating. They had such a number of relatives, not to mention friends.

# Chapter 44

August blended into September faster than Selena could have imagined, and September, in turn, had raced into October. They were but a week away from her wedding, and she was both excited and apprehensive. She wanted everything to go well, from the comfort and entertainment contrived for their numerous guests, to the wedding and the celebration. But mostly, she was looking forward to spending the rest of her life with the man she loved.

She and Flavia were astounded by the number of family members and friends who accepted the invitations to their weddings. Aunt Rowena's prediction had been correct. Finding housing for all the guests had been a massive undertaking. Thankfully, their closest neighbors, as well as some of their Rotherby friends, including the Sizers, were more than willing to help with the lodging. Flavia confessed to Selena that she was disappointed she and Orland would not be spending their wedding night in the remodeled hunting lodge that was to be their home until their new house could be built.

Sitting on a bench in the garden, Flavia pouted her lips and complained, "The lodge must be used to house Lady Edgerton's numerous relatives. Orland and I will be spending our wedding night in his bedchamber. Fact is, we will not be able to settle into our home together until Lady Edgerton's relatives leave. For all I know, we will not have our home until we return from your brother Giles's wedding."

As Giles's wedding was set for the first week in November, but little more than two weeks after Selena's and Flavia's weddings, Selena would not be surprised if Flavia's fears were accurate. Friends and relatives, who came great distances over often poorly maintained highways, were unlikely to return to their homes until they had enjoyed a lengthy visit.

Some guests were already arriving. Selena's father had returned a week past, and her cousin Timandra and her husband and three children, which included Timandra's-six-month-old son, had arrived four days after Selena's father. Having come all the way from Northumberland, and not knowing what road conditions they would encounter, they had come with a full accompaniment of servants, from Timandra's personal maid, to two nurses, two footmen, an outrider, and the coachman and postilion, as well as their riding horses and spare coach horses.

Timandra and her husband made a handsome couple, Timandra with her dark hair and regal carriage, and Gavin with his blond hair and laughing blue eyes. The evening the Merritts arrived, Calder had been scheduled to take supper at Whimbrel. He and Timandra's husband, Gavin, took an instant liking to one another. Though destined to inherit two large manors, a partnership in a couple of coal mines, and four coal barges, plus the title of Baron of Kirkwood, Gavin Merritt displayed no conceit. He knew a lot about the needs of keeping an estate profitable, especially as concerned sheep and cattle and their fodder. Calder invited Gavin to visit his farm, and Gavin readily accepted the invitation. After the visit, he told Selena and Calder he was vastly impressed.

"From the health and care of your herds and flocks to the state of your equipment and buildings, 'tis no wonder you prosper," Gavin said, and Selena had beamed. She loved to hear Calder praised.

Timandra said she expected her younger sister, Vivien, and her husband, Durand Laibrook, future baron of Blackhorn, and their young son to arrive any day. They, too, had a great distance to travel, coming from the coast of Lancashire. Timandra was disappointed her mother, Lady Grasmere, Phillida Lotterby, and her father Berold Lotterby, the Earl of Grasmere, were not coming, but Selena and Flavia had received a loving letter from their Aunt Phillida explaining her situation. Having returned home from her long sojourn in London with their cousin, Elizabeth, she had not the desire to again make that lengthy trip. Also, she wanted to be close to hand should her brother, Kenrick, the Earl of Tyneford, and the head of the senior line of the D'Arcy family, need her. They feared Kenrick's wife, Blanch, Elizabeth's mother, would soon die. She had fought off the consumption for a number of years, but she was losing the battle. Despite knowing the inevitable would come, Aunt Phillida believed her brother would be devastated.

Flavia, having been fostered with her Aunt Phillida for a number of years, was sorely disappointed her beloved aunt would not be at her wedding, but she could understand her aunt's unwillingness to undertake the journey she herself had so hated. Due to his mother's illness, Robert, Kenrick's oldest son, and heir to the Tyneford Earldom, was also staying close to home, but Elizabeth, now settled into her new home in London, would be coming to their weddings. Her husband, having been absent from his business as a broker for their lengthy visit to their families after their wedding, believed he could not afford to accompany her. He would have the opportunity to meet more of Elizabeth's family at Giles's wedding in November. Elizabeth would be escorted to the wedding by Selena's brother, Giles.

Giles's betrothed, Mistress Caroline Yelverton, was unable to attend. She was over-whelmed by the planning of her own wedding. But she sent sweet notes to Selena and Flavia wishing them a beautiful ceremony, and she expressed her eagerness to see them at her own wedding. Being an orphan, Caroline had only an elderly cousin to help her with the necessary preparations. As the wedding was to be held in London, not at Caroline's home in Essex, she was not working with people or areas familiar to her. With Giles being heir to the Rygate Earldom, and the godson of King Charles, who was planning to attend the wedding, everything from the ceremony to the following celebration would need to be deftly coordinated and eloquent, yet artfully unpretentious. Selena's mother was helping where she could, and she had helped write Caroline's and Giles's invitations. Lady Rygate presently abided in the Rygate apartment in London, that she might offer support and encouragement to her future daughter-in-law.

In some ways, Selena pitied Caroline. Yes, she was an heiress of a substantial fortune, the only child of Viscount, John Yelverton, Lord Brockhurst, but both her parents had died when she was young, and she had been reared by her aged maternal grandparents and a governess. She had led near a cloistered life on the family manor, Lombard Meadows, in Essex. Until she met Giles, her social life had consisted of small entertainments with neighboring families. Now, she was being thrown into the massive and raucous D'Arcy family. It would be quite a change for her.

Turning her thoughts back to Flavia, Selena asked, "Did I understand you to say that the Elliotts and Adkins have offered to lodge Lord Edgerton's various family members? If so, are we responsible for their entertainment?"

Shedding her pout, Flavia said, "Yes, both families have been lovely offering to lodge Lord Edgerton's family and friends. Lord Edgerton has but a couple of cousins attending, his family being small. His other guests are friends, peers from Parliament. However, his friends will be bringing their spouses, so seeing to their needs, from housing them to bedding their servants and stabling and feeding their horses, will entail considerable expense. I am but hoping they will not come early or stay long as the D'Arcy family seems to be doing. But, we are not responsible for the Edgerton guests' entertainment, except for the celebration after our wedding. The Edgertons must see to their guests as we see to ours.

"Speaking of which, I spoke with Maris Nibley yesterday. She came by while you were taking a ride with Gavin and Timandra. She is amazed and pleased with the change in her step-mother. She says she and Mistress Nibley have discussed several plays, poems, and books, and not once has Mistress Nibley attempted to criticize her manner of dress."

Selena had to smile. She could imagine how Mistress Nibley, always impeccably dressed, but intent on nurturing her relationship with her husband's daughter, must have fought down her urge to help Maris improve her appearance. Maris seemed to care little about the latest fashions or hair styles. She wore her thin brown hair in a neat bun, a style that did nothing to flatter her round face with its too large nose, too small mouth, and receding chin. Her round gray eyes and bright smile were her best features, but she could in no way be considered pretty. Still, she had confessed to Flavia that Wally Shandy, in his shy way, was courting her. Maris had hopes, as Wally's fortune continued to prosper, her father would overlook his previous status as a landless laborer and consent to her marrying Wally. She was very pleased to say, she had Mistress Nibley on her side. The good-hearted woman, never having known or seen Wally before Ewen and his friends transformed him into a gentleman, found him most pleasing. Selena guessed neither Maris nor Mistress Nibley would have thought a man as handsome as Wally would be interested in Maris. But both women were pleased with the situation, and Selena could not help but believe the gentle, sweet-hearted Wally had truly formed a tender for Maris.

Interrupting Selena's musing, Flavia said, "Maris says Mistress Nibley is beside herself with excitement. She cannot believe she is to house the Marquess of Sedmouth, and the future marchioness, our cousin Amabel, and Amabel's parents."

Selena laughed. "'Twill be delightful to see Amabel again. Such fun to learn she is also Calder's cousin through her mother, Donnet. He says Donnet's mother, who lives in London, cannot at her age make the journey here, but her children and some of their children – they are all Calder's cousins – are coming to the wedding." She pursed her lips thoughtfully. "If I am correct, one cousin and her family are to stay with Calder's sister, Eloisa, in Rotherby. Others are staying at Lord Penhaligon's hunting lodge. They are, after all, his cousins, too.

"Lord Penhaligon asked Avis to ready the lodge for his many guests. Apparently his lodge has been used over the years for the Cardington, Huddleston, and Grantham family gatherings. Avis says she hired a couple of women from Whimbrel to get the whole place cleaned, the bedchambers aired, and the kitchen scrubbed." Placing her hand to heart and heaving a sigh, Selena added, "Avis says Lord Penhaligon's wife, Lady Penhaligon, who has only been here once before, is coming and will be hostess to all the guests. She is bringing her own cook and kitchen staff, a couple of chamber maids, footmen, and who knows what else."

Flavia giggled. "Who would have guessed Calder Grantham, a prosperous farmer, and yet a yeoman, not a member of the gentry, would have so many prestigious family members."

Selena nodded. "I mean to thank Lord Penhaligon for pointing out the connections to Father. I know that helped convince Father to consent to my betrothal to Calder. Did I tell you that the reason Lord Penhaligon came here was because of a letter Avis wrote him. Or at least had her husband write to him. Told him a boar was tearing up his park. Avis said that was really just to give him an excuse to come to White Acres. In the letter, she added the information about Calder and me. Told him she feared my father would not approve of Calder. She says she knew Lord Penhaligon would help. He is not one to think himself superior to others, just because he was the first born son of an earl. Avis says his father was the same way. In fact, she says the old Earl was the least pompous man she ever knew." Selena giggled. "She said that is including her husband. Everyone was very sad when the old Earl died."

Flavia nodded. "I am not certain whether Father and Mother ever knew the older Lord Penhaligon, but they have always liked the present Lord Penhaligon. He has often dined with us when he visits White Acres. He seems ever cheerful."

"Avis thinks highly of him. The Huddleston home will be full with Mister Huddleston's brother and his family, and some of his Cardington cousins. Calder says his Aunt Alba and her husband and their children and grandchildren are coming. Some of the cousins are staying at Calder's, but his youngest cousin and her family are staying with his sister. Eloisa will have a full house with two sets of cousins and their families."

"I like Eloisa Tusket," Flavia said. "You are fortunate that you will have such a sweet and pretty sister-in-law. She is as pretty as your Calder is handsome." She frowned. "Orland has no siblings. I could wish he had a married sister. Someone Lady Edgerton could visit more often than she visits her siblings."

Selena burst into a laugh that had her hugging her stomach. "I know what you mean," she managed to gasp out. "How I would hate to have Lady Edgerton for a mother-in-law. Lord Edgerton is fun, but oh my, Lady Edgerton – when she frowns, she could curdle milk."

Snickering, Flavia said, "Orland says the servants are ready to rebel. Lady Edgerton has been working them from early morning until late into the evening. She wants all perfect when her relatives arrive. Orland believes, was it not for his father, half the servants would have quit, despite their contracts."

Still chuckling, Selena said, "I can understand her wanting things to be perfect. Has not your mother brought in extra help from Whimbrel village?"

"Aye, she has," Flavia admitted with a nod.

"Hannah and Hermia have been cleaning and baking, along with all the other jobs they have been doing during the harvesting and winnowing," Selena said, making her admiration for the two women evident. "Calder has been more than a little busy, what with obligatory suppers or dinners here. He has had to meet with the brick mason, who will be adding onto our house, and with the stone mason who will be building our new stables and coach house. The lower portion of the stables and coach house will be stone like the barn, the upper portion will be timber framed with wood slats and slate roofing. I do hope Calder will not be unhappy with all the changes to his home and farm. He says as long as we can be together, naught else matters, but … I wonder."

"Nonsense," Flavia said. "You and he are so perfectly suited for one another, just as Orland and I are. You will have nothing but joyful days ahead of you. With the extra hands to help on the farm, and the extra income from your Lincolnshire manor, all will go well."

Selena gave her cousin a hug. "You are so dear. I am glad we will be neighbors, and our children will grow up together."

"Yes, is that not wonderful," Flavia answered, returning the hug and then rising. "We had best see if Mother needs help, what with more and more of the family arriving."

"Agreed," Selena said, and linking arms, she and Flavia set off for the house.

# Chapter 45

"I thank you again for agreeing to come with me to meet Calder's family, Flavia," Selena said, taking the lead as they set off through the woods. "I am not certain why I feel so nervous, and yet, I do."

"I think 'tis natural to be nervous," Flavia answered from behind Selena. "I was terribly nervous when I met Lady Edgerton's sister and her husband and two daughters yesterday. I was so glad to have Orland standing next to me. Turned out Mistress Fairwell is not nearly so overbearing as is Lady Edgerton. I would guess your Calder's family members are total delights, or he would have warned you to beware." She giggled when Selena looked back over her shoulder at her and grimaced. "Besides, you know I always enjoy this walk whether we are going to the Nibley's or to Calder's. 'Tis good to stretch the legs after another filling dinner, and it helps clear my head. I just keep hoping we have not forgotten to invite someone or order something or that … oh, who knows what could go wrong."

"Naught will go wrong, Flavia," Selena said, hoping she sounded confident. She, too, was having many of the same worries, though for no good reason. Banns had been posted and read on three straight Sundays. Their wedding gowns were finished and carefully tucked away in their armoires. Arrangements for the housing of all the guests, their servants, their horses, and their coaches had been accomplished. The new Whimbrel school that would serve as the church for their wedding was completed. It was scrubbed clean, and all the debris outside had been cleared away. The benches and tables, books and slates that would soon be serving the students were stored in Mister Hall's granary barn until after the ceremony, and a podium for the Rotherby vicar had been put in place, that he might stand behind it to give his sermon after the wedding ceremony at the church door. Widow Forester and several other Whimbrel women had volunteered to decorate the inside of the school with bunches of autumn leaves and sheaths of wheat tied with bright ribbons the day before the wedding.

Barrels of beer, wine, and cider were stored in the cellar buttery, and Uncle Nate was taking Ewen and his multitude of friends hunting on the morrow, not just to amuse them, but with the hope of bringing home deer, pheasants, and hares to be prepared for the wedding feast. Extra trestle tables, chairs, and benches had been borrowed and awaited being set up on the day of the weddings. Plates, goblets, mugs, pitchers, napkins, and table cloths had also been borrowed. Providing seating and place settings for the large number of guests had been a master chore undertaken by Aunt Rowena and her ever helpful cousin Carola. "Bless the dear woman," Aunt Rowena was often wont to say.

Sheep, ducks, geese, doves, and an ox had been selected and would be taken to the butcher in Whimbrel two days before the wedding. The butcher had assured Aunt Rowena he would have enough men on hand to help him with the butchering. Even though many of the pastries would be made by the Whimbrel baker, pipes of flour for bread, rolls, pies, thickening, and cakes had been delivered to Aunt Rowena's prized cook, and he was busy with his baking. Extra help had been hired to aid the cook in his many tasks.

The same musicians who had played for Flavia's welcome home party would play for the wedding celebration. Once the feast was ended, the hall would be cleared but for chairs and benches along the walls, and the dancing would begin. Since they could not know whether the weather would cooperate, gaming tables would be set up in the parlor rather than outside, but in the hopes the weather would be sunny, they would also set up croquet and bowling on the green to add to the entertainment.

"I am eager to meet your brother Reggie's new wife," Flavia said, bringing Selena's myriad thoughts back to the present. "Father says Amaryllis is truly beautiful."

"Aye," Selena agreed. "She is not just beautiful but is sweet and brave. Much like you, dear cousin."

Flavia thanked Selena for the pretty compliment, then asked, "Should we keep our visit with Calder short, what with Reggie and Amaryllis, and Vivien and her family due to arrive at any time today, at least, according to the note Mother received from Cecily yesterday?"

"I suppose we must, but I hope I may not appear rude. Does Hannah offer refreshments, as I am certain she will, we can stay for that, and then make our excuses. What think you?"

"I think that would be perfect. When did Calder's family start arriving?"

"I believe they all arrived last evening, which is why Calder could not join us for supper. Poor dear has been so busy, between preparing for his guests and seeing to the threshing and winnowing of his grain, not to mention all the other everyday chores that need attending, and then he has been expected to join us every evening for supper. He has hired one new laborer, a youth from Rotherby, but being young, the boy will need to be trained in his duties."

"Do you know when construction will start on your stables and the addition to the house?"

"Calder, with input from Father, has approved the plans for both, and construction should start a couple of days before we leave for Giles's wedding," Selena answered, as they broke into the clearing where they normally stopped for a short breather. "I am excited about…"

Her sentence went unfinished as a man leaped up from a spot where he had been sitting in the bushes. "Ah, Lady Selena, I thank the good Lord you have finally come. I have been waiting here for three days."

"Well, sir, what is it I may help you with?" Selena asked. She thought she recognized the man as being one of the men who had abducted her for Darnell.

Lifting his arm, the man pointed at gun at her. Selena took a step back and Flavia gasped.

"I be that sorry milady, but I fear I must abduct you."

"Oh, not again," Selena said, slowly wagging her head from side to side. She looked back at Flavia. "What can Orland be up to now?"

"Nay, Lady Selena, 'tis not for Mister Darnell that I must abduct you. 'Tis for my own dire need." He looked past Selena to Flavia. "I am that glad you be here, too, Lady Flavia. You can take a message back to

Lady Selena's father. Tell him no harm will come to Lady Selena, and I will be contactin' him on how he may get her safely back." He waved his pistol at Flavia. "You be on your way. Be quick about it. Me time be runnin' out."

Flavia looked at Selena and Selena said, "Do as he says, Flavia. Tell Father I am fine. I cannot think this man means to harm me."

"Indeed she is right!" the man said. "I mean her no harm. Now, be off with you."

Flavia gave Selena a hurried hug and whispered, "Be brave, love," before dashing off.

"Milady, I need you to be comin' with me," the man said, and he waved the pistol toward a break in the copse of trees. The man was well muscled, but his dress was shabby and worn, and his shoes had long since seen better days. His dark brown eyes looked sad and weary, and his grizzled chin and cheeks indicated he had not shaved in many a day. He appeared to be a man very down on his luck.

Pushing branches and bushes aside, he herded Selena down a narrow path that Selena guessed had previously only been used by small animals. "Careful of your gown here, milady," her abductor said, pulling back a thorny bush. "I am that sorry to be puttin' you through this, but I got me no choice."

"Why have you no choice, Mister...? Oh, I am sorry I cannot remember your name."

"Silas, milady, Silas Barn. But I be no Mister."

"Well, Silas, why must you abduct me?"

"'Tis a bit of a story, milady."

"It would seem we have the time for it," she answered, noticing that they had entered a different woods. These trees were large and tall and no underbrush snagged at her skirts. She guessed they must have crossed into the Nibley woods. The squire had not needed to cut his forest and sell his wood, as her uncle had, in order to pay for the construction of his house.

Silas half chuckled, but it was not a happy chuckle. "Aye, 'tis ashamed I am to be doin' this to you, milady, but I must get a hundred pounds from your father in order to save me sister and her family."

"A hundred pounds! Good heavens, what do they need with a hundred pounds?"

"'Tis not what they need. 'Tis what that Shylock, Andrus, is demandin' I be payin' him, or else, do I not, me sister's husband could meet with a bad accident. Then where would me sister and her three little ones be with no husband to be supportin' 'em."

Selena stopped and looked directly into Silas's eyes. "Are you telling me someone is threatening your family?"

"Aye," he said, giving her a little nudge in the back with his pistol to get her moving again. "'Tis not far now."

Selena started walking again, but questioned, "Who is Andrus?"

"He be the man I must pay a hundred pounds to."

"But why? Did you borrow that amount? Now you cannot repay it?"

"Nay, I borrowed but twenty pounds to be buyin' me the sweetest little colt. He looked to be a weaklin' but I could tell by the spark in his eyes, that he was meant for greatness. I raised him up, took the best of care of him. He was all I thought he would be. Would have won me back the twenty pounds and more."

He stopped when they entered a small area under a large oak tree, and Selena could see a three-legged stool and a grime-coated rope rested under the tree.

"Here we be, milady. You just have you a seat on that stool."

"But what happened to your colt, Silas? Why did he not win you back your twenty pounds?" Selena asked, looking at Silas before glancing at the stool.

"Do sit, milady," Silas urged.

"Not until you tell me what happened to the colt." She raised her chin and planted her feet firmly. She had no fear that Silas would shoot her.

Heaving a sigh, Silas said, "He was fast, was my Inkspot." He looked at Selena and smiled, showing dark gums with several teeth missing. "I named him that because he was brown with a white blaze on his nose and one black spot, like a spot of ink there near the end of his nose." He touched his own crooked nose. It looked as though it had been broken a time or two.

"I bought him from Mister Manger, the man I worked for." He shook his head. "Worked for him for nigh on thirty years. Started workin' in his stable, muckin' out the stalls and such, when I was no more than five or six. But I was good with the horses, and by the time I was ten, he had me ridin' the horses, trainin' 'em, so to say. By the time I was a full growed man, I was in charge of his stables, breedin' his horses, trainin' em, and all else that had to do with the horses. Me wages was twelve pounds a year.

"Mister Manger thought Inkspot was worthless, so he laughed and sold him to me. I borrowed the twenty from a friend, and I used my wages to pay for Inkspot's keep. Then I did what odd jobs I could find after work at the stables to pay for extra oats for the colt. He grew big and strong, and could he run."

A grin spreading across his face, he looked so proud. Then the grin disappeared, and he gestured toward the stool. "Milady, do please have a seat. I must be tyin' you up so I can be gettin' the note to your father."

She shook her head. "You have yet to tell me what happened to Inkspot."

"Do you please sit. I promise I will tell you."

Slanting her eyes at him, she debated whether she could trust him. Deciding she could, she sat on the stool. It wobbled a bit, but she righted it, then looked up at Silas. "Well?"

He nodded, at the same time picking up the rope, but he just stood holding it and twisting it a little. "When Mister Manger saw how fast Inkspot was, he said he wanted to buy him back from me, but I said no. Manger said did I not sell him Inkspot, he would dismiss me, but still I said no. So he dismissed me. Then I no longer had a place to keep Inkspot, or to train him. My friend let me keep him in his barn. 'Twas not a fittin' place for a horse as fine as Inkspot, but 'twas a roof o'er his head, and I slept there with him."

Squatting beside Selena, Silas said, "Milady, I must tie one of your hands. I will leave the other free, do you get an itch or some such, but I must tie one hand."

Selena frowned, but let him wrap the rope around her wrist. "Very well, but do continue the story."

"Yes, milady. I did what jobs I could find, and trained Inkspot where and when I could. Then came the day to enter the race. I scraped up the fee, and I had no doubt Inkspot would win. And he would have won." He started wrapping the rope around the tree and Selena's waist. It was a large tree, but he had a long rope. From behind the tree where he was tying the rope, he said, "We was out in front, runnin' neck and neck with a big bruiser of a horse, and Inkspot was startin' to pull ahead. Well, that belswagger, that scum ridin' the bruiser, nudged that big horse into Inkspot, knocked him off balance, and he and I both went down."

"Oh, no!" Selena gasped trying to peek around the tree. "Was Inkspot hurt?"

Silas came back around to stand in front of Selena. "Aye. He will ne'er run again. Good for naught but pullin' a hay wagon, which is what he does now. Gave him to my friend. Better than havin' him go to someone who would treat him poorly."

"How sad." She was wondering if she could maybe buy the horse and give him a good home once her new stables were built. She looked up at Silas. "But that does not explain why you owe this man Andrus a hundred pounds."

"Ah. My friend needed the twenty pounds he had loaned me, and I had no way to pay him, so he sold my loan to another man. I made what payments I could but not fast enough to suit my new lender, so he sold my loan to Andrus. Andrus charges double the interest, and no matter how hard I tried, I could not keep up with the interest. Next thing I know, Andrus says I owe him a hundred pounds. Says he wants it within a week, and he sends a bullyhuff to collect it. The man says Andrus cares not what I have to do to get the hundred pounds, but can I not pay, bad things will happen to me family. In particular to me sister's husband."

"How dreadful! I have heard some of these men who loan money are ruthless. Fact is, my brother and I once saved my cousin from borrowing from such a person." Selena started to stand, but realized she could not. "Silas, abducting me is not a good answer. Once I explain this to my father, I am certain he will give you the hundred pounds you need."

Silas shook his head. "Nay, milady. I cannot be takin' that chance. Mayhap he would and mayhap he would not. You should be safe here. There be no ferocious animals in these woods. I will send the note to your father. He will leave the money where I tell him, and he will come and set you free. Again, I am that sorry to be doin' this to you."

He turned to leave, and Selena called after him. "Silas, you are making a mistake. This will not work. Oh, do please listen to me." But her cries were useless. He was soon hidden by the trees, and she was left to wonder how long she would have to wait to be rescued.

# Chapter 46

Breathless, Flavia raced past the lake and headed for the house. Seeing the footman, Jimmy, heading for the stables, she called to him, and he came running to her.

"Lady Flavia," he cried, "what is amiss? Where is Lady Selena? Has she been hurt?"

"She is not hurt yet, Jimmy, but you must go quickly and bring Mister Grantham. Tell him it is urgent."

"What do I tell him of Lady Selena?"

"Say naught of her. Just tell him to hurry. Now go!" she ordered, and after a little shake of his head, Jimmy raced back to the stables, and Flavia, holding her aching side, ran up the terrace steps and entered the house, calling for her mother and her father.

Finding her parents as well as Selena's father and Timandra and Gavin in the parlor, she blurted out her story between gasps for breath.

Her father took hold of her shoulders and forced her to look up at him. "You say you knew this man, this abductor?"

She nodded. "'Tis not that I know him, I but think he was …" She stopped herself. How could she tell them that Orland had attempted to abduct Selena to force her to marry him. It was before he realized he was not really in love with Selena, but he loved her.

"Go on child. If you know who this man is, you must tell us," her father demanded.

She glanced at her mother then at Selena's father. He looked so frightened. The blood had drained from his face, and fear shone in his eyes. She had no choice, she had to tell them something. At least a partial truth. "'Twas a joke Orland meant to play on us," she at last said. "'Twas while his mother was away. He used the coach and hired three men to pretend to abduct Selena and me while we were walking through the woods to the Nibleys'. As happened, 'twas not funny," she looked to her mother, "and 'twas how I came home with a twisted ankle."

"I knew there was more to that story than what I was told," her mother said.

"Yes, well, one of the men who pretended to abduct us was the man who has now abducted Selena. He had a pistol, and he said he had been waiting three days in the clearing where Selena and I always stop to catch our breath. He said he would send a boy with a note telling you where to leave the hundred pounds. He said he was desperate."

"I have not more than twenty pounds on me," her uncle said.

"Not to worry on that count," Flavia's father said. "I have more than what is needed in my strong box, though a hundred pounds seems a small sum for the man to be taking such a risk. However, I doubt we will have to give the scoundrel anything."

"What do you mean? I will take no chances with Selena's life," Uncle Ranulf said.

Flavia's father narrowed his eyes and cocked his head. "Nay, but remember, I spent near ten years being places I was not expected to be. I was more than a little good at surprising my prey. But as you say, we will take no chances with Selena's life. That I guarantee you." He looked to Flavia's mother. "Should we not send for Grantham?"

"I have sent for him," Flavia said. "I saw Jimmy and told him to bring Calder at once."

"Good girl," her father said. "All we can do is wait for the note to be delivered."

The wait was not easy on any of them. The footman, Plocket, had been told when a boy arrived, he should be directed immediately into the parlor. Flavia, twisting her hands together, sat next to her mother on the couch. Her mother had an arm around Flavia's shoulders and from time to time would pat her arm. Concern vivid on their faces, Timandra and Gavin watched Uncle Ranulf and Flavia's father as they paced about the room.

"I believe 'tis a good thing you sent Ewen and his friends off to Rotherby," Gavin said. "At least they are not underfoot or tossing out brazen plans to nab the abductor."

330

"Aye," Flavia's father agreed with a nod of his head, but said nothing else.

After a visit with cousin Elizabeth in London, Ewen had returned with a multitude of friends. All the youths were the sons of the men from her father's former highwaymen gang. Ewen thought it fitting to have his father's old friends represented by their sons at Flavia's wedding. Fortunately, Lord Penhaligon was housing Ewen and his friends in his hunting lodge.

Flavia was glad Orland had gone with Ewen. She would not like to have Uncle Ranulf confronting him about his attempt at abduction. She would have to warn Orland to have a care and would have to tell him the half-truth she had told about the incident.

Flavia's father had planned numerous activities to keep Ewen and his friends from underfoot, and Orland was included in most of the plans. This afternoon, her father had arranged for a fencing master, who had won several contests, to give a demonstration with one of his top students at the Rotherby Assembly Hall. After the demonstration, the master would give lessons to the young men. On the morrow, her father had arranged for a hunt in his three-hundred-acre park. The day after that, Lord Penhaligon was having a hunt in his four-hundred-acre park. She had no knowledge of what other plans her father might have scheduled, but she knew he would do his best to keep the youths away from Whimbrel Hall, except at meal time.

Flavia jumped when Plocket knocked on the door and opened it to admit a young boy of around ten. A shock of blond hair stood up on the boy's head when he pulled off his cap, and freckles paled on his face when he flushed a bright red. He seemed embarrassed to have so many eyes bearing down on him.

"Come in, boy," Flavia's father said. "No need to be afraid. Have you a note for us?"

"Aye," the boy said, holding out a grubby piece of paper in a trembling hand. "The man said I was to give this paper to Lady Selena's father. He said you would give me a penny for delivering it."

"I am her father," Uncle Ranulf said, taking the paper from the boy.

"Here is your penny," Flavia's father said, pulling a coin from his purse. "I will give you two more if you can tell me if you know the man or where you spoke to him."

The boy took the penny and thanked Flavia's father, but said, "I ne'er saw the man afore. He had dark hair and dark eyes and grubby clothes. I was on me way home after helpin' with the threshin' at Mister Hall's farm when he called to me. Said was important Lady Selena's father got the note quickly, so I agreed to bring it here."

His eyes wide, he added, "I like Lady Selena. She got that new school built for us, so we are not havin' to walk all the way to Rotherby. Is she in some kind of trouble?"

Flavia's father put his hand on the boy's shoulder. "Nay. You need have no worry for her. Now, here are two more pennies for you."

"Thank you, Lord Rotherby." Pocketing the pennies, the boy turned, and Plocket, having waited at the doorway, escorted him out.

"What does the note say?" Gavin asked. He and Timandra were on their feet, as were Flavia and her mother.

"Says to leave the hundred pounds in a knot hole in a lone oak tree in a field on the road to Rotherby. At least I think that is what it says. The spelling is so poor, and the paper so grimy. Says when he gets the money, he will leave a note telling where to find Selena."

"Let me see it," Flavia's father said, taking the note from her uncle. "Yes. That is what it says, and I know just where it is. Good location. The tree is close to the woods, but far from the road. He can watch what you do and wait for you to return to the road before he retrieves the money. He can be back in the woods before you could catch him. Even if you are on horseback.

"However," Flavia's father grinned. "I know a back way into those woods. I can catch him when he, thinking he has escaped, returns to the woods. I will take your man, Billings, with me. Between us, we will nab him." He held up his hand as Uncle Ranulf started to protest. "Nay, Ranulf, I promise, we will do nothing until the lout has the money and has left the note."

"I could go with you," Gavin said.

Flavia's father shook his head. "No, best not. We will need to move quietly through the woods. More than two would mean more risk of making noise. I know Billings to be a good man. He is all I need."

"Aye," Uncle Ranulf said. "Billings is good with a gun or a sword or a knife. Angelica will not let me travel any distance without him. She swears he keeps me safe on our sometimes treacherous highways."

"Let me get the hundred pounds, and we will be on our way." He called to Plocket. "Have my horse and Lord Rygate's horse saddled, and Billings' horse, also. Tell Billings he is going with us on an errand and to bring his pistol."

"Yes, my lord," Plocket said and hurried off to do his lord's bidding.

❧ ❧ ❧

Sitting around the dinner table with his visiting family, Calder was expecting Selena to arrive at any moment. His Aunt Alba and Uncle Kleef Mowbray were staying with an old friend of Aunt Alba's in Rotherby, but they had come to have dinner with Calder, so they could meet Selena before the wedding. Two of Aunt Alba's adult children, Noam and Laycia, and their spouses and children were staying with him. Aunt Alba's youngest daughter, Melia, her husband, and two-year-old son were staying with his sister, Eloisa. Calder accepted that his house would be crowded, but this was by no means the first time his extended family had congregated for various events. His wedding was considered the perfect time for all the family to gather—that included his more distant cousins, the Cardingtons and their offspring and spouses. Most would be staying at White Acres in Lord Penhaligon's hunting lodge. Beorn Huddleston, Ware's younger brother, and his family were also coming, and, of course, would stay with Ware.

When Calder's great grandmother's sister Cordelia had been alive, the gatherings had been frequent, often annual, but since Cordelia's death, the families only gathered for special occasions. The last gathering had been three years back when Ware's sister Troth had returned from Europe for a visit with her new husband.

The hall table had been extended to accommodate all the guests, plus Calder's laborers. The weather being warm, the door to the hall was left open. Lying peacefully in the doorway, Rollo insured no chickens wandered into the house. Though enjoying the conversation and banter around the table, Calder was keeping a keen lookout for Selena. He was surprised to see the footman, Jimmy, ride up, jump from his horse, barely bothering to tie the animal to the hitching post, and dash toward the house. On his feet before Jimmy entered, Calder grabbed the youth by his coat when he darted inside, and with fear in his voice, cried, "Has something happened to Selena?" Why else would the footman be in such a hurry?

"I know not, Mister Grantham," Jimmy said, catching his breath. "Lady Flavia came running from the woods, and bid me come to get you immediately. She would not take the time to tell me aught. She but ran for the house, and I ran to saddle the horse."

Calder looked at his family. "Something is amiss. I must go at once to Whimbrel."

"I will go with you," his cousin, Noam, said. "I need but saddle my horse."

"Take my horse," his father said. "I wanted the exercise, so I chose to ride, though your mother chose to come in the coach."

Jimmy said, "You take the horse I rode, Mister Grantham. I will walk back."

Noam's wife Angeny asked, "Should I come, Calder, that I may report back to the family? We are all very concerned."

Calder looked at the anxious eyes peering up at him. His son, Pascal, had gripped Hannah's hand. Fear was recognizable on their faces. "No need, Angeny. I will send Jimmy back with a report when I have more details. I suspect naught but a sprained ankle or some such." His heart was thundering in his chest, but he wanted to assure his son and family that all would be well. All would be well. All had to be well.

When Calder and Noam arrived at Whimbrel, they were quickly apprised of the situation. They were told Selena's father and uncle had just left with the hundred pounds requested by the abductor. "You are certain she was not hurt?" Calder demanded of Flavia.

Flavia shook her head. "She was not hurt. In fact, I cannot say she even seem frightened. But I was. The man had a pistol."

"He was definitely on foot? You saw no signs of a horse?" Noam asked, his blue eyes, so like Calder's, were glued on Flavia. Near Calder in age, when younger, the two had often been mistaken for brothers, though Noam was a tad shorter and stockier than Calder.

"Nay, I saw no horse," Flavia answered.

Nodding, Noam said, "Good," and he looked at Calder. "My guess is Lady Selena is being held not far from where she was abducted. Otherwise, the man could not have secured her, found the boy to deliver his note, and made it to his hiding place in so short a pace of time. I suggest we go search for her."

"Yes!" Calder cried, jumping on the idea. Better to do something than stand around and wait. He looked at Flavia. "You took the path you normally take?"

She nodded. "Yes, and 'twas in the bower where he accosted us."

"I know where that is," Calder said.

"Then do we hurry, we should be able to pick up the trail," Noam said.

"I will go with you," Gavin said, "and we will get my outrider, Tombs. I swear, the man can near track anything."

"Then let us get him and be on our way," Noam said.

Calder was grateful to his cousin. Noam, employed by a firm that did numerous and varied types of investigations, from finding people, to searching out the financial security of an investment, had quickly sensed the probability that Selena could not be detained at too distant a location. Hopefully they would quickly find her.

Gavin's outrider, Tombs, a fierce looking man with broad shoulders and a craggy visage, was showing some gray at his temples, but he moved out with a steady trot, easily keeping up with the younger men. In no time they had reached the bower. There, Tombs took over, and with little apparent effort, found the trail that Calder prayed would lead them to Selena.

# Chapter 47

Fearing some harm would come to Silas, poor man, Selena wished she could have persuaded him not to pursue his desperate course. He really had no chance against her Uncle Nate. Silas might be asking Selena's father for the money, but Uncle Nate would be involved. If only she could have made Silas wait and listen to her. She knew she could convince her father to loan Silas the hundred pounds. He could pay it back by working for her and Calder. She was going to need a man who truly knew horses. Jimmy would make a good coachman, but she wanted a groomsman who could keep the horses, especially the riding horses, in top condition.

Bored, and having given up any attempt to reach behind the tree to untie her binds or to slip her wrist free, she tried to amuse herself by going over the list of guests coming to her and Flavia's weddings. Ticking them off on her fingers, she had soon gone over the list twice. She next turned her attention to the foods they intended to serve. Having so many guests for such an extended stay had meant enormous planning and incredible expense for her uncle and aunt, but her father was paying half the expenses. The real burden, though, the organization, the ordering of multiple supplies had fallen on Aunt Rowena. Carola had been a great help, offering to run any and all kinds of errands. Today, right after dinner, Carola had set off for Whimbrel to go over various and sundry things with the baker, the women who would be decorating the school, those brewing the ale, and the youths who would be directing the coachmen where to park their coaches. The granary owner, Mister Hall, having a field closest to the village, and having completed his harvesting, had volunteered his field for the coaches, but his sheep, currently grazing on the chaff, would need to be removed to safe quarters until after the coaches departed.

As they so often did, her thoughts drifted to Calder. He would be wondering when she would arrive. She hoped he would not be worried about her. Mayhap Flavia would send him word. But then, did he learn of her plight, that might worry him even more. She pictured Calder, the way his eyes shone when he looked at her. She could see his love for her in those beautiful blue eyes. She loved being held in his arms, loved his kisses, his gentle fondles.

She knew what to expect on their wedding night. Aunt Rowena had given her and Flavia a talk, but she and Flavia had already discussed the matter. They had not lived around animals all their lives and not learned a few facts. Aunt Rowena declared the act of making love the most beautiful way for two people in love to express their love for each other. She said for some women, the first time they made love could be painful, but after that first time, there would be no more pain, just intense pleasure. For some, even the first time brought no pain. Selena was a little nervous about that first time, but she had no doubt, with Calder, it would be thrilling, and as beautiful as Aunt Rowena promised.

Squiggling on her stool and trying to get more comfortable, her attention was caught by the sound of barking. She recognized one deep-throated bark. The dogs had to belong to Squire Nibley. Poaching in his woods had resumed, so the squire's kennel man, Deaver, must have the dogs out, hoping the hounds would pick up a scent. Was she lucky, mayhap they would chance upon her and set her free. Hearing rustling in the woods, she was hopeful her wish had been answered. Instead, two bearded and shabbily dressed men burst into the clearing around the oak tree. Both men were carrying dead hares, and both stopped in utter surprise when they saw her. Poachers. They had to be poachers.

"Well, now what have we here?" the older of the two men said, brushing past the young one. "A pretty maid, an' she be all trussed up."

Selena was wary of the way the man was looking at her, but she raised her chin and said, "Sir, and I would be pleased would you untie me. My family must be worried about me."

The man chuckled. "Now, who would have tied up such a pretty maid? Mayhap your husband for disobeying him, or some lover you crossed?"

"'Tis not like that. I am Lady Selena D'Arcy, and this has been a grave mistake. But do you release me, I will see you are well rewarded."

The man laughed again and handed his hare to the younger man. "Hold this, Willy. I mean to take me a closer look at this bound up laaady." He stretched out the word lady in a mocking sort of way, his lips curling in a disgusting smile.

The younger man, little more than a boy, Selena thought, said, "I hear the dogs, Mort. We need to be on our way."

"Ah, now, Willy, we got time enough for me to see what the laaady has to offer," the older man said, drawing closer to Selena.

Her skin crawled, and the man's smell assaulted her nostrils. He would not save her. He was intent on assaulting her. When he reached out and took a hold on her skirt, she slapped him with her free hand, and kicked out at him. Her defensive gestures made him chuckle again.

"Feisty now are ye? Mayhap that is why your master bound you to this tree. T' teach ye to be more civil." He narrowed his eyes and cocked his head. "More accommodatin'."

When he reached for her again, she let out as loud a scream as she could muster. Mayhap Deaver or someone would hear her. As she screamed, the man reached his filthy hand to her mouth, but she twisted and turned on her stool and screamed a second time. With her second scream, the younger poacher took off at a run.

A nasty look crossed the older man's face, and he raised his hand to backhand her, but she ducked his swing, tipping over her stool in the process, and leaving her struggling to find some kind of seating or footing. Her back scrapped on the tree bark, tearing her gown and scratching her skin, but she managed another scream.

❧ ❧ ❧

At Selena's first scream, Calder pushed past Tombs and thrashed his way toward the sound of her voice. Her second scream sent his pulse pounding in his ears, and at her third scream, he burst into the clearing. His heart stopped in his throat when he saw Selena bound to a tree with a disreputable looking man bending over her.

"Selena!" he cried, and the man jerked around to face him, but Tombs, entering the clearing on Calder's heels, thrust past Calder and grabbed the man, freeing Calder to go to Selena. In an instant, Calder had Selena on his knee, propping her up so the rope was not cutting into her. He swept out a knife, cut her free, and pulled her into his arms.

"My dear one, my dear, dear Selena," he cried into her neck, crushing her to his chest.

Selena wrapped her arms around his neck and sighed, "Oh, my wonderful Calder."

Rising, he pulled her up with him, but still held her close in his arms. "Are you hurt, my love? Did the blackguard hurt you?"

"Did he lay a finger on Lady Selena, he could well be a dead man," Tombs said.

The vile man, cowering on his knees in front of Tombs, had blood running down his beard from his busted lip and more blood dribbled from his nose onto the ground. Tombs had a pistol pointed at the man's head. Cold anger evident in his voice, Tombs said, "From my years of service, first to Lord Grasmere, and then Lady Timandra, I have known Lady Selena since she was little higher than my knees. A sprite she is, never a mean bone in her body. Never hurt a soul in her life. I will not take it kindly has this scum harmed her."

Gavin clamped a hand on Tombs shoulder. "We will take him back to Whimbrel and determine what is to be done with him. And, yes, has he hurt Lady Selena, he will pay."

Selena pulling a little away from Calder said, "I am not badly hurt. Only the back of my gown is torn and my back a little scraped, but all of you came to my rescue before he could do me any real harm." Her gaze lingered on Calder before looking at Tombs, Gavin, and Noam. "Thank you. Thank you all."

She looked back up at Calder. "I see a gentleman, I know not."

He smiled down at her. That was Selena. She would not want to appear ungrateful. She would want to know whom she was thanking. "My cousin, Noam Mowbray." He held a hand out to his cousin and said, "Noam, may I make known to you my soon to be bride, Lady Selena."

Stepping closer, Noam bowed over Selena's hand. "Lady Selena, 'tis an honor."

"'Twas Noam had the idea you could not be far from where you were abducted. 'Twas his idea we come looking for you. Tombs easily picked up the trail." He looked over again at Gavin Merritt's loyal outrider. "I owe you, Tombs."

"Nay. I am but happy we have Lady Selena safe and secure. I have long had a fondness for the Lady Selena." He looked kindly at Selena. "Ever since I watched her champion a waif what had been nabbed for stealing a loaf of bread." He chuckled. "Not much more than a tot was she, but she stood right up to that beadle and told him he would not be taking the lad off to jail. I am happy to say, that lad is now in the Merritt employ. Could not ask for a better groomsman, now could we Mister Merritt?"

"You are right there, Tombs" Gavin said. "You took the boy under your wing, and I could not be happier with his service." He looked at Selena. "We thank you for saving the lad."

Selena laughed, the sound tinkling out joyfully. Its sound made the man who had been assaulting her look up in surprise. "I think I was so young then," Selena said, "I barely remember the incident, but I am pleased the lad has prospered."

Tombs looked down at the man at his feet. "Be this the man who abducted you, milady?"

Selena shook her head. "No. He is a poacher. He and another man each had a hare. The other man ran off with both hares. I heard Squire Nibley's dogs barking and thought they might bring the squire's man, Deaver, to my rescue." Slanting her eyes upward at Calder, she said, "I am much happier that you are the one who rescued me."

"Well, I think we should be getting back to Whimbrel," Gavin said. "Are you able to walk all right, Selena?"

"Oh, yes. Really, I am fine. I am just happy to be free. I was so bored."

Calder kissed her nose. "My sweet darling. Let us get you home. Flavia and your aunt are beside themselves with worry. And I must send word to my family that you are safe."

"Then let us hurry. I have no wish to let them continue to worry."

"On your feet," Tombs said, dragging the culprit to his feet.

"I ne'er dreamed she were a real lady," the man said in a whimpering voice. "How could I know a lady would be so bound up."

"You should know better than to mistreat any woman," Tombs said, giving the man a shove. "You will get no sympathy from me. Now move."

With the baying of the dogs still in the distance, Calder guessed Deaver was keeping them on a leash, or the dogs would have found Selena. Tombs led the way, pushing the poacher in front of him. Gavin followed him, and Noam brought up the rear. He was there to help hold tree limbs and bushes back as Calder aided Selena along the narrow trail back to the bower and the path leading to Whimbrel. Selena had limped a little at first, but she said she but needed to work out the cricks. Soon she was moving with her usual pace, and Calder was able to breathe easier. He knew her back had to hurt, but she made no complaint.

In telling him the gist of her abduction, she astounded him by saying she wanted to hire the man who had abducted her. Wanted him to be able to work off the hundred pounds he would owe. He knew horses, she said. She also wanted to buy the man's injured horse. Calder wanted nothing more than to thrash the abductor. Ye gads, the man had endangered Selena. Calder hated to think what might have happened had he not arrived in time to stop the poacher's assault on Selena. Yet, he knew he would acquiesce to Selena's wishes. It would seem, at least according to Tomb's tale, Selena had been defending the less fortunate since she was a child.

He had been interested to learn Selena had impressed Tombs by saving a youth from the gaol. He was impressed with Tombs, not only for his skills, but because he had apparently given the waif a home and guidance. He wondered how many other people Selena had helped over the years, and how many more would she be helping. Certainly the new school would benefit the youths of the parish, including Pascal. And to think what she had done for Wally Shandy. He had little doubt but what there would be many more recipients of Selena's largess. God, what a woman he was lucky enough to be marrying.

# Chapter 48

Ranulf's heart dropped, and his breath caught in his throat when he, his brother Nate, Billings, and the man, Silas Barn, arrived at the oak tree where Barn had left Selena, only to find Selena was not there. "But I left her right there. I made her as comfy as I could, there on the stool," Barn said, his fear evident in the quivering of his voice.

"Looks to have been a struggle here," Billings said, pointing to a flattened bush and churned up dirt. "Bit of blood, on the ground here."

Ranulf grabbed Barn by his coat and shook him. "Has my daughter been injured, I swear you are a dead man!"

"Easy," Nate said. "The rope here has been cut. I am guessing someone freed Selena. Let us go back to the house. Could be she is there waiting for us to return."

Still holding Barn close, Ranulf shook him again. "She had best be there."

"Billings," Nate said, "you take the trail back. Just on the off chance you see the path diverges. We will take the horses and Barn back to the house. Is Lady Selena not there, we will come from the opposite direction. Leave us a signal if you take a different path."

With a quick nod, Billings answered, "Aye sir," and set off at a fast clip.

"Shall we return home?" Nate asked, looking at Ranulf.

Having released Barn, Ranulf was still glaring at him, but he pushed him in the direction of the road where they had left the horses. Nate's plan had worked perfectly. No sooner had Barn collected the hundred pounds from the knot in the tree and left a map showing where he had left Selena, than Nate and Billings, springing from the woods, had pounced upon him. Weeping, the man had proclaimed he never meant to harm Lady Selena. Told them, without the hundred pounds, they might as well kill him. Instead, they forced him to lead them to where he had left Selena. He had stumbled along, moaning that all was now lost. He moaned about his poor sister and her children, but Ranulf paid little attention to the man's woes. He but wanted to see his daughter, safe and sound.

❋ ❋ ❋

After receiving multiple hugs from Flavia, Aunt Rowena, and Timandra, Selena allowed herself to be escorted up to her room to be made over by the three women and her maid Alice. After stripping down, she relaxed as Alice rinsed her back and face and hands with fresh warm water. Her hair was combed out, tiny twigs and leaves dispatched, and then Alice put it up in a neat bun. Aunt Rowena fussed over her back and put a soothing salve on it and a soft bandage, and finally she was helped on with clean hose, petticoats, bodice, and skirt.

"Do you feel up to going back downstairs," Aunt Rowena asked. "You have had quite an ordeal. I am certain Calder would understand did you wish to rest."

Selena laughed. "Nay, Aunt Rowena. I feel fine. I am eager to become better acquainted with Calder's cousin, Noam. Calder said it was his cousin's idea to search for me."

"So it was," Flavia said. "Have you noticed how closely Mister Mowbray resembles Calder. Oh, not as handsome, but same blue eyes, same hair."

"No one could be as handsome as my Calder," Selena said with a giggle, "but yes, that they are related is easy to discern. So… let us go down and join the men."

They were descending the stairs when Selena's father burst through the front door. His eyes went immediately to Selena. "Daughter!" he cried. "You are safe!"

"Father!" Selena said, hurrying to him.

He grasped her in his arms and held her tightly. She could not remember him ever clinging to her in such a fashion, and he kept saying, "My daughter, my daughter, thank the good lord you are safe."

The voices in the hall brought Calder, Gavin, and Noam from the parlor, and from over her father's shoulder, Selena gave Calder a smile.

"Come now, Ranulf," Uncle Nate said, "let me give the gel a hug, too."

Selena's father slowly released her, and she was swept into her uncle's arms. She giggled. "I must remember to be abducted more often. I get so much attention."

"Never say such a thing," her father said. "I have near had an apoplectic fit."

"Aye, he has been a sight," Uncle Nate said, "but we have apprehended your abductor and retrieved the hundred pounds. However, you must tell us how you were freed."

He was not to immediately learn about her rescue, for Selena looked past her father to the open door where the footman Plocket was guarding her abductor. Silas, shoulders slumped, hands tied behind him, raised his head. His defeated, hopeless eyes met Selena's. "Oh, Father," Selena said, "you must release poor Silas. He meant me no harm, in fact …"

Her father interrupted her with a choked bray. "Meant you no harm! The scum abducted you, child!"

"He is not scum, Father. He is really very nice, but he had a misfortunate incident that put him in debt to a vicious man named Andrus, who has threatened his sister and her family. So you see, he only needed the money to save his brother-in-law from being killed or injured."

"I care not what he needed the money for," her father thundered, his face turning red with his anger. "He abducted you!"

"Did you say he owes the money to Andrus? Andrus of London?" Noam asked, and everyone turned to look at him.

"Yes," Selena said, addressing Calder's cousin. "Silas borrowed twenty pounds from a friend to buy a horse, but when his horse was brutalized in a race, Silas could not repay his friend. The friend sold the debt to another man who sold the debt to that mean man, Andrus, and the twenty pound debt, became a hundred pounds. Andrus sent a man to threaten Silas that if he failed to pay what Andrus claimed he was owed, the man would hurt Silas's sister's family. That is why Silas had to have the money. To save his family."

"That sounds like Andrus," Noam said. "I know people who have had dealings with him. The man is ruthless, and did he say he would do injury unless he received his payment, indeed, he would do someone an injury. He charges outrageous interest that no one can pay, and then threatens those who miss their payments to him."

Selena's father, narrowing his eyes, glared at Noam. "Who, sir, are …"

Stepping forward, Calder interrupted Selena's father, "Lord Rygate, Lord Rotherby, may I present my cousin, Noam Mowbray." Selena's father drew himself up and, like Selena's uncle, politely acknowledged the introduction, but he still eyed Noam suspiciously as Calder continued. "Noam works with a London firm that does various kinds of investigations, from financial to criminal. Fact is, I just learned today that the Drescott Firm has done work for Sir William Hayward, Selena's cousin Lady Elizabeth's husband. Noam would know of what he speaks."

"Done work for Hayward have you?" Uncle Nate asked.

"Yes, Lord Rotherby," Noam said, "primarily financial. At times Sir William wants a company investigated. He wants to know if they are as sound as they declare, and would they make a good investment for a client. But I have worked with a client or two who have had dealings with Andrus. Unsavory character he is, beyond any doubt."

"Why, I think I remember that name," Timandra said, turning to her husband. "Gavin, was that not the name of the man the Bakers were in debt to? Do you not remember?"

"Yes," Gavin said, "'Twas their fear of Andrus that forced their hand and led to their apprehension, but the family is familiar with that story. No need to rehash it."

"You see, Father," Selena said, putting a hand on her father's chest, "that is why you must loan Silas the money. So he can pay Andrus off, because Andrus is threatening Silas's sister's husband. Who would support Silas's sister, did she lose her husband."

Her father stared down at her and shook his head. "Nay, Selena, I cannot see why you should want me to give the man a hundred pounds." Raising his voice, he repeated again, "The man abducted you!"

"Yes, Father, but he never meant to harm me. He but needs the money, and when I receive my settlement, I can pay you back, and Silas can pay Calder and me back by being our groomsman. He really knows horses, and we will need a man who is good with horses."

"Wait a minute. Are you saying you want this man to work for you?" Her father looked at Calder. "Are you aware of this, Grantham?"

Calder looked from Selena's father to Selena. "She did say that was her wish, sir. I would prefer to thrash the man, but does Selena think he would be a good groomsman, I cannot argue with her. I know little of carriage horses or fine riding horses. I must trust her judgement on that. Besides, I do need another laborer to help ready things that we may attend her brother's wedding next month."

Uncle Nate started chuckling. "Give up, Ranulf. You know you can never win an argument with your daughter. If she wishes to help the man, so be it."

Selena's father glared at her. "I cannot believe I am worried sick about you. But thanks to Nate, we apprehend the villain. Now, you not only want me to give that man a hundred pounds, you want to give him employment."

Smiling at her father, Selena nodded and said, "Yes, Father. Poor Silas needs our help."

Her father frowned and shrugged. "Well, you will have your way as you always do. I will loan Barn the hundred pounds. You will refund me from your settlement, but how Barn will ever pay you back is beyond me." He turned to Plocket. "Release him."

Silas was staring uncomprehendingly, first at Selena, and then her father, as Plocket unbound his hands. "I… I am not to hang. I…I…am to have the money?"

"Yes, Silas," Selena said, "and you are to have a job with Mister Grantham and me. So you may pay off your loan and be free of that horrid Andrus."

"With your approval Lord Rotherby," interrupting, Noam looked at Selena's uncle. "I recommend someone like Tombs go with Barn to pay the loan. Andrus is devious. He could come up with another reason that Barn owes him still more. 'Twould be best, did someone like Tombs impress upon the man collecting the hundred pounds, that he communicate to Andrus that Barn is under your protection, sir. That the loan is considered paid. Does anything vile happen to Barn or his family, Andrus would be answering to you. Andrus tries to stay clear of the peers."

"Good thinking Mowbray," Uncle Nate said. "We will send Billings and Tombs. Fact is, I will give the hundred pounds into Billings' care. That way we know for certain this is not an all-out fabrication."

"So, Silas, you see," Selena said with a broad smile, "had you listened to me in the first place, this would all have been much more simple."

"Lady Selena, I will ne'er be able to thank you enough," Silas said, his eyes glowing. He looked to her father and then her uncle. "Or you, Lord Rygate, or you Lord Rotherby."

Patting Silas on the shoulder, Selena said, "You will thank us by showing up at Mister Grantham's farm early tomorrow morning, cleaned and shaven and ready to go to work. You will be given housing in the loft above the barn where Mister Grantham's other laborers have accommodations. When we have a stable built, you will be in charge of our horses."

"You are a lucky man, Barn," Uncle Nate said. "But I think you know it."

"Indeed, sir, I do know it," Silas said. Stepping back, he bowed to Selena. "Milady, I will do whatever you wish me to do, and when you have your horses, I will care for them like they was my own. I will ne'er let you down, on that you can depend."

His tone harsh, Selena's father said, "Just make certain your word is good, or you will answer to me."

Standing on tiptoe, Selena kissed her father's cheek. "Never fear father, all will be well. Silas will be an outstanding laborer and groomsman, of that I am certain."

"As usual, you will have your own way," her father said with a shake of his head.

"That would be the Lady Selena I know and have grown to love," came a bristly voice from the door. "Still collecting strays, I see."

Selena jerked around to see a tall, aging, but august woman with bright gray eyes, a long slender nose, and graying hair, standing stiffly and leaning on a cane in the doorway. "Mistress Sermon! How wonderful!" Selena cried and pushed past everyone to embrace her friend.

"Easy, gel, you will knock me over," Mistress Sermon grunted.

Loosening her hold, Selena grinned and placed a kiss on Mistress Sermon's cheek. Looking past her friend, she was pleased to see Mistress Sermon's nephew, Richard Toms. Beside him was a small, pretty, brown-haired woman who looked to be in her early twenties. Her eyes met Selena's, and dimples popped to her cheeks when she smiled.

"Oh, Mister Toms, so grand you are here," Selena exclaimed. "And the lovely woman at your side must be your betrothed, Mistress Tidewell. All of you do come in."

Aunt Rowena had hurried to the door to introduce herself and to welcome the newcomers into her home. "You must forgive the fuss, Mistress Sermon," she said, drawing the woman into the hall. "We have been having a most eventful afternoon."

"So it would seem," Mistress Sermon said, "but does it involve Lady Selena, then I am not surprised. I have known her but a short time, but I know her motives are ever on the side of right and goodness." She looked to Selena's father. "Lord Rygate, if I may be so bold, I will tell you I greatly admire your daughter, and I believe you are most fortunate to have raised such a remarkable young woman."

Selena could not help but chuckle at the look on her father's face. What infuriated him about his daughter, Mistress Sermon now praised. Controlling her glee, Selena said, "Father, allow me to introduce Mistress Jane Sermon, and her nephew, Mister Richard Toms. You already know them, Uncle Nate." He nodded, and she looked to her father. "They are the dear friends I met on our journey from home to Whimbrel. Reggie, Amaryllis, and I owe them much. The lovely lady with Mister Toms is his betrothed, Mistress Clotilda Tidewell."

Both men bowed to the ladies and nodded to Toms before Selena began introducing the other people gathered in the hall. She saved the introduction to Calder to the last. "This is the man who stole my heart, and who will soon be my husband. Mister Calder Grantham," she said, slipping an arm around Calder's waist.

Toms, his gray eyes dancing, his pointed, foxlike nose aquiver, said, "I cannot tell you how pleased I am to meet you, Mister Grantham. Anyone who could capture Lady Selena's heart must be a fine fellow indeed."

"Thank you, Mister Toms," Calder said, "and believe me, I know how fortunate I am."

"Suppose we all go into the parlor," Aunt Rowena said. "Plocket can see about some refreshments for our guests. She took Mistress Sermon's arm. "You must be exhausted. Please come in here and let us make you comfortable. After you have some refreshment, Selena and my daughter will take you and Mistress Tidewell upstairs to freshen up. Would you care for some ale, or perhaps some sherry?"

As the women and Toms followed Aunt Rowena into the parlor, Selena noticed the men hung back. "We have a matter to deal with in the stables," she heard Calder tell her father, and Gavin nodded.

"Aye, Rotherby," Gavin said. "My man, Tombs, has a true villain in custody. I believe we need deal with him before we send Tombs and Billings off with Barn."

Selena's uncle nodded. "Let us be to it then," he said and turned to lead the men toward the back of the house. Selena knew they would be dealing with the poacher. She could not feel sorry for the man. He was cruel, but she hoped the younger man, who had run away, would run far enough he would not be caught. Poaching was a crime, but many poachers were but trying to feed their families. Life was a hard row for many people.

Selena arrived in the parlor to hear her aunt telling Mistress Sermon they should send their coach and servants on to the Nibleys'. "You should stay and have supper here. Then after supper, when you arrive at Nibley Hall, your servants will have your rooms readied. Cousins of ours will also be staying with the Nibleys', as will Lord Sedmouth. He is betrothed to our young cousin, Amabel Harmon. They are due to arrive tomorrow."

"We will be delighted to stay to supper with you, Lady Rotherby," Mistress Sermon said.

"Indeed we will," Clotilda Tidewell said. She looked at Selena. "I thank you, Lady Selena, for including me in the invitation to your wedding. I must admit to being eager to meet you. Richard has had such praise for you."

Selena laughed. "He is being kind. I was also eager to meet you. Both Mister Toms and Mistress Sermon," she glanced at the older woman seated next to Aunt Rowena, "have had great praise for you. Fact is, Mistress Sermon has said you are the perfect woman for her nephew. Now that I have met you, I can see she is right."

"Aye," Toms said with a chuckle. "Clotilda will keep me on a straight path." He looked around the room. "But where are the other men? Am I missing out on some sport?"

"Nay," Selena said. "They had a little matter with today's events that needed to be settled. They will return soon. Now, do tell me how you have fared since last we met."

Mistress Sermon began by telling about the completion of her home repair after a fire, while Aunt Rowena excused herself long enough to write a note to the Nibleys that Mistress Sermon's maid could give to them. Selena, glad to have Silas's dilemma resolved, settled back in her chair to enjoy her friends.

# Chapter 49

Ranulf learned from Calder and Gavin about the poacher and how the villain had attacked Selena. Had he known about the attack on Selena before he agreed to help Barn, he never would have agreed to give Barn the needed funds. He wanted nothing more than to throttle the man. Was it not for Barn, Selena would never have been put in such danger. But, he had given his word. Barn would get his hundred pounds, but Ranulf hoped he would never have to see the man again. Now, his attention was on the man who had assaulted his daughter.

"I would recommend, Lord Rygate," Tombs said, "that you let Billings and me have some time with him. When we finish with him, he is not apt to come round this neighborhood again. Better than making the Lady Selena have to testify against him in court."

"Oh, aye, I would not have Selena testify in court. No. No way!" Ranulf was aghast at the thought of Selena having to appear in court. Having to explain how she came to be in a situation that the poacher could assault her. No. That would never do.

"I am in agreement," Calder said. "Does Tombs make it clear to the poacher that he will not live another day does he show his face anywhere in this parish ever again, then I think he should be released without any charges being pressed."

"Then I would think we are all in agreement," Nate said, looking at Tombs. "We will leave the poacher to you and Billings. When you have finished and sent him on his way, come collect the funds from me, and take Barn to pay off this Andrus fellow's henchman."

"Yes, Lord Rotherby," Tombs said, before turning to Barn and telling him, "Wait outside by the door. You will not, I think, wish to witness this."

Barn blanched and nodded, then looked questioningly to Ranulf. "Go on," Ranulf said. "Wait by the door. And be grateful 'tis not you Tombs is educating."

Calder said, "I have sent word to my family that Selena is well and unharmed. They are all eager to meet her, however, I think now is not the time."

"Nonsense," Nate said. "Bring them all here for supper. Rowena told the cook to be prepared to serve any number of people for dinner or supper. You and Mister Mowbray go home and get your family and bring them here. I will tell Rowena you are coming. How many should she expect?"

Ranulf was not surprised by Calder's hesitancy.

"Are you certain that would not be an imposition, Lord Rotherby?" Calder asked.

"I am certain. Rowena is already prepared to serve Ewen and all his friends, and I would guess the new arrivals will be staying for supper, so what do a few more matter. So how many?"

Still looking wary, Calder said, "Seven counting me."

"Fine, fine," Nate said with a flick of his hand. "You and Mowbray hurry on back and get your family here. I will explain to Selena that you will be returning soon. I know she will want you to become acquainted with the new arrivals, and she will be wanting to meet your family."

"Very well," Calder said, beckoning to his cousin. "Noam, let us go. We can bring everyone over in your mother's and your sister's coaches. We will leave the children with Hannah and Hermia. They will see they have their supper and are tucked into their cots."

"Are you not adding to Rowena's burden?" Ranulf asked, as he and his brother and Gavin started back to the house.

Nate chuckled. "Nay. Rowena, knowing any number of guests could descend upon us at any time, already told the footmen to set up all the trestle tables for every meal. The extra maids we have hired might as well get some work setting the tables. What dishes are not used can be picked up and put out again on the morrow. So seven more will make little difference."

Ranulf was not so certain, but his concern was forgotten upon returning to the parlor to find his son, Reginald, and his lovely wife, Amaryllis, had arrived.

"Saw what I took to be Toms's coach driving away as we arrived," Reginald was saying as Ranulf entered the room. "Was I pleased to find 'twas but his servants leaving." Turning, he saw his father and exclaimed, "Father!" and hurried to embrace Ranulf.

"I hoped you might be arriving today," Ranulf said, giving his son a hug before embracing his lovely new daughter-in-law.

"We would have been here sooner, but we had to stop for a short visit with Cecily and her brood," Reginald said, his dark eyes alight. He then looked to Rowena. "As Milo and Godwin and their families are staying with Cecily, they intend to settle in there for the night, but they send their love and promise to be here for dinner tomorrow. Cousin Vivien and her husband and little Thelan should be here shortly." He chuckled. "Vivien and Cecily were having a discussion about when to move a child out of a crib. Oh, and I am to tell you, Aunt Rowena, that your brother and his wife will be arriving on the morrow. They were to leave a day behind us."

Rowena nodded. "Thank you, Reggie. I have their room and yours and Amaryllis's all prepared. Now, I think 'tis time we ladies go upstairs to refresh ourselves before supper."

"One moment, Rowena," Nate said. "As Selena was unable to meet Grantham's family today, I told him to bring them here for supper. So there will be seven more coming."

Ranulf noted Rowena never blinked an eye, she merely smiled and said, "I will let the cook know, but to my understanding, he is prepared with numerous soups, puddings, and pies, so did we have twenty more arriving, I believe he would not be perturbed." She looked to Selena. "You see, Selena, your uncle has solved your dilemma, and you will soon again have Calder at your side."

Selena's bright laughter tinkled out over the room, and she gave her uncle a kiss on the cheek. "Thank you, Uncle Nate. And thank you, Father, for helping poor Silas. I would guess all is now under control."

Ranulf smiled at his daughter. Could any man love a daughter more. She had ever been a bright spot in his life. From the moment she was born, and her tiny hand clasped his finger, she had held his heart in a vice. He loved his four sons. Was proud of each one of them. But Selena … well, she was lightness and gaiety. She had a genuine love for humankind as well as for animals. Watching her happiness shine forth in her eyes, he was glad Rowena had not made a polished and cultivated lady of her. He would not like Selena to be anyone but Selena. That Selena had chosen the right man for her was also apparent. She would be happy with her farmer, and that made Ranulf happy.

"Yes, daughter, all is well," he said.

# Chapter 50

Selena stood on the terrace and gave thanks for the glorious day. The brisk fall weather was stimulating, but not cold, as the sun shone brightly in a clear blue sky. Her wedding could not have been more perfect. The walk through Whimbrel on her father's arm from the coach to the church, soon to be the school, had met with no obstacles. No twisted ankles, no noisome animals loose to disrupt the parade of guests following in the wedding parties' wake. Whimbrel villagers, dressed in their finest, had lined the path. Then, when the vows were taken at the church door, the villagers witnessed the ceremony.

After the ceremony, as husband and wife, Selena and Calder entered the church. They were followed by Flavia and Darnell, who had also taken their vows at the door. As many of their guests as could, crowded into the building. Everyone, even the elderly, had to stand. There was no room for chairs. The vicar kept his lecture short, and soon offered a blessing. Selena and Calder and Flavia and Darnell then walked back through the village to the hurrahs and good wishes of the villagers, as well as the traditional shower of wheat.

Selena's father and Uncle Nate had provided a feast for the villagers, four large boars, numerous mince pies, and several marzipan cakes, accompanied by cider and ale. It was a day of celebration for all. Hannah, Hermia, and Calder's laborers, including his newest laborer, Silas, had been in attendance, as had a number of the tenants from neighboring manors and farms. Calder's former in-laws, marveling at Calder's rise in society, had wished him and Selena long lives and much happiness. Selena told them they must visit whenever they should choose, after all, the Hadrians were Pascal's kin.

Before she knew it, they were in the coach and headed back up to the house for the wedding breakfast. Trestle tables covered in white cloths had been set up in the grand hall. Colorful fall wreaths and late blooming flowers decorated the walls. Maids and footmen stood ready to serve the multitude of guests. Along with their nurses, the children, who had been allowed to attend the wedding, were fed in the family dinning chamber. The youngest children would then be taken back to the nursery for play time and naps; the slightly older children could go outside to enjoy the sunshine and the games. Selena was pleased Pascal and the Huddleston children quickly made friends with her young cousins.

With the breakfast ended and everyone waiting for the hall to be cleared and for the musicians to start playing, the outside grounds were alive with strolling couples and lively chatter. Smiling, Selena watched her new husband mingle with their guests. She could not expect him to remember all her cousins, but then, she was not sure she could remember all his cousins, most of whom were staying with Lord and Lady Penhaligon at the Penhaligon hunting lodge. Selena had been impressed with Lady Penhaligon, as had Aunt Rowena. A bright, intelligent, gracious woman, Lady Penhaligon had seen to the comfort of her husband's numerous cousins, as well as to the needs of Ewen's young friends being housed in the lodge hall.

Seeing cousins that she had not seen in three years filled Selena's heart with a warm joy. She knew many had come to Flavia's and her weddings because they would be going on to London for Giles's wedding in two weeks. With Giles being heir to the Rygate earldom, his wedding was considered important, especially as the King himself would be attending. Giles, and Selena's youngest brother Thayer and her cousin Elizabeth had arrived but a day before the wedding. They would stay but one day after the wedding before returning to London.

Selena greatly enjoyed her cousin Elizabeth. At the D'Arcy reunions, she, Elizabeth, and Flavia had always been inseparable. The night before the wedding, the three cousins stayed up late talking and laughing. Elizabeth had assured Selena and Flavia that the marriage night would be heavenly. "And it will keep getting better," Elizabeth promised with a joyous giggle.

"Lady Selena." Selena's thoughts were interrupted by Leighton Plaisance, a distant cousin of Aunt Rowena. "I wish to again thank you and Lady Flavia for including me in your list of guests," he said, his dark brown eyes warm and thoughtful. He was a nice-looking young man, but other than his dark eyes, he looked nothing like Aunt Rowena or any of her children. Still, he had a winning smile, polite manners, and a well-modulated voice. She liked him. Eventually, when Aunt Rowena's brother died, Leighton Plaisance would be the senior head of the Plaisance family, and he would inherit the Plaisance coat of arms.

"Mister Plaisance, I am pleased you have come. My cousins have made you welcome?"

"Indeed, they have been most welcoming. 'Tis nice after all these years to meet some of my cousins. Sutherlin, as his friends do address him, I especially enjoy."

Selena laughed. "Yes, Ewen is a bit of a scoundrel at times, but he is always good fun."

"I have told him that I would welcome him and any of his friends in my home in York." He cleared his throat and hawed a bit before saying, "Lady Selena. I am attracted to Mistress Oriole Cardington. Do you think I would be impertinent, did I ask her if I might write to her?"

"I barely know Mistress Cardington myself, Mister Plaisance. She is one of my husband's cousins." She liked referring to Calder as her husband. "But I can see how you would be attracted to her. She is lovely and seems to have a delightful sense of humor. I would say, she would not be offended, did you ask permission to write to her."

"Thank you." He smiled broadly and headed off in the direction of Mistress Cardington.

Selena joined Cecily, who was immersed in conversation with Calder's sister, Eloisa, and Eloisa's cousins. Their conversation was centered around babies and children, nurses and tutors."

Turning to Selena, Cecily said, "I like all your new relatives."

"So do I," Selena said, and, leaning closer to Cecily, whispered, "I hope Flavia will be as happy with hers. I will say, Lady Edgerton's sister seems kind."

Cecily chuckled. "Yes, Mistress Fairwell and her husband and daughters seem pleasant. However, Lady Edgerton is a strong-willed woman. I worry Flavia may let her intimidate her. But good news. Your sweet cousin Amabel's betrothed, the Marquess of Sedmouth, has offered Flavia and Orland to stay in their house in London for the season. Apparently his house, though old, is huge, has something like twenty-six bedchambers. He and Amabel and her parents are returning to London and will be staying in his home until Amabel and Sedmouth's wedding in December. He has said his door is open to any and all of us."

"Yes." Selena smiled. "He is most generous. He made the same offer to the Nibleys. They are thrilled. They never dreamed they would be invited to the home of a Marquess. I do think Amabel's marriage to Sedmouth will be a good one, even though he is twenty years her senior. He dotes on her, and he is an attractive man."

"I, too, think it will be a good marriage," Cecily said, tilting her head to one side. "Amabel, with her pale skin, fair hair, and silvery-blue eyes, looks like a fairy princes. And she is so sweet. She deserves someone to dote on her. To spoil her."

Hearing music, Selena gave Cecily a hug before heading for her husband. The hall was cleared, and the musicians had started playing. Selena was excited. This would be Calder's and her first time to dance together. She hoped it would go well. Everyone would be watching her and Calder and Flavia and Darnell dance the first dance. Calder said Ware's wife, Avis, had taught him a couple of the more sedate dances. He had never done any but lively country dances. It mattered not. Soon the dance floor would be crowded with other dancers.

When she joined Calder, he looked down at her with such love in his eyes, it made her head spin. How she wished she and Calder could go home this instant. But no, they would have to stay for several more hours. They would not be able to politely leave until late afternoon. The celebration would go on for hours after they left. The trestle tables would be set back up and supper would be served. As the air chilled, the revelers would saunter about inside the house. Some would play cards or other games set up in the parlor. Then, when the tables were again cleared and removed, they would have more dancing. At some point, people would send for their coaches and begin to leave. Those with children would leave first. Hosts with guests expressing weariness would be next. No doubt Ewen and his friends would be among the last to leave.

The servants would work long into the night. Some would have to help masters and mistresses to bed. Others would have to clean up the mess and set the tables up once again for all the guests who would be having breakfast at Whimbrel. Aunt Rowena would be playing hostess to a number of family members for several days to come. At some point, the last of the guests would depart, and Aunt Rowena would be able to ready herself to go to London for Giles's wedding. Much as Aunt Rowena hated going to London, Giles's wedding she could not avoid.

Taking her husband's arm, Selena made a mental note to thank her aunt for all she had done to make her wedding celebration so special. Yes, she had already thanked Aunt Rowena numerous times over, but she needed to come up with a special thanks. Well, she would think of something. For now, she but wanted to enjoy this day of days and her new husband.

# *Chapter 51*

The sun was low on the horizon and the air had a slight nip to it when Selena and Calder arrived at their home in the coach they shared with Calder's cousin Noam, his wife Angeny and a very tired Pascal. Selena had spotted Noam and Angeny readying to leave, and asked if she and Calder might share their coach. "Aunt Rowena said we could take their coach," Selena said, "but as you are set to depart, it would seem simpler than troubling Uncle Nate's coachman."

"We welcome your company," Angeny said, her gray eye twinkling, her slim lips curved in a winsome smile. "We are departing at this time, because little Ajax, our baby, has seldom been this long away from me. He is barely turned a year but is good at getting into everything. I fear Nancy, our nursemaid, will have had her hands full."

Hugs, good wishes, and a couple of ribald jokes followed Selena and Calder out the door and to the coach where Selena tossed her bouquet of rosemary, parsley, and pink and purple asters. She thought she saw Maris Nibley catch the bouquet and clutch it to her breast. Despite the jocular pleas of a couple of Ewen's friends, she had no intention of tossing her garters. Shooing them away with her hand, she turned to her father, and he handed her up into the coach. To her joy, as he helped her settle her gown, he told her he was proud of her, and he believed she had made a good choice. To Calder, he said, "I know you will take good care of my darling girl."

Nodding, Calder said, "Indeed, I will, sir." He then joined Selena, Pascal, and his cousins in the coach, and Selena's father closed the door. Leaning out the window, Selena waved and blew kisses. She saw tears come to Aunt Rowena's eyes, but a huge smile encompassed Uncle Nate's face. Flavia and Elizabeth and Amaryllis continued to wave until the coach turned a bend. Flavia and Darnell would soon be heading for their home, or at least Darnell's room in his parents' home.

Well, it was but for two nights, then they would be headed for London with Elizabeth and Selena's brothers, Giles and Thayer. In London, they had their choice of staying with Elizabeth or with Amabel at Sedmouth's. As Elizabeth would soon be housing Timandra's and Vivien's families, Flavia said she was leaning toward accepting Amabel's invitation. Besides, she admitted to being curious to see a house of such immense size and prestige.

The Mowbray coach was not grand, and the Mowbrays had but the coachman and one footman, but the four horses were well matched and spirited. Good bloodlines, Selena thought. At their arrival, Silas hurried out from the barn to take the horses' reins as the footman jumped off the back of the coach to let down the steps and open the door. Selena had to smile. Silas was petting the lead horses and talking soothingly to them. Oh, he was going to be a good addition to their staff. Calder had not liked the idea of hiring Silas, but he was now pleased with him. He told her Silas had already made friends with the other laborers. Plus, Silas promised Joseph he would help him cut the rest of the wood he needed to frame the house he was building so he and Hermia could be married. Silas said he had helped build several different types of houses, from wattle and dab to clapboard, and he would help Joseph build his house. Yes, Silas was an asset.

The door to the house was immediately opened by Hermia. "Oh, Lady Selena, we have been expecting you any time now," she said, dropping a quick curtsy before stepping back to allow Selena and Calder to enter. Rollo, hurrying up from wherever he had been, gave a yap, and Selena bent to give his head a pat.

"Good Rollo," Pascal said, looking first at the dog and then to Selena. "I wonder if he knows you will now be living here?"

"Now, how could he be knowing that?" demanded Hannah, having joined them at the door, still wiping her hands on her apron. "Do come into your new home, Lady Selena. I have just been whipping up a wee supper for you."

"Oh, Hannah, you are too good," Selena said, her heart soaring, but before she could enter her new home, Calder stopped her.

"No, my dear wife," he said, "this is one ancient tradition I will not forsake." With the grin she so adored, he scooped her up and carried her over the threshold with Pascal and Rollo trotting in on his heels.

Giggling, Selena gave Calder a kiss on the cheek before he set her back on her feet, and Hannah proclaimed, "'Tis right and proper. Right and proper, I say."

Selena gave Hannah a hug and said, "I hope you were able to enjoy the festivities in Whimbrel before you came back here."

"We had a grand time, milady" Hermia said, bobbing a curtsy. "Let me take your wrap."

"Here, I will take it," Alice said. "In fact, I will take it right up to your room, milady. I have all your things moved in, and I hope you will find everything to your satisfaction."

"Dear Alice," Selena said, "I am sure all is perfect. I could not ask for a better maid. That you agreed to remain in my service makes me very happy."

Blushing, Alice said, "Lady Selena, with all you have done for my family … why I will remain with you for as long as I can still do my duty."

"Do your duty by taking her wrap," Hannah said. "We have left Mistress Mowbray just standing in the doorway."

"Oh, dear." Selena turned to draw Angeny, followed by her husband, into the house. "How rude of me," Selena said.

Angeny chuckled. "Not in the least. You are entering your new home. 'Tis right everyone should make you welcome."

"Momma!" came a piping voice from the staircase, and Selena looked up to see a little boy, squiggling in his nurse's arms. As the nurse brought him downstairs, the little fellow, who could have been Pascal as a baby with his light brown curls and huge blue eyes, was holding out his arms to his mother. No sooner did the nurse reach the bottom step, and the baby squirmed free, and with a running toddle, headed for Angeny. His little stubby legs were moving so fast, he stumbled, and might have fallen had Rollo not been close to hand. The boy grabbed the dog's fur, balanced himself and resumed his rush.

Laughing, Angeny reached down and hefted her sturdy son up. His little arms went around her neck, and she gave him a hug and a kiss. "Did you miss me, son?"

"I believe he only truly started missing you when he got up from his afternoon nap," the youthful nurse said, her brown eyes soft, a sweet smile touching her lips. "Clarissant kept him amused most of the day, but he started looking for you, and then calling for you a couple of hours ago. He never cried though. He was a brave boy."

"Were you a brave boy, my little love?" Angeny said, giving her son another kiss. "But, here, you must meet the new mistress of the Grantham household." She turned to Selena. "Lady Selena, may I present my son Ajax." Detaching her son's arms from her neck, she said, "Ajax, this is Lady Selena Grantham."

The little boy looked at Selena curiously, his head tilted to one side, and Selena could not help but laugh. Her laughter brought Ajax's head up straight, and his eyes grew even larger, then he too burst into a bubbly glee that quickly had everyone laughing.

"What a joyful scene," came a voice from the staircase, and another young woman, holding the hand of a pretty, little, blond child, descended into the hall.

"Lady Selena…," began Angeny, but Selena interrupted her. "Please, you must call me Selena. We are cousins and cousins stand on no such formality."

Angeny gave Selena a bright smile and said, "Very well, Cousin Selena. Let me present Ajax's nurse, Nancy, and Clarissant's nurse, Hilda." Both young women dropped curtsies to Selena. "The pretty little girl with Hilda is Noam's sister's youngest daughter, Clarissant."

The little girl, copying the nurses, made a sweet curtsy, and Selena squatted down next to the child. "You are very pretty, Clarissant," she said. "I understand you helped take care of Ajax today. That was very good of you. How old are you?"

Clarissant held up three fingers, and her nurse said, "Yes, that is right, Clarissant, you are three years old."

Bobbing her head and making her curls bounce, Clarissant proclaimed in a piping little voice, "Yes, tree. I am tree."

Rising with Clarissant in her arms, Selena looked down at Pascal. "You looked to be having a good time with any number of young boys."

Pascal, slumped against a bench at the table, had been drooping, but he perked up at Selena's statement. "Indeed I did, Lady…" He stopped and looked questioningly at Selena. "What do I call you now?"

"Well, I intend to call you my son, so you may choose to call me Mother or if you prefer, you may just call me Selena."

A broad smile spread across Pascal's face. "I will call you, Mother," he said.

"Splendid. So tell me, did you have a good time?"

"I did. I cannot think when I ever had a finer time."

"Oh, my," declared Angeny. "I had best go up and change my gown and see about feeding this young fellow." She bounced the chuckling child in her arms.

"He ate his pap with no complaints," the nurse Nancy said, but the way he was pawing at his mother's breast indicated he was ready for his supper.

"After he is fed, and I have changed, I will be back down," Angeny said, heading up the stairs. She looked back at her husband. "Noam, you had best come along and change, too. We are due to have dinner tomorrow at the lodge, and do you soil that coat or your breeches, we have naught else with us for you to wear."

"Humph. I made it through the wedding breakfast without mussing my clothing," Noam said, following after his wife.

"Yes, but this evening, you will be drinking more and having good sport with Calder's laborers. You will not be thinking to mind your manners."

He looked back at Selena and Calder before heading up the stairs. "She is always right."

Calder chuckled, "Indeed, 'tis near time for supper." He looked at Selena. "The hands will soon be returning from celebrating in Whimbrel and will be ready for their supper."

"Silas, being the new man, came back with us to see to the needs of the animals. He seems a good worker," Hannah said, before turning to Hermia. "Best be getting the table set. For you, Lady Selena, and Calder, we set a table up in your bedchamber. I have your supper near ready, and your father left a lovely bottle of claret for your celebratory supper. It is already up in your room. Alice did a fine job getting the room ready for you, so you two go on up and enjoy your supper in peace. Alice and Hermia will be bringing supper up to you soon as you have time to wash and tidy up."

Looking at Calder, Hannah added, "When you have had your supper, Calder, come back down here, and Alice and Mistress Mowbray will see to Lady Selena's needs." She fluttered her hands at them. "Go on with you."

Upon entering the bedchamber, Selena gazed in wonder at the transformation Alice had worked. The room had been bright and lovely before, but now, it was not only a bedchamber, it was a parlor for her and Calder. Two chairs and a small table draped with a white cloth were set by the window on the right side of the hearth. A thick white candle in a blue bowl was in the center of the table. The open bottle of claret and two stemmed glass goblets awaited Selena's and Calder's pleasure.

To insure Selena would feel the room was her room as well as Calder's, the armoire Aunt Rowena and Uncle Nate had given her as a wedding gift had been placed on the far side of the bed. A comfy chair that Selena's mother had sent her from her room at Rygate was situated under a window, and a table with a decorative lantern was next to the chair. Extra pillows with lace trimmed cases decorated the blue coverlet on the bed, and four white candles in shiny bronze candlesticks gave the room a flickering glow.

"Everything is so lovely," Selena breathily said.

"Do you truly like it?" Alice asked, her eyes wide with hope.

"How could I not? I cannot think of anything else I could wish for."

"Hannah and Hermia and Mister Grantham and I all worked on it."

"Yes," Calder said, "but most of the credit must go to Alice. She knew where you would want things, and how the room should be arranged. 'Twas her idea to give us our own table, for when we want to dine in privacy. I have to admit, I like that idea a lot."

"There's warm water in the pitcher and clean towels on the rack," Alice said. "While you wash up, I will just pop down and see is your supper ready."

"Thank you, Alice. Thank you very much," Selena said, giving her maid a hug.

Alice blushed, bobbed a curtsy, and hurried out the door.

Turning to Calder, Selena walked into his arms and surrendered to the first real kiss they had shared in many a day. They would have their supper, and soon, very soon, they would slip into bed together. She could not think how she could possibly be any happier.

<h1 style="text-align:center">Chapter 52</h1>

Selena thought she would be unable to eat her supper, she was so excited, but as she had not eaten anything since her wedding breakfast, she found she had a hearty appetite. She and Calder ate slowly, sipped their claret, and talked of many subjects; the perfection of their wedding, their confusion in trying to keep all their new relatives straight, the trials they would face with the building that would soon be starting, and the trips they would have to take to London for Giles's wedding in two weeks, then for Cousin Amabel's wedding in December.

"How will you manage to be away from the farm? You have so much that needs your attention," Selena said. "I cannot bear the thought of going without you like Elizabeth has done, coming here for our wedding without her new husband. She misses William terribly, she says."

"You will not be going anywhere without me. I have made Abner my steward. When I am unable to attend matters that need attending, he will be in charge. He has been with me enough years that I believe I can trust him to see all gets done. Of course, that means I have increased his wages, but it would seem with all the new hires we now have, including Jimmy and Alice, and Silas, Abner's increase is but a fraction of our labor costs. Still, do we mind our expenditures, your dowry should cover all without any skimping."

"I hope you will not mind all these changes to your life," Selena said. "Pascal will also have to adjust to the changes."

"Neither Pascal nor I will mind any of the changes. Nor will Hannah. My love for you is so great, had your father declared we must live in your manor in Lincolnshire, I would have moved there with never a bat of my eye. You, my dear bride, are my life, my heartbeat."

"Dear husband! I feel the same." Selena rose from her chair and went over to put her arms around her husband's neck. "I cannot imagine my life without you in it."

Calder pulled her down on his lap, and his lips found hers. At first his kiss was soft and gentle, then it became more demanding, and Selena's heart took off at a rapid pace. Since their betrothal, they had stolen but a few moments together. They had kissed, and he had touched her in ways that made enticing prickles race up her spine. She wanted to claim him as her own. Now. She wanted him now. Instead, he pulled away from her, saying, "I have been told I must go back downstairs so that Alice and Angeny can prepare you for bed."

"Nonsense." Selena tried to pull his mouth back to hers. "I need no one to help me but you."

He chuckled. "Nay, Selena, we would not want to offend those who wish to help. Besides, we will need the table cleared, and, with all that noise downstairs, I think I had best see what is causing such a ruckus."

Sighing, Selena let him gently force her from his lap, so he could stand. "Should I come down, too? It really has gotten noisy. I half thought I heard my brother Reggie's voice."

Calder kissed her forehead. "No. You must wait here for Alice and Angeny to ready you in that frilly bit of fluff laid out on the bed. I am looking forward to seeing you in it. Then I am looking forward to seeing you out of it."

His words, and the look he gave her, made her knees turn to mush. As he turned to leave, she sank back onto her chair. My but she hoped Alice and Angeny would soon have her ready for bed. The thought of her body pressed against Calder's had her mad with desire. She had wondered if she would ever know such overpowering love. Would she ever know the love that her parents knew, that Uncle Nate and Aunt Rowena knew, or would she end her days alone and longing for an unknown bliss. She had almost been afraid to hope, but she had dreamed. Oh, yes, she had dreamed. And now her dreams had come true. How lucky could she be?

She frowned, the noise from downstairs had become a roar. How much had Calder's laborers been drinking? Well, 'twas right they should have a day to celebrate. Lord knew they worked hard, day in and day out. Why should they not have a reward?

Hearing footsteps, she rose, thinking she would help stack the dishes, but hearing giggles and laughter, she paused as the door burst open. To her amazement, Alice and Angeny were not the only ones who would be readying her for bed.

"Oh! Dear one." Amaryllis, her blue eyes sparkling, laughed with glee. "If you could but see your face."

Her brother Reggie's beautiful new bride was first to enter the bedchamber and first to give Selena a hug. "What a perfect husband for you is your Calder. Reggie thinks so, too. We are so glad you are to remain the dear Selena we love so much."

"She is right," Selena's cousin, Timandra, said, moving in to give Selena a hug, when Amaryllis stepped aside. "Calder is perfect for you. And so handsome. I had thought no one could be more handsome than my husband, but Calder is one to turn heads."

Laughing as more of her friends and family crowded into her bedchamber, Selena said, "How came you all to be here?"

"You cannot think you would not receive as loving a bedchamber bedecking as you and Fonda gave me," Amaryllis said.

Aunt Rowena's daughter-in-law, Fonda Crossly, was next to hug Selena. "Dear Selena," Fonda said in her soft purr, "did I not tell you all would be well. You are as lovely a lady as your dear mother could wish you to be, and yet, here with your new husband, you will have the freedom you so desire."

Fonda was not a beautiful woman, but her sultry voice and joyful vivacity charmed all who knew her. Selena returned Fonda's hug with warmth and fervor, before next being engulfed in an embrace by Mistress Sermon.

"My lovely child," Mistress Sermon said, her aging body stiff, but her gray eyes dancing, "were you my own daughter, I could not love you more or be any happier for you. All I ask is that you continue with our correspondence. I so enjoy your letters. And, an occasional visit would make my old heart happy."

"Mayhap you could come to Mere Manse," Clotilda Tidewell, Toms's betrothed, said. "Once Dicky and I are married, we will be looking to have visitors. Of course, we do hope you and Mister Grantham will be able to attend our wedding. We will have the wedding in my parish in Hemel Hempstead, and I know that is some distance from here, but it is not as far as London. The wedding is being planned for April."

Freed from Mistress Sermon's embrace, Selena took Clotilda's hand. "On our trip to Leicester, Mister Toms was so very kind to us when the wheel on our coach broke, and we were stranded. I have so enjoyed meeting you, Clotilda. You are as lovely and bright as Mister Toms and Mistress Sermon described you. Spring is a busy time for a farmer, and my husband is a farmer, but does he think he can be away for a few days, we will love to attend your wedding."

"Splendid," Mistress Sermon said. "Do you come, you must plan to stay with me in Watford. 'Tis but ten miles to Hemel Hempstead. And 'tis a well-maintained road, even in the rainy season."

"You are both so kind. I hope we may attend," Selena said, before accepting a hug from Mistress Nibley and then a tighter embrace from Maris Nibley.

Maris whispered in her ear, "I cannot thank you and Flavia enough for bringing Wally into my life. And, I thank you for the change you have wrought in my step-mother. We are becoming allies." Stepping back she added in a normal voice, "I have formed new friendships with your cousin, Amabel, and with Clotilda." She looked from one brightly smiling young woman to the other. "We intend to correspond, and as I have been invited to both weddings, I hope to attend both."

Clotilda caught Maris's hand. "I will be counting on you. When I come to London to shop for my trousseau, I will look forward to meeting your friend, Mister Shandy. I already love his stories."

"I will hope to soon meet him also," Amabel said, after taking her turn to hug Selena. She then gave Selena a second hug. "This one is from Elizabeth. She, and Flavia's mother, and Lady Edgerton and her sister and daughters, and Flavia's sister, Cecily, and Cecily's daughter, Brilliana, and Timandra's sister, Vivian, and Flavia's sister-in-law, Mary, and…" She waved her delicate hand in the air, and her silvery-blue eyes danced. "Oh, everyone who is not here went to give Flavia's bedchamber the same lovely bedecking we intend to do for you."

"We can thank Mistress Nibley and her impressive conservatory for the lovely flowers, and for all the flower petals we intend to sprinkle about this room," Mistress Sermon said.

Mistress Nibley blushed. "I am but so pleased my flowers have done so well this year."

"She furnished plenty for Flavia's bedchamber, too," Amabel said. "She and Squire Nibley made us ever so comfortable during our stay. Sedmouth says he has seldom been so well fed, or so well entertained when not in one of his own manor houses."

"I agree," Mistress Sermon said. "We were treated like royalty, were we not, Clotilda?"

Clotilda clasped Mistress Nibley in a light embrace. "Your hospitality is unequalled."

"Well," Angeny said, "are we to get this room bedecked and Selena into bed, we had best step back and allow Alice and Hermia to finish clearing the table."

Alice, a lock of her blond hair escaping from under her cap, a smidge of moisture on her brow, and her pink cheeks glowing, looked pretty despite her hurried efforts to tidy the table. Hermia, her arms loaded with used dishes, her limp brown hair hanging in wet strands beneath her cap, her wayward eye straying to one side, gave a bright smile, and in her sweet voice, said, "We are near done here, Mistress Mowbray, but do one of you put the table into the corner and push the chairs under it, we would appreciate it."

"I will attend that," Calder's sister, Eloisa, said, and as Hermia and Alice exited, Eloisa and her cousin, Melia, maneuvered the table and chairs into the corner.

"'Tis my turn to give you a hug, my new dear cousin," Laycia, Noam's sister, said, and nodding to her younger sister, Melia, added, "We are so happy to welcome you into our family."

"We certainly are," Eloisa said, taking her turn to hug Selena after Laycia released her. "I am so glad Calder has found a life partner as right for him as you are. I foresee a wonderful future ahead for the two of you."

"Oh, yes," Amaryllis said. "I am certain you are correct. They could not be more perfect for one another."

Selena agreed. No one could suit her better than Calder. She found it satisfying that her friends and family recognized the perfection of her and Calder's bond. Happy as she was to bask in the love of her friends and family, she wondered when the bedecking was to begin? When could she change into the frilly nightshift draped across the bed? The one Calder wanted to see her in before he removed it. That thought sent a delightful tingle racing up her spine.

Fonda must have noticed her shiver, for she chuckled and said, "As soon as Alice returns, she, Angeny, and I will ready you for bed while the others turn this chamber into a bower."

She had barely spoken, and Alice came hurrying back into the room. "Oh, milady, I am so sorry to be tardy. 'Tis such mayhem downstairs, Hermia and I could scarce make our way through to set down our loads."

"What is going on down there?" Selena asked. "'Tis definitely noisy."

"'Tis all the men," Timandra said. "They are having any number of drinks. I am guessing lots of toasts to Calder and you. When you are finally in the bed, looking the lovely bride you are, the men will escort Calder up here to you."

Selena giggled and looked at Amaryllis. "'Twas as we did with you. Now 'tis my turn, huh?" Beckoning to Alice, she said, "Let us get on with it."

"I have a screen here, milady," Alice said, pulling a screen out from behind the armoire and setting it up near the bed.

"Ah," Fonda said. "That is perfect." Speaking loudly over the happy chatter in the room, and the roar from downstairs, she addressed the others. "Angeny and I will help Selena's maid ready Selena for bed while the rest of you commence with the bedecking."

Taking Selena's hand, Fonda pulled Selena behind the screen, where she and Angeny began undressing her. Selena could see nothing that was going on in the rest of the room, but hearing all the laughter and bright giggles, she smiled. The room was becoming brighter and brighter, and she guessed besides the flowers and rose petals provided by Mistress Nibley, someone had also provided any number of candles. She laughed when a flurry of rose petals was tossed over the screen to land on her head and float down to her feet.

"What do you wish done with your garters," Fonda asked.

A smile creeping over her face, Selena raised an eyebrow. "Put them under my pillow."

Fonda returned her smile. "That is an impish smile, my sweet imp. Have a plan, do you?" Expecting no answer, Fonda did as Selena requested.

Once Selena was in her nightshift, Alice took her hair down and combed it until it floated lightly about her shoulders. Looking at Fonda, Alice asked, "What say you, Lady Crossly, is she ready for bed?"

Fonda nodded. "Aye, Alice, she is ready. Go ahead and put away the screen."

When Alice removed the screen, Selena stared in wonder at her bedchamber's changed décor. Pink and red rose petals were bedecking everything, including the bed coverlet. Flowers beautifully arranged in vases were on every flat surface. The table in the corner and the mantel held silver tripods of glowing white candles. Blue cushions trimmed with lace had been placed on the two chairs, and blue and white streamers were swirled around various items and hung about the windows.

"Oh, 'tis beautiful," Selena said. "'Tis like a room for a fairy princess."

"You are beautiful, Selena," Amaryllis said. "You could be that fairy princess. Fonda, have you held the mirror up for her to see herself?"

"No, but 'tis time to unveil it, I think. Alice, I believe it is stored in the armoire."

"Yes, Lady Crossly, it is. Shall I get it out?"

"Please do."

Opening the doors of the armoire, Alice pulled out a package wrapped in soft white wool and tied with a gold, silk ribbon. She handed it to Fonda, who presented it to Selena. "'Tis but a token to show our love for you. Do open it."

Placing it on the bed, Selena untied the ribbon, folded back the wool covering and stared at her reflection in a gilt-framed mirror. "Oh," she whispered, "'tis lovely."

"Yes, you are," Fonda said, and Selena giggled.

"I meant the mirror. Thank you, dear Fonda." She embraced her friend. "I will have Calder hang it over the wash basin stand tomorrow."

"I have a little something for you," Amaryllis said, and handed Selena a silver candle snuffer. "This should make it easier to extinguish all these candles when you and Calder are ready to go to sleep. It and the silver tripods are Reggie's and my gift to you and Calder."

"Thank you, Amaryllis. They are exquisite. But I feel guilty. I never gave you and Reggie a gift. Never even thought to do so."

"Nonsense. You gave me more than I can ever repay. You gave me my brother's life. You gave me Reggie. Where I would be had you not entered my life, I hate to think."

"She is ever like that, is she not?" Mistress Sermon said, before Selena could answer Amaryllis. "That is what I love about her. Ever there, ready with a helping hand."

"Yes," Amabel said, "I still remember the time Selena climbed up that tree at Walling House to rescue my new kitten. Tore her gown coming down, but Lady Tibble was safe."

"I remember that," Fonda said. "It happened at the first reunion I went to. Milo and I had only been married two years. We had a quiet wedding. Milo would wait only the three weeks for the banns to be read, so there was no time to plan a large wedding. I had met some of the D'Arcy family, but I was not prepared for one of the D'Arcy reunions, despite Milo's warnings. Then when Selena came tumbling out of the tree with the kitten – and her brothers did naught but laugh, I realized I had married into a most entertaining family."

"I was not in the least bit injured," Selena said, "but mother's dear maid, Esmeralda, hurried me off to get my gown changed before Mother could see me. Mother would have worried, and we always try to protect her from any worry."

"I am looking forward to hearing more of these stories about your adventures, Selena," Angeny said. "Pascal has already told us several in just the time that he has known you. But now, I think 'tis time we get you into bed so your husband may join you. I am guessing he is growing tired of all the carousing downstairs."

"She is right," Fonda said. "Let us get you settled." The coverlet and sheet were pulled back, and Selena crawled into the bed. The bed she would soon be sharing with Calder. Fonda helped her settle her nightshift and arrange her hair about her shoulders. Then Fonda and everyone else stepped back and looked at Selena. Selena started laughing. "I feel like a prize filly at a horse show with all of you staring at me."

"You are a prize filly, my dear," Mistress Sermon said. "Indeed, you are one of a kind."

"Who is to fetch Calder?" his cousin, Laycia, asked. "Shall I, or maybe Eloisa should?"

"Yes," Angeny said, "I think Eloisa should bring him up."

When Eloisa left, everyone started chattering again, and Angeny, slipping over next to Selena, whispered, "I want you to know that the chair cushions were made for you by Alice and Hermia. They wanted to do something special for you."

Looking up at Angeny, Selena said, "Thank you so much for telling me. I will want to thank them. The cushions are lovely."

"As you know, Squire and Mistress Nibley furnished all the flowers for you and Lady Flavia. The vases are a gift from Mistress Sermon and Mister Toms."

"Everyone has been so kind," Selena said, looking about the room at all her friends.

"There is more," Angeny said, her gray eyes soft, her smile sweet. "These silken sheets are from Laycia and Melia and their husbands." Selena ran an appreciative hand over the shimmering sheets. "The goblets you drank your claret from are from Noam and me." Before Selena could thank her, Angeny continued, "Tomorrow you will learn you have many more gifts awaiting you downstairs. Lord and Lady Penhaligon have gifted you with a twelve piece, cobalt-blue and white porcelain dinnerware set. It includes chargers, bowls, and smaller plates."

Widening her eyes, Selena gasped. "Why, I barely know them. Why would they …"

Interrupting her, Angeny said, "In marrying you, Calder has married into the large D'Arcy family. But you, Selena, have married into the equally large Cardington family. Lord Penhaligon is not a Cardington, but Cordelia Cardington was his beloved aunt, his father's half-sister. She was Calder's and Noam's great, great aunt, and Ware Huddleston's great aunt. Lord Penhaligon and his father and his younger brother, Sir Elton, often attended the Cardington family gatherings. So, though

Lord Penhaligon is not closely related to the Granthams or the Huddlestons, he, and his father before him, have always acknowledged an attachment to Cordelia's less aristocratic family members.

"And he has always been generous. He and Lady Penhaligon gave a twelve piece set of silver knives and spoons to Noam's sister, Laycia, and her husband. He gave Melia and her husband a coach. He gave Noam and me a beautiful little cottage not far from our employer's residence. We could never have bought such a house ourselves. 'Tis not large, but 'tis comfy and has lovely grounds."

Selena stared at her new cousin in utter disbelief. Not only had Lord Penhaligon helped to convince Selena's father that he should allow her to marry Calder, but now, to give them such a gift. But apparently, he was as Angeny said, most generous. And very kind and caring.

"I tell you this, Selena," Angeny said, "because when I married into this family, I was at a loss to keep up with all Noam's cousins. It took me forever to learn who gave us which gifts and to send appropriate thank you letters. I feared I would thank the wrong cousin for the wrong item. Anyway, I know most of them better now, and do you wish, tomorrow, Laycia and I can help you sort through the gifts and help you place the right cousin with the appropriate item."

"Oh, yes, Angeny. That would be so helpful. Thank you." Selena was grateful to have help with the gifts. At least the gifts from the D'Arcy side were at Aunt Rowena's, and she had already seen most of them, and had connected the giver to the gift.

The sound of loud footsteps and boisterous voices turned Selena's attention from Angeny to the door. Bright smiles on their faces, all the women in the room also turned expectantly to the door. It burst open, and Calder stepped into the bedchamber.

# Chapter 53

A herd of men followed Calder into the room, and when he stopped in his tracks, a couple of the men bumped into him. Selena giggled, her tinkling laughter floating out over the room. God, she looked lovely. Pushing his followers back, Calder stepped closer to the bed. He wanted nothing more than to be rid of the mass of people in his bedchamber. He wanted to prove his love for his new wife.

At first, his gaze only on Selena, it took him a few moments before he realized the room was ablaze with candlelight, and a floral scent was perfuming the air. Flowers and rose petals seemed to be everywhere. "Even with all the flowers in this room, my wife, you are the loveliest flower of them all," he said, drawing closer to the bed. "If I could but convince all our guests to depart, I would dearly love to be alone with you."

Selena blushed and her father said, "My new son-in-law is correct in all he says. You do look so lovely, my daughter, and indeed, 'tis time we all headed back to Whimbrel. I understand Lady Penhaligon and Carola Mead have undertaken the duties of seeing to our supper while Lord and Lady Rotherby see Lady Flavia settled into her love nest." He chuckled. "So. Let us depart."

"But Father," Reggie said, "we have not toasted the happy couple here in their room, nor have we serenaded them."

Calder looked aghast at Selena's brother. All four of her brothers had been keeping his hall entertained with their lively songs. They had also offered numerous toasts. Each of their toasts had been answered by his cousin, Noam, or Noam's two brothers-in-law, or Reggie's friend, Toms. Calder's laborers had also merrily joyed in, but 'twas Ewen's friends, Ansel Yardley and Silvester Preston, who would not be outdone. Nary a toast went unchallenged. Calder wondered why the two could not have gone with Ewen, and Ewen's other friends he had brought to the wedding, to toast Lady Flavia and Darnell, instead of coming to his house. At least Selena's father and Squire Nibley and Lord Sedmouth had been circumspect. What a mess had been left downstairs for Hannah and Hermia to clean up, before they could set up the sleeping cots and finally retire to their own beds.

To his chagrin, Selena's brothers burst into a song. Even the dignified Giles, heir to the Rygate Earldom, was singing away in his booming baritone. Selena was laughing again and clapping her hands. That was one of the many things he loved about her. She was never cross, and she appreciated every service, large or small, that was rendered her.

When the song ended, and everyone applauded, Lady Fonda raised her sensuous voice and said, "Lord Rygate has already mentioned we could well be holding up supper at Whimbrel. I believe we need to leave these newlyweds to their bower and be on our way." She beckoned to her husband. "Milo, would you see the coach is ready, please?"

Smiling affectionately at his wife, Lord Crossly said, "I will see to it immediately," and he was the first to exit. As he left, Calder's sister entered the room. She carried Clarissant, Laycia's daughter, in her arms.

"She wants to see the pretty fairy princess, before she will go to bed," Eloisa declared.

"Oh, Isa, you spoil my daughter," Laycia said, coming to take Clarissant from Eloisa. "There, you see. Is Lady Selena not the loveliest bride?"

"Oooh," Clarissant said, her eyes wide as she surveyed the glowing room. Then she looked at Selena. "Yes. She is just like a fairy princess."

Selena laughed, and Clarissant's childish gurgle echoed Selena's gay laughter.

"Now, you are off to bed," Laycia said, bouncing the child in her arms as she left the room amidst Clarissant's protest.

"The rest of you," Angeny said. "Let us be gone. Calder is fast losing patience with all of us, and rightfully so."

Calder breathed a welcome sigh as Angeny and Fonda began herding everyone from the room, but as Preston and Yardley, amidst protest, started to exit, Selena called to Preston. "Silvester," she cried, and when he turned, she whipped something from under her pillow and tossed it at him. It was one of her garters, but her aim was off. Yardley, rather than Preston, caught the prize.

Waving it above his head, Yardley cheered and said, "I will sport this on my arm until I find me a bride as lovely and worthy as you, Selena."

His sleepy-eyed gaze twinkling, Preston gave Selena a wicked grin. "Oh, no, Selena. 'Twas a good try, but you will not be finding me eager to tie the knot." He clamped Yardley on the back. "I will that fate to Yardley here."

With both men chuckling, they left, and soon only Eloisa was left in the room. Her eyes, so like her brother's, glowed, and rising on tiptoe, she kissed Calder's cheek. "I could not be happier for you," she said and looked over at Selena. "Dear new sister, welcome to our family."

"Thank you," Selena said, as Eloisa turned and exited, softly closing the door behind her.

Turning to again gaze upon Selena, Calder said, "I cannot help but think I must be the luckiest man in the world."

"I know I am the luckiest woman," Selena said and patted the bed beside her. "Do please join me. I seem to have been waiting forever for this day, this night."

Calder was eager to comply with her request, but in looking about the room, he said, "I think mayhap I should put out a few of these candles first."

Selena reached behind her and pulled the candle snuffer Amaryllis had given her from the table beside the bed. Smiling seductively, she held it out to Calder. He had to harness all his will power not to simply forget about the candles and hop into bed with his bride. Inhaling deeply, he set about extinguishing all the candles but the two on the tables on either side of the bed.

After placing the snuffer on the mantle, and with his eyes on Selena, he removed his coat and hung it over the back of a chair. Next came his waistcoat and his cravat, then he sat down to remove his shoes and stockings. Finally he rose and slipped off his breeches. He stood before his wife in naught but his shirt.

His eyes had not left her face, and he liked that she had watched his every move. Her head tilted slightly to one side, a smile touching her lips, she looked him up and down. Her gaze traveled up him from his bare feet until her eyes again met his. She held out her arms, and he was undone. In an instant he was at the bedside slipping his shirt off over his head and scrambling under the sheet to take his wife into his arms.

❈ ❈ ❈

Nestling into Calder's arms, Selena reveled in the feel of her husband's bare skin. She ran her hands up and down his back, and the two of them slid down in the bed. "I love the silkiness of your night rail, my love," Calder said, "but I am eager to touch your skin. Do you mind if we remove the shift?"

"Not in the least," she answered in a wispy breath. She wanted to feel her skin tightly pressed against his. She feared being too aggressive. Torn, not knowing what would make him happy, she was hesitant to act too wanton. But she wanted, oh so much, to make him happy, to pleasure him as his touch pleasured her.

Sitting up, she pulled the sheet back in order to get the shift off over her head. She then tossed the silky garment to the foot of the bed. In doing so, she exposed her naked body to his view and his to hers. She loved what she saw. Broad, near-hairless chest, flat, taut stomach, and sturdy, muscled legs and arms. Having admired his body, she raised her gaze to his face to find his gaze perusing her body.

"Gads, Selena, but you are so lovely, so desirable," he said, his voice husky with emotion. His lips found hers and again the two of them slipped down in the bed. One of his arms went around her back, and he pressed her to his chest.

"Selena, Selena," he said. "I want so much to make this a pleasurable experience for you, but do you touch me in this manner, I fear I will explode before we are joined as one."

"Then let us join as one," she said, feeling like her heart was in her throat. "I want you now. I need to make you mine. Mine, forever and ever."

"Then so shall we join as husband and wife," he answered.

When they joined, she reveled in claiming him as her own, and when he reached his release, she sighed in contentment. For a few moments he continued to cling to her, his weight resting lightly on her, then he rolled off her but pulled her into an embrace at his side. "That was the most beautiful experience of my entire life," he whispered, then kissed her brow. "But 'twas not so great for you, was it?"

"Why 'twas beautiful," Selena said in surprise. "Though I was told to expect some pain the first time, I felt no pain at all. I just felt love for you, and joy that I can now call you mine. You made me very happy."

"I intend to make you happier," he replied, and soon, in response to his gentle but stimulating touch, she erupted into a scintillating passion that sent her vaulting into heaven, before returning to find Calder's lips sweetly covering hers as he held her tightly in his arms.

Pulling away from him just enough to see his face, she sighed, "That was wonderful. That must be what Aunt Rowena was referring to."

Calder chuckled lightly. "I would guess you must be right. In the future, I intend you shall know such pleasure ere I find mine. Mayhap we may at some point find our pleasure at the same time, but does that never happen, I still mean our loving to always be a shared moment that we can both delight in."

"If you have just demonstrated for me such a delight, I am eager to experience it again any time you are willing to so prove your love for me."

"Hmmm, I think we should first extinguish these sputtering bedside candles, my love, and then I see no reason we should not enjoy a slower, more seductive loving."

With the candles extinguished, the room was intensely dark, but in a few moments Selena's eyes adjusted, and the moonlight, just beginning to peep through the window, showed her Calder's handsome face. He was so dear to her. Her heart swelling with her love for him, she relaxed in his arms and let him introduce her to the beauty of timeless love. When he again brought her to the height of ecstasy, and then found his pleasure, she thought she could finally understand why her mother had wanted her to experience such a love. It was beautiful and fulfilling beyond words, beyond description.

She experienced a satisfaction that had her bursting with excitement. At the same time, she felt contented and ready to drift into sleep. Cuddled in Calder's arms, her head resting on his shoulder, she heard his breathing slowing, and after kissing her brow, he whispered, "Good night, my sweet love. May your dreams be as sweet as you are."

"Good night, my wondrous husband," she whispered. "You have made me so very happy. I love you more than I can ever express."

"That feeling is mutual," he said, giving her nose a kiss.

She kissed his cheek, and before long she heard his regular breathing and knew he had drifted into sleep. She expected sleep would soon claim her, but as the drowsiness crept over her, she replayed the day, the fabulous day.

Though sleepy, her thoughts turned to the future. On the morrow, she and Calder would be busy from morning to evening. They would take dinner with Lord and Lady Penhaligon and Calder's many cousins. They would then go to Whimbrel for supper with her family. The following day, Lord Penhaligon had a hunt scheduled for the men, mainly to keep the younger men occupied. Selena's father and Uncle Nate were helping coordinate the hunt. While the men were immersed in their hunt, the women would have a relaxing gathering at Whimbrel, as the women of the two large families became better acquainted.

Selena wished her cousin Elizabeth would be there, but Elizabeth wanted to return to her new husband. Selena could not blame her for that. Elizabeth would be accompanied by Selena's brothers, Giles and Thayer, who also needed to return to London, Giles to help his betrothed with their wedding plans, Thayer to his studies. At the age of ten, Thayer had already determined his future. He meant to be a Member of Parliament. His less serious older brothers thought he would outgrow the notion, but Selena believed her youngest brother would not be dissuaded from his goal. Serious, studious, and fair-minded, he would someday make a good MP.

Other guests would also soon be leaving, especially those of Calder's family, and Calder would be able to resume his work on the farm, but Selena knew a number of her cousins would be staying for at least a week before going to London for Giles's wedding. As Flavia and Orland were headed to London with Elizabeth, Selena would be needed at

Whimbrel to help Aunt Rowena entertain the remaining cousins. That would mean daytime separation from Calder. That she hated, but she owed much to her aunt and uncle. She would do her part.

Snuggling closer to her husband, Selena finally let sleep overtake her as she reveled in her joy and the delightful future that lay ahead of her with the man she loved so intensely. Yes, dreams could come true.

384

The End

## Deceptive Deceptions
### By Celia Martin

# Chapter 1

**Theatre Royal – Drury Lane – March 1684**

Calantha Matherly, alias Marvella Blessing, sank into a deep curtsy and let the applause flow over her. The audiences still loved her. But for how much longer? She had turned thirty-one on her last birthday. How much longer could she continue to be Marvelous Marvella? When youths had first started calling her by that name, she had scoffed at them, but over the years, she became accustomed to it. She still could not say she liked it, but the company manager liked it, as did the writers. Not to be immodest, she knew she was not only beautiful, she was a good actress. Her Lady Macbeth the previous year had been widely acclaimed, and the queues waiting to get into the theater to see her current performance had been as long as any of her past shows.

The only productions that drew longer queues were ones where she played a woman pretending to be a male, and she appeared on stage in tight breeches and hose that put her legs on display. The men in the audience were often beside themselves. Rising and leaving the stage, Calantha hurried to her changing room and bolted the door. King Charles had commanded men from the audience to stay out of the backstage area where the women changed, but many of the peerage decided they were exempt from the King's command. They moseyed back at will. But Calantha was lucky. Worverton had paid royally to have Calantha given her own private changing chamber. He wanted no other men ogling the woman he loved. Plus, the privacy helped Calantha maintain her disguise.

It had not always been so, however. Until Worverton entered her life, she had been as subject to men's bold stares and propositions as the other women. Many of the women were not offended by the men. Most hoped to become the mistress of one of their wealthier admirers. Calantha had never expected to become anyone's mistress, but then, she had not expected to fall in love with Lord Worverton. After removing the wig she had worn for her performance, she began to carefully remove but a portion of her face paint. Her gray eyes with the dark kohl accenting them stared back at her as she combed out her light-brown hair. After re-pinning it atop her head, she put on the golden-blond wig she would wear home. Satisfied with her appearance, she had just risen when a knock sounded at her door.

"Who is it?"

"'Tis, I. Dicken, Mistress Blessing. You have visitors."

"Visitors?" The youth Dicken, and the other members of the cast, knew she would see no admirers. And Worverton would not need Dicken to announce him.

"'Tis Lady Elizabeth Hayward and Mistress Elsworth. And Lord Albin, Mistress. They wish a word with you."

Confused, she opened the door a crack. Sure enough, behind Dicken were two ladies and the chubby Lord Albin. She knew Albin. He was friends with Hayward, who was friends with Worverton, and from time to time, Albin had joined them in a late night supper in a quiet inn.

"Good heavens, Lord Albin, what do you mean bringing these ladies back here? This is no place for them to be seen." She looked at Dicken. "And you. You should know better."

Dicken bowed his head, but looked back up. "Lord Albin and I both know better, Mistress Blessing, but if Lady Elizabeth wants something, it does no good to gainsay her. She will have her way. Did Lord Albin and I not escort her back here, she would come on her own."

"He speaks the truth, Mistress Blessing," the pretty, dark-haired woman said. "Mistress Elsworth and I are determined to have speech with you, so you might as well let us in."

Shrugging, not knowing what else she could do, Calantha stepped back and opened the door. "Do come in Lady Elizabeth and Mistress Elsworth." Lady Elizabeth was a beautiful woman with her dark hair, clear complexion, and blue-green eyes. Her friend, Mistress Elsworth would, by many, be considered plain, with her slightly pointed nose and thin lips, but her pale, silvery-blue eyes were bright with humor and intelligence. She seemed to be there to support Lady Elizabeth, for she let Lady Elizabeth do the talking.

Lady Elizabeth thanked Dicken for bringing her to Calantha's door, then told Albin, "Wait for us near the exit, Lord Albin. We will not be long."

Albin started to sputter. "But … but …, Lady Elizabeth, what will Hayward say do I leave you unaccompanied?"

"He will never know. Besides, we will be safe inside Mistress Blessing's chamber. Now, do please go. We will rejoin you soon." She fluttered her hand at Albin, then turning back to Calantha, she smiled brightly, and she and Mistress Elsworth entered Calantha's changing room.

"This is a surprise, my lady," Calantha said, with a brief curtsy first to Lady Elizabeth and then to her friend. "What can I do for you?"

"'Tis what we can do for you, Mistress Blessing," Lady Elizabeth said. "I know you must be exhausted after your wonderful performance, so we will make this brief." She took out a piece of paper from her pocket and handed it to Calantha.

Warily accepting the paper, Calantha looked at it. On the paper was Lady Elizabeth's name, her address, a date and day of the week, and a time. She looked up and cocked her head. "What is this for?"

"That paper gives you my address and the date and time I expect you to be at my home. I say expect, because, do you not come to me, I will come to you. I have learned where you live, and I will not be put off." She half-turned to her friend. "Mistress Elsworth and I will not be put off."

"But why? What is this about?"

"You will learn everything when you come to my house. Now, do I have your guarantee you will come? Remember, do you not come, we will come to you."

"If you think I have been having an affair with your ..."

Before she could finish speaking, Lady Elizabeth started laughing. "Oh, good heavens, no. Having an affair with William. Indeed, no. Now, do I have your word? If so, we can depart. I know Lord Albin must be getting anxious."

Bewildered, Calantha looked down again at the paper before slowly nodding her head. "It would seem I have no choice. But I do wish you would tell me why I must obey this summons." She looked back up into Lady Elizabeth's determined eyes. Calantha was feeling angry, but Lady Elizabeth was smiling brightly. The lady reached out and patted Calantha's hand. "All will be well. Now, we will leave you, that you may finish whatever it is you were doing. Good evening." With that, the two ladies turned and exited the room.

Tired as she was, this being her first week back on the stage with the theater reopening after the end of the Lenten season, Calantha was too befuddled to head for home. Closing the door, she sat down on the bench before her mirror. What in the world was all this about? How she wished Worverton was in town that she might ask him to discover what was afoot. Being friends with Hayward, surely he could learn why Lady Elizabeth Hayward was insisting she visit her home.

# *Biography*

Celia Martin is a former Social Studies/English teacher. Her love of history dates back to her earliest memories when she sat enthralled as her grandparents recounted tales of their past. As a child, she delighted in the make-believe games that she played with her siblings and friends, but as she grew up and had to put aside the games, she found she could not set aside her imagination. So, Celia took up writing stories for her own entertainment.

She is an avid reader. She loves getting lost in a romance, but also enjoys good mysteries, exciting adventure stories, and fact-loaded historical documentaries. When her husband retired and they moved from California to the glorious Kitsap Peninsula in the state of Washington, she was able to begin a full-fledged writing career. And has never been happier.

When not engaged in writing, Celia enjoys travel, keeping fit, and listening to a variety of different music styles.

---

*Visit my web site at:*
**https://tinyurl.com/cmartinbooks**

---

www.ingramcontent.com/pod-product-compliance
Lightning Source LLC
Chambersburg PA
CBHW070734190726

48292CB00002B/253